W9-DGO-649

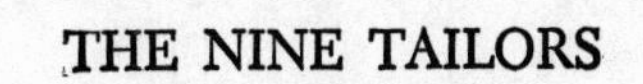

THE NINE TAILORS

THE NINE TAILORS

CHANGES

Rung on an Old Theme

IN

Two Short Touches

AND

Two Full Peals

DOROTHY L. SAYERS

HARCOURT, BRACE & WORLD, INC.
NEW YORK

Printed in the United States of America

Quality Printing and Binding by:
THE MAPLE-VAIL BOOK MANUFACTURING GROUP
Pine Camp Drive
Binghamton, N.Y. 13902 U.S.A.

ISBN 0-151-65897-8

FOREWORD

FROM *time to time complaints are made about the ringing of church bells. It seems strange that a generation which tolerates the uproar of the internal combustion engine and the wailing of the jazz band should be so sensitive to the one loud noise that is made to the glory of God. England, alone in the world, has perfected the art of change-ringing and the true ringing of bells by rope and wheel, and will not lightly surrender her unique heritage.*

I have to ask the indulgence of all change-ringers for any errors I may have made in dealing with their ancient craft. The surnames used in these books are all such as I have myself encountered among the people of East Anglia, but every place and person described is wholly fictitious, as are also the sins and negligences of those entirely imaginary bodies, the Wale Conservancy Board, the Fen Drainage Board and the East Level Waterways Commission.

My grateful thanks are due to Mr. W. J. Redhead, who so kindly designed for me the noble Parish Church of Fenchurch St. Paul and set it about with cherubims.

DOROTHY L. SAYERS

CONTENTS

A SHORT TOUCH OF STEDMAN'S TRIPLES

FIVE PARTS

A FULL PEAL OF KENT TREBLE BOB MAJOR

THREE PARTS

1

A SHORT TOUCH OF

Kent Treble Bob Major

TWO COURSES

704

BY THE COURSE ENDS

64352

23456

8TH THE OBSERVATION.

Call her in the middle with a double, before wrong and home.

Repeated once.

TROYTE

THE FIRST COURSE

The Bells Are Rung Up

The coil of rope which it is necessary to hold in the hand, before, and whilst raising a bell, always puzzles a learner; it gets into his face, and perhaps round his neck (in which case he may be hanged!).

TROYTE ON CHANGE-RINGING

"THAT'S TORN IT!" said Lord Peter Wimsey.

The car lay, helpless and ridiculous, her nose deep in the ditch, her back wheels cocked absurdly up on the bank, as though she were doing her best to bolt to earth and were scraping herself a burrow beneath the drifted snow. Peering through a flurry of driving flakes, Wimsey saw how the accident had come about. The narrow, hump-backed bridge, blind as an eyeless beggar, spanned the dark drain at right angles, dropping plump down upon the narrow road that crested the dyke. Coming a trifle too fast across the bridge, blinded by the bitter easterly snowstorm, he had overshot the road and plunged down the side of the dyke into the deep ditch beyond, where the black spikes of a thorn hedge stood bleak and unwelcoming in the glare of the headlights.

Right and left, before and behind, the fen lay shrouded. It was past four o'clock and New Year's Eve; the snow that had fallen all day gave back a glimmering greyness to a sky like lead.

"I'm sorry," said Wimsey. "Whereabouts do you suppose we've got to, Bunter?"

The manservant consulted a map in the ray of an electric torch.

"I think, my lord, we must have run off the proper road at Leamholt. Unless I am much mistaken, we must be near Fenchurch St. Paul."

As he spoke, the sound of a church clock, muffled by the snow, came borne upon the wind; it chimed the first quarter.

"Thank God!" said Wimsey. "Where there is a church, there is civilization. We'll have to walk it. Never mind the suitcases; we can send somebody for them. Br'rh! it's cold. I bet that when Kingsley welcomed the wild northeaster he was sitting indoors by a good fire, eating muffins. I could do with a muffin myself. Next time I accept hospitality in the Fen-country, I'll take care that it's at midsummer, or else I'll go by train. The church lies to windward of us, I fancy. It would."

They wrapped their coats about them and turned their faces to the wind and snow. To left of them, the drain ran straight as a rule could make it, black and sullen, with a steep bank shelving down to its slow, unforgiving waters. To their right was the broken line of the sunk hedge, with, here and there, a group of poplars or willows. They tramped on in silence, the snow beating on their eyelids. At the end of a solitary mile the gaunt shape of a windmill loomed up upon the farther bank of the drain, but no bridge led to it, and no light showed.

Another half-mile, and they came to a signpost and a secondary road that turned off to the right. Bunter turned his torch upon the signpost and read upon the single arm:

"Fenchurch St. Paul."

There was no other direction; ahead, road and dyke marched on side by side into an eternity of winter.

"Fenchurch St. Paul for us," said Wimsey. He led the way into the side-road, and as he did so, they heard the clock again—nearer—chiming the third quarter.

A few hundred yards of solitude, and they came upon the first sign of life in this frozen desolation: on their left, the roofs of a farm, standing some way back from the road, and, on the right, a small, square building like a box of bricks, whose sign, creaking in the blast, proclaimed it to be the Wheatsheaf public-house. In front of it stood a small, shabby car, and from windows on the ground and first floors light shone behind red blinds.

Wimsey went up to it and tried the door. It was shut, but not locked. He called out, "Anybody about?"

A middle-aged woman emerged from an inner room.

"We're not open yet," she began, abruptly.

"I beg your pardon," said Wimsey. "Our car has come to grief. Can you direct us——?"

"Oh, I'm sorry, sir. I thought you were some of the men. Your car broke down? That's bad. Come in. I'm afraid we're all in a muddle——"

"What's the trouble, Mrs. Tebbutt?" The voice was gentle and scholarly, and, as Wimsey followed the woman into a small parlour, he saw that the speaker was an elderly parson.

"The gentlemen have had an accident with their car."

"Oh, dear," said the clergyman. "Such a terrible day, too! Can I be of any assistance?"

Wimsey explained that the car was in the ditch, and would certainly need ropes and haulage to get it back to the road again.

"Dear, dear," said the clergyman again. "That would be coming over Frog's Bridge, I expect. A most dangerous place, especially in the dark. We must see what can be done about it. Let me give you a lift into the village."

"It's very good of you, sir."

"Not at all, not at all. I am just getting back to my tea. I am sure you must be wanting something to warm you up. I trust you are not in a hurry to reach your destination. We should be delighted to put you up for the night."

Wimsey thanked him very much, but said he did not want to trespass upon his hospitality.

"It will be a great pleasure," said the clergyman, courteously. "We see so little company here that I assure you you will be doing my wife and myself a great favour."

"In that case——" said Wimsey.

"Excellent, excellent."

"I'm really most grateful. Even if we could get the car out tonight, I'm afraid the axle may be bent, and that means a blacksmith's job. But couldn't we get rooms at an inn or something? I'm really ashamed——"

"My dear sir, pray don't think twice about it. Not but what I am sure Mrs. Tebbutt here would be delighted to take you in and would make you very comfortable—very comfortable indeed; but her husband is laid up with this dreadful influenza—we are suffering from quite an epidemic of it, I am sorry to say—and I fear it would not be altogether convenient, would it, Mrs. Tebbutt?"

"Well, sir, I don't know as how we could manage very well, under the circumstances, and the Red Cow has only one room——"

"Oh, no," said the clergyman, quickly, "not the Red Cow; Mrs. Donnington has visitors already. Indeed, I will take no denial. You must positively come along to the Rectory. We have ample accommodation—too much, indeed, too much. My name, by the way, is Venables—I should have mentioned it earlier. I am, as you will have gathered, rector of the parish."

"It's extremely good of you, Mr. Venables. If we're really not putting you out, we will accept your invitation with pleasure. My name is Wimsey—here is my card—and this is my man, Bunter."

The Rector fumbled for his glasses, which, after disentangling the cord, he perched very much askew on his long nose, in order to peer at Wimsey's card.

"Lord Peter Wimsey—just so. Dear me! The name seems familiar. Have I not heard of it in connection with—ah! I have it! *Notes on the Collection of Incunabula*, of course. A very scholarly little monograph, if I may say so. Yes. Dear me. It will be charming to exchange impressions with another book-collector. My library is, I fear, limited, but I have an edition of the *Gospel of Nicodemus* that may interest you. Dear me! Yes. Delightful to have met you like this. Bless my heart, there's five o'clock striking. We must be off, or I shall get a scolding from my wife. Good afternoon, Mrs. Tebbutt. I hope your good man will be much improved by tomorrow; I really think he is looking better already."

"Thank you, sir; Tom's always so pleased to see you. I'm sure you do him a lot of good."

"Tell him to keep his spirits up. Such a nasty, depressing complaint. But he's over the worst now. I will send a little bottle of port wine as soon as he is able to take it. Tuke Holdsworth '08," added the Rector, in an aside to Wimsey; "couldn't harm a fly, you know. Yes. Dear me! Well! We really must be going. I'm afraid my car is not much to boast of, but there's more room in it than one would think. Many's the christening party we've managed to squeeze into it, eh, Mrs. Tebbutt? Will you sit beside me, Lord Peter? Your man and your—dear me! have you any luggage? . . . Ah! down at Frog's Bridge? I will send my gardener to fetch it. It will be quite safe where it is; we're all honest people about here, aren't we, Mrs. Tebbutt? That's right. You must have this rug about your legs—yes, I insist. No, no, thank you. I can start her up quite well. I am so well accustomed to do it. There, you see! A few good pulls and she comes up as brisk as a bell. All right behind, my man? Good. Excellent. *Good* afternoon, Mrs. Tebbutt!"

The ancient car, shuddering to her marrow-bones, lurched away down the straight and narrow road. They passed a cottage, and then, quite suddenly, on their right, there loomed out of the whirling snow a grey, gigantic bulk.

"Great Heavens!" exclaimed Wimsey, "is that your church?"

"Yes, indeed," said the Rector, with pride. "You find it impressive?"

"Impressive!" said Wimsey. "Why, it's like a young cathedral. I'd no idea. How big is your parish, then?"

"You'll be surprised when I tell you," said the Rector, with a chuckle. "Three hundred and forty souls—no more. Astonishing, is it not? But you find the same thing all over the Fens. East Anglia is famous for the size and splendour of its parish churches. Still, we flatter ourselves we are almost unique, even in this part of the world. It was an abbey foundation, and in the old days Fenchurch St. Paul must have been quite an important place. How high should you say our tower was?"

Wimsey gazed up at the great pile.

"It's difficult to tell in this darkness. Not less than a hundred and thirty feet, surely."

"Not a bad guess. A hundred and twenty-eight, to be exact, to the top of the pinnacles, but it looks more, because of the comparative lowness of the clerestory roof. There aren't many to beat us. St. Peter Mancroft, of course—but that's a town church. And St. Michael's, Coventry, is one hundred and thirty feet without the spire. But I would venture to back Fenchurch St. Paul against them all for beauty of proportion. You will see that better when we turn the corner. Here we are. I always blow my horn here; the wall and the trees make it so very dangerous. I sometimes think we ought to have the churchyard wall set back a little, in the public interest. Ah! now you get a little idea. Very fine, is it not, the piling of the aisle and clerestory? You will be able to judge better in daylight. Here is the Rectory—just opposite the church. I always blow my horn at the gate for fear anybody should be about. The bushes make it so very dark. Ah! safely negotiated. I'm sure you will be glad to get into the warm and have a cup of tea—or possibly something stronger. I always blow my horn at the door, so as to tell my wife I am back. She gets nervous when I am out after lighting-up time; the dykes and drains make these roads so very awkward, and I am not as young as I was. I fear I am already a little late. Ah! here is my wife. Agnes, my dear, I am sorry to be a little behind time, but I have brought a guest back with me. He has had an accident with his car and will stay the night with us. The rug! Allow me! I fear that seat is something of a *res angusta*. Pray be careful of your head. Ah! all is well. My dear—Lord Peter Wimsey."

Mrs. Venables, a plump and placid figure in the lamplight from the open door, received the invasion with competent tranquillity.

"How fortunate that my husband should have met you. An accident? I do hope you are not hurt. I always say these roads are perfect death-traps."

"Thank you," said Wimsey. "There is no harm done. We stupidly ran off the road—at Frog's Bridge, I understand."

"A very nasty place—quite a mercy you didn't go into the Thirty-foot Drain. Do come in and sit down and get yourselves warm. Your man? Yes, of course. Emily! Take this gentleman's manservant into the kitchen and make him comfortable."

"And tell Hinkins to take the car and go down to Frog's Bridge for the luggage," added the Rector. "He will find Lord Peter's car there. He had better go at once, before the weather gets worse. And, Emily! tell him to send over to Wilderspin and arrange to get the car out of the dyke."

"Tomorrow morning will do for that," said Wimsey.

"To be sure. First thing tomorrow morning. Wilderspin is the blacksmith—an excellent fellow. He will see to the matter most competently. Dear me, yes! And now, come in, come in! We want our tea. Agnes, my dear, have you explained to Emily that Lord Peter will be staying the night?"

"That will be all right," said Mrs. Venables, soothingly. "I do hope, Theodore, you have not caught cold."

"No, no, my dear. I have been well wrapped up. Dear me, yes! Ha! What do I see? Muffins?"

"I was just wishing for muffins," said Wimsey.

"Sit down, sit down and make a good meal. I'm sure you must be famished. I have seldom known such bitter weather. Would you prefer a whisky-and-soda, perhaps?"

"Tea for me," said Wimsey. "How jolly all this looks! Really, Mrs. Venables, it's tremendously good of you to take pity upon us."

"I'm only so glad to be able to help," said Mrs. Venables, smiling cheerfully. "Really, I don't think there's anything to equal the dreariness of these fen roads in winter. It's most fortunate your accident landed you comparatively close to the village."

"It is indeed." Wimsey gratefully took in the cosy sitting-room, with its little tables crowded with ornaments, its fire roaring behind a chaste canopy of velvet overmantel, and the silver tea-vessel winking upon the polished tray. "I feel like Ulysses, come to port after much storm and peril."

He bit gratefully into a large and buttery muffin.

"Tom Tebbutt seems a good deal better today," observed the Rector. "Very unfortunate that he should be laid up just now, but we must be thankful that it is no worse. I only hope there are no further casualties. Young Pratt will manage very well, I think; he went through two long touches this morning without a single mistake, and he is extremely keen. By the way, we ought, perhaps, to warn our visitor——"

"I'm sure we ought," said Mrs. Venables. "My husband has asked you to stay the night, Lord Peter, but he ought to have mentioned that you will probably get very little sleep, being so close to the church. But perhaps you do not mind the sound of bells."

"Not at all," said Wimsey.

"My husband is a very keen change-ringer," pursued Mrs. Venables, "and, as this is New Year's Eve——"

The Rector, who seldom allowed anybody else to finish a sentence, broke in eagerly.

"We hope to accomplish a real feat tonight," he said, "or rather, I should say, tomorrow morning. We intend to ring the New Year in with—you are not, perhaps, aware that we possess here one of the finest rings in the country?"

"Indeed?" said Wimsey. "Yes, I believe I have heard of the Fenchurch bells."

"There are, perhaps, a few heavier rings," said the Rector, "but I hardly know where you would rival us for fullness and sweetness of tone. Number seven, in particular, is a most noble old bell, and so is the tenor, and the John and Jericho bells are also remarkably fine—in fact, the whole ring is most 'tuneable and sound,' as the old motto has it."

"It is a full ring of eight?"

"Oh, yes. If you are interested, I should like to show you a very charming little book, written by my predecessor, giving the whole history of the bells. The tenor, Tailor Paul, was actually cast in a field next the churchyard in the year 1614. You can still see the depression in the earth where the mould was made, and the field itself is called the Bell-Field to this day."

"And have you a good set of ringers?" inquired Wimsey, politely.

"Very good indeed. Excellent fellows and most enthusiastic. That reminds me. I was about to say that we have arranged to ring the New Year in tonight with no less," said the Rector, emphatically, "no less than fifteen thousand, eight hundred and forty Kent Treble Bob Majors. What do you think of that? Not bad, eh?"

"Bless my heart!" said Wimsey. "Fifteen thousand——"

"Eight hundred and forty," said the Rector.

Wimsey made a rapid calculation.

"A good many hours' work there."

"Nine hours," said the Rector, with relish.

"Well done, sir," said Wimsey. "Why, that's equal to the great performance of the College Youths in eighteen hundred and something."

"In 1868," agreed the Rector. "That is what we aim to emulate. And, what's more, but for the little help I can give, we shall be obliged to do as well as they did, and ring the whole peal with eight ringers only. We had hoped to have twelve, but unhappily, four of our best men have been laid low by this terrible influenza, and we can get no help from Fenchurch St. Stephen (which has a ring of bells, though not equal to ours) because there they have no Treble Bob ringers and confine themselves to Grandsire Triples."

Wimsey shook his head, and helped himself to his fourth muffin.

"Grandsire Triples are most venerable," he said solemnly, "but you can never get the same music——"

"That's what I say," crowed the Rector. "You never can get the same music when the tenor is rung behind—not even with Stedman's, though we are very fond here of Stedman's and ring them, I venture to say, very well. But for interest and variety and for sweetness in the peal, give me Kent Treble Bob every time."

"Quite right, sir," said Wimsey.

"You will never beat it," said Mr. Venables, soaring away happily to the heights of the belfry, and waving his muffin in the air, so that the butter ran down his cuff. "Take even Grandsire Major —I cannot help feeling it as a defect that the blows come behind so monotonously at the bobs and singles—particularly at the singles, and the fact that the treble and second are confined to a plain hunting course——"

The rest of the Rector's observations on the Grandsire method of change-ringing were unhappily lost, for at that moment Emily made her appearance at the door, with the ominous words:

"If you please, sir, could James Thoday speak to you for a moment?"

"*James* Thoday?" said the Rector. "Why, certainly, of course. Put him in the study, Emily, and I will come in a moment."

The Rector was not long gone, and when he returned his face was as long as a fiddle. He let himself drop into his chair in an attitude of utter discouragement.

"This," he ejaculated, dramatically, "is an irreparable disaster!"

"Good gracious, Theodore! What in the world is the matter?"

"William Thoday! Of all nights in the year! Poor fellow, I ought not to think of myself, but it is a bitter disappointment—a bitter disappointment."

"Why, what has happened to Thoday?"

"Struck down," said the Rector, "struck down by this wretched scourge of influenza. Quite helpless. Delirious. They have sent for Dr. Baines."

"T'chk, t'chk," said Mrs. Venables.

"It appears," went on the Rector, "that he felt unwell this morning, but insisted—most unwisely, poor man—on driving in to Walbeach on some business or other. Foolish fellow! I thought he looked seedy when he came in to see me last night. Most fortunately, George Ashton met him in the town and saw how bad he was and insisted on coming back with him. Poor Thoday must have taken a violent chill in all this bitter cold. He was quite collapsed when they got home and they had to put him to bed instantly, and now he is in a high fever and worrying all the time because he cannot get to the church tonight. I told his brother to make every effort to calm his mind, but I fear it will be difficult. He is so enthusiastic, and the thought that he has been incapacitated at this crisis seems to be preying on his mind."

"Dear, dear," said Mrs. Venables, "but I expect Dr. Baines will give him something to quiet him down."

"I hope so, sincerely. It *is* a disaster, of course, but it is distressing that he should take it so to heart. Well, well. What can't be cured must be endured. This is our last hope gone. We shall be reduced to ringing minors."

"Is this man one of your ringers, then, padre?"

"Unfortunately, he is, and there is no one now to take his place. Our grand scheme will have to be abandoned. Even if I were to take a bell myself, I could not possibly ring for nine hours. I am not getting younger, and besides, I have an Early Service at 8 o'clock, in addition to the New Year service which will not release me till after midnight. Ah, well! Man proposes and God disposes—unless"—the Rector turned suddenly and looked at his guest—"you were speaking just now with a good deal of feeling about Treble Bob—you are not, yourself, by any chance, a ringer?"

"Well," said Wimsey, "I used at one time to pull quite a pretty rope. But whether, at this time of day——"

"Treble Bob?" inquired the Rector, eagerly.

"Treble Bob, certainly. But it's some time since——"

"It will come back to you," cried the Rector, feverishly. "It will come back. Half an hour with the handbells——"

"My dear!" said Mrs. Venables.

"Isn't it wonderful?" cried the Rector. "Is it not really providential? That just at this moment we should be sent a guest who is actually a ringer and accustomed to ringing Kent Treble Bob?" He rang for the maid. "Hinkins must go round at once and call the lads together for a practice ring on the handbells. My dear, I am afraid we shall have to monopolize the dining-room, if you don't mind. Emily, tell Hinkins that I have here a gentleman who can ring the peal with us and I want him to go round immediately——"

"One moment, Emily. Theodore, is it quite fair to ask Lord Peter Wimsey, after a motor accident, and at the end of a tiring day, to stay up ringing bells from midnight to nine o'clock? A short peal, perhaps, if he really does not mind, but even so, are we not demanding rather a lot of his good nature?"

The Rector's mouth drooped like the mouth of a hurt child, and Wimsey hastened to his support.

"Not in the least, Mrs. Venables. Nothing would please me more than to ring bells all day and all night. I am not tired at all. I really don't need rest. I would far rather ring bells. The only thing that worries me is whether I shall be able to get through the peal without making stupid mistakes."

"Of course you will, of course you will," said the Rector, hurriedly. "But as my wife says—really, I am afraid I am being very thoughtless. Nine hours is too much. We ought to confine ourselves to five thousand changes or so——"

"Not a bit of it," said Wimsey. "Nine hours or nothing. I insist upon it. Probably, once you have heard my efforts, it will be nothing."

"Pooh! nonsense!" cried the Rector. "Emily, tell Hinkins to get the ringers together here by—shall we say half-past six? I think they can all be here by then, except possibly Pratt, who lives up at Tupper's End, but I can make the eighth myself. How delightful this is! Positively, I cannot get over the amazing coincidence of your arrival. It shows the wonderful way in which Heaven provides even for our pleasures, if they be innocent. I hope, Lord Peter, you will not mind if I make a little reference to it in my sermon tonight? At least, it will hardly be a sermon—only a few thoughts appropriate to the New Year and its opportunities. May I ask where you usually ring?"

"Nowhere, nowadays; but when I was a boy I used to ring at Duke's Denver, and when I go home at Christmas and so on, I occasionally lay hand to a rope even now."

"Duke's Denver? Of course—St. John ad-Portam-Latinam—a beautiful little church; I know it quite well. But I think you will admit that our bells are finer. Well, now, if you will excuse me, I will just run and put the dining-room in readiness for our practice."

He bustled away.

"It is very good of you to indulge my husband's hobby," said Mrs. Venables; "this occasion has meant so much to him, and he has had so many disappointments about it. But it seems dreadful to offer you hospitality and then keep you hard at work all night."

Wimsey again assured her that the pleasure was entirely his.

"I shall insist on your getting a few hours' rest at least," was all Mrs. Venables could say. "Will you come up now and see your room? You will like a wash and brush-up at any rate. We will have supper at 7.30, if we can get my husband to release you by then, and after that, you really must go and lie down for a nap. I have put you in here—I see your man has everything ready for you."

"Well, Bunter," said Wimsey, when Mrs. Venables had departed, leaving him to make himself presentable by the inadequate light of a small oil-lamp and a candle, "that looks a nice bed—but I am not fated to sleep in it."

"So I understand from the young woman, my lord."

"It's a pity you can't relieve me at the rope, Bunter."

"I assure your lordship that for the first time in my existence I regret that I have made no practical study of Campanology."

"I am always so delighted to find that there are things you cannot do. Did you ever try?"

"Once only, my lord, and on that occasion an accident was only narrowly averted. Owing to my unfortunate lack of manual dexterity I was very nearly hanged in the rope, my lord."

"That's enough about hanging," said Wimsey, peevishly. "We're not detecting now, and I don't want to talk shop."

"Certainly not, my lord. Does your lordship desire to be shaved?"

"Yes—let's start the New Year with a clean face."

"Very good, my lord."

. . . . . .

Descending, clean and shaven, to the dining-room, Wimsey found the table moved aside and eight chairs set in a circle. On seven of the chairs sat seven men, varying in age from a gnarled old gnome with a long beard to an embarrassed youth with his hair plastered into a cow-lick; in the centre, the Rector stood twittering like an amiable magician.

"Ah! there you are! Splendid! excellent! Now, lads, this is Lord Peter Wimsey, who has been providentially sent to assist us out of our difficulty. He tells me he is a little out of practice, so I am sure you will not mind putting in a little time to enable him to get his hand in again. Now I must introduce you all. Lord Peter, this is Hezekiah Lavender, who has pulled the Tenor for sixty years and means to pull it for twenty years longer, don't you, Hezekiah?"

The little gnarled man grinned toothlessly and extended a knobby hand.

"Proud to meet you, my lord. Yes, I've pulled old Tailor Paul a mort o' times now. Her and me's well acquainted, and I means to go on a-pulling of her till she rings the nine tailors for me, that I do."

"I hope you will long be spared to do it, Mr. Lavender."

"Ezra Wilderspin," went on the Rector. "He's our biggest man, and he pulls the smallest bell. That's often the way of things, isn't it? He is our blacksmith, by the way, and has promised to get your car put right for you in the morning."

The blacksmith laughed sheepishly, engulfed Wimsey's fingers in an enormous hand and retired to his chair in some confusion.

"Jack Godfrey," continued the Rector. "Number Seven. How's Batty Thomas going now, Jack?"

"Going fine, thank you, sir, since we had them new gudgeons put in."

"Jack has the honour of ringing the oldest bell we have," added the Rector. "Batty Thomas was cast in 1338 by Thomas Belleyetere of Lynn; but she gets her name from Abbot Thomas who re-cast her in 1380—doesn't she, Jack?"

"So she do, sir," agreed Mr. Godfrey. Bells, it may be noted, like ships and kittens, have a way of being female, whatever names they are given.

"Mr. Donnington, the landlord of the Red Cow, our churchwarden," went on the Rector, bringing forward a long, thin man with a squint. "I ought to have mentioned him first of all, by right of his office, but then, you see, though he himself is very distinguished, his bell is not so ancient as Tailor Paul or Batty Thomas. He takes charge of Number Six—Dimity, we call her—a comparative newcomer in her present shape, though her metal is old."

"And a sweeter bell we haven't got in the ring," averred Mr. Donnington, stoutly. "Pleased to meet you, my lord."

"Joe Hinkins, my gardener. You have already met, I think. He pulls Number Five. Harry Gotobed, Number Four; our sexton, and what better name could a sexton have? And Walter Pratt—our youngest recruit, who is going to ring Number Three and do it very well indeed. So glad you were able to get here in time, Walter. That's all of us. You, Lord Peter, will take poor William Thoday's bell, Number Two. She and Number Five were recast in the same year as Dimity—the year of the old Queen's Jubilee; her name is Sabaoth. Now, let's get to work. Here is your handbell; come and sit next to Walter Pratt. Our good old friend Hezekiah will be the conductor, and you'll find he can sing out his calls as loud and clear as the bells, for all he's seventy-five years past. Can't you, Grand-dad?"

"Ay, that I can," cried the old man, cheerfully. "Now, boys, if you be ready, we'll ring a little touch of 96, just to put this gentleman in the way of it, like. You'll remember, my lord, that you starts by making the first snapping lead with the treble and after that you goes into the slow hunt till she comes down to snap with you again."

"Right you are," said Wimsey. "And after that I make the thirds and fourths."

"That's so, my lord. And then it's three steps forward and one step back till you lay the blows behind."

"Carry on, sergeant major."

The old man nodded, adding: "And you Wally Pratt, mind what you're about, and don't go a-follerin' your course bell beyond thirds place. I've telled yew about that time and again. Now, are you ready, lads—go!"

. . . .

The art of change-ringing is peculiar to the English, and, like most English peculiarities, unintelligible to the rest of the world. To the musical Belgian, for example, it appears that the proper thing to do with a carefully-tuned ring of bells is to play a tune upon it. By the English campanologist, the playing of tunes is considered to be a childish game, only fit for foreigners; the proper use of bells is to work out mathematical permutations and combinations. When he speaks of the music of his bells, he does not mean musicians' music—still less what the ordinary man calls music. To the ordinary man, in fact, the pealing of bells is a monotonous jangle and a nuisance, tolerable only when mitigated by remote distance and sentimental association. The change-ringer does, indeed, distinguish musical differences between one method of producing his permutations and another; he avers, for instance, that where the hinder bells run 7, 5, 6, or 5, 6, 7, or 5, 7, 6, the music is always prettier, and can detect and approve, where they occur, the consecutive fifths of Tittums and the cascading thirds of the Queen's change. But what he really means is, that by the English method of ringing with rope and wheel, each several bell gives forth her fullest and her noblest note. His passion—and it is a passion—finds its satisfaction in mathematical completeness and mechanical perfection, and as his bell weaves her way rhythmically up from lead to hinder place and down again, he is filled with the solemn intoxication that comes of intricate ritual faultlessly performed. To any disinterested spectator, peeping in upon the rehearsal, there might have been something a little absurd about the eight absorbed faces; the eight tense bodies poised in a spell-bound circle on the edges of eight dining-room chairs; the eight upraised right hands, decorously wagging the handbells upward and downward; but to the performers, everything was serious and important as an afternoon with the Australians at Lord's.

Mr. Hezekiah Lavender having called three successive bobs, the bells came back into rounds without mishap.

"Excellent," said the Rector. "You made no mistake about that."

"All right, so far," said Wimsey.

"The gentleman will do well enough," agreed Mr. Lavender. "Now, boys, once again. What 'ull we make it this time, sir?"

"Make it a 704," said the Rector, consulting his watch. "Call her in the middle with a double, before, wrong and home, and repeat."

"Right you are, sir. And you, Wally Pratt, keep your ears open for the treble and your eyes on your course bell, and don't go gapin' about or you'll have us all imbrangled."

The unfortunate Pratt wiped his forehead, curled his boots tightly round the legs of his chair, and took a firm hold of his bell. Whether out of nervousness or for some other cause, he found himself in trouble at the beginning of the seventh lead, "imbrangled" himself and his neighbors very successfully and broke into a severe perspiration.

"Stand!" growled Mr. Lavender, in a disgusted tone. "If that's the way you mean to set about it, Wally Pratt, we may just so well give up the ringing of this here peal. Surely you know by this time what to do at a bob?"

"Come, come," said the Rector. "You mustn't be disheartened, Wally. Try again. You forgot to make the double dodge in 7, 8, didn't you?"

"Yes, sir."

"Forgot!" exclaimed Mr. Lavender, waggling his beard. "Now, just yew take example by his lordship here. *He* didn't go forgettin' things, none the more for bein' out o' practice."

"Come, come, Hezekiah," cried the Rector again. "You mustn't be hard on Wally. We haven't all had sixty years' experience."

Mr. Lavender grunted, and started the whole touch again from the beginning. This time Mr. Pratt kept his head and his place and the ringing went successfully through to its conclusion.

"Well rung all," cried the Rector. "Our new recruit will do us credit, I think, Hezekiah?"

"I almost fell down in the second lead, though," said Wimsey, laughing. "I as nearly as possible forgot to lay the four blows in fourths place at the bob. However, nearly isn't quite."

"You'll keep your place all right, my lord," said Mr. Lavender. "As for you, Wally Pratt——"

"I think," said the Rector, hastily, "we'd better run across to the church now and let Lord Peter get the feel of his bell. You may as well all come over and ring the bells up for service. And, Jack, see to it that Lord Peter's rope is made comfortable for him. Jack

Godfrey takes charge of the bells and ropes," he added in explanation, "and keeps them in apple-pie order for us."

Mr. Godfrey smiled.

"We'll need to let the tuckings down a goodish bit for his lordship," he observed, measuring Wimsey with his eye; "he's none so tall as Will Thoday, not by a long chalk."

"Never you mind," said Wimsey. "In the words of the old bell-motto: I'd have it to be understood that though I'm little, yet I'm good."

"Of course," said the Rector, "Jack didn't mean anything else. But Will Thoday is a very tall man indeed. Now where did I put my hat? Agnes, my dear! Agnes! I can't find my hat. Oh, here, to be sure. And my muffler—I'm so much obliged to you. Now, let me just get the key of the belfry and we—dear me, now! When did I have that key last?"

"It's all right, sir," said Mr. Godfrey. "I have all the keys here, sir."

"The church-key as well?"

"Yes, sir, and the key of the bell-chamber."

"Oh, good, good—excellent. Lord Peter will like to go up into the bell-chamber. To my mind, Lord Peter, the sight of a ring of good bells—I beg your pardon, my dear?"

"I said, Do remember dinner-time, and don't keep poor Lord Peter too long."

"No, no, my dear, certainly not. But he will like to look at the bells. And the church itself is worth seeing, Lord Peter. We have a very interesting twelfth-century font, and the roof is considered to be one of the finest specimens—yes, yes, my dear, we're just going."

The hall-door was opened upon a glimmering world. The snow was still falling fast; even the footprints made less than an hour earlier by the ringers were almost obliterated. They straggled down the drive and crossed the road. Ahead of them, the great bulk of the church loomed dark and gigantic. Mr. Godfrey led the way with an old-fashioned lantern through the lych-gate and along a path bordered with tombstones to the south door of the church, which he opened, with a groaning of the heavy lock. A powerful ecclesiastical odour, compounded of ancient wood, varnish, dry rot, hassocks, hymn-books, paraffin lamps, flowers and candles, all gently baking in the warmth of slow-combustion stoves, billowed out from the interior. The tiny ray of the lantern picked out here the poppy-head on a pew, here the angle of a stone pillar, here the gleam of brass from a mural tablet. Their footsteps echoed queerly in the great height of the clerestory.

"All Transitional here," whispered the Rector, "except the Late Perpendicular window at the end of the north aisle, which of course you can't see. Nothing is left of the original Norman foundation but a couple of drums at the base of the chancel arch, but you can trace the remains of the Norman apse, if you look for it, underneath the Early English sanctuary. When we have more light, you will notice—Oh, yes, Jack, yes, by all means. Jack Godfrey is quite right, Lord Peter—we must not waste time. I am apt to be led away by my enthusiasm."

He conducted his guest westwards under the tower arch, and thence, in the wake of Jack Godfrey's lantern, up a steep and winding belfry stair, its stone treads worn shallow with the feet of countless long-dead ringers. After a turn or so, the procession halted; there was a jingling of keys and the lantern moved away to the right through a narrow door. Wimsey, following, found himself in the ringing-chamber of the belfry.

It was in no way remarkable, except in being perhaps a little loftier than the average, on account of the exceptional height of the tower. By daylight, it was well lit, having a fine window of three lights on each of its three exterior sides, while low down in the eastern wall, a couple of unglazed openings, defended by iron bars against accident, gave upon the interior of the church, a little above the level of the clerestory windows. As Jack Godfrey set the lantern on the floor, and proceeded to light a paraffin lamp which hung against the wall, Wimsey could see the eight bell-ropes, their woollen sallies looped neatly to the walls, and their upper ends vanishing mysteriously into the shadows of the chamber roof. Then the light streamed out and the walls took shape and colour. They were plainly plastered, with a painted motto in Gothic lettering running round below the windows: "They Have Neither Speech nor Language but their Voices are Heard Among Them, their Sound is Gone Forth into All Lands." Above this, various tablets of wood, brass and even stone, commemorated the ringing of remarkable peals in the past.

"We shall hope to put up a new tablet after tonight," said the Rector's voice in Wimsey's ear.

"I only hope I may do nothing to prevent it," said Wimsey. "I see you have the old regulations for your ringers. Ah! 'Keep stroak of time and goe not out, Or elles you forfeit out of doubt For every fault a Jugg of beer.' It doesn't say how big a jug, but there is something about the double g that suggests size and potency. 'If a bell you overthrow 'Twill cost you sixpence ere you goe.' That's cheap, considering the damage it does. On the other hand, sixpence for every swear or curse is rather on the dear side, I think, don't you, padre? Where's this bell of mine?"

"Here, my lord." Jack Godfrey had unhitched the rope of the second bell, and let down to its full length the portion of rope below the sallie.

"When you've got her raised," he said, "we'll fix them tuckings proper. Unless you'd like me to raise her for you?"

"Not on your life," said Wimsey. "It's a poor ringer that can't raise his own bell." He grasped the rope and pulled it gently downwards, gathering the slack in his left hand. Softly, tremulously, high overhead in the tower, Sabaoth began to speak, and her sisters after her as the ringers stood to their ropes. "Tin-tin-tin," cried Gaude in her silvery treble; "tan-tan," answered Sabaoth; "din-din-din," "dan-dan-dan," said John and Jericho, climbing to their places; "bim, bam, bim, bam," Jubilee and Dimity followed; "bom," said Batty Thomas; and Tailor Paul, majestically lifting up her great bronze mouth, bellowed "bo, bo, bo," as the ropes hauled upon the wheels.

Wimsey brought his bell competently up and set her at back-stroke while the tuckings were finally adjusted, after which, at the Rector's suggestion, a few rounds were rung to let him "get the feel of her."

"You can leave your bells up, boys," said Mr. Hezekiah Lavender, graciously, when this last rehearsal was concluded, "but don't you go a-taking that for what they calls a preceedent, Wally Pratt. And listen here, all on you; don't make no mistake. You comes here, sharp at the quarter to eleven, see—and you rings same as usual for service, and after Rector has finished his sermon, you comes up here again quiet and decent and takes your places. Then, while they're a-singin' their 'ymn, I rings the nine tailors and the 'alf-minute passing-strokes for Old Year, see. Then you takes your ropes in hand and waits for the clock to strike. When she's finished striking I says 'Go!' and mind as you're ready to go. And when Rector's done down below, he's promised to come up and give a 'and from time to time to any man as needs a rest, and I'm sure it's very kind of him. And I take leave to suppose, Alf Donnington, as you won't forget the usual."

"Not me," said Mr. Donnington. "Well, so long, boys."

The lantern led the way from the ringing-chamber, and a great shuffling of feet followed it.

"And now," said the Rector, "and now, Lord Peter, you will like to come and see—dear me!" he ejaculated, as they groped upon the dark spiral stair, "where in the world is Jack Godfrey? Jack! He has gone on down with the others. Ah, well, poor fellow, no doubt he wants to get home to his supper. We must not be selfish. Unfortunately he has the key of the bell-chamber, and without it we cannot conduct our researches. However, you will see much better tomorrow. Yes, Joe, yes—we are coming. Do be careful of these stairs—they are very much worn, especially on the inside. Here we are, safe and sound. Excellent! Now, before we go, Lord Peter, I should so much like to show you——"

The clock in the tower chimed the three-quarters.

"Bless my heart!" cried the Rector, conscience-stricken, "and dinner was to be at half-past! My wife—we must wait till tonight. You will get a general idea of the majesty and beauty of our church if you attend the service, though there are many most interesting details that a visitor is almost bound to miss if they are not pointed out to him. The font, for instance—Jack! bring the lantern here a moment—there is one point about our font which is most uncommon, and I should like to show it to you. Jack!"

But Jack, unaccountably deaf, was jingling the church keys in the porch, and the Rector, sighing a little, accepted defeat.

"I fear it is true," he said, as he trotted down the path, "that I am inclined to lose count of time."

"Perhaps," replied Wimsey politely, "the being continually in and about this church brings eternity too close."

"Very true," said the Rector, "very true—though there are mementoes enough to mark the passage of time. Remind me tomorrow to show you the tomb of Nathaniel Perkins—one of our local worthies and a great sportsman. He refereed once for the great Tom Sayers, and was a notable figure at all the 'mills' for miles around, and when he died—Here we are at home. I will tell you later about Nathaniel Perkins. Well, my dear, we're back at last! Not so *very* late after all. Come along, come along. You must make a good dinner, Lord Peter, to fit you for your exertions. What have we here? Stewed oxtail? Excellent! Most sustaining! I trust, Lord Peter, you can eat stewed oxtail. For what we are about to receive . . ."

THE SECOND COURSE

The Bells in Their Courses

When mirth and pleasure is on the wing we ring;
At the departure of a soul we toll.

RINGERS' RULES AT SOUTHILL, BEDFORDSHIRE

AFTER DINNER, Mrs. Venables resolutely asserted her authority. She sent Lord Peter up to his room, regardless of the Rector, who was helplessly hunting through a set of untidy bookshelves in search of the Rev. Christopher Woollcott's *History of the Bells of Fenchurch St. Paul.*

"I can't imagine what has become of it," said the Rector: "I fear I'm sadly unmethodical. But perhaps you would like to look at this—a trifling contribution of my own to campanological lore. I know, my dear, I know—I must not detain Lord Peter—it is thoughtless of me."

"You must get some rest yourself, Theodore."

"Yes, yes, my dear. In a moment. I was only——"

Wimsey saw that the one way to quiet the Rector was to desert him without compunction. He retired, accordingly, and was captured at the head of the stairs by Bunter, who tucked him firmly up beneath the eiderdown with a hot-water bottle and shut the door upon him.

A roaring fire burned in the grate. Wimsey drew the lamp closer to him, opened the little brochure presented to him by the Rector, and studied the title-page:

An Inquiry into
the Mathematical Theory
of the
IN AND OUT OF COURSE

together with
Directions for
Calling Bells into Rounds
from any position
in all the recognized Methods
upon a
New and Scientific Principle
by
Theodore Venables, M.A.

Rector of Fenchurch St. Paul
sometime Scholar of Caius Coll: Camb:
author of
"Change-ringing for Country Churches,"
"Fifty Short Touches of Grandsire Triples," etc.
"God is gone up with a merry noise."

MCMII

The letter-press was of a soporific tendency; so was the stewed ox-tail; the room was warm; the day had been a tiring one; the lines swam before Lord Peter's eyes. He nodded; a coal tinkled from the grate; he roused himself with a jerk and read: ". . . if the 5th is in course after the 7th (says Shipway), and 7th after the 6th, they are right, when the small bells, 2, 3, 4, are brought as directed in the preceding peals; but if 6, 7 are together without the 5th, call the 5th into the hunt. . . ."

Lord Peter Wimsey nodded away into dreams.

. . . . . .

He was roused by the pealing of bells.

For a moment, memory eluded him—then he flung the eider-down aside and sat up, ruffled and reproachful, to encounter the calm gaze of Bunter.

"Good God! I've been asleep! Why didn't you call me? They've begun without me."

"Mrs. Venables gave orders, my lord, that you were not to be disturbed until half-past eleven, and the reverend gentleman instructed me to say, my lord, that they would content themselves with ringing six bells as a preliminary to the service."

"What time is it now?"

"Nearly five minutes to eleven, my lord."

As he spoke, the pealing ceased, and Jubilee began to ring the five-minute bell.

"Dash it all!" said Wimsey. "This will never do. Must go and hear the old boy's sermon. Give me a hair-brush. Is it still snowing?"

"Harder than ever, my lord."

Wimsey made a hasty toilet and ran downstairs, Bunter following him decorously. They let themselves out by the front door, and, guided by Bunter's electric torch, made their way through the shrubbery and across the road to the church, entering just as the organ boomed out its final notes. Choir and parson were in their places and Wimsey, blinking in the yellow lamplight, at length discovered his seven fellow-ringers seated on a row of chairs beneath the tower. He picked his way cautiously over the cocoa-nut matting towards them, while Bunter, who had apparently acquired all the necessary information beforehand, made his unperturbed way to a pew in the north aisle and sat down beside Emily from the Rectory. Old Hezekiah Lavender greeted Wimsey with a welcoming chuckle and thrust a prayer-book under his nose as he knelt down to pray.

"Dearly beloved brethren——"

Wimsey scrambled to his feet and looked round.

At the first glance he felt himself sobered and awe-stricken by the noble proportions of the church, in whose vast spaces the congregation—though a good one for so small a parish in the dead of a winter's night—seemed almost lost. The wide nave and shadowy aisles, the lofty span of the chancel arch—crossed, though not obscured, by the delicate fan-tracery and crenellated moulding of the screen—the intimate and cloistered loveliness of the chancel, with its pointed arcading, graceful ribbed vault and five narrow east lancets, led his attention on and focused it first upon the remote glow of the sanctuary. Then his gaze, returning to the nave, followed the strong yet slender shafting that sprang fountain-like from floor to foliated column-head, spraying into the light, wide arches that carried the clerestory. And there, mounting to the steep pitch of the roof, his eyes were held entranced with wonder and delight. Incredibly aloof, flinging back the light in a dusky shimmer of bright hair and gilded outspread wings, soared the ranked angels, cherubim and seraphim, choir over choir, from corbel and hammer-beam floating face to face uplifted.

"My God!" muttered Wimsey, not without reverence. And he softly repeated to himself: "He rode upon the cherubims and did fly; He came flying upon the wings of the wind."

Mr. Hezekiah Lavender poked his new colleague sharply in the ribs, and Wimsey became aware that the congregation had settled down to the General Confession, leaving him alone and agape upon his feet. Hurriedly he turned the leaves of his prayer-book and applied himself to making the proper responses. Mr. Lavender, who had obviously decided that he was either a half-wit or a heathen, assisted him by finding the Psalms for him and by bawling every verse very loudly in his ear.

". . . Praise Him in the cymbals and dances: praise Him upon the strings and pipe."

The shrill voices of the surpliced choir mounted to the roof, and seemed to find their echo in the golden mouths of the angels.

"Praise Him upon the well-tuned cymbals; praise Him upon the loud cymbals.

"Let everything that hath breath praise the Lord."

. . . .

The time wore on towards midnight. The Rector, advancing to the chancel steps, delivered, in his mild and scholarly voice, a simple and moving little address, in which he spoke of praising God, not only upon the strings and pipe, but upon the beautiful bells of their beloved church, and alluded, in his gently pious way, to the presence of the passing stranger—"please do not turn round to stare at him; that would be neither courteous nor reverent"—who had been sent "by what men call chance" to assist in this work of devotion. Lord Peter blushed, the Rector pronounced the Benediction, the organ played the opening bars of a hymn and Hezekiah Lavender exclaimed sonorously: "Now, lads!" The ringers, with much subdued shuffling, extricated themselves from their chairs and wound their way up the belfry stair. Coats were pulled off and hung on nails in the ringing-chamber, and Wimsey, observing on a bench near the door an enormous brown jug and nine pewter tankards, understood, with pleasure, that the landlord of the Red Cow had, indeed, provided "the usual" for the refreshment of the ringers.

The eight men advanced to their stations, and Hezekiah consulted his watch.

"Time!" he said.

He spat upon his hands, grasped the sallie of Tailor Paul, and gently swung the great bell over the balance.

Toll-toll-toll; and a pause; toll-toll-toll; and a pause; toll-toll-toll; the nine tailors, or teller-strokes, that mark the passing of a man. The year is dead; toll him out with twelve strokes more, one for every passing month. Then silence. Then, from the faint, sweet tubular chimes of the clock overhead, the four quarters and the twelve strokes of midnight. The ringers grasped their ropes.

"Go!"

The bells gave tongue: Gaude, Sabaoth, John, Jericho, Jubilee, Dimity, Batty Thomas and Tailor Paul, rioting and exulting high up in the dark tower, wide mouths rising and falling, brazen tongues clamouring, huge wheels turning to the dance of the leaping ropes. Tin tan din dan bim bam bom bo—tan tin din dan bam bim bo bom—tin tan dan din bim bam bom bo—tan tin dan din bam bim bo bom—tan dan tin bam din bo bim bom—every bell in her place striking tuneably, hunting up, hunting down, dodging, snapping, laying her blows behind, making her thirds and fourths, working down to lead the dance again. Out over the flat, white wastes of fen, over the spear-straight, steel-dark dykes and the wind-bent, groaning poplar trees, bursting from the snow-choked louvres of the belfry, whirled away southward and westward in gusty blasts of clamour to the sleeping counties went the music of the bells—little Gaude, silver Sabaoth, strong John and Jericho, glad Jubilee, sweet Dimity and old Batty Thomas, with great Tailor Paul bawling and striding like a giant in the midst of them. Up and down went the shadows of the ringers upon the walls, up and down went the scarlet sallies flickering roofwards and floorwards, and up and down, hunting in their courses, went the bells of Fenchurch St. Paul.

Wimsey, his eye upon the ropes and his ear pricked for the treble's shrill tongue speaking at lead, had little attention to give to anything but his task. He was dimly conscious of old Hezekiah, moving with the smooth rhythm of a machine, bowing his ancient back very slightly at each pull to bring Tailor Paul's great weight over, and of Wally Pratt, his face anxiously contorted and his lips moving in the effort to keep his intricate course in mind. Wally's bell was moving down now towards his own, dodging Number Six and passing her, dodging Number Seven and passing her, passing Number Five, striking her two blows at lead, working up again, while the treble came down to take her place and make her last snapping lead with Sabaoth. One blow in seconds place and one at lead, and Sabaoth, released from the monotony of the slow hunt, ran out merrily into her plain hunting course. High in the air above them the cock upon the weathervane stared out over the snow and watched the pinnacles of the tower swing to and fro with a slowly widening sweep as the tall stalk of stone gathered momentum and rocked like a wind-blown tree beneath his golden feet.

The congregation streamed out from the porch, their lanterns and torches flitting away into the whirling storm like sparks tossed from a bonfire. The Rector, pulling off surplice and stole, climbed in his cassock to the ringing-chamber and sat down upon the bench, ready to give help and counsel. The clock's chimes came faintly through the voices of the bells. At the end of the first hour the Rector took the rope from the hand of the agitated Wally and released him for an interval of rest and refreshment. A soft glugging sound proclaimed that Mr. Donnington's "usual" was going where it would do most good.

Wimsey, relieved at the end of the third hour, found Mrs. Venables seated among the pewter pots, with Bunter in respectful attendance beside her.

"I do hope," said Mrs. Venables, "that you are not feeling exhausted."

"Far from it; only rather dry." Wimsey remedied this condition without further apology, and asked how the peal sounded.

"Beautiful!" said Mrs. Venables, loyally. She did not really care for bell-music, and felt sleepy; but the Rector would have felt hurt if she had withdrawn her sympathetic presence.

"It's surprising, isn't it?" she added, "how soft and mellow it sounds in here. But of course there's another floor between us and the bell-chamber." She yawned desperately. The bells rang on. Wimsey, knowing that the Rector was well set for the next quarter of an hour, was seized with a fancy to listen to the peal from outside. He slipped down the winding stair and groped his way through the south porch. As he emerged into the night, the clamour of the bells smote on his ears like a blow. The snow was falling less heavily now. He turned to his right, knowing that it is unlucky to walk about a church widdershins, and followed the path close beneath the wall till he found himself standing by the west door. Sheltered by the towering bulk of the masonry, he lit a sacrilegious cigarette, and, thus fortified, turned right again. Beyond the foot of the tower, the pathway ended, and he stumbled among grass and tombstones for the whole length of the aisle, which, on this side, was prolonged to the extreme east end of the church. Midway between the last two buttresses on the north side he came upon a path leading to a small door; this he tried, but found it locked, and so passed on, encountering the full violence of the wind as he rounded the east end. Pausing a moment to get his breath, he looked out over the Fen. All was darkness, except for a dim stationary light which might have been shining from some cottage window. Wimsey reckoned that the cottage must lie somewhere along the solitary road by which they had reached the Rectory, and wondered why anybody should be awake at three o'clock on New Year's morning. But the night was bitter and he was wanted back at his job. He completed his circuit, re-entered by the south porch and returned to the belfry. The Rector resigned the rope to him, warning him that he had now to make his two blows behind and not to forget to dodge back into eighths place before hunting down.

At six o'clock, the ringers were all in pretty good case. Wally Pratt's cow-lick had fallen into his eyes, and he was sweating freely, but was still moving well within himself. The blacksmith was fresh and cheerful, and looked ready to go on till next Christmas. The publican was grim but determined. Most unperturbed of all was the aged Hezekiah, working grandly as though he were part and parcel of his rope, and calling his bobs without a tremor in his clear old voice.

At a quarter to eight the Rector left them to prepare for his early service. The beer in the jug had sunk to low tide and Wally Pratt, with an hour and a half to go, was beginning to look a little strained. Through the southern window a faint reflection of the morning light came, glimmering frail and blue.

At ten minutes past nine the Rector was back in the belfry, standing watch in hand with a beaming smile on his face.

At thirteen minutes past nine the treble came shrilling triumphantly into her last lead.

Tin tan din dan bim bam bom bo.

Their long courses ended, the bells came faultlessly back into rounds, and the ringers stood.

"Magnificent, lads, magnificent!" cried Mr. Venables. "You've done it, and it couldn't have been better done."

"Eh!" admitted Mr. Lavender, "it was none so bad." A slow toothless grin overspread his countenance. "Yes, we done it. How did it sound from down below, sir?"

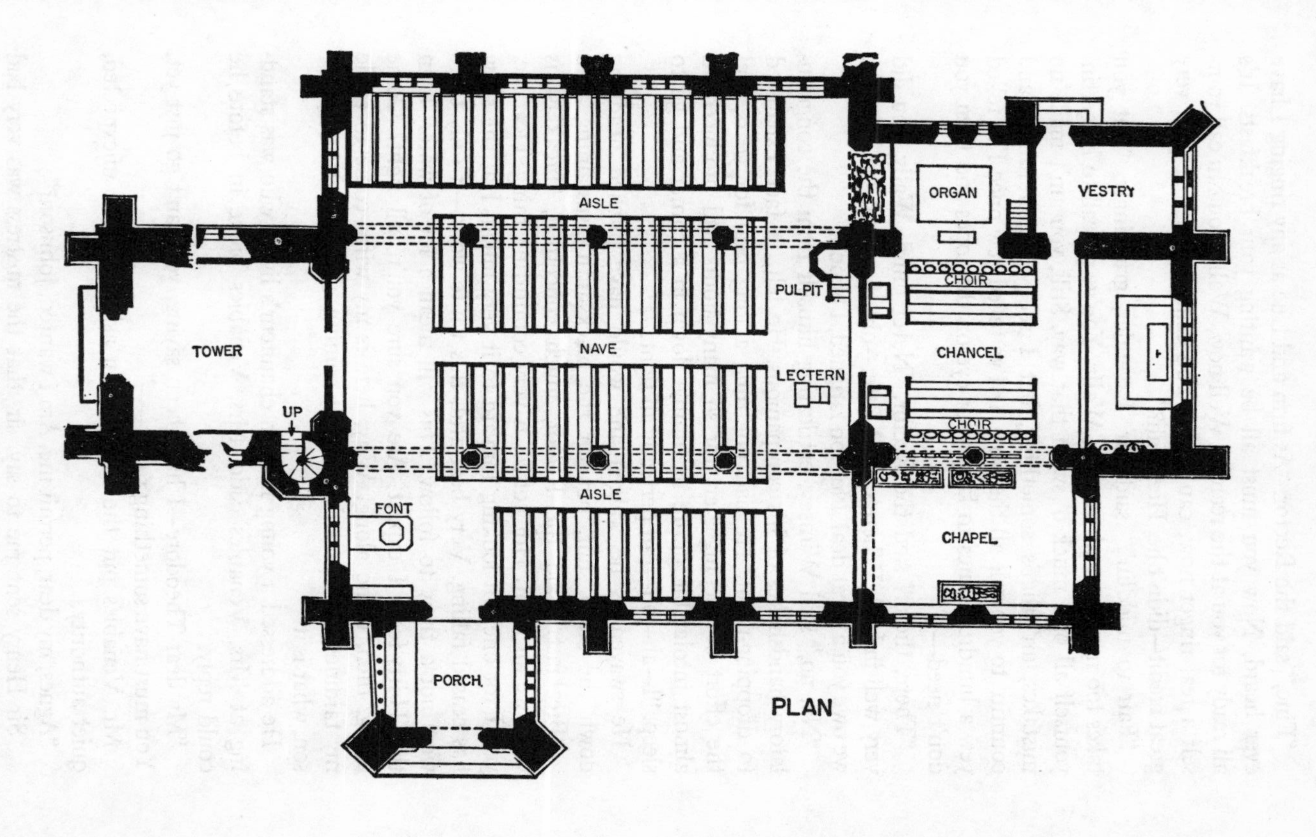
AISLE
ORGAN
VESTRY
PULPIT
CHOIR
TOWER
NAVE
CHANCEL
LECTERN
UP
CHOIR
AISLE
FONT
CHAPEL
PORCH
PLAN

"Fine," said the Rector. "As firm and true as any ringing I have ever heard. Now you must all be wanting your breakfasts. It's all ready for you at the rectory. Well now, Wally, you can call yourself a real ringer now, can't you? You came through it with very great credit—didn't he, Hezekiah?"

"Fair to middlin'," said Mr. Lavender, grudgingly. "But you takes too much out o' yourself, Wally. You've no call to be gettin' yourself all of a muck o' sweat that way. Still, you ain't made no mistakes, an' that's something, but I see you a-mumblin' and countin' to yourself all the time. If I've telled yew once I've telled yew a hundred times to keep your eye on the ropes and then you don't need——"

"There, there!" said the Rector. "Never mind, Wally, you did very well indeed. Where's Lord Peter—oh! there you are. I'm sure we owe you a great deal. Not too fatigued, I hope?"

"No, no," said Wimsey, extricating himself from the congratulatory handshakes of his companions. He felt, in fact, exhausted to dropping-point. He had not rung a long peal for years, and the effort of keeping alert for so many hours had produced an almost intolerable desire to tumble down in a corner and go to sleep. "I—ah—oh—I'm perfectly all right."

He swayed as he walked and would have pitched headlong down the steep stair, but for the blacksmith's sustaining arm.

"Breakfast," said the Rector, much concerned, "breakfast is what we all want. Hot coffee. A very comforting thing. Dear me, yes, I for one am looking forward to it very much. Ha! the snow has ceased falling. Very beautiful, this white world—if only there were not a thaw to follow. This will mean a lot of water down the Thirty-foot, I expect. Are you sure you're all right? Come along, then, come along! Why, here is my wife—come to chide my tardiness, I expect. We're just coming, my dear—Why, Johnson, what is it?"

He addressed a young man in chauffeur's livery who was standing at Mrs. Venables' side. Mrs. Venables broke in before he could reply.

"My dear Theodore—I have been saying, you can't go just yet. You must have something to eat——"

Mr. Venables put the interruption aside with an unexpected, quiet authority.

"Agnes, my dear, permit me. Am I wanted, Johnson?"

"Sir Henry sent me to say, sir, that the mistress was very bad this morning, and they're afraid she's sinking, sir, and she is very anxious to receive the sacrament if you could see your way——"

"Good Heavens!" exclaimed the Rector. "So ill as that? Sinking? I am terribly grieved to hear it. Of course, I will come immediately. I had no idea——"

"No more hadn't any of us, sir. It's this wicked influenza. I'm sure nobody ever thought yesterday——"

"Oh, dear, oh, dear! I hope it's not as bad as you fear! But I mustn't delay. You shall tell me about it as you go. I will be with you in one moment. Agnes, my dear, see that the men get their breakfast and explain to them why I cannot join them. Lord Peter, you must excuse me. I shall be with you later. Bless my heart! Lady Thorpe—what a scourge this influenza is!"

He trotted hurriedly back into the church. Mrs. Venables looked ready to cry, between anxiety and distress.

"Poor Theodore! After being up all night—of course he has to go, and we ought not to think about ourselves. Poor Sir Henry! An invalid himself! Such a bitter morning, and no breakfast! Johnson, please say to Miss Hilary how sorry I am and ask if there is anything I can do to help Mrs. Gates. The housekeeper, you know, Lord Peter—such a nice woman, and the cook away on holiday, it does seem so hard. Troubles never come singly. Dear me, you must be famished. Do come along and be looked after. You'll be sure to send round, Johnson, if you want any help. Can Sir Henry's nurse manage, I wonder? This is such an isolated place for getting any help. Theodore! are you sure you are well wrapped up?"

The Rector, who now rejoined them, carrying the Communion vessels in a wooden case, assured her that he was well protected. He was bundled into the waiting car by Johnson, and whirled away westwards towards the village.

This untoward incident cast a certain gloom over the breakfast table, though Wimsey, who felt his sides clapping together like an empty portmanteau, was only too thankful to devour his eggs and bacon and coffee in peace. Eight pairs of jaws chumped steadily, while Mrs. Venables dispensed the provisions in a somewhat distracted way, interspersing her hospitable urgings with ejaculations of sympathy for the Thorpe family and anxiety for her husband's well-being.

"Such a lot of trouble as the Thorpes have had, too, one way and another," she remarked. "All that dreadful business about old Sir Charles, and the loss of the necklace, and that unfortunate girl and everything, though it was a merciful thing the man died, after killing a warder and all that, though it upset the whole family very much at the time. Hezekiah, how are you getting on? A bit more bacon? Mr. Donnington? Hinkins, pass Mr. Godfrey the cold ham. And of course, Sir Henry never has been strong since the War, poor man. Are you getting enough to eat down there, Wally? I do hope the Rector won't be kept too long without his breakfast. Lord Peter, a little more coffee?"

Wimsey thanked her, and asked what, exactly, was the trouble about old Sir Charles and the necklace.

"Oh, of course, you don't know. So silly of me! Living in this solitary place, one imagines that one's little local excitements are of world-wide importance. It's rather a long story, and I shouldn't have mentioned it at all"—here the good lady lowered her voice—"if William Thoday had been here. I'll tell you after breakfast. Or ask Hinkins. He knows all about it. How is William Thoday this morning, I wonder? Has anybody heard?"

"He's mortal bad, ma'am, I'm afeard," replied Mr. Donnington, taking the question to himself. "I saw my missus after service, and she told me she'd heard from Joe Mullins as he was dreadfully delirious all night, and they couldn't hardly keep him in his bed, on account of him wanting to get up and ring."

"Dear, dear! It's a good thing for Mary that they've got James at home."

"So it is," agreed Mr. Donnington. "A sailor's wonderful handy about the house. Not but what his leave's up in a day or two, but it's to be hoped as they'll be over the worst by then."

Mrs. Venables clucked gently.

"Ah!" said Hezekiah. "'Tis a mortal bad thing, this influenza. And it do take the young and strong cruel often, and leave the old uns be. Seems like old fellers like me is too tough fer it."

"I hope so, Hezekiah, I'm sure," said Mrs. Venables. "There! Ten o'clock striking, and the Rector not back. Well, I suppose one couldn't expect—why, there's the car coming up the drive! Wally, would you please ring that bell. We want some fresh eggs and bacon for the Rector, Emily, and you'd better take the coffee out and hot it up for him."

Emily took out the jug, but returned almost immediately.

"Oh, if you please, ma'am, the Rector says, will you all excuse him, please, and he'll take his breakfast in the study. And oh! if you please, ma'am, poor Lady Thorpe's gone, ma'am, and if Mr. Lavender's finished, he's please to go over to the church at once and ring the passing bell."

"Gone!" cried Mrs. Venables. "Why, what a terrible thing!"

"Yes, ma'am. Mr. Johnson says it was dreadful sudden. The Rector hadn't hardly left her room, ma'am, when it was all over, and they don't know how they're to tell Sir Henry."

Mr. Lavender pushed his chair back and quavered to his ancient feet.

"In the midst of life," he said solemnly, "we are in death. Terrible true that is, to be sure. If so be as you'll kindly excuse me, ma'am, I'll be leaving you now, and thank you kindly. Good mornin' to you all. That were a fine peal as we rung, none the more for that, and now I'll be gettin' to work on old Tailor Paul again."

He shuffled sturdily out, and within five minutes they heard the deep and melancholy voice of the bell ringing, first the six tailors for a woman and then the quick strokes which announce the age of the dead. Wimsey counted them up to thirty-seven. Then they ceased, and were followed by the slow tolling of single strokes at half-minute intervals. In the dining-room, the silence was only broken by the shy sound of hearty feeders trying to finish their meal inconspicuously.

The party broke up quietly. Mr. Wilderspin drew Wimsey to one side and explained that he had sent round to Mr. Ashton for a couple of farm-horses and a stout rope, and hoped to get the car out of the ditch in a very short time, and would then see what was needed in the way of repairs. If his lordship cared to step along to the smithy in an hour or so, they could go into consultation about the matter. His (Mr. Wilderspin's) son George was a great hand with motors, having had considerable experience with farm engines, not to mention his own motor-bike. Mrs. Venables retired into the study to see that her husband had everything he wanted and to administer such consolation as she might for the calamity that had befallen the parish. Wimsey, knowing that his presence at Frog's Bridge could not help and would probably only hinder the break-down team, begged his hostess not to trouble about him, and wandered out into the garden. At the back of the house, he discovered Joe Hinkins, polishing the Rector's aged car. Joe accepted a cigarette, passed a few remarks about the ringing of the peal, and thence slid into conversation about the Thorpe family.

"They live in the big red-brick house t'other side the village. A rich family they were once. They do say as they got their land through putting money into draining of the Fen long ago under the Earl of Bedford. You'd know all about that, my lord, I dare say. Anyhow, they reckon to be an old family hereabouts. Sir Charles, he was a fine, generous gentleman; did a lot of good in his time, though he wasn't what you'd call a rich man, not by no means. They do say his father lost a lot of money up in London, but I don't know how. But he farmed his land well, and it was a rare trouble to the village when he died along of the burglary."

"What burglary was that?"

"Why, that was the necklace the mistress was talking about. It was when young Mr. Henry—that's the present Sir Henry—was married. The year of the War, it was, in the spring—April 1914—I remember it very well. I was a youngster at the time, and their wedding-bells was the first long peal I ever rang. We gave them 5,040 Grandsire Triples, Holt's Ten-part Peal—you'll find the record of it in the church yonder, and there was a big supper at the Red House afterwards, and a lot of fine visitors came down for the wedding. The young lady was an orphan, you see, and some sort of connection with the family, and Mr. Henry being the heir they was married down here. Well, there was a lady come to stay in the house, and she had a wonderful fine emerald necklace—worth thousands and thousands of pounds it was—and the very night after the wedding, when Mr. Henry and his lady was just gone off for their honeymoon, the necklace was stole."

"Good lord!" said Wimsey. He sat down on the running-board of the car and looked as encouraging as he could.

"You may say so," said Mr. Hinkins, much gratified. "A big sensation it made at the time in the parish. And the worst part of it was, you see, that one of Sir Charles' own men was concerned in it. Poor gentleman, he never held up his head again. When they took this fellow Deacon and it came out what he'd done——"

"Deacon was——?"

"Deacon, he was the butler. Been with them six years, he had, and married the housemaid, Mary Russell, that's married to Will Thoday, him as rings Number Two and has got the influenzy so bad."

"Oh!" said Wimsey. "Then Deacon is dead now, I take it."

"That's right, my lord. That's what I was a-telling you. You see, it 'appened this way. Mrs. Wilbraham woke up in the night and saw a man standing by her bedroom window. So she yelled out, and the fellow jumped out into the garden and dodged into the shrubbery, like. So she screamed again, very loud, and rang her bell and made a to-do, and everybody came running out to see what was the matter. There was Sir Charles and some gentlemen that was staying in the house, and one of them had a shot-gun. And when they got downstairs, there was Deacon in his coat and trousers just running out at the back door, and the footman in pyjamas; and the chauffeur as slept over the garage, he came running out too, because the first thing as Sir Charles did, you see, was to pull the house-bell what they had for calling the gardener. The gardener, he came too, of course, and so did I, because you see, I was the gardener's boy at the time, and wouldn't never have left Sir Charles, only for him having to cut down his establishment, what with the War and paying Mrs. Wilbraham for the necklace."

"Paying for the necklace?"

"Yes, my lord. That's just where it was, you see. It wasn't insured, and though of course nobody could have held Sir Charles responsible, he had it on his conscience as he ought to pay Mrs. Wilbraham the value of it, though how anybody calling herself a lady could take the money off him I don't understand. But as I was a-saying, we all came out and then one of the gentlemen see the man a-tearing across the lawn, and Mr. Stanley loosed off the shot-gun at him and hit him, as we found out afterwards, but he got away over the wall, and there was a chap waiting for him on the other side with a motor-car, and he got clear away. And in the middle of it all, out comes Mrs. Wilbraham and her maid, a-hollering that the emerald necklace has been took."

"And didn't they catch the man?"

"Not for a bit, they didn't, my lord. The chauffeur, he gets the car out and goes off after them, but by the time he'd got started up, they was well away. They went up the road past the church, but nobody knew whether they'd gone through Fenchurch St. Peter or up on to the Bank, and even then they might have gone either by Dykesey and Walea or Walbeach way, or over the Thirty-foot to Leamholt or Holport. So the chauffeur went after the police. You see, barring the village constable at Fenchurch St. Peter there's no police nearer than Leamholt, and in those days they didn't have a car at the police-station even there, so Sir Charles said to send the car for them would be quicker than telephoning and waiting till they came."

"Ah!" said Mrs. Venables, suddenly popping her head in at the garage door. "So you've got Joe on to the Thorpe robbery. He knows a lot more about it than I do. Are you sure you aren't frozen to death in this place?"

Wimsey said he was quite warm enough, thanks, and he hoped the Rector was none the worse for his exertions.

"He doesn't seem to be," said Mrs. Venables, "but he's rather upset, naturally. You'll stay to lunch, of course. No trouble at all. Can you eat shepherd's pie? You're sure? The butcher doesn't call today, but there's always cold ham."

She bustled away. Joe Hinkins passed a chamois leather thoughtfully over a headlight. "Carry on," said Wimsey.

"Well, my lord, the police did come and of course they hunted round a good bit, and didn't we bless them, the way they morrised over the flower-beds, a-looking for footprints and breaking down the tulips. Anyhow, there 'twas, and they traced the car and got the fellow that had been shot in the leg. A well-known jewel thief he was, from London. But you see, they said it must have been a inside job, because it turned out as the fellow as jumped out o' the window wasn't the same as the London man, and the long and the short of it was, they found out as the inside man was this here Deacon. Seems the Londoner had been keeping his eye on that necklace, like, and had got hold of Deacon and got him to go and steal the stuff and drop it out of the window to him. They was pretty sure of their ground—I think they found finger-prints and such like—and they arrested Deacon. I remember it very well, because they took him one Sunday morning, just a-coming out of church, and a terrible job it was to take him; he near killed a constable. The robbery was on the Thursday night, see? and it had took them that time to get on to it."

"Yes, I see. How did Deacon know where to find the jewels?"

"Well, that was just it, my lord. It came out as Mrs. Wilbraham's maid had let out something, stupid-like, to Mary Russell—that is, her as had married Deacon, and she, not thinking no harm, had told her husband. Of course, they had them two women up too. All the village was in a dreadful way about it, because Mary was a very decent, respectable girl, and her father was one of our sidesmen. There's not an honester, better family in the Fenchurches than what the Russells are. This Deacon, he didn't come from these parts, he was a Kentish man by birth. Sir Charles brought him down from London. But there wasn't no way of getting him out of it, because the London thief—Cranton, he called himself, but he had other names—he blew the gaff and gave Deacon away."

"Dirty dog!"

"Ah! but you see, he said as Deacon had done him down and so, if Cranton was telling the truth, he had. Cranton said as Deacon dropped out nothing but the empty jewel-case and kept the necklace for himself. He went for Deacon 'ammer-and-tongs in the dock and tried for to throttle him. But of course, Deacon swore as it was all a pack of lies. His tale was, that he heard a noise and went to see what was the matter, and that when Mrs. Wilbraham saw him in her room, he was just going to give chase to Cranton. He couldn't deny he'd been in the room, you see, because of the finger-prints and that. But it went against him that he'd told a different story at the beginning, saying as how he'd gone out by the back door, hearing somebody in the garden. Mary supported that, and it's a fact that the back door was unbolted when the footman got to it. But the lawyer on the other side said that Deacon had unbolted the door himself beforehand, just in case he had to get out by the window, so as to leave himself a way back into the house. But as for the necklace, they never could settle that part of it, for it wasn't never found. Whether Cranton had it, and was afraid to get rid of it, like, or whether Deacon had it and hid it, I don't know and no more does nobody. It ain't never turned up to this day, nor yet the money Cranton said he'd given Deacon, though they turned the place upside-down looking for both on 'em. And the upshot was, they acquitted the two women, thinking as how they'd only been chattering silly-like, the way women do, and they sent Cranton and Deacon to prison for a good long stretch. Old Russell, he couldn't face the place after that, and he sold up and went off, taking Mary with him. But when Deacon died——"

"How was that?"

"Why, he broke prison and got away after killing a warder. A bad lot, was Deacon. That was in 1918. But he didn't get much good by it, because he fell into a quarry or some such place over Maidstone way, and they found his body two years later, still in his prison clothes. And as soon as he heard about it, young William Thoday, that had always been sweet on Mary, went after her and married her and brought her back. You see, nobody here ever believed as there was anything against Mary. That was ten year ago, and they've got two fine kids and get along first-class. This fellow Cranton got into trouble again after his time was up and was sent back to prison, but he's out again now, so I'm told, and Jack Priest—that's the bobby at Fenchurch St. Peter—he says he wouldn't wonder if we heard something about that necklace again, but I don't know. Cranton may know where it is, and again he may not, you see."

"I see. So Sir Charles compensated Mrs. Wilbraham for the loss of it."

"Not Sir Charles, my lord. That was Sir Henry. He came back at once, poor gentleman, from his honeymoon, and found Sir Charles terrible ill. He'd had a stroke from the shock, when they took Deacon, feeling responsible-like, and being over seventy at the time. After the verdict, Mr. Henry as he was then, told his father he'd see that the thing was put right, and Sir Charles seemed to understand him; and then the War came and Sir Charles never got over it. He had another stroke and passed away, but Mr. Henry didn't forget, and when the police had to confess as they'd almost give up hope of the necklace, then he paid the money, but it came very hard on the family. Sir Henry got badly wounded in the Salient and was invalided home, but he's never been the same man since, and they say he's in a pretty bad way now. Lady Thorpe dying so sudden won't do him no good, neither. She was a very nice lady and very much liked."

"Is there any family?"

"Yes, my lord; there's one daughter, Miss Hilary. She'll be fifteen this month. She's just home from school for the holidays. It's been a sad holiday for her, and no mistake."

"You're right," said Lord Peter. "Well, that's an interesting tale of yours, Hinkins. I shall look out for news of the Wilbraham emeralds. Ah! here's my friend Mr. Wilderspin. I expect he's come to say that the car's on deck again."

This proved to be the case. The big Daimler stood outside the Rectory gate, forlornly hitched to the back of a farm waggon. The two stout horses who drew it seemed, judging by their sleek complacency, to have no great opinion of it. Messrs. Wilderspin senior and junior, however, took a hopeful view of the matter. A little work on the front axle, at the point where it had come into collision with a hidden milestone would, they thought, do wonders with it, and, if not, a message could be sent to Mr. Brownlow at Fenchurch St. Peter, who ran a garage, to come and tow it away, with his lorry. Mr. Brownlow was a great expert. Of course, he might be at home or he might not. There was a wedding on at Fenchurch St. Stephen, and Mr. Brownlow might be wanted there to take the wedding-party to church, they living a good way out along Digg's Drove, but if necessary the postmistress could be asked to telephone and find out. She would be the right party to do it, since, leaving out the post-office, there was no other telephone in the village, except at the Red House, which wouldn't be convenient at a time like the present.

Wimsey, looking dubiously at his front axle, thought it might perhaps be advisable to procure the skilled assistance of Mr. Brownlow and said he would approach the postmistress for that purpose, if Mr. Wilderspin would give him a lift into the village. He scrambled up, therefore, behind Mr. Ashton's greys, and the procession took its way past the church for the better part of a quarter of a mile, till it reached the centre of the village.

The parish church of Fenchurch St. Paul, like a good many others in that part of the country, stands completely isolated from the village itself, with only the Rectory to neighbour it. The village itself is grouped about a cross-roads, one arm of which runs southward to Fenchurch St. Stephen and northwards to join the Fenchurch St. Peter road a little south of the Thirty-foot; while the other, branching off from the same road by the church, degenerates at the western end of the village into a muddy drove by which, if you are not particular about your footing, you may, if you like, emerge once more on to the road by the Thirty-foot at Frog's Bridge. The three Fenchurches thus form a triangle, with St. Paul to the north, St. Peter to the south, and St. Stephen to the west. The L.N.E.R. line connects St. Peter with St. Stephen, passing north to cross the Thirty-foot at Dykesey Viaduct on its way to Leamholt.

Of the three, Fenchurch St. Peter is the largest and most important, possessing in addition to a railway-station, a river with two bridges. It has, however, but a bare and uninteresting church, built in the latest and worst period of Perpendicular, with a slate spire and no bells to speak of. Fenchurch St. Stephen has a railway-station—though only as it were, by accident, through lying more or less upon the direct line between Leamholt and St. Peter. Still, there the station is; moreover, there is a church with a respectable fourteenth-century tower, a rather remarkable rood-screen, a Norman apse and a ring of eight bells. Fenchurch St. Paul is the smallest village, and has neither river nor railway; it is, however, the oldest; its church is by far the largest and the noblest, and its bells beyond question the finest. This is due to the fact that St. Paul is the original abbey foundation. The remains of the first Norman church and a few stones which mark the site of the old cloisters may still be seen to east and south of the existing chancel. The church itself, with the surrounding

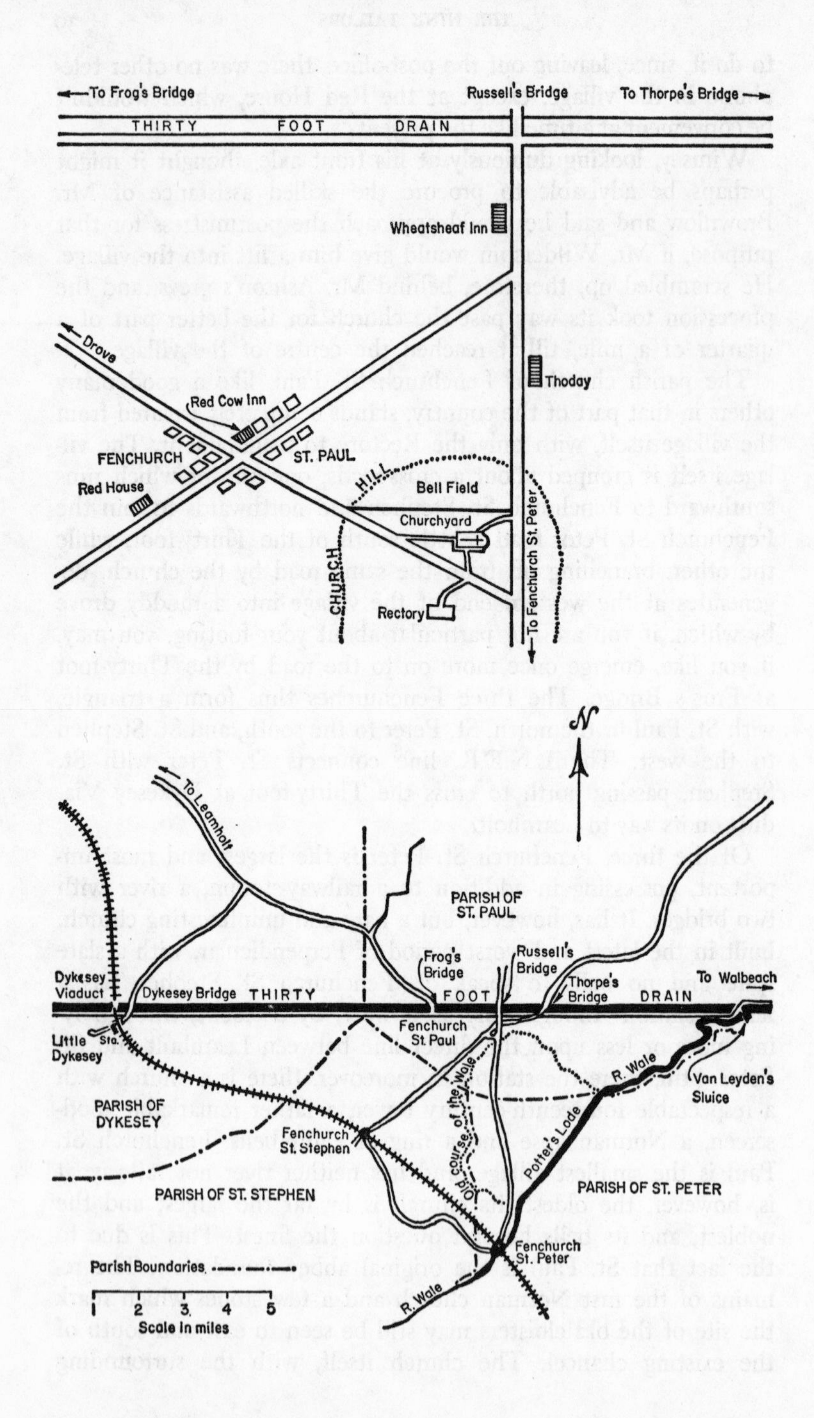

To Frog's Bridge
Russell's Bridge
To Thorpe's Bridge
THIRTY FOOT DRAIN
Wheatsheaf Inn
Drove
Thoday
Red Cow Inn
FENCHURCH
ST. PAUL
Red House
CHURCH HILL
Bell Field
Churchyard
Rectory
To Fenchurch St. Peter
N
To Leamholt
PARISH OF ST. PAUL
Frog's Bridge
Russell's Bridge
Dykesey Viaduct
Dykesey Bridge
THIRTY
FOOT
Thorpe's Bridge
DRAIN
To Walbeach
Little Dykesey
Sta.
Fenchurch St. Paul
R. Wale
Van Leyden's Sluice
PARISH OF DYKESEY
Fenchurch St. Stephen
Old course of the Wale
Potter's Lode
PARISH OF ST. STEPHEN
PARISH OF ST. PETER
Fenchurch St. Peter
Parish Boundaries
R. Wale
1 2 3 4 5
Scale in miles

glebe, stands on a little mound rising some ten or twelve feet above the level of the village—an elevation which, for the Fens, is considerable and, in ancient times, was sufficient to save church and abbey from inundation during the winter months. As for the river Wale, Fenchurch St. Peter has no right to boast about that, for did not the old course of the Wale run close by St. Paul's church, until the cutting of Potter's Lode in King James I's time drained away its waters by providing them with a shorter and more direct channel? Standing on the roof of the tower at Fenchurch St. Paul, you can still trace the old river bed, as it wanders circuitously across meadow and ploughland, and see where the straight green dyke of Potter's Lode spans it like a string to a bow. Outside the group of the Fenchurches, the land rises slightly all round, being drained by cross-dyking into the Wale.

Lord Peter Wimsey, having seen the front axle of the Daimler taken down and decided that Mr. Brownlow and Mr. Wilderspin could probably fix it up between them, dispatched his message from the post-office, sent a wire to the friends who were expecting him at Walbeach, and then cast about him for some occupation. The village presented nothing of interest, so he determined to go and have a look at the church. The tolling of the bell had ceased and Hezekiah had gone home; the south door was, however, open, and entering, he discovered Mrs. Venables putting fresh water in the altar vases. Catching sight of him as he stood gazing at the exquisite oak tracery of the screen, she came forward to greet him.

"It *is* beautiful, isn't it? Theodore is so proud of his church. And he's done a lot, since we've been here, to keep it looking nice. Fortunately the man before us was conscientious and did his repairs properly, but he was *very* Low and allowed all manner of things that quite shocked us. This beautiful chapel, for instance, would you *believe* that he allowed it to be used for furnace-coke? Of course, we had all that cleared out. Theodore would like a lady-altar here, but we're afraid the parishioners would think it popish. Yes—it's a magnificent window, isn't it? Later than the rest, of course, but so fortunate that it's kept its old glass. We were so afraid when the Zeppelins came over. You know, they dropped a bomb at Walbeach, only twenty miles off, and it might just as easily have been here. Isn't the parclose lovely? Like lace, I always think. The tombs belong to the Gaudy family. They lived here up to Queen Elizabeth's time, but they've all died out now. You'll find the name on the Treble bell: GAUDE, GAUDY, DOMINI IN

LAUDE. There used to be a chantry on the north side, corresponding to this: Abbot Thomas' chantry, it was, and that's his tomb. Batty Thomas is named after him—a corruption of 'Abbot,' of course. Some vandal in the nineteenth century tore down the screen behind the choir stalls to put the organ in. It's a hideous thing, isn't it? We put in a new set of pipes a few years ago, and now the bellows want enlarging. Poor Potty has his work cut out to keep the windchest filled when Miss Snoot is using the full organ. They all call him Potty Peake, but he's not really potty, only a little lacking, you know. Of course, the angel-roof is our great show-piece—I think myself it's even lovelier than the ones at March or Needham Market, because it has all the original colouring. At least, we had it touched up here and there about twelve years back, but we didn't add anything. It took ten years to persuade the churchwardens that we could put a little fresh gold-leaf on the angels without going straight over to Rome, but they're proud of it now. We hope to do the chancel roof too, one day. All these ribs ought to be painted, you can still see traces of colour, and the bosses ought to be gilt. The east window is Theodore's *bête noire*. That dreadful crude glass—about 1840, I think it is. Quite the worst period, Theodore says. The glass in the nave has all gone, of course—Cromwell's men. Thank goodness they left part of the clerestory. I suppose it was rather a job to get up there. The pews are modern; Theodore got them done ten years ago. He'd have preferred chairs, but the congregation wouldn't have liked it, being used to pews, and he had them copied from a nice old design that wasn't too offensive. The old ones were terrible—like bathrooms—and there was a frightful gallery along both sides, blocking the aisle windows completely and ruining the look of the pillars. We had that taken down at the same time. It wasn't needed, and the school-children *would* drop hymn-books and things on people's heads. Now, the choir-stalls are different. *They* are the original monks' stalls, with misereres. Isn't the carving fine? There's a piscina in the sanctuary, but not a very exciting one."

Wimsey admitted that he was unable to feel great excitement about piscinas.

"And the altar-rails are very poor, of course—Victorian horrors. We want very much to put up something better in their place when we can find the money. I'm sorry I haven't the key to the tower. You'd like to go up. It's a wonderful view, though it's all ladders above the ringing-chamber. It makes my head swim, especially going over the bells. I think bells are rather frightening, somehow. Oh, the font! You must look at the font. That carving is supposed to be quite remarkable. I forget exactly what it is that's so special about it—stupid of me. Theodore must show you, but he's been sent for in a hurry to take a sick woman off to hospital, right away on the other side of the Thirty-foot, across Thorpe's Bridge. He rushed off almost before he'd finished his breakfast."

("And they say," thought Wimsey, "that Church of England parsons do nothing for their money.")

"Would you like to stay on and look round? Do you mind locking the door and bringing the key back? It's Mr. Godfrey's key—I can't *think* where Theodore has put his bunch. It does seem wrong to keep the church locked, but it's such a solitary place. We can't keep an eye on it from the Rectory because of the shrubbery and there are sometimes very unpleasant-looking tramps about. I saw a most horrible man go past only the other day, and not so long ago someone broke open the alms-box. That wouldn't have mattered so much, because there was very little in it, but they did a lot of wanton damage in the sanctuary—out of disappointment, I suppose, and one can't really allow that, can one?"

Wimsey said, No, one couldn't, and Yes, he would like to look round the church a little longer and would remember about the key. He spent the first few minutes after the good lady had left him in putting a suitable donation into the alms-box and in examining the font, whose carvings were certainly curious and, to his mind, suggestive of a symbolism neither altogether Christian nor altogether innocent. He noted a heavy old cope-chest beneath the tower, which, on being opened, proved to contain nothing more venerable than a quantity of worn bell-ropes, and passed on into the north aisle, noticing that the corbels supporting the principals of the angel-roof were very appropriately sculptured with cherubs' heads. He brooded for a little time over the tomb of Abbot Thomas, with its robed and mitred effigy. A stern old boy, he thought, this fourteenth-century cleric, with his strong, harsh face, a ruler rather than a shepherd of his people. Carved panels decorated the sides of the tomb, and showed various scenes in the life of the abbey; one of them depicted the casting of a bell, no doubt of "Batty Thomas," and it was evident that the Abbot had taken particular pride in his bell, for it appeared again, supporting his feet, in place of the usual cushion. Its decorations and mottoes were realistically rendered: on the shoulder: + NOLI +

ESSE + INCREDVLVS + SED + FIDELIS +; on the sound-bow: + *Abbat Thomas sett mee heare + and bad mee ringe both lovd and cleer* + 1380 +; and on the waist: O SANCTE THOMA, which inscription, being embellished with an abbot's mitre, left the spectator in a pleasing uncertainty whether the sanctity was to be attributed to the Apostle or the ecclesiastic. It was as well that Abbot Thomas had died long before the spoliation of his house by King Henry. Thomas would have made a fight for it, and his church might have suffered in the process. His successor, douce man, had meekly acquiesced in the usurpation, leaving his abbey to moulder to decay, and his church to be purified peaceably by the reformers. So, at least, the Rector informed Wimsey over the shepherd's pie at lunch.

It was only very reluctantly that the Venables consented to let their guest go; but Mr. Brownlow and Mr. Wilderspin between them had made such good progress on the car that it was ready for use by two o'clock, and Wimsey was anxious to press on to Walbeach before dusk set in. He started off, therefore, speeded by many handshakes and much earnest solicitation to come again soon and help to ring another peal. The Rector, at parting, thrust into his hands a copy of *Venables on the In and Out of Course*, while Mrs. Venables insisted on his drinking an amazingly powerful hot whisky-and-water, to keep the cold out. As the car turned right along the Thirty-foot Bank, Wimsey noticed that the wind had changed. It was hauling round to the south, and, though the snow still lay white and even over the Fen, there was a softness in the air.

"Thaw's coming, Bunter."

"Yes, my lord."

"Ever seen this part of the country when the floods are out?"

"No, my lord."

"It looks pretty desolate; especially round about the Welney and Mepal Washes, when they let the waters out between the Old and New Bedford Rivers, and across the Fen between Over and Earith Bridge. Acres of water, with just a bank running across it here and there or a broken line of willows. Hereabouts, I think it's rather more effectively drained. Ah! look—over to the right—that must be Van Leyden's Sluice that turns the tide up the Thirty-foot Drain—Denver Sluice again on a smaller scale. Let's look at the map. Yes, that's it. See, here's where the Drain joins the Wale, but it meets it at a higher level; if it wasn't for the sluice, all the Drain water would turn back up the Wale and flood the whole place. Bad engineering—but the seventeenth-century engineers had to work piecemeal and take things as they found 'em. That's the Wale, coming down through Potter's Lode from Fenchurch St. Peter. I shouldn't care for the sluice-keeper's job —dashed lonely, I should think."

They gazed at the ugly little brick house, which stood up quaintly on their right, like a pricked ear, between the two sides of the Sluice. On the one side a weir, with a small lock, spanned the Thirty-foot, where it ran into the Wale six feet above the course of the river. On the other, the upper course of the Wale itself was spanned by a sluice of five gates, which held the Upper Level waters from turning back up the river.

"Not another house within sight—oh, yes—one cottage about two miles further up the bank. Boo! Enough to make one drown one's self in one's own lock. Hullo! what happens to the road here? Oh, I see; over the Drain by the bridge and turn sharp right —then follow the river. I do wish everything wasn't so rectangular in this part of the world. Hoops-a-daisy, over she goes! There's the sluice-keeper running out to have a look at us. I expect we're his great event of the day. Let's wave our hats to him—Hullo-ullo! Cheerio!—I'm all for scattering sunshine as we pass. As Stevenson says, we shall pass this way but once—and I devoutly hope he's right. Now then, what's this fellow want?"

Along the bleak white road a solitary figure, plodding towards them, had stopped and extended both arms in appeal. Wimsey slowed the Daimler to a halt.

"Excuse me stopping you, sir," said the man, civilly enough. "Would you be good enough to tell me if I'm going right for Fenchurch St. Paul?"

"Quite right. Cross the bridge when you come to it and follow the Drain along in the direction you are going till you come to the signpost. You can't miss it."

"Thank you, sir. About how far would it be?"

"About five and a half miles to the signpost and then half a mile to the village."

"Thank you very much, sir."

"You've got a cold walk, I'm afraid."

"Yes, sir—not a nice part of the country. However, I'll be there before dark, that's a comfort."

He spoke rather low, and his voice had a faint London twang; his drab overcoat, though very shabby, was not ill-cut. He wore a short, dark, pointed beard and seemed to be about fifty years old, but kept his face down when talking as if evading close scrutiny.

"Like a fag?"

"Thank you very much, sir."

Wimsey shook a few cigarettes out of his case and handed them over. The palm that opened to receive them was calloused, as though by heavy manual labour, but there was nothing of the countryman about the stranger's manner or appearance.

"You don't belong to these parts?"

"No, sir."

"Looking for work?"

"Yes, sir."

"Labourer?"

"No, sir. Motor mechanic."

"Oh, I see. Well, good luck to you."

"Thank you, sir. Good afternoon, sir."

"Good afternoon."

Wimsey drove on in silence for about half a mile. Then he said: "Motor mechanic possibly, but not recently, I think. Stone-quarrying's more about the size of it. You can always tell an old lag by his eyes, Bunter. Excellent idea to live down the past, and all that, but I hope our friend doesn't put anything across the good Rector."

2

A FULL PEAL OF

Grandsire Triples

HOLT'S TEN-PART PEAL

5,040

BY THE PART ENDS

First Half

246375
267453
275634
253746
235476

Second Half

257364
276543
264735
243657
234567

2ND THE OBSERVATION.

Call her: 1st Half

Out of the hunt, middle, in and out at 5, right, middle, wrong, right, middle and into the hunt (4 times repeated).

2nd Half

Out of the hunt, wrong, right, middle, wrong, right, in and out at 5, wrong and into the hunt (4 times repeated).

The last call in each half is a single; Holt's Single must be used in ringing this peal.

THE FIRST PART

Mr. Gotobed Is Called Wrong with a Double

Thou shalt pronounce this hideous thing
With cross, and candle, and bell-knelling.

JOHN MYRC: INSTRUCTIONS FOR PARISH PRIESTS (15TH CENTURY)

SPRING AND Easter came late together that year to Fenchurch St. Paul. In its own limited, austere and almost grudging fashion the Fen acknowledged the return of the sun. The floods withdrew from the pastures; the wheat lifted its pale green spears more sturdily from the black soil; the stiff thorns bordering dyke and grass verge budded to a softer outline; on the willows, the yellow catkins danced like little bell-rope sallies, and the silvery pussies plumped themselves for the children to carry to church on Palm Sunday; wherever the grim banks were hedge-sheltered, the shivering dog-violets huddled from the wind.

In the Rectory garden, the daffodils were (in every sense of the word) in full blow, for in the everlasting sweep and torment of wind that sweeps across East Anglia, they tossed desperately and madly. "My poor daffodils!" Mrs. Venables would exclaim, as the long leaf-tufts streamed over like blown water, and the golden trumpets kissed the ground, "this dreadful old wind! I don't know how they stand it!" She felt both pride and remorse as she cut them—sound stock varieties, Emperor, Empress, Golden Spur—and took them away to fill the altar-vases and the two long, narrow, green-painted tin troughs that on Easter Sunday stood one on either side of the chancel screen. "The yellow looks so bright," thought Mrs. Venables, as she tried to persuade the blossoms to stand upright among the glossy green of periwinkle and St. John's wort, "though it really seems a shame to sacrifice them."

She knelt before the screen on a long red cushion, borrowed from a pew-seat to protect her "bones" from the chill of the stone floor. The four brass altar-vases stood close beside her, in company with a trug full of flowers and a watering-can. Had she tried to fill them at the Rectory and carry them over, the sou'-wester would have blown them into ruin before she had so much as crossed the road. "Tiresome things!" muttered Mrs. Venables, as the daffodils flopped sideways, or slid down helplessly out of sight into the bottom of the trough. She sat up on her heels and reviewed her work, and then turned, hearing a step behind her.

A red-haired girl of fifteen, dressed in black, had come in, bearing a large sheaf of pheasant-eye narcissi. She was tall and thin and rather gawky, though with promise of becoming some day a striking-looking woman.

"Are these any use to you, Mrs. Venables? Johnson's trying to get the arums along, but the wind's so terrific, he's afraid they'll be broken all to bits in the barrow. I think he'll have to pack them into the car, and drive them down in state."

"My dear Hilary, how kind of you! Yes, indeed—I can do with all the white flowers I can get. These are beautiful, and *what* a delicious scent! Dear things! I thought of having some of our plants stood along there in front of Abbot Thomas, with some tall vases among them. And the same on the other side under old Gaudy. But I am *not*"—here she became very much determined—"I am *not* going to tie bunches of greenery on to the font and the pulpit this year. They can have that at Christmas and Harvest Festival, if they like, but at Easter it's unsuitable and absurd, and now that old Miss Mallow's gone, poor dear, there's no need to go on with it."

"I hate Harvest Festivals. It's a shame to hide up all this lovely carving with spiky bits of corn and vegetable marrows and things."

"So it is, but the village people like it, you know. Harvest Festival is *their* festival, Theodore always says. I suppose it's wrong that it should mean so much more to them than the Church seasons, but it's natural. It was much worse when we came here—before you were born or thought of, you know. They actually used to drive spikes into the pillars to hold up wreaths of evergreens. Quite wicked. Just thoughtlessness, of course. And at Christmas they had horrible texts all across the screens and along that abominable old gallery—done in cotton-wool on red flannel. Disgusting, dirty old things. We found a great bundle of them in the vestry when we came here, full of moths and mice. The Rector put his foot down about *that*."

"And I suppose half the people went over to the Chapel."

"No, dear—only two families, and one of them has come back since—the Wallaces, you know, because they had some sort of dispute with the Minister about their Good Friday beanfeast. Something to do with the tea-urns, but I forget what. Mrs. Wallace is a funny woman; she takes offence rather easily, but so far —touch wood"—(Mrs. Venables performed this ancient pagan rite placidly on the oak of the screen)—"so far, I've managed to work in quite smoothly with her over the Women's Institute. I wonder if you'd just step back a little way and tell me if these two sides match."

"You want a few more daffs on the decani side, Mrs. Venables."

"Here? Thank you, dear. Is that better? Well, I think it will have to do. Oo-oh! my poor old bones! Yes, it'll pass in a crowd with a push, as they say. Oh, here's Hinkins with the aspidistras. People may say what they like about aspidistras, but they do go on all the year round and make a background. That's right, Hinkins. Six in front of this tomb and six the other side—and have you brought those big pickle-jars? They'll do splendidly for the narcissi, and the aspidistras will hide the jars and we can put some ivy in front of the pots. Hinkins, you might fill up my watering-can. How is your father today, Hilary? Better, I hope."

"I'm afraid he isn't any better, Mrs. Venables. Doctor Baines is very much afraid he won't get over it. Poor old Dad!"

"Oh, my dear! I'm terribly sorry. This has been a dreadful time for you. I'm afraid the shock of your dear mother's death coming so suddenly was too much for him."

The girl nodded.

"We'll hope and pray it isn't as bad as the doctor thinks. Dr. Baines always takes a pessimistic view of everything. I expect that's why he's only a country practitioner, because I think he's really very clever; but patients do like a doctor to be cheerful. Why don't you get a second opinion?"

"We're going to. There's a man called Hordell coming down on Tuesday. Dr. Baines tried to get him today, but he's away for Easter."

"Doctors oughtn't to go away," said Mrs. Venables, rather uncharitably. The Rector never took holidays at the greater festivals, and scarcely ever at any other time, and she could not quite see that there was any necessity for the rest of the world to do so.

Hilary Thorpe laughed rather ruefully.

"I feel a little like that myself. But he's supposed to be the very best man there is, and we're hoping that a couple of days won't make all that difference."

"Good gracious, no, I hope not," said the Rector's wife. "Is that Johnson with the arums? Oh, no, it's Jack Godfrey. I expect he's going up to grease the bells."

"Is he? I'd like to watch him. May I go up to the belfry, Mrs. Venables?"

"I'm sure you may, my dear. But do be careful. I never think those great high ladders are really safe."

"Oh, I'm not afraid of them. I love looking at the bells."

Hilary hastened down the church and caught Jack Godfrey up just as he emerged from the winding stair into the ringing-chamber.

"I've come to watch you do the bells, Mr. Godfrey. Shall I be in your way?"

"Why, no, Miss Hilary, I'd be very pleased for you to come. You better go first up them ladders, same as I can help you if you was to slip."

"I shan't slip," said Hilary, scornfully. She climbed briskly up the thick and ancient rungs, to emerge into the chamber which formed the second story of the tower. It was empty, except for the case which housed the chiming mechanism of the church clock, and the eight bell-ropes rising through the sallie-holes in the floor to vanish through the ceiling in the same way. Jack Godfrey followed her up soberly, carrying his grease and cleaning-rags.

"Be a bit careful of the floor, Miss Hilary," he urged, "it's none so good in places."

Hilary nodded. She loved this bare, sun-drenched room, whose four tall walls were four tall windows. It was like a palace of glass lifted high into the air. The shadows of the splendid tracery of the South window lay scrawled on the floor like a pattern of wrought iron on a gate of brass. Looking down through the dusty panes, she could see the green fen spread out mile upon mile.

"I'd like to go up to the top of the tower, Mr. Godfrey."

"All right, Miss Hilary; I'll take you up, if so be as there's time when I've done with the bells."

The trap-door that led to the bell-chamber was shut; a chain ran down from it, vanishing into a sort of wooden case upon the wall. Godfrey produced a key from his bunch and unlocked this case, disclosing the counterpoise. He pulled it down and the trap swung open.

"Why is that kept locked, Mr. Godfrey?"

"Well, Miss Hilary, now and again it has happened as the ringers has left the belfry door open, and Rector says it ain't safe. You see, that Potty Peake might come a-traipsing round, or some of they mischeevious lads might come up here and get larking about with the bells. Or they might go up the tower and fall off and hurt theirselves. So Rector said to fix a lock the way they couldn't get the trap-door open."

"I see." Hilary grinned a little. "Hurt theirselves" was a moderate way of expressing the probable result of a hundred-and-twenty-foot fall. She led the way up the second ladder.

By contrast with the brilliance below, the bell-chamber was sombre and almost menacing. The main lights of its eight great windows were darkened throughout their height; only through the slender panelled tracery above the slanting louvres the sunlight dripped rare and chill, striping the heavy beams of the bell-cage with bars and splashes of pallid gold, and making a curious fantastic patterning on the spokes and rims of the wheels. The bells, with mute black mouths gaping downwards, brooded in their ancient places.

Mr. Godfrey, eyeing them with the cheerful familiarity born of long use, fetched a light ladder that stood against the wall, set it up carefully against one of the cross-beams, and prepared to mount.

"Let me go up first, or I shan't see what you're doing."

Mr. Godfrey paused and scratched his head. The proposal did not seem quite safe to him. He voiced an objection.

"I shall be quite all right; I can sit on the beam. I don't mind heights one bit. I'm very good at gym."

Sir Henry's daughter was accustomed to have her own way, and got it—with the stipulation that she should hold on very tightly by the timber of the cage and not let go or "morris about." The promise being given, she was assisted to her lofty perch. Mr. Godfrey, whistling a lively air between his teeth, arranged his materials methodically about him and proceeded with his task, greasing the gudgeons and trunnions, administering a spot of oil to the pulley-axle, testing the movement of the slider between the blocks and examining the rope for signs of friction where it passed over wheel and pulley.

"I've never seen Tailor Paul as close as this before. She's a big bell, isn't she?"

"Pretty fair," said Jack Godfrey, approvingly, giving the bell a friendly pat on her bronze shoulder. A shaft of sunshine touched the soundbow, lighting up a few letters of the inscription, which ran, as Hilary very well knew:

NINE+TAYLERS+MAKE+A+MANNE+IN+CHRIST+
IS+DETH+ATT+END+IN+ADAM+YAT+BEGANNE+
1614

"She've done her bit in her time, have old Tailor Paul—many a good ring have we had out of her, not to say a sight of funerals and passing-bells. And we rung her with Gaude for them there Zeppelin raids, to give the alarm like. Rector was saying the other day as she did soon ought ter be quarter-turned, but I don't know. Reckon she'll go a bit longer yet. She rings out true enough to my thinking."

"You have to ring the passing-bell for everyone that dies in the parish, don't you, whoever they are?"

"Yes, dissenter and church alike. That was laid down by old Sir Martin Thorpe, your great-great-grandfather, when he left the money for the bell-fund. 'Every Christian soul' was the words in his will. Why, we even had to ring for that woman as lived up the Long Drove, as was a Roman Catholic. Old Hezekiah was rare put out." Mr. Godfrey chuckled reminiscently. " 'What, ring old Tailor Paul for a Roman?' he says, 'you wouldn't call the like o' them Christians, would you, Rector?' he says. 'Why, Hezekiah,' says Rector, 'we was all Romans in this country once; this church was built by Romans,' he says. But Hezekiah, he wouldn't see it. He never had much education, you see. Well, now, Miss Hilary, that'll do for Tailor Paul, I'm thinking, so if you'll give me your hand I'll be helping you down."

Gaude, Sabaoth, John, Jericho, Jubilee and Dimity each in her turn was visited and anointed. When, however, it came to the turn of Batty Thomas, Mr. Godfrey displayed a sudden and unexpected obstinacy.

"I'm not taking you up to Batty Thomas, Miss Hilary. She's an unlucky bell. What I mean, she's a bell that has her fancies and I wouldn't like for to risk it."

"What *do* you mean?"

Mr. Godfrey found it difficult to express himself more plainly.

"She's my own bell," he said; "I've rung her close on fifteen year now and I've looked after her for ten, ever since Hezekiah got too old for these here ladders. Her and me knows one another and she've no quarrel with me nor I with her. But she's queer-tempered. They do say as how old Batty down below, what had her put up here, was a queer sort of man and his bell's took after him. When they turned out the monks and that—a great many years ago, that'd be—they do say as Batty Thomas tolled a whole night through on her own like, without a hand laid to the rope. And when Cromwell sent his men to break up the images an' that, there was a soldier come up here into the belfry, I don't know for what, maybe to damage the bells, but anyhow, up he come; and some of the others, not knowing he was here, began to haul on the ropes, and it seems as how the bells must have been left mouth up. Careless ringers they must have been in those days, but anyhow, that's how 'twas. And just as this soldier was leaning over to look at the bells, like, Batty Thomas came swinging down and killed him dead. That's history, that is, and Rector says as how Batty Thomas saved the church, because the soldiers took fright and ran away, thinking it was a judgment, though to my thinking, it was just carelessness, leaving the bell that fashion. Still, there it was. And then, there was a poor lad in old Rector's time learning to ring, and he tried to raise Batty Thomas and got hisself hanged in the rope. A terrible thing that was, and there again, I say it was carelessness and the lad didn't ought to have been let practise all alone, and it's a thing Mr. Venables never will allow. But you see, Miss Hilary, Batty Thomas has killed two men, and while it's quite understandable as there was carelessness both times or it wouldn't have happened—well! I wouldn't like to take any risks, like I said."

And with this as his last word on the subject, Mr. Godfrey mounted aloft to grease the gudgeons of Batty Thomas unassisted. Hilary Thorpe, dissatisfied but recognizing an immovable obstacle when she met one, wandered vaguely about the belfry, scuffing up the dust of ages with her square-toed, regulation-pattern school shoes and peering at the names which bygone rustics had scrawled upon the plastered walls. Suddenly, in a remote corner, something gleamed white in a bar of sunlight. Idly she picked it up. It was a sheet of paper, flimsy and poor in quality and ruled in small, faint squares. It reminded her of the letters she occasionally received from a departed French governess and, when she examined it, she saw that it was covered with writing in the very same purple ink that she associated with "Mad'm'selle," but the hand was English—very neat, and yet somehow not the hand of a well-educated person. It had been folded in four and its under side was smeared with fine dust from the floor on which it had lain, but it was otherwise fairly clean.

"Mr. Godfrey!"

Hilary's voice was so sharp and excited that Jack Godfrey was quite startled. He very nearly fell off the ladder, adding thereby one more to Batty Thomas' tale of victims.

"Yes, Miss Hilary?"

"I've found such a funny thing here. Do come and look at it."

"In one moment, Miss Hilary."

He finished his task and descended. Hilary was standing in a splash of sunshine that touched the brazen mouth of Tailor Paul and fell all about her like Danaë's shower. She was holding the paper where the light could catch it.

"I found this on the floor. Do listen to it. It's absolutely loony. Do you think Potty Peake could have written it?"

Mr. Godfrey shook his head.

"I couldn't say, I'm sure, Miss Hilary. He's queer, is Potty, and he did use to come up here one time, before Rector locked up the trap-door chain. But that don't look to me like his writing."

"Well, I don't think anybody but a lunatic could have written it. Do read it. It's so funny." Hilary giggled, being of an age to be embarrassed by lunacy.

Mr. Godfrey set down his belongings with deliberation, scratched his head and perused the document aloud, following the lines with a somewhat grimy forefinger.

> "I thought to see the fairies in the fields, but I saw only the evil elephants with their black backs. Woe! how that sight awed me! The elves danced all around and about while I heard voices calling clearly. Ah! how I tried to see—throw off the ugly cloud—but no blind eye of a mortal was permitted to spy them. So then came minstrels, having gold trumpets, harps and drums. These played very loudly beside me, breaking that spell. So the dream vanished, whereat I thanked Heaven. I shed many tears before the thin moon rose up, frail and faint as a sickle of straw. Now though the Enchanter gnash his teeth vainly, yet shall he return as the Spring returns. Oh, wretched man! Hell gapes, Erebus now lies open. The mouths of Death wait on thy end."

"There, now," said Mr. Godfrey, astonished. "That's a funny one, that is. Potty it is, but, if you follow me, it ain't Potty neither. Potty ain't no scholar. This here, now, about Ereebus—what do you take that to mean?"

"It's a kind of an old name for hell," said Hilary.

"Oh, that's what it is, is it? Chap that wrote this seems to have got that there place on his mind, like. Fairies, too, and elephants. Well, I don't know. Looks like a bit of a joke, don't it now? Perhaps" (his eye brightened with an idea), "perhaps somebody's been copying out something out of a book. Yes, I wouldn't wonder if that's what that is. One of them old-fashioned books. But it's a funny thing how it got up here. I'd show it to Rector, Miss Hilary, that's what I'd do. He knows a lot of books, and maybe he'd know where it come from."

"That's a good idea. I will. But it's awfully mysterious, isn't it? Quite creepy. Can we go up the tower now, Mr. Godfrey?"

Mr. Godfrey was quite willing, and together they climbed the last long ladder, stretching high over the bells and leading them out by way of a little shelter like a dog-kennel on to the leaded roof of the tower. Leaning against the wind was like leaning against a wall. Hilary pulled off her hat and let her thick bobbed hair blow out behind her, so that she looked like one of the floating singing angels in the church below. Mr. Godfrey had no eyes for this resemblance; he thought Miss Hilary's angular face and straight hair rather unattractive, if the truth were known. He contented himself with advising her to hold tight by the iron stays of the weathercock. Hilary paid no attention to him, but advanced to the parapet, leaning over between the pierced battlements to stare out southward over the Fen. Far away beneath her lay the churchyard, and, while she looked, a little figure, quaintly foreshortened, crawled beetle-like from the porch and went jogging down the path. Mrs. Venables, going home to lunch. Hilary watched her struggle with the wind at the gate, cross the road and enter the Rectory garden. Then she turned and moved to the east side of the tower, and looked out along the ridged roofs of the nave and chancel. A brown spot in the green churchyard caught her eye and her heart seemed to turn over in her body. Here, at the north-east angle of the church, her mother lay buried, her grave not yet turfed over; and now it looked as though, before long, the earth would have to be opened up again to let the husband join his wife. "Oh, God!" said Hilary, desperately, "don't let Dad die—You can't—You simply can't." Beyond the churchyard wall lay a green field, and in the middle of the field there was a slight hollow. She knew that hollow well. It had been there now for over three hundred years. Time had made it shallower, and in three hundred years more it might disappear altogether, but there it still was—the mark left by the great pit dug for the founding of Tailor Paul.

Jack Godfrey spoke close beside her.

"Time I was getting along now, Miss Hilary."

"Oh, yes. I'm sorry. I wasn't thinking. Are you ringing a peal tomorrow?"

"Yes, Miss Hilary. We're going to have a try at Stedman's. They're difficult to ring, are Stedman's, but very fine music when you get them going proper. Mind your head, Miss Hilary. A full peal of 5,040 we're going to give them—that's three hours. It's a fortnit thing as Will Thoday's all right again, because neither Tom Tebbutt nor young George Wilderspin is what you might call reliable in Stedman's, and of course, Wally Pratt's no good at all. Excuse me one minute, Miss Hilary, while I gathers up my traps. But to my mind, there's more interest, as you might say, in Stedman's than in any other method, though it takes a bit of thinking about to keep it all clear in one's head. Old Hezekiah don't so much care about it, of course, because he likes the tenor rung in. Triples ain't much fun for him, he says, and it ain't to be wondered at. Still, he's an old man now, and you couldn't hardly expect him to learn Stedman's at his age, and what's more, if he could, you'd never get him to leave Tailor Paul. Just a moment, Miss Hilary, while I lock up this here counterpoise. But give me a nice peal of Stedman's and I ask no better. We never had no Stedman's till Rector come, and it took him a powerful long time to learn us to ring them. Well I mind the trouble we had with them. Old John Thoday—that's Will's father, he's dead and gone now—he used to say, 'Boys,' he said, 'it's my belief the Devil himself couldn't get no sense out of this dratted method.' And Rector fined him sixpence for swearing, like it says in they old rules. Mind you don't slip on the stair, Miss Hilary, it's terrible worn. But we learned Stedman to rights, none the more for that, and to my mind it's a very pretty method of ringing. Well, good morning to you, Miss Hilary."

. . . .

The peal of 5,040 Stedman's Triples was duly rung on Easter Sunday morning. Hilary Thorpe heard it from the Red House, sitting beside the great old four-poster bed, as she had sat on New Year's morning to hear the peal of Treble Bob Major. Then the noise of the bells had come full and clear; today, it reached her only in distant bursts, when the wind, rollicking away with it eastward, bated for a moment or veered round a little to the south.

"Hilary!"

"Yes, Dad."

"I'm afraid—if I go west this time—I'll be leaving you rottenly badly off, old girl."

"I don't care a dash about that, old thing. Not that you are going west. But if you did, I should be quite all right."

"There'll be enough to send you to Oxford, I dare say. Girls don't seem to cost much there—your uncle will see to it."

"Yes—and I'm going to get a scholarship, anyway. And I don't want money. I'd rather make my own living. Miss Bowler says she doesn't think anything of a woman who can't be independent." (Miss Bowler was the English mistress and the idol of the moment.) "I'm going to be a writer, Dad. Miss Bowler says she wouldn't wonder if I'd got it in me."

"Oh? What are you going to write? Poetry?"

"Well, perhaps. But I don't suppose that pays very well. I'll write novels. Best-sellers. The sort that everybody goes potty over. Not just bosh ones, but like *The Constant Nymph*."

"You'll want a bit of experience before you can write novels, old girl."

"Rot, Daddy. You don't want experience for writing novels. People write them at Oxford and they sell like billy-ho. All about how awful everything was at school."

"I see. And when you leave Oxford, you write one about how awful everything was at college."

"That's the idea. I can do that on my head."

"Well, dear, I hope it'll work. But all the same, I feel a damned failure, leaving you so little. If only that rotten necklace had turned up! I was a fool to pay that Wilbraham woman for it, but she as good as accused the old Governor of being an accessory, and I——"

"Oh, Dad, please—*please* don't go on about that silly necklace. Of course you couldn't do anything else about it. And I don't want the beastly money. And anyhow, you're not going to peg out yet."

But the specialist, arriving on Tuesday, looked grave and, taking Dr. Baines aside, said to him kindly:

"You have done all you could. Even if you had called me in earlier, it could have made no possible difference."

And to Hilary, still kindly:

"We must never give up hope, you know, Miss Thorpe. I can't disguise from you that your father's condition is serious, but Nature has marvellous powers of recuperation. . . ."

Which is the medical man's way of saying that, short of miraculous intervention, you may as well order the coffin.

. . . .

On the following Monday afternoon, Mr. Venables was just leaving the cottage of a cantankerous and venomous-tongued old lady on the extreme outskirts of the parish, when a deep, booming sound smote his ear from afar. He stood still with his hand upon the gate.

"That's Tailor Paul," said the Rector to himself.

Three solemn notes, and a pause.

"Man or woman?"

Three notes, and then three more.

"Man," said the Rector. He still stood listening. "I wonder if poor old Merryweather has gone at last. I hope it isn't that boy of Hensman's." He counted twelve strokes, and waited. But the bell tolled on, and the Rector breathed a sigh of relief. Hensman's boy, at least, was safe. He hastily reckoned up the weaklings of his flock. Twenty strokes, thirty strokes—a man of full age. "Heaven send," thought the Rector, "it isn't Sir Henry. He seemed better when I saw him yesterday." Forty strokes, forty-one, forty-two. Surely it must be old Merryweather—a happy release for him, poor old man. Forty-three, forty-four, forty-five, forty-six. Now it must go on—it could not stop at that fatal number. Old Merryweather was eighty-four. The Rector strained his ears. He must have missed the next stroke—the wind was pretty strong, and his hearing was perhaps not as good as it had been.

But he waited full thirty seconds before Tailor Paul spoke again; and after that there was silence for another thirty seconds.

The cantankerous old lady, astonished to see the Rector stand so long bare-headed at her gate, came hobbling down the garden path to know what it was all about.

"It's the passing-bell," said Mr. Venables, "they have rung the nine tailors and forty-six strokes, and I'm afraid it must be for Sir Henry."

"Oh, dear," said the cantankerous old woman, "that's bad. Terrible bad, that is." A peevish kind of pity came into her eyes. "What's to become of Miss Hilary now, with her mother and father gone so quick, and her only fifteen, and nobody to keep her in check? I don't hold with girls being left to look arter themselves. They're troublesome at the best and they didn't ought to have their parents took away from them."

"We mustn't question the ways of Providence," said the Rector.

"Providence?" said the old woman. "Don't yew talk to me about Providence. I've had enough o' Providence. First he took my husband, and then he took my 'taters, but there's One above as'll teach him to mend his manners, if he don't look out."

The Rector was too much distressed to challenge this remarkable piece of theology.

"We can but trust in God, Mrs. Giddings," he said, and pulled up the starting-handle with a jerk.

. . . . . .

Sir Henry's funeral was fixed for the Friday afternoon. This was an occasion of mournful importance to at least four persons in Fenchurch St. Paul. There was Mr. Russell, the undertaker, who was a cousin of that same Mary Russell who had married William Thoday. He was determined to excel himself in the matter of polished oak and brass plates, and his hammer and plane had been keeping up a dismal little harmony of their own during the early part of the week. His, also, was the delicate task of selecting the six bearers so that they might be well-matched in height and step. Mr. Hezekiah Lavender and Mr. Jack Godfrey went into conference about the proper ringing of a muffled peal—Mr. Godfrey's business being to provide and adjust the leather buffets about the clappers of the bells, and Mr. Lavender's to arrange and conduct the ringing. And Mr. Gotobed, the sexton, was concerned with the grave—so much concerned that he had declined to take part in the peal, preferring to give his whole mind to the graveside ceremonies, although his son, Dick, who assisted him with the spadework, considered himself quite capable of carrying on on his own. There was not, indeed, very much to do in the way of digging. Rather to Mr. Gotobed's disappointment, Sir Henry had expressed a wish to be buried in the same grave with his wife, so that there was little opportunity for any fine work in the way of shaping, measuring and smoothing the sides of the grave. They had only to cast out the earth—scarcely yet firm after three rainy months—make all neat and tidy and line the grave with fresh greenery. Nevertheless, liking to be well beforehand with his work, Mr. Gotobed took measures to carry this out on the Thursday afternoon.

The Rector had just come in from a round of visits, and was about to sit down to his tea, when Emily appeared at the sitting-room door.

"If you please, sir, could Harry Gotobed speak to you for a moment?"

"Yes, certainly. Where is he?"

"At the back door, sir. He wouldn't come in on account of his boots being dirty."

Mr. Venables made his way to the back door; Mr. Gotobed stood awkwardly on the step, twirling his cap in his hands.

"Well, Harry, what's the trouble?"

"Well, sir, it's about this here grave. I thought I better come and see you, being as it's a church matter, like. You see, when Dick and me come to open it up, we found a corpus a-laying inside of it, and Dick says to me——"

"A corpse? Well, of course there's a corpse. Lady Thorpe is buried there. You buried her yourself."

"Yes, sir, but this here corpus ain't Lady Thorpe's corpus. It's a man's corpus, that's what it is, and it du seem as though it didn't have no right to be there. So I says to Dick——"

"A man's corpse! What do you mean? Is it in a coffin?"

"No, sir, no coffin. Just an ordinary suit o' clothes, and he du look as though he's abeen a-laying there a goodish while. So Dick says, 'Dad,' he says, 'this looks like a police matter to me. Shall I send for Jack Priest?' he says. And I says, 'No,' I says, 'this here is church property, this is, and Rector did ought to be told about it. That's only right and respectful,' I says. 'Throw a bit o' summat over it,' I says, 'while I goes and fetches Rector, and don't let any o' they boys come into the churchyard.' So I puts on my coat and comes over, because we don't rightly know what to do about it."

"But what an extraordinary thing, Harry!" exclaimed the Rector, helplessly. "I really—I never—who is this man? Do you know him?"

"It's my belief, sir, his own mother wouldn't know him. Perhaps you'd like to step across and take a look at him?"

"Why, yes, of course, I'd better do that. Dear me, dear me! how very perplexing. Emily! Emily! have you seen my hat anywhere? Ah, thank you. Now, Harry. Oh, Emily, please tell Mrs. Venables that I am unexpectedly detained, and not to wait tea for me. Yes, Harry, I'm quite ready now."

Dick Gotobed had spread a tarpaulin over the half-open grave, but he lifted this as the Rector approached. The good gentleman gave one look and averted his eyes rather hastily. Dick replaced the tarpaulin.

"This is a very terrible thing," said Mr. Venables. He had removed his clerical felt in reverence for the horrid thing under the tarpaulin, and stood bewildered, his thin grey hair ruffled by the wind. "We must certainly send for the constable—and—and——" here his face brightened a little—"and for Dr. Baines, of course. Yes, yes—Dr. Baines will be the man. And, Harry, I think I have read that it is better in these cases to disturb things as little as possible. Er—I wonder who this poor fellow can possibly be. It's nobody belonging to the village, that's certain, because if anybody was missing we should have heard about it. I cannot imagine how he can have come here."

"No more can't we, sir. Looks like he was a proper stranger. Excuse me, sir, but didn't we ought to inform the coroner of this here?"

"The coroner? Oh, dear! yes, naturally; I suppose there will have to be an inquest. What a dreadful business this is! Why, we haven't had an inquest in the village since Mrs. Venables and I came to the Rectory, and that's close on twenty years. This will be a very shocking blow for Miss Thorpe, poor child. Her parents' grave—such a fearful desecration. Still, it can't be hushed up, of course. The inquest—well, well, we must try to keep our wits about us. I think, Dick, you had better run up to the post-office and get a call put through to Dr. Baines and ask him to come over at once and you had better ring through to St. Peter and get someone to send a message to Jack Priest. And you, Harry, had better stay here and keep an eye on—on the grave. And I will go up to the Red House myself and break the shocking news to Miss Thorpe, for fear she should hear it in an abrupt and painful way from somebody else. Yes, I think that is what I had better do. Or perhaps it would be more suitable if Mrs. Venables were to go round. I must consult her. Yes, yes, I must consult Mrs. Venables. Now, Dick, off you go, and be sure you don't say a word about this to anybody till the constable comes."

There is no doubt that Dick Gotobed did his best in the matter, but, since the post-office telephone lived in the postmistress's sitting-room, it was not altogether easy to keep any message confidential. At any rate, by the time that P.C. Priest arrived, rather blown, upon his push-cycle, a small knot of men and women had gathered in and about the churchyard, including Hezekiah Lavender, who had run as fast as his ancient legs could carry him from his cottage-garden, and was very indignant with Harry Gotobed for not letting him lift the tarpaulin.

"'Ere!" said the constable, running his machine adroitly into the midst of a bunch of children clustered round the lych gate and tipping himself off bodily sideways. "'Ere! what's all this? You run along home to yer mothers, see? And don't let me catch you here again. 'Afternoon, Mr. Venables, sir. What's the trouble here?"

"There's been a body found in the churchyard," said Mr. Venables.

"Body, eh?" said the constable. "Well, it's come to the right place, ain't it? What have your done with it? Oh, you've left it where you found it. Quite right, sir. And where might that be? Oh, 'ere. *I* see. All right; let's have a look at him. Oh! ah! that's it, is it? Why, Harry, whatever have you been a-doing of? Tryin' to bury him?"

The Rector began to explain, but the constable stopped him with an upraised hand.

"One moment, sir. We'll take this here matter in the proper and correct order. Just a moment while I gets out my notebook. Now, then. Date. Call received 5.15 pee hem. Proceeded to the churchyard, arriving 5.30 pee hem. Now, who found this here body?"

"Dick and me."

"Name?" said the constable.

"Go on, Jack. You knows me well enough."

"That don't matter. I've got to do it in the proper way. Name?"

"Harry Gotobed."

"Hoccupation?"

"Sexton."

"Righto, Harry. Go ahead."

"Well, Jack, we was a-openin' this here grave, which is Lady Thorpe's grave what died last New Year's Day, for to be ready for her 'usband's body, see, what's to be buried tomorrow. We begins to shovel away the earth, one at each end, like, and we hadn't got much more than a foot or so below ground level, as you might say, when Dick drives his spade down a good spit, and he says to me, 'Dad,' he says, 'there's something in here.' And I says to him, 'What's that?' I says, 'what do you mean? Something in here?' and then I strikes my spade hard down and I feels something sort of between hard and soft, like, and I says, 'Dick,' I says, 'that's a funny thing, there *is* something here.' So I says, 'Go careful, my boy,' I says, 'because it feels funny-like to me,' I says. So we starts at one end and shovels away gentle, and arter a bit we sees something sticking up like it might be the toe of a boot. So I says, 'Dick,' I says, 'that's a boot, that is.' And he says, 'You're right, Dad, so 'tis.' So I says, 'Looks to me like we begun at the wrong end of this here, so to say.' So he says, 'Well, Dad, now we've gone so far we may so well have a look at him.' So we gets a-shovellin' again, still going very careful, and arter a bit more we sees something lookin' like 'air. So I says, 'You put that there shovel away and use your 'ands, because we don't want to spile it.' And he says, 'I don't like.' And I says, 'Don't you be a fool, my boy. You can wash your 'ands, can't you, when you've done?' So we clears away very careful, and at last we sees him plain. And I says, 'Dick, I don't know who he is nor yet how he got here, but he didn't ought to be here.' And Dick says, 'Shall I go for Jack Priest?' And I says, 'No. 'Tis Church ground and we better tell Rector.' So that's what we done."

"And I said," put in the Rector, "that we had better send at once for you and for Dr. Baines—and here he is, I see."

Dr. Baines, a peremptory-looking little man, with a shrewd Scotch face, came briskly up to them.

"Good afternoon, Rector. What's happened here? I was out when your message came, so I—good Lord!"

A few words put him in possession of the facts, and he knelt down by the graveside.

"He's terribly mutilated—looks as though somebody had regularly beaten his face in. How long has he been here?"

"That's what we'd like you to tell us, Doctor."

"Half a minute, half a minute, sir," interrupted the policeman. "What day was it you said you buried Lady Thorpe, Harry?"

"January 4th, it were," said Mr. Gotobed, after a short interval for reflection.

"And was this here body in the grave when you filled it up?"

"Now don't you be a fool, Jack Priest," retorted Mr. Gotobed. "'Owever can you suppose as we'd fill up a grave with this here corpus in it? It ain't a thing as a man might drop in careless like, without noticing. If it was a pocketknife, or a penny-piece, that'd be another thing, but when it comes to the corpus of a full-grown man, that there question ain't reasonable."

"Now, Harry, that ain't a proper answer to my question. I knows my duty."

"Oh, all right. Well, then, there weren't no body in that there grave when I filled it up on January 4th—leavin' out, of course, Lady Thorpe's body. That was there, I don't say it wasn't, and for all I know it's there still. Unless him as put this here corpus where it is took the other away with him, coffin and all."

"Well," said the doctor, "it can't have been here longer than three months, and so far as I can tell, it hasn't been there much less. But I'll tell you that better when you get it out."

"Three months, eh?" Mr. Hezekiah Lavender had pushed his way to the front. "That 'ud be about the time that stranger chap disappeared—him as was stayin' at Ezra Wilderspin's and wanted a job to mend up moty-cars and sich. He had a beard, too, by my recollection."

"Why, so he had," cried Mr. Gotobed. "What a head you have on you, Hezekiah! That's who it is, sure-lie. To think o' that, now! I always thought that chap was after no good. But who could have gone for to do a thing like this here?"

"Well," said the doctor. "If Jack Priest has finished with his interrogation, you may as well get the body dug out. Where are you going to put it? It won't be a very nice thing to keep hanging about."

"Mr. Ashton have a nice airy shed, sir. If we was to ask him, I dessay he could make shift to move his ploughs out for the time being. And it's got a decent-sized window and a door with a lock to it."

"That'll do well. Dick, run round and ask Mr. Ashton and get him to lend us a cart and a hurdle. How about getting hold of the coroner, Rector? It's Mr. Compline, you know, over at Leamholt. Shall I ring him up when I get back?"

"Oh, thank you, thank you. I should be very grateful."

"All right. Can they carry on now, Jack?"

The constable signified his assent, and the digging was resumed. By this time the entire village seemed to have assembled in the churchyard, and it was with the greatest difficulty that the children were prevented from crowding round the grave, since the grown-ups who should have restrained them were themselves struggling for positions of vantage. The Rector was just turning upon them with the severest rebuke he knew how to utter, when Mr. Lavender approached him.

"Excuse me, sir, but did I ought to ring Tailor Paul for that there?"

"Ring Tailor Paul? Well, really, Hezekiah, I hardly know."

"We got to ring her for every Christian soul dyin' in the parish," persisted Mr. Lavender. "That's set down for us. And seemin'ly he must a-died in the parish, else why should anybody go for to bury him here?"

"True, true, Hezekiah."

"But as for bein' a Christian soul, who's to say?"

"That, I fear, is beyond me, Hezekiah."

"As to bein' a bit behindhand with him," went on the old man, "that ain't no fault of ours. We only knowed today as he'd died, so it stands to reason we couldn't ring for him earlier. But Christian—well, there! that's a bit of a puzzle, that is."

"We'd better give him the benefit of the doubt, Hezekiah. Ring the bell by all means."

The old man looked dubious, and at length approached the doctor.

"How old?" said the latter, looking round in some surprise. "Why, I don't know. It's hard to say. But I should think he was between forty and fifty. Why do you want to know? The bell? Oh, I see. Well, put it at fifty."

So Tailor Paul tolled the mysterious stranger out with nine strokes and fifty and a hundred more, while Alf Donnington at the Red Cow and Tom Tebbutt at the Wheatsheaf did a roaring trade, and the Rector wrote a letter.

THE SECOND PART

Lord Peter Is Called Into the Hunt

Hunting is the first part of change-ringing which it is necessary to understand.

TROYTE ON CHANGE-RINGING

"MY DEAR Lord Peter (wrote the Rector),—

"Since your delightful visit to us in January, I have frequently wondered, with a sense of confusion, what you must have thought of us for not realizing how distinguished an exponent of the methods of Sherlock Holmes we were entertaining beneath our roof. Living so very much out of the world, and reading only *The Times* and the *Spectator*, we are apt, I fear, to become somewhat narrow in our interests. It was only when my wife wrote to her cousin Mrs. Smith (whom you may know, perhaps, as she lives in Kensington) and mentioned your stay with us, that we were informed, by Mrs. Smith's reply, what manner of man our guest was.

"In the hope that you will pardon our lamentable ignorance, I venture to write and ask you to give us some advice out of your great experience. This afternoon we have been jerked rudely out of 'the noiseless tenor of our way,' by a most mysterious and shocking occurrence. On opening the grave of the late Lady Thorpe to receive the body of her husband—whose sad death you no doubt saw in the obituary columns of the daily press—our sexton was horrified to discover the dead body of a completely strange man, who appears to have come by his end in some violent and criminal manner. His face has been terribly mutilated, and—what seems even more shocking—the poor fellow's hands have been cut right off at the wrists! Our local police have, of course, the matter in hand, but the sad affair is of peculiar and painful interest to me (being in some sort connected with our parish church), and I am somewhat at a loss to know how I, personally, should proceed. My wife, with her usual great practical ability, suggested that we should seek your aid and advice, and Superintendent Blundell of Leamholt, with whom I have just had an interview, most obligingly says that he will give you every facility for investigation should you care to look into the matter personally. I hardly like to suggest to so busy a man that you should actually come and conduct your investigations on the spot, but, in case you thought of doing so, I need not say how heartily welcome you would be at the Rectory.

"Forgive me if this letter is somewhat meandering and confused; I am writing in some perturbation of mind. I may add that our Ringers retain a most pleasant and grateful recollection of the help you gave us with our famous peal, and would, I am sure, wish me to remember them to you.

"With kindest regards from my wife and myself,

"Most sincerely yours,

"THEODORE VENABLES.

"P.S.—My wife reminds me to tell you that the inquest is at 2 o'clock on Saturday."

This letter, dispatched on the Friday morning, reached Lord Peter by the first post on Saturday. He wired that he would start for Fenchurch St. Paul at once, joyfully cancelled a number of social engagements, and at 2 o'clock was seated in the Parish Room, in company with a larger proportion of the local population than had probably ever gathered beneath one roof since the spoliation of the Abbey.

The coroner, a florid-faced country lawyer, who seemed to be personally acquainted with everybody present, got to work with the air of an immensely busy person, every moment of whose time was of value.

"Come, now, gentlemen. . . . No talking over there *if* you please . . . all the jury this way. . . . Sparkes, give out these Testaments to the jury . . . choose a foreman, please. . . . Oh! you have chosen Mr. Donnington . . . very good. . . . Come along, Alf . . . take the Book in your right hand . . . diligently inquire . . . Sovereign Lord the King . . . man unknown . . . body . . . view . . . skill and knowledge . . . help you God . . . kiss the Book . . . sit down . . . table over there . . . now the rest of you . . . take the Book in your right hand . . . your *right hand*, Mr. Pratt . . . don't you know your left hand from your right, Wally? . . . No laughing, please, we've no time to waste . . . same oath that your foreman . . . you and each of you severally to keep . . . help you God . . . kiss the Book . . . on that bench by Alf Donnington. . . . Now then, you know what we're here for . . . inquire how this man came by his death . . . witnesses to identity . . . understood no witnesses to identify. . . .

Yes, Superintendent? . . . Oh, I see . . . why didn't you say so? Very well . . . this way, please. . . . I beg your pardon, sir? . . . Lord Peter . . . do you mind saying that again . . . Whimsy? Oh, no H . . . just so . . . Wimsey with an E . . . quite . . . occupation? . . . what? . . . Well, we'd better say, Gentleman . . . now then, my lord, you say you can offer evidence as to identity?"

"Not exactly, but I rather think . . ."

"One moment, please . . . take the Book in your right hand . . . evidence . . . inquiry . . . truth, whole truth and nothing but the truth . . . kiss the Book . . . yes . . . name, address, occupation, we've got all that. . . . If you can't keep that baby quiet, Mrs. Leach, you'll have to take it out. . . . Yes?"

"I have been taken to see the body, and from my observation I think it possible that I saw this man on January 1st last. I do not know who he was, but if it is the same man he stopped my car about half a mile beyond the bridge by the sluice and asked the way to Fenchurch St. Paul. I never saw him again, and had never seen him before to my knowledge."

"What makes you think it may be the same man?"

"The fact that he is dark and bearded and that the man I saw also appeared to be wearing a dark blue suit similar to that worn by deceased. I say 'appeared,' because he was wearing an overcoat, and I only saw the legs of his trousers. He seemed to be about fifty years of age, spoke in a low voice with a London accent and was of fairly good address. He told me that he was a motor-mechanic and was looking for work. In my opinion, however . . ."

"One moment. You say you recognize the beard and the suit. Can you swear . . . ?"

"I cannot swear that I definitely recognize them. I say that the man I saw resembled the deceased in these respects."

"You cannot identify his features?"

"No; they are too much mutilated."

"Very well. Thank you. Are there any more witnesses to identity?"

The blacksmith rose up rather sheepishly.

"Come right up to the table, please. Take the Book . . . truth . . . truth . . . truth . . . Name Ezra Wilderspin. Well now, Ezra, what have you got to say?"

"Well, sir, if I was to say I recognized the deceased, I should be telling a lie. But it's a fact that he ain't unlike a chap that come along, same as his lordship here says, last New Year's Day a-looking for a job along of me. Said he was a motor-mechanic out o' work. Well, I told him I might do with a man as knowed somethin' about motors, so I takes him on and gives him a trial. He did his work pretty well, near as I could judge, for three days, livin' in our place, and then, all of a sudden, off he goes in the middle of the night and we never seen no more of him."

"What night was that?"

"Same day as they buried her ladyship it was . . ."

Here a chorus of voices broke in:

"January 4th, Ezra! that's when it were."

"That's right. Saturday, January 4th, so 'twere."

"What was the name of this man?"

"Stephen Driver, he called hisself. Didn't say much; only that he'd been trampin' about a goodish time, lookin' for work. Said he'd been in the Army, and in and out of work ever since."

"Did he give you any references?"

"Why, yes, sir, he did, come to think on it. He give me the name of a garridge in London where he'd been, but he said it had gone bankrupt and shut up. But he said if I was to write to the boss, he'd put in a word for him."

"Have you got the name and address he gave you?"

"Yes, sir. Leastways, I think the missus put it away in the teapot."

"Did you take up the reference?"

"No, sir. I did think of it, but being no great hand at writing I says to myself I'd wait till the Sunday, when I'd have more time, like. Well, you see, before that he was off, so I didn't think no more about it. He didn't leave nothing behind him, bar an old toothbrush. We 'ad to lend him a shirt when he came."

"You had better see if you can find that address."

"That's right, sir. Liz!" (in a stentorian bellow). "You cut off home and see if you can lay your 'and on that bit o' paper what Driver give me."

Voice from the back of the room: "I got it here, Ezra," followed by a general upheaval, as the blacksmith's stout wife forced her way to the front.

"Thanks, Liz," said the coroner. "Mr. Tasker, 103 Little James St., London, W.C. Here, Superintendent, you'd better take charge of that. Now, Ezra, is there anything more you can tell us about this man Driver?"

Mr. Wilderspin explored his stubble with a thick forefinger.

"I dunno as there is, sir."

"Ezra! Ezra! don't yew remember all them funny questions he asked?"

"There now," said the blacksmith, "the missus is quite right. That was a funny thing about them questions, that was. He said he 'adn't never been in this here village before, but he knowed a friend as had and the friend had told him to ask after Mr. Thomas. 'Mr. Thomas!' I says. 'There ain't no Mr. Thomas in this here village, nor never has been to my knowledge.' 'That's queer,' he says, 'but maybe he's got another name as well. Far as I can make out,' he says, 'this Thomas ain't quite right in his 'ead. My friend said as he was potty, like.' 'Why,' I says, 'you can't mean Potty Peake? Because Orris is his Chrissen name.' 'No,' he says, 'Thomas was the name. Batty Thomas, that's right. And another name my friend gi'n me,' he says, 'was a fellow called Paul—a tailor or some'in o' that, living next door to him, like.' 'Why,' I says to him, 'your friend's been havin' a game with you. Them ain't men's names, them's the names of bells,' I says. 'Bells?' he says. 'Yes,' I says, 'church bells, that's what they is. Batty Thomas and Tailor Paul, they call 'em.' And then he went on and asked a sight o' questions about they bells. 'Well,' I says, 'if you want to know about Batty Thomas and Tailor Paul, you better ask Rector,' I says. 'He knows all about they old bells.' I dunno if he ever went to Rector, but he come back one day—that were the Friday—and says he been in the church and see a bell carved on old Batty Thomas' tomb, like, and what did the writing on it mean. And I says to ask Rector, and he says: 'Did all bells have writing on 'em,' and I says, 'Mostly'; and arter that he didn't say no more about it."

Nobody being able to make very much sense out of Mr. Wilderspin's revelations, the Rector was called, who said that he remembered having seen the man called Stephen Driver on one occasion when he was distributing the parish magazine at the smithy, but that Driver had said nothing then, or at any other time, about bells. The Rector then added his own evidence about finding the body and sending for the police, and was dismissed in favour of the sexton.

Mr. Gotobed was very voluble, repeating, with increased circumlocutory detail and reference to what he had said to Dick and Dick to him, the account he had originally given to the police. He then explained that Lady Thorpe's grave had been dug on the 3rd of January and filled in on the 4th, immediately after the funeral.

"Where do you keep your tools, Harry?"

"In the coke-house, sir."

"Where's that?"

"Well, sir, it's down underneath the church—where Rector says the old cryp used to be. Makes a sight o' work, that it du, a-carryin' coke up and down they stairs and through the chancel and sweepin' up arter it. You can't 'elp it a-dribbling out o' the scuttle, do as you like."

"Is the door kept locked?"

"Oh, yes, sir, always kept locked. It's the little door under the organ, sir. You can't get to it without you have the key and the key of the West door as well. That is to say, either the key of the West door or one of the church keys, sir, if you take my meaning. I has the West door key, bein' 'andiest for me where I live, but either of the others would do as well."

"Where do you keep these keys?"

"Hanging up in my kitchen, sir."

"Has anybody else got a key to the coke-house door?"

"Yes, sir; Rector has all the keys."

"Nobody else?"

"Not as I knows on, sir. Mr. Godfrey has them all, only the key of the cryp."

"I see. When these keys are in your kitchen, I suppose any of your family has access to them?"

"Well, sir, in a manner of speakin', yes, but I 'opes as how you ain't tryin' to put anything on me and my missus, nor yet Dick, let alone the children. I been sexton in this here village twenty year follerin' on Hezekiah, and none of us ain't never yet been suspected of 'ittin' strangers over the 'ead and buryin' of them. Come to think of it, this chap Driver came round to my place one morning on a message, and 'ow do I know what he did? Not but what, if he'd a-took the keys, I'd be bound to miss them; still, none the more for that . . ."

"Come, come, Harry! Don't talk nonsense. You don't suppose this unfortunate man dug his own grave and buried himself? Don't waste time."

(Laughter, and cries of, "That's a good 'un, Harry!")

"Silence, *if* you please. Nobody's accusing you of anything. Have you in fact ever missed the keys at any time?"

"No, sir" (sulkily).

"Or ever noticed that your tools had been disturbed?"

"No, sir."

"Did you clean them after digging Lady Thorpe's grave?"

"'Course I cleaned 'em. I always leaves my tools clean."

"When did you use them next after that?"

This puzzled Mr. Gotobed for a moment. The voice of Dick supplied helpfully: "Massey's baby."

("Don't prompt the witness, please!")

"That's right," agreed Mr. Gotobed. "Massey's baby it were, as you can see by the Register. And that 'ud be about a week later—ah! just about."

"You found the tools clean and in their right place when you dug the grave for Mrs. Massey's baby?"

"I ain't noticed nothing different."

"Not at any time since?"

"No, sir."

"Very well. That will do. Constable Priest."

The constable, taking the oath briskly, informed the court of his having been called to the scene of action, having communicated with Superintendent Blundell, having assisted at the removal of the body and of having helped to search the clothes of the deceased. He then made way for the Superintendent, who corroborated his evidence and produced a brief list of the dead man's belongings. These were: a suit of navy-blue serge of poor quality, much deteriorated by its burial in the earth, but apparently purchased fairly recently from a well-known firm of cheap outfitters; much-worn vest and pants, bearing (unexpectedly enough) the name of a French manufacturer; a khaki shirt (British army type); a pair of working-man's boots, nearly new; a cheap spotted tie. In his pockets they had found a white cotton handkerchief; a packet of woodbines; twenty-five shillings and eightpence in cash; a pocket-comb; a ten-centime piece; and a short length of stiff wire, bent at one end into a hook. The body had worn no overcoat.

The French money and underclothing and the piece of wire were the only objects which seemed to suggest any kind of clue. Ezra Wilderspin was recalled, but could not bring to mind that Driver had ever said anything about France, beyond mentioning that he had served in the War; and the Superintendent, asked whether he thought the wire could be anything in the nature of a pick-lock, shook his head, and said it didn't look like anything of that sort to *him*.

The next witness was Dr. Baines, and his evidence produced the only real sensation of the day. He said:

"I have examined the body of deceased and made an autopsy. I should judge the subject to be a man aged between 45 and 50. He appears to have been well-nourished and healthy. Taking into account the nature of the soil, which tends to retard putrefaction, the position of the body when found, that is, about two feet beneath the level of the churchyard and from three to four feet beneath the actual surface of the mound, I should judge the extent of decomposition found to indicate that deceased had been lying in the grave between three and four months. Decay does not proceed so rapidly in a buried body as in one exposed to the air, or in a clothed body as in a naked body. In this case, the internal organs and the soft tissues generally were all quite distinguishable and fairly well preserved. I made a careful examination and could discover no signs of external injury on any part of the body except upon the head, arms, wrists and ankles. The face had apparently been violently battered in with some blunt instrument, which had practically reduced all the anterior—that is, the front—part of the skull to splinters. I was not able to form any exact estimate of the number of blows inflicted, but they must have been numerous and heavy. On opening the abdomen——"

"One moment, Doctor. I take it we may assume that the deceased died in consequence of one or some of these blows upon the skull?"

"No; I do not think that the blows were the cause of death."

At this point an excited murmur ran round the little hall, and Lord Peter Wimsey was distinctly observed to rub his finger-tips lightly together with a gratified smile.

"Why do you say that, Dr. Baines?"

"Because, to the best of my judgment and belief, all the blows were inflicted after death. The hands also were removed after death, apparently with a short, heavy knife, such as a jack-knife."

Further sensation; and Lord Peter Wimsey audibly observed: "Splendid!"

Dr. Baines added a number of technical reasons for his opinion, chiefly connected with the absence of any extravasation of blood and the general appearance of the skin; adding, with proper modesty, that he was, of course, not an expert and could only proffer his opinion for what it was worth.

"But why should anybody inflict such savage injuries on a dead body?"

"That," said the doctor drily, "is outside my province. I am not a specialist in lunacy or neurosis."

"That is true. Very well, then. In your opinion, what was the cause of death?"

"I do not know. On opening the abdomen I found the stomach, intestine, liver and spleen considerably decomposed, the kidneys, pancreas and oesophagus in a fairly good state of preservation." (Here the doctor wandered off into medical detail.) "I could not see," he resumed, "any superficial signs of disease or injury by poison. I, however, removed certain organs" (he enumerated them) "and placed them in sealed jars" (further technical details), "and propose dispatching them today for expert examination by Sir James Lubbock. I should expect to receive his report in about a fortnight's time—possibly earlier."

The coroner expressed himself satisfied with this suggestion, and then went on:

"You mentioned injuries to the arms and ankles, Doctor; what was the nature of those?"

"The skin of the ankles seemed to have been very much broken and abraded—as though the ankles had been tightly bound with cord or rope which had cut through the socks. The arms also showed the pressure marks of a rope above the elbows. These injuries were undoubtedly inflicted before death."

"You suggest that somebody tied the deceased up with ropes, and then, by some means or other, brought about his death?"

"I think that the deceased was undoubtedly tied up—either by another person or by himself. You may remember that there was a case in which a young man at one of the universities died in circumstances which suggested that he had himself bound his own wrists and arms."

"In that case, the cause of death was suffocation, I believe?"

"I believe it was. I do not think that was the case here. I found nothing to indicate it."

"You do not, I suppose, suggest that the deceased went so far as to bury himself?"

"No; I do not suggest that."

"I am glad to hear it," said the coroner, sarcastically. "Can you suggest any reason why, if a man had accidentally or intentionally killed himself by tying himself up——?"

"After tying himself up; the tying of the arms and ankles would not in themselves be likely to cause death."

"After tying himself up—why somebody else should then come along, smash his face in and then bury him secretly?"

"I could suggest a variety of reasons; but I do not think that is my province."

"You are very correct, Doctor."

Dr. Baines bowed.

"He might, I suppose, have perished of starvation, if he had tied himself up and been unable to free himself?"

"No doubt. Sir James Lubbock's report will tell us that."

"Have *you* anything further to tell us?"

"Only that, as a possible aid to identification, I have made as careful a note as I can—in view of the extensive mutilation of the jaws—of the number and condition of deceased's teeth, and of the dental work done upon them at various times. I have handed this note over to Superintendent Blundell in order that he may issue an inquiry."

"Thank you, Doctor; that will no doubt be very helpful."

The coroner paused, glanced through his notes and then turned to the Superintendent.

"In the circumstances, Superintendent, it seems to me advisable to adjourn the inquest until you have completed your investigations. Shall we say, till today fortnight? Then, if you should see your way to making any charge against anybody in connection with this crime, or accident, or whatever it is, we may if you like adjourn the inquiry *sine die*."

"I think that would be the best way, Mr. Compline."

"Very well. Gentlemen, we will adjourn until today fortnight."

The jury, a little puzzled and disappointed at not being asked for any opinion, filed slowly out from behind the long trestle table at which they had been seated—a table dedicated, under happier circumstances, chiefly to parish teas.

"A beautiful case," said Lord Peter, enthusiastically, to Mr. Venables. "Quite charming. I am uncommonly grateful to you for drawing my attention to it. I wouldn't have missed it for the world. I like your doctor."

"We consider him a very able man."

"You must introduce me to him; I feel that we should get on well together. The coroner doesn't like him. Some trifling personal antagonism, no doubt. Why, here is my old friend Hezekiah! How do you do, Mr. Lavender? How's Tailor Paul?"

There was general greeting. The Rector caught the arm of a tall, thin man hurrying past their little group.

"Just a moment, Will. I want to introduce you to Lord Peter

Wimsey. Lord Peter, this is Will Thoday, whose bell you rang on your last visit."

Hands were shaken.

"Very sorry I was to miss that peal," said Thoday. "But I was pretty bad, wasn't I, Rector?"

"You were indeed. You don't look to have quite got over it yet."

"I'm all right, sir, except for being troubled by a bit of a cough. But that'll pass away with the spring weather coming."

"Well, you must take care of yourself. How's Mary?"

"Fine, sir, thank you. She was for coming to this here inquest, but I said as it wasn't no place for a woman. I'm thankful I got her to stop at home."

"Yes; the doctor's evidence was very disagreeable. Children all right? That's splendid. Tell your wife Mrs. Venables will be coming round to see her in a day or two. Yes, she's very well, thank you—distressed, naturally, by all this sad business. Ah! There's Dr. Baines. Doctor! Lord Peter Wimsey wants very much to make your acquaintance. You'd better come and have a cup of tea at the Rectory. Good day, Will, good day! . . . I don't like the looks of that fellow," added the Rector, as they turned towards the Rectory. "What do you think of him, Doctor?"

"He's looking a bit white and strained today. Last week I thought he was a lot better, but he had a bad bout of it and he's rather a nervous subject. You don't expect farm-labourers to have nerves, do you, Lord Peter? But they're human, like the rest of us."

"And Thoday is a very superior man," said the Rector, as though superiority conveyed a licence to keep a nervous system. "He used to farm his own land till these bad times set in. Now he works for Sir Henry—that is to say, he did. I'm sure I don't know what will happen now, with only that poor child left at the Red House. I suppose the trustee will let the place, or put in a steward to run it for her. It doesn't bring in very much these days, I fear."

At this point a car overtook them and stopped a little way ahead. It proved to contain Superintendent Blundell and his assistants, and the Rector, apologizing fussily for his remissness, made him and Wimsey acquainted with one another.

"Pleased to meet you, my lord. I've heard of you through my old friend Inspector Sugg. He's retired now—did you know?—and got a nice little place the other side of Leamholt. He often talks about you. Says you used to pull his leg something cruel. This is a bad job, this is. Between you and me, my lord, what was it you were going to say when the coroner interrupted you—about this chap Driver's not being a motor-mechanic?"

"I was going to say that he gave me the impression of having done most of his manual labour lately at Princetown or somewhere like that."

"Ah!" said the Superintendent, thoughtfully. "Struck you that way, did he? How was that?"

"Eyes, voice, attitude—all characteristic, what?"

"Ah!" said the Superintendent again. "Ever heard of the Wilbraham emeralds, my lord?"

"Yes."

"You know that Nobby Cranton's out again? And it seems he ain't reported himself lately, neither. Last heard of six months ago in London. They've been looking for him. Maybe we've found him. In any case, I wouldn't be surprised if we was to hear of those emeralds again before very long."

"Loud cheers!" said Wimsey. "I'm all for a treasure-hunt. This is confidential, of course?"

"If you please, my lord. You see, if somebody thought it worth while to kill Cranton and smash him up and bury him, *and* cut off his hands, where he keeps his fingerprints, there's somebody in this village that knows something. And the less they think we guess, the more free they'll act and speak. And that's why, my lord, I was rather glad when the reverend gentleman suggested you coming down here. They'll talk freer to you than to me—see?"

"Perfectly. I'm a terrific success at pottering round asking sloppy questions. And I can put away quite a lot of beer in a good cause."

The Superintendent grinned, begged Wimsey to come and see him at any time, clambered into his car and drove off.

. . . .

The great difficulty about any detective inquiry is knowing where to start. After some thought, Lord Peter made out the following list of queries:

A. *Identity of the Corpse.*

1. Was it Cranton?—Wait for report on teeth and police report.

2. Consider the question of the ten-centime piece and the French underclothing. Has Cranton been in France? When? If not Cranton, is anyone known in the village also known to have been in France at any period since the War?
3. The destruction of the hands and features after death suggests that the murderer had an interest in making recognition impossible. If the body is Cranton, who knew Cranton (a) by sight? (b) personally?
(Note: Deacon knew him; but Deacon is dead. Did Mary Thoday know him?) Many people must have seen him at the trial.

B. *The Wilbraham Emeralds.*

1. Resulting from the above: Was Mary Thoday (formerly Mary Deacon, née Russell) really after all concerned in the theft?
2. Who really had the emeralds—Deacon or Cranton?
3. Where are the emeralds now? Did Cranton (if it was Cranton) come to Fenchurch St. Paul to look for them?
4. If the answer to 3 is "Yes," why did Cranton wait till now to make his search? Because some fresh information had lately reached him? Or merely because he was continuously in prison till just lately? (Ask the Superintendent.)
5. What is the meaning of "Driver's" interest in Batty Thomas and Tailor Paul? Is anything to be gained from a study of the bells and/or their mottoes?

C. *The Crime.*

1. What did deceased die of? (Wait for experts' report.)
2. Who buried (and presumably also killed) him?
3. Can any clue to the time of the burial be gained by looking up the weather reports? (Snow? rain? footprints?)
4. Whereabouts did the murder take place? The churchyard? the church? somewhere in the village?
5. If the sexton's tools were used, who had access to them? ("Driver," apparently, but who else?)

Quite a lot of questions, thought his lordship, and some of them unanswerable till outside reports came in. The matter of the bell-mottoes could, of course, be looked into at once. He sought the Rector and asked whether he could, without too much trouble, lay his hand on Woollcott's *History of the Bells of Fenchurch St. Paul*, which he had once spoken about. The Rector thought he could, and after he had hunted through all his study shelves and enlisted the aid of Mrs. Venables and Emily, the book was in fact discovered in a small room devoted to the activities of the Clothing Club ("and how it could have got there, I cannot imagine!"). From this work Wimsey distilled the following facts, interesting to archæologists, but not immediately suggestive of anything in the way of corpses or emeralds:

Batty Thomas (No. 7. Weight 30½ cwt. Note: D). The oldest bell in the ring in her present form, and older still in her original metal. First cast by Thomas Belleyetere of Lynn in 1338. Re-cast, with additional metal, by Abbot Thomas of Fenchurch (fl: 1356–1392) in 1380. This abbot also built the tower and the greater part of the existing nave, though the aisle windows were enlarged in Perpendicular style by Abbot Martin circ. 1423).

Inscriptions:

Shoulder —NOLI + ESSE + INCREDVLVS + SED + FIDELIS +
Waist —O SANCTE THOMA.
Soundbow—ABBAT . THOMAS . SETT . MEE . HEARE . AND . BAD . MEE . RINGE . BOTH . LOVD . AND . CLEER . 1380 .

No record of any other bells at this time, though there was probably at least one other. We know, however, that in the reign of Elizabeth there was a ring of five bells in D of which

John (No. 3. Weight 8 cwt. Note: A) was the original treble. She bears the name of her founder, John Cole, an itinerant founder of the period.

Inscription:

Soundbow—JHON . COLE . MAD . MEE . JHON PRESBYTER . PAYD . MEE . JHON . EVAGELIST . AID . MEE . MDLVII .

Jericho (No. 4. Weight 8½ cwt. Note: G) was the No. 2 of the old peal, and her maker seems to have thought aggressively well of her.

Inscription:

Shoulder —FROM . IERICHO . TO . IOHN . AGROAT . YB . IS . NOE . BELLE . CAN . BETTER . MY . NOTE . 1559 .

Of the original No. 4, nothing is known. The original No. 3 (F ♯) was a poor bell, flat in pitch and weak in quality. In James I's reign, this bell was further flattened by the grinding away of its inner surface so as to produce some sort of approximation to F ♯, and the great tenor bell was added to make a ring of six in C.

Tailor Paul (No. 8. Weight 41 cwt. Note: C)—A very noble bell of superb truth and tone. She was cast in the Bellfield by the church. (See parish records.)

Inscriptions:

Shoulder —PAVLE + IS + MY + NAME + HONOVR + THAT + SAME +
Soundbow—NINE + TAYLERS + MAKE + A + MANNE + IN + CHRIST + IS + DETH + ATT + END + IN + ADAM + YAT + BEGANNE + 1614

The bells survived the tumults of the Great Rebellion, and in the later part of the century, when the fashion for change-ringing set in, a new treble and second were added to bring the number up to eight.

Gaude (Treble. Weight 7 cwt. Note: C). The gift of the Gaudy family, she bears a "canting" motto.

Inscription:

Soundbow—GAVDE . GAUDY . DÑI . IN . LAVDE . MDCLXVI .

The No. 2 of that period was known as *Carolus*, having been given in honour of the King's Restoration. This bell, however, was cracked in the 18th century, as a result of the abominable practice of "clapping" the two smallest bells for occasional services, so that the ring was again reduced to six, of which No. 5 (F ♯) had always been unsatisfactory. In the first half of the

19th century (that period of ecclesiastical apathy) the worm was allowed to get into the timbers of the bell-cage, as a result of which No. 6 (the Elizabethan No. 4) fell and was broken. Nothing was done until the 'eighties, when an energetic High-Church rector called public attention to the bad state of the bells. Subscriptions were raised, the framework of the bell-cage was repaired and put in order, and three bells were re-cast:

Sabaoth (No. 2. Weight 7¼ cwt. Note: B) was the gift of the Rector.

Inscriptions:

Shoulder —SANCTUS . SANCTUS . SANCTUS . DOMINUS . DEUS . SABAOTH .
Soundbow—RECAST BY JOHN TAYLOR OF LOUGHBOROUGH 1887.

Dimity (No. 6. Weight 14 cwt. Note: E) was given in memory of Sir Richard Thorpe, who died 1883.

Inscriptions:

Shoulder —RECAST BY JOHN TAYLOR OF LOUGHBOROUGH 1887.
Soundbow—IN . PIAM . MEMORIAM . RICARDI . THORPE . ARMIGERI . NUNC . DIMITTIS . DOMINE . SERVUM . TUUM . IN . PACE .

Jubilee (No. 5. Weight 9½ cwt. Note: F ♯). The funds for this bell were raised by public subscription in commemoration of the Queen's Jubilee.

Inscriptions:

Shoulder —JUBILATE . DEO . OMNIS . TERRA .
Waist —RECAST . IN . THE . YEAR . OF . THE . QUEEN'S . JUBILEE . BY . JOHN . TAYLOR . AND . CO . E. HINKINS . AND . B. DONNINGTON . CHURCHWARDENS .

Wimsey puzzled his head for some time over this information, but without very much result. The dates, the weights and the mottoes—was there anything here that could serve as a guide to buried treasure? Batty Thomas and Tailor Paul had been particularly mentioned, but try as he would, for him they had neither speech nor language. After a time he gave up his calculations. Possibly there was something about the bells themselves that did not appear in Mr. Woollcott's work. Something written or carved on the timbers, possibly. He must go up and look some time.

It was Sunday morning. As he lifted his head from his calculations, he heard the bells begin to ring for matins. He hastened out in the hall, where he found his host winding the grandfather clock.

"I always wind it when the bells begin on a Sunday morning," explained Mr. Venables, "otherwise I might forget. I fear I am none too methodical. I hope you will not feel obliged to come to church, merely because you are our guest. I always make a point of telling our visitors that they are quite free to do as they wish. What time do *you* make it? Ten thirty-seven—we will put the hands at 10.45. He always loses about a quarter of an hour during the week, you see, and by putting him a little forward each time he is wound, we strike a happy mean. If you will just remember that he is always *fast* on Sundays, Mondays and Tuesdays, *right* on Wednesdays, and *slow* on Thursdays, Fridays and Saturdays, you will find him a very reliable guide."

Wimsey said he was sure of it, and turned to find Bunter at his elbow, offering him with one hand his hat and with the other two leather-bound volumes on a small salver.

"You see, padre, we have every intention of going to Church; we have, in fact, come prepared. Hymns A & M—I suppose that is the right work?"

"I took the liberty of ascertaining as much beforehand, my lord."

"Of course you did, Bunter. You always ascertain everything. Why, padre, what's the trouble? Have you lost anything?"

"I—er—it's very odd—I could have declared that I laid them down just here. Agnes! Agnes, my dear! Have you seen those banns anywhere?"

"What is it, Theodore?"

"The banns, my dear. Young Flavel's banns. I know I had them with me. I always write them out on a slip of paper, you see, Lord Peter; it is so very inconvenient to carry the register to the lectern. Now what in the world——?"

"Are they on top of the clock, Theodore?"

"My dear, what a——! Bless me, though, you are quite right.

How did that come about, I wonder? I must have put them up there unconsciously when I was picking up the key. Very strange, indeed, but the little mishap is now remedied, thanks to my wife. She always knows where I have put things. I believe she knows the workings of my mind better than I do myself. Well, I must go across to the Church now. I go early, because of the choir-boys. My wife will show you the Rectory pew."

The pew was conveniently situated for observation, towards the rear of the nave on the north side. From it, Mrs. Venables was able to survey the south porch, by which the congregation entered, and also to keep an admonitory eye on the school children who occupied the north aisle, and to frown at those who turned round to stare or make faces. Lord Peter, presenting a placid front to the inquisitive glances of his fellow-worshippers, also watched the south porch. There was a face he was particularly anxious to see. Presently he saw it. William Thoday came in, and with him a thin, quietly dressed woman accompanied by two little girls. He guessed her to be about forty, though, as is frequently the case with country women, she had lost most of her front teeth and looked older. But he could still see in her the shadow of the smart and pretty parlour-maid that she must have been sixteen years before. It was, he thought, an honest face, but its expression was anxious and almost apprehensive—the face of a woman who had been through trouble and awaited, with nervous anticipation, the next shock which fate might hold in store for her. Probably, thought Wimsey, she was worried about her husband. He did not look well; he, too, had the air of being braced in self-defence. His uneasy eyes wandered about the church and then returned, with a curious mingling of wariness and protective affection, to his wife. They took their seats almost immediately opposite the Rectory pew, so that Wimsey, from his corner seat, was able to watch them without any appearance of particularity. He gained the impression, however, that Thoday felt his scrutiny and resented it. He turned his eyes away, therefore, and fixed them on the splendours of the angel roof, lovelier than ever in the soft spring sunshine that streamed through the rich reds and blues of the clerestory windows.

The pew which belonged to the Thorpe family was empty, except for an upright middle-aged gentleman who was pointed out in a whisper by Mrs. Venables as being Hilary Thorpe's uncle from London. The housekeeper, Mrs. Gates, and the Red House servants sat in the south aisle. In the pew immediately in front of Wimsey was a stout little man in a neat black suit, who, Mrs. Venables further informed him, was Mr. Russell, the village undertaker, and a cousin of Mary Thoday. Mrs. West, the postmistress, arrived with her daughter, and greeted Wimsey, whom she remembered from his last visit, with a smile and something between a nod and a bob. Presently, the bells ceased, with the exception of the five-minutes bell, and the ringers came clattering up to their places. Miss Snoot, the schoolmistress, struck into a voluntary, the choir came in from the vestry with much noise of hobnailed boots, and the Rector entered his stall.

The service was devoid of incident, except that Mr. Venables again mislaid the banns, which had to be fetched from the vestry by the tenor on the cantoris side, and that, in his sermon, he made a solemn little allusion to the unfortunate stranger whose funeral was to take place on the morrow, whereat Mr. Russell nodded, with an air of importance and approbation. The Rector's progress to the pulpit was marked by a loud and gritty crunching, which caused Mrs. Venables to mutter in an exasperated tone, "That's the coke again—Gotobed *will* be so careless with it." At the conclusion, Wimsey found himself stranded with Mrs. Venables in the porch, while handshakings and inquiries passed.

Mr. Russell and Mr. Gotobed came out together, busily talking, and the former was introduced to Lord Peter.

"Where are they a-putting of him, Harry?" asked Mr. Russell, eagerly turning from ceremony to business.

"Over on north side, next to old Susan Edwards," replied the sexton. "We got him dug last night, all very fit and proper. Maybe his lordship would like to come and see."

Wimsey expressed suitable interest, and they made their way round to the other side of the church.

"We're giving him a nice bit of elm," said Mr. Russell, with some satisfaction, when the handsome proportions of the grave had been duly admired. "He did ought by rights to have come on the parish, and that means deal, as you know, but Rector says to me, 'Poor fellow,' he says, 'let's put him away nice and seemly, and I'll pay for it,' he says. And I've trued up the boards good and tight, so there won't be no unpleasantness. Of course, lead would be the right thing for him, but it ain't a thing as I'm often asked for, and I didn't think as I could get it in time, and the fact is, the sooner he's underground again, the better. Besides, lead is cruel 'ard work on the bearers. Six of them we're giving him—I wouldn't want to be thought lacking in respect for the dead, however come by, so I says to Rector, 'No, sir,' I says, 'not that old handcart,' I says, 'but six bearers just the same as if he was one of ourselves.' And Rector, he quite agreed with me. Ah! I daresay there'd be a sight of folk come in from round about, and I wouldn't like them to see the thing done mean or careless like."

"That's right," said Mr. Gotobed. "I've heerd as there's a reg-lar party comin' from St. Stephen in Jack Brownlow's sharrer. It'll be a rare frolic for 'em."

"Rector's giving a wreath, too," pursued Mr. Russell, "and Miss Thorpe's sending another. And there'll be a nice bunch o' flowers from the school-children and a wreath from the Women's Institute. My missus was round collecting the pennies just as soon as we knowed we'd have the buryin' of him."

"Ah! she's a quick worker and no mistake," said the sexton, admiringly.

"Ah! and Mrs. Venables, she made the money up to a guinea, so it'll be a real good one. I like to see a nice lot of flowers at a funeral. Gives it tone, like."

"Is it to be choral?"

"Well, not what you might call fully choral, but just a 'ymn at the graveside. Rector says, 'Not too much about parted friends,' he says. ''Twouldn't be suitable, seeing we don't know who his friends was.' So I says, 'What about *god moves in a myster'ous way?*' I says. 'That's a good solemn-like, mournful 'ymn, as we all knows the tune on, and if anything can be said to be myster'ous, it's this here death,' I says. So that's what was settled."

"Ah!" said the voice of Mr. Lavender, "you're right there, Bob Russell. When I was a lad, there wasn't none o' this myster'ous-ness about. Everything was straightforward an' proper. But ever since eddication come in, it's been nothing but puzzlement, and fillin' up forms and 'ospital papers and sustificates and such, be-fore you can even get as much as your Lord George pension."

"That may be, Hezekiah," replied the sexton, "but to my mind it all started with that business of Jeff Deacon at the Red House, bringin' strangers into the place. First thing as 'appened arter that was the War, and since then we been all topsy-turvy, like."

"As to the War," said Mr. Russell, "I daresay we'd a-had that anyhow, Jeff Deacon or no Jeff Deacon. But in a general way you're quite right. He was a bad 'un, was Jeff, though even now, poor Mary won't hear a word again' him."

"That's the way with women," said Mr. Lavender, sourly. "The wusser a man is, the more they dotes on him. Too soft-spoken he were, to my liking, were that Deacon. I don't trust these London folk, if you'll excuse me, sir."

"Don't mention it," said Wimsey.

"Why, Hezekiah," remonstrated Mr. Russell, "you thought a sight o' Jeff Deacon yourself at one time. Said he was the quickest chap at learning Kent Treble Bob as you ever had to do with."

"That's a different thing," retorted the old gentleman. "Quick he was, there ain't no denyin', and he pulled a very good rope. But quickness in the 'ed don't mean a good 'eart. There's many evil men is as quick as monkeys. Didn't the good Lord say as much? The children o' this world is wiser in their generation than the children o' light. He commended the unjust steward, no doubt, but he give the fellow the sack just the same, none the more for that."

"Ah, well," said the sexton, "Jeff Deacon 'ull be put in his proper place where he've gone, and the same with this poor chap, whoever he be. We ain't got nothing to meddle wi' that, only to do our dooties in the station whereto we are called. That's Scripture, that is, and so I says, Give him a proper funeral, for we don't know when it may be our turn next."

"That's very true, Harry; very true, that is. It may be you or me to be 'it on the 'ed one o' these days—though who can be going about to do such things beats me. Now then, Potty, what do you want here?"

"Nothing, nothing, Bob. Only to see where you was a-putting of the dead 'un. Ah! he were reglar smashed up, he were, weren't he? Beat all to a pulp, eh? Whack! whack! I a-liked to a-seen that, I would."

"Clear off," said the undertaker. "I'm disgusted wi' you, Potty. Fair disgusted. Don't you get talkin' that a-way, or I'll tell Rector on you, and he won't let you blow the organ no more. See? What you mean by it?"

"Nothing, Bob, nothing."

"That's a good thing."

Mr. Russell watched the imbecile uneasily as he shuffled away, his big head rolling and his hands swinging loosely at his sides.

"He's getting very queer, is Potty," said he. "I 'ope as he's safe. I reckon he did ought to be shut up."

"No, no," said the sexton. "Potty's safe enough. I don't 'old with these 'ere asylums."

At this point Mrs. Venables joined them to take possession of her guest.

"Poor little Hilary Thorpe wasn't in church," she observed. "Such a nice child. I should have liked you to see her. But she's quite prostrated, poor child, so Mrs. Gates tells me. And you know, the village people do stare so at anybody who's in trouble, and they will want to talk and condole. They mean well, but it's a terrible ordeal. I'll take you along to the Red House one day. Come along now—I'm sure you want your dinner."

THE THIRD PART

Lord Peter Is Taken from Lead and Makes Thirds Place

The bell that the treble takes from lead makes thirds place and returns to lead again; while the bells in 4, 5 and 6, 7 dodge when the place is made.

RULES FOR RINGING GRANDSIRE TRIPLES

LORD PETER watched the coffin borne up the road.

"Here comes my problem," said he to himself, "going to earth on the shoulders of six stout fellows. Finally, this time, I suppose, and I don't seem to have got very much out of it. What a gathering of the local worthies—and how we are all enjoying it! Except dear old Venables—he's honestly distressed. . . . This everlasting tolling makes your bones move in your body. . . . Tailor Paul . . . Tailor Paul . . . two mortal tons of bawling bronze. . . . 'I am the Resurrection and the Life . . .' that's all rather sobering. This chap's first resurrection was ghastly enough—let's hope there won't be another this side of Doomsday. . . . Silence that dreadful bell! . . . Tailor Paul . . . though even that might happen, if Lubbock finds anything funny. . . . 'Though after my skin worms destroy this body . . .' How queer that fellow Thoday looks . . . something wrong there, I shouldn't wonder. . . . Tailor Paul . . . 'We brought nothing into this world and it is certain we can carry nothing out . . .' except our secrets, old Patriarch; we take those with us all right." The deep shadows of the porch swallowed up priest, corpse and bearers, and Wimsey, following with Mrs. Venables, felt how strange it was that he and she should follow that strange corpse as sole and unexpected mourners.

"And people may say what they like," thought Wimsey again, "about the services of the Church of England, but there was genius in the choosing of these psalms. 'That I may be certified how long I have to live'—what a terrifying prayer! Lord, let me never be certified of anything of the kind. 'A stranger with Thee and a sojourner'—that's a fact, God knows. . . . 'Thou hast set our misdeeds before Thee' . . . very likely, and why should I, Peter Wimsey, busy myself with digging them up? I haven't got so very much to boast about myself, if it comes to that. . . . Oh, well! . . . 'world without end, Amen.' Now the lesson. I suppose we sit down for this—I'm not very well up in the book of the words. . . . Yes. . . . This is the place where the friends and relations usually begin to cry—but there's nobody here to do it—not a friend, nor a—How do I know that? I don't know it. Where's the man or woman who would have recognized that face, if the murderer hadn't taken all those pains to disfigure it? . . . That red-haired kid must be Hilary Thorpe . . . decent of her to come . . . interesting type . . . I can see her making a bit of a splash in five years' time. . . . 'I have fought with beasts at Ephesus' . . . what on earth has that got to do with it? . . . 'raised a spiritual body'—what does old Donne say? 'God knows in what part of the world every grain of every man's dust lies. . . . He whispers, he hisses, he beckons for the bodies of his saints' . . . do all these people believe that? Do I? Does anybody? We all take it pretty placidly, don't we? 'In a flash, at a trumpet crash, this Jack, joke, poor potsherd, patch, matchwood, immortal diamond is—immortal diamond.' Did the old boys who made that amazing roof believe? Or did they just make those wide wings and adoring hands for fun, because they liked the pattern? At any rate, they made them *look* as though they believed something, and that's where they have us beat. What next? Oh, yes, out again to the grave, of course. Hymn 373 . . . there must be some touch of imagination in the good Mr. Russell to have suggested this, though he looks as if he thought of nothing but having tinned salmon to his tea. . . . 'Man that is born of a woman . . .' not very much further to go now; we're coming into the straight. . . . 'Thou knowest, Lord, the secrets of our hearts. . . .' I knew it, I knew it! Will Thoday's going to faint. . . . No, he's got hold of himself again. I shall have to have a word with that gentleman before long . . . 'for any pains of death, to fall from Thee.' Damn it! that goes home. Why? Mere splendour of rhythm, I expect—there are plenty of worse pains. . . . 'Our dear brother here departed' . . . *brother* . . . we're all dear when we're dead, even if beforehand somebody hated us enough to tie us up and . . . Great Scott, yes! What about that rope?"

The problem of the rope—absurdly overlooked and now absurdly insistent—took such possession of Wimsey that he forgot to join in the Lord's Prayer; nor had he even wits to spare for a sardonic commentary on the means used by Providence to deliver this our brother out of the miseries of this sinful world. He was amazed that he had not earlier seized upon the rope as a clue to the labyrinth. For the tying-up of the dead man implied so much.

Where had the rope come from? How had it happened to be handy for the tying-up, and where had that tying taken place? You might kill a man in hot blood, but you did not first tie him. The death of a bound man meant premeditation—a calf roped for the shambles. The rope had been removed before burial; there was a horrid thrift about that. . . . At this point Wimsey shook himself. There was no need to fancy things; there were plenty of other reasons for the removal of the rope. It had been removed before death. It had been removed and replaced where it came from, lest its absence should arouse suspicion. It had been removed for the same reason that the face had been mutilated—lest anyone finding the body should recognize it. Finally, it had been removed because it had tied the body *to* something—and that, perhaps, was the likeliest reason. For the body must have been brought from somewhere—how? Car, lorry, cart, waggon, wheelbarrow, truck . . . ? It reminded one of "Tinker, tailor . . ."

"Everything *very* nicely done, Mr. Russell," said Mrs. Venables.

"Yes'm?" said Mr. Russell. "Very glad you think so, 'm. We done what we could to the best of our ability."

"I'm sure," said Mrs. Venables, "that if his own people had been here, they couldn't have wished for anything *nicer*."

"No'm," agreed Mr. Russell, much gratified, "and it's a pity they couldn't a-been present, for there's no doubt a handsome funeral is a great comfort to them as is left. Of course, it ain't so grand as a London funeral would be——" He glanced wistfully at Wimsey.

"But much nicer," said Wimsey, in a ridiculous echo of Mrs. Venables. "You see, it has so much more of the personal touch."

"That's very true," said the undertaker, much encouraged. "Why, I dessay these London men get as much as three or four funerals every week, and it stands to reason as they can't put the same 'eart into it—let alone not knowing the parties. Well, I'll be getting along now. There's someone wants to speak to you, my lord."

"No," said Wimsey, firmly, to a gentleman in well-worn tweeds, who approached briskly. "I have no story for the *Morning Star*. Nor for any other paper. Hop it. I have other things to do."

"Yes," added Mrs. Venables, addressing the reporter as though he were an importunate child at a school treat, "run away now, the gentleman's busy. How tiresome these newspapers are! You must get sick to death of them. Come along. I want to introduce you to Hilary Thorpe. Hilary, my dear, how are you? Very sweet of you to come—so trying for you. How is your uncle? This is Lord Peter Wimsey."

"I'm ever so glad to meet you, Lord Peter. Dad used to read all about your cases—he'd have loved to have a talk with you. You know, I think he'd have been frightfully amused to think of being mixed up in one himself—if only it hadn't been Mother's grave. I'm glad he didn't know about that. But it is a mystery, isn't it? And he was—well, quite a kid about mysteries and things."

"Was he? I should have thought he'd had about enough of them."

"You mean about the necklace? That was pretty awful for him, poor dear. Of course, it all happened before I was born, but he often used to talk about it. He always used to say he believed Deacon was the worst of the two men, and that Grand-dad ought never to have had him in the house. It was funny, but I believe he rather took a liking to the other man—the London thief. He only saw him at the trial, of course, but he said he was an amusing beggar and he believed he was telling the truth."

"That's dashed interesting." Lord Peter turned suddenly and savagely on the young man from the *Morning Star*, who still hovered at a little distance. "See here, my lad, if you don't make a noise like a hoop and roll away, I shall have something to say to your editor. I will not have this young lady followed about and bothered by you. Go right away, and if you're good I'll see you later and tell you any lies you like. See? Now vanish! . . . Curse the Press!"

"That lad's a sticker," said Miss Thorpe. "He badgered poor Uncle nearly out of his senses this morning. That's Uncle, talking to the Rector. He's a Civil Servant, and he disapproves of the Press altogether. He disapproves of mysteries, too. It's rotten for Uncle."

"I expect he'll disapprove of me."

"Yes, he does. He thinks your hobby unsuited to your position in life. That's why he's rather carefully avoiding an introduction. Uncle's a comic old bird, but he isn't a snob and he's rather decent, really. Only he's not a bit like Dad. You and Dad would have got on splendidly. Oh, by the way—you know where Dad and Mother are buried, don't you? I expect that was the first place you looked at."

"Well, it was; but I'd rather like to look at it again. You see, I'm wondering just exactly how the—the——"

"How they got the body there? Yes, I thought you'd be wondering that. I've been wondering, too. Uncle doesn't think it's nice of me to wonder anything of the sort. But it really makes things easier to do a little wondering, I mean, if you're once interested in a thing it makes it seem less real. That's not the right word, though."

"Less personal?"

"Yes; that's what I mean. You begin to imagine how it all happened, and gradually it gets to feel more like something you've made up."

"H'm!" said Wimsey. "If that's the way your mind works, you'll be a writer one day."

"Do you think so? How funny! That's what I want to be. But why?"

"Because you have the creative imagination, which works outwards, till finally you will be able to stand outside your own experience and see it as something you have made, existing independently of yourself. You're lucky."

"Do you really think so?" Hilary looked excited.

"Yes—but your luck will come more at the end of life than at the beginning, because the other sort of people won't understand the way your mind works. They will start by thinking you dreamy and romantic, and then they'll be surprised to discover that you are really hard and heartless. They'll be quite wrong both times—but they won't ever know it, and *you* won't know it at first, and it'll worry you."

"But that's just what the girls say at school. How did you know? . . . Though they're all idiots—mostly, that is."

"Most people are," said Wimsey, gravely, "but it isn't kind to tell them so. I expect you do tell them so. Have a heart; they can't help it. . . . Yes, this is the place. Well, you know, it isn't very much overlooked, is it? That cottage is the nearest—whose is that?"

"Will Thoday's."

"Oh, is it? . . . And after that, there's only the Wheatsheaf and a farm. Whose is the farm?"

"That's Mr. Ashton's place. He's quite a well-to-do kind of man, one of the churchwardens. I liked him very much when I was a kid; he used to let me ride on the farm-horses."

"I've heard of him; he pulled my car out of the ditch one day—which reminds me. I ought to call and thank him personally."

"That means you want to ask him questions."

"If you *do* see through people as clearly as that, you oughtn't to make it so brutally plain to them."

"That's what Uncle calls my unfeminine lack of tact. He says it comes of going to school and playing hockey."

"He may be right. But why worry?"

"I'm not worrying—only, you see, Uncle Edward will have to look after me now, and he thinks it's all wrong for me to be going to Oxford. . . . What are you looking at? The distance from the South gateway?"

"Uncomfortably discerning woman—yes, I was. You could bring the body in a car and carry it round without too much difficulty. What's that, there, close up by the north wall of the churchyard? A well?"

"Yes; that's the well where Gotobed gets the water for washing out the porch and scrubbing the chancel and all that. I think it's rather deep. There used to be a pump there at one time, but the village people used to come and use it for drinking water, when the village well ran dry, and Mr. Venables had to stop it, because he said it wasn't sanitary, drinking water out of a graveyard; so he took the pump away, and paid for having the village well dug deeper and put in order. He's a frightfully good old sort. When Gotobed wants water he has to haul it up as best he can in a bucket. He grumbles a lot about it. The well's a great nuisance, anyway, because it makes the graves on that side very damp, and sometimes in the winter you can't dig them properly. It was worse before Mr. Venables had the churchyard drained."

"Mr. Venables seems to do a lot for the parish."

"He does. Dad used to subscribe to things, of course, but Mr. Venables generally starts things, when it's anything to do with the Church. At least, when it's things like drains, it's probably Mrs. Venables. Why did you want to know about the well?"

"I wanted to know whether it was used or disused. As it's used, of course nobody would think of hiding anything large in it."

"Oh, you mean the body? No, that wouldn't have done."

"All the same," said Wimsey. . . . "Look here! forgive my asking, but, supposing your father hadn't died when he did, what sort of tombstone would he have been likely to put up to your mother? Any idea?"

"None at all. He hated tombstones and wouldn't discuss them, poor darling. It's horrid to think that he's got to have one."

"Quite. So that for all anybody knew, he might have had a flat stone put down, or one of those things with a marble kerb round and chips in the middle."

"A thing like a fender? Oh, no! he'd never have had *that*. And certainly not chips. They always reminded him of that fearfully genteel kind of coffee-sugar you get at the sort of places where everything's served on mats and all the wine-glasses are coloured."

"Ah! but did the murderer know your father's feelings about coffee-sugar and wine-glasses?"

"Sorry—I don't know what you're driving at."

"My fault; I'm always so incoherent. I mean—when there are such lots of good places for putting bodies in—dykes and drains and so on, why cart one at great risk and trouble to a churchyard to plant it where it might quite easily be dug up by a stonemason smoothing away the earth for a fenderful of marble chips? I know the body was a good two feet below ground-level, but I suppose they have to dig down a bit when they set up gravestones. It all seems so odd and so rash. And yet, of course, I can see the fascination of the idea. You'd think a grave was about the last place where anyone would look for a stray body. It was sheer bad luck that it should have had to be opened up again so soon. All the same—when you think of the job of getting it here, and digging away at night in secret——! But it looks as though it must have been done that way, because of the rope-marks, which show that the man was tied up somewhere first. It must, I mean, all have been deliberate and thought-out beforehand."

"Then the murderer couldn't have thought about it earlier than New Year's Day when Mother died. I mean, he couldn't have counted on having a grave handy."

"Of course he couldn't; but it may have happened at any time since."

"Surely not at *any* time. Only within a week or so after Mother died."

"Why?" asked Wimsey, quickly.

"Why, because old Gotobed would be certain to notice if anybody had been digging his grave about after the earth had been firmed up properly. Don't you think it must have happened quite soon—probably while the wreaths were still on the grave? They stayed there for a week, and then they looked dead and beastly, and I told Gotobed to chuck them away."

"That's an idea," said Wimsey. "I never thought about that—not having had very much to do with the digging of graves. I must ask Gotobed about it. I say! Can you remember how long the snow lay after your mother died?"

"Let me see. It stopped snowing on New Year's Day, and they swept the path up to the south door. But it didn't start to thaw till—wait! I know! It was during the night of the second, though it had been getting sort of warmer for two days, and the snow was kind of damp. I remember quite well now. They dug the grave on the third, and everything was all sloshy. And on the day of the funeral it rained like billy-oh! It was dreadful. I don't think I shall ever forget it."

"And that took all the snow away, of course."

"Oh, yes."

"So it would have been easy enough for anybody to get to the grave without leaving footprints. Yes. I suppose you never noticed yourself that the wreaths had been moved, or anything?"

"Oh, no! As a matter of fact, I didn't come here much. Dad was so ill, I had to be with him—and anyway, I didn't think of Mother as being *here*, you know. Lord Peter, I think all this business about graves is hateful, don't you? But I'll tell you who would have noticed anything, and that's Mrs. Gates—our housekeeper, you know. She came down every day. She's a perfect ghoul. She kept on trying to talk to me about it, and I wouldn't listen to her. She's quite nice, really, but she ought to live in a Victorian novel, where people wear crape and weep into the tea-cups. . . . Oh, dear! there's Uncle Edward looking for me. He looks quite dyspeptic with disapproval. I'm going to introduce you to him, just to embarrass the poor dear. . . . Uncle Edward! This is Lord Peter Wimsey. He's been so kind. He says I have a creative imagination, and ought to be a writer."

"Ah! how do you do?" Mr. Edward Thorpe, forty-four, very correct and formal, presented a bland Civil-Service front to the impact of Wimsey's personality. "I believe I have met your brother, the Duke of Denver. I hope he is quite well . . . Quite . . . quite so. . . . It is very good of you to take an interest in my niece's young ambitions. All these young women mean to do great things, don't they? But I tell her, authorship is a good stick, but a bad crutch. Very distressing business, this. I am so sorry she should be dragged into it, but of course, in her position, the village people expect her to—ah!—enter into their—ah!—their—um——"

"Amusements?" suggested Wimsey. It came upon him with a shock that Uncle Edward could not be many years older than himself. He felt for him the apprehensive reverence which one feels for a quaint and brittle piece of antiquity.

"For anything which touches them nearly," said Mr. Thorpe. Gallant fellow! Deeply disapproving, he yet sought to defend his niece against criticism. "But I am taking her away for a little peace and quietness," he added. "Her aunt, unhappily, was unable to come to Fenchurch—she suffers sadly from rheumatoid arthritis—but she is looking forward to seeing Hilary at home."

Wimsey, glancing at Hilary's sullen face, saw rebellion rising; he knew exactly the kind of woman who would have married Uncle Edward.

"In fact," said Mr. Thorpe, "we are leaving tomorrow. I am so sorry we cannot ask you to dine, but under the circumstances——"

"Not at all," said Wimsey.

"So I fear it must be a case of Hail and Farewell," continued Mr. Thorpe, firmly. "Delighted to have met you. I could wish that it were under happier circumstances. Ah—good afternoon. Please remember me to your brother when you see him."

. . . .

"Warned off!" said Wimsey, when he had shaken hands with Uncle Edward and bestowed on Hilary Thorpe a grin of understanding sympathy. "Why? Corrupting the morals of youth? Or showing too much zeal about digging up the family mystery? Is Uncle Edward a dark horse or a plain ass, I wonder? Did he go to his brother's wedding? I must ask Blundell. Where is Blundell? I wonder if he is free tonight?"

He hastened to catch the Superintendent, who had dutifully attended the funeral, and arranged to run over to Leamholt after dinner. Gradually the congregation melted away. Mr. Gotobed and his son Dick removed their official "blacks" and fetched the spades that leaned against the wall near the covered well.

As the earth thudded heavily upon the coffin lid, Wimsey joined the small group that had gathered to discuss the ceremony and read the cards upon the wreaths. He stooped idly to examine an exceptionally handsome and exotic floral tribute of pink and purple hothouse exhibits, wondering who could have gone to so much expense for the unknown victim. With a slight shock he read, on a visiting card: "With reverent sympathy. Lord Peter Wimsey. St. Luke XII. 6."

"Very appropriate," said his lordship, identifying the text after a little thought (for he had been carefully brought up). "Bunter, you are a great man."

. . . .

"What I really want to know," said Lord Peter, as he stretched comfortable legs upon the Superintendent's hearth, "is the relation between Deacon and Cranton. How did they get into touch? Because a lot seems to turn on that."

"So it does," agreed Mr. Blundell; "but the trouble is, we have only got their words to go on, and which was the biggest liar, the Lord God only knows, though Mr. Justice Bramhill made a guess. There's no doubt of one thing, and that is that they knew each other in London. Cranton was one of those smooth-spoken, gentlemanly sort of crooks that you meet hanging about the lounge in cheap-smart restaurants—you know the type. He'd been in trouble before, but he gave out he was a reformed character, and made quite a spot of money writing a book. At least, I suppose somebody wrote it for him, but he had his name put on the cover, and all that. There've been several of that sort since the War, but this chap was a smart lad—a bit ahead of his time, really. He was thirty-five in 1914; not educated anything to speak of, but with a kind of natural wit, sharpened by having had to look out for himself, if you take my meaning."

"Just so. A graduate in the University of the world."

"That's very well put," said Mr. Blundell, welcoming the cliché as an inspiration. "Very cleverly put indeed. Yes—that's just what he was. Deacon, now, he was different. A very superior man indeed, he was, and a great reader. In fact, the chaplain down at Maidstone said he was quite a remarkable scholar in his way, with a poetic imagination, whatever that may be exactly. Sir Charles Thorpe took quite a fancy to the fellow, treated him friendly and all that, and gave him the run of the library. Well, these two met in some dance place or other, some time in 1912, when Sir Charles was staying in London. Cranton's story is that some girl that Deacon had picked up—Deacon was always after a skirt—pointed him out to Deacon as the author of this book I was telling you about, and that Deacon made out to be tremendously interested in the book and pumped him a lot about crooks and their doings and the way they worked their little games and all that. He said Deacon made a dead set at him and wouldn't leave him alone, and was always kind of hinting that he was bound to go back to the old life in the end. Deacon said different. He said that what interested him was the literary side of the business, as he called it. Says he thought, if a crook could write a book and make money, why not a butler? According to him, it was Cranton made a dead set at *him*, and started pumping him about what sort of place he'd got, and suggesting if there was anything to be pinched, they should pinch it together and go shares, Deacon working the inside part of the job and Cranton seeing to the rest—finding a fence and settling the terms and so on. I daresay it was six of one and half-a-dozen of the other, if you ask me. A pretty pair they were, and no mistake."

The Superintendent paused to take a long draught of beer from a pewter mug and then resumed.

"You understand," he said, "this was the story they told after we'd got hold of 'em both for the robbery. At first, naturally, they both lied like Ananias and swore they'd never seen each other before in their lives, but when they found what the prosecution had up against them, they changed their tune. But there was this about it. As soon as Cranton realized that the game was up, he adopted this story and stuck to it. In fact, he pleaded guilty at the trial and his one idea seemed to be to get Deacon into trouble and have him gaoled good and hard. He said Deacon had double-crossed him and he was out to get his own back—though whether there was any truth in that, or whether he thought he would get off easy by making himself out to be the poor unfortunate victim of temptation, or whether it was all pure malice, I don't know. The jury had their own idea about it, and so had the judge.

"Well, now. In April 1914 this wedding of Mr. Henry Thorpe's came along, and it was pretty well known that Mrs. Wilbraham was going to be there with her emerald necklace. There wasn't a thief in London that didn't know all about Mrs. Wilbraham. She's a sort of cousin of the Thorpes, a lot of times removed, and a long way back, and she's got a stack of money and the meanness of fifty thousand Scotch Jews rolled into one. She'll be about eighty-six or seven now and getting childish, so I'm told; but in those days she was just eccentric. Funny old lady, stiff as a ramrod, and always dressed in black silks and satins—very old-fashioned—with jewels and bangles and brooches and God knows what stuck all over her. That was one of her crazes, you understand. And another was, that she didn't believe in insurance and she didn't believe a lot in safes, neither. She had a safe in her town house, naturally, and kept her stuff locked up in it, but I don't suppose she'd have done that if the safe hadn't been put in by her husband when he was alive. She was too mean to buy as much as a strongbox for herself, and when she went away on a visit, she preferred to trust to her own wits. Mad as a March Hare, she must have been," said the Superintendent, thoughtfully, "but there! you'd be surprised what a lot of these funny old ladies there are going about loose in the world. And of course, nobody ever liked to say anything to her, because she was disgustingly rich and had the full disposal of her own property. The Thorpes were about the only relations she had in the world, so they invited her to Mr. Henry's wedding, though it's my belief they all hated the sight of her. If they hadn't have asked her, she'd have taken offence, and—well, there! You can't offend your rich relations, can you?"

Lord Peter thoughtfully refilled his own beer-mug and said, "Not on any account."

"Well, then," pursued the Superintendent, "here's where Cranton and Deacon tell different tales again. According to Deacon, he got a letter from Cranton as soon as the wedding-day was announced, asking him to come and meet him at Leamholt and discuss some plan for getting hold of the emeralds. According to Cranton, it was Deacon wrote to him. Neither of 'em could produce a scrap of evidence about it, one way or the other, so, there again, you paid your money and you took your choice. But it was proved that they did meet in Leamholt and that Cranton came along the same day to have a look at the house.

"Very good. Now Mrs. Wilbraham had a lady's maid, and if it hadn't been for her and Mary Thoday, the whole thing might have come to nothing. You'll remember that Mary Thoday was Mary Deacon then. She was housemaid at the Red House, and she'd got married to Deacon at the end of 1913. Sir Charles was very kind to the young couple. He gave them a nice bedroom to themselves away from the other servants, just off a little back stair that runs up by the butler's pantry, so that it was quite like a little private home for them. The plate was all kept in the pantry, of course, and it was supposed to be Deacon's job to look after it.

"Now, this maid of Mrs. Wilbraham's—Elsie Bryant was her name—was a quick, smart sort of girl, full of fun and high spirits, and it so happened that she'd found out what Mrs. Wilbraham did with her jewels when she was staying away from home. It seems the old girl wanted to be too clever by half. I think she must have been reading too many detective stories, if you ask me, but anyway, she got it into her head that the best place to keep valuables wasn't a jewel case or a strong-box or anything of that kind, that would be the first thing a burglar would go for, but some fancy place where nobody would think of looking, and to cut a long story short, the spot she pitched upon was, if you'll excuse me mentioning it, underneath one of the bedroom utensils. You may well laugh—so did everybody in court, except the judge, and he happened to get a fit of coughing at the time and his handkerchief was over his face, so nobody could see how he took it. Well, this Elsie, she was a bit inquisitive, as girls are, and one day—not very long before the wedding—she managed to take a peep through a keyhole or something of that kind, and caught the old lady just in the act of putting the stuff away. Naturally, she couldn't keep a thing like that to herself, and when she and her mistress got to Fenchurch—which they did a couple of days before the wedding, the first thing she had to do was to strike up a bosom friendship with Mary Deacon (as she was then) for the express purpose, as it seems to me, of telling her all about it in confidence. And of course, Mary, being a devoted wife and all that, had to share the joke with her husband. I dare say it's natural. Anyhow, counsel for the defence made a big point of it, and there's no doubt it was that utensil kept Elsie and Mary out of quod. 'Gentlemen,' he said to the jury, in his speech, 'I see you all smiling over Mrs. Wilbraham's novel idea of a safe-deposit, and I've no doubt you're looking forward to passing the whole story on to your wives when you get home. And that being so, you can very well enter into the feelings of my client Mary Deacon and her friend, and see how—in the most innocent manner in the world—the secret was disclosed to the one man who might have been expected to keep it quiet.' He was a clever lawyer, he was, and had the jury eating out of his hand by the time he'd done with them.

"Now we've got to guess again. There was a telegram sent off to Cranton from Leamholt—no doubt about that, for we traced it. He said it came from Deacon, but Deacon said that if anybody sent it, it must have been Elsie Bryant. She and Deacon were both in Leamholt that afternoon, but we couldn't get the girl at the post-office to recognize either of them, and the telegram was written in block letters. To my mind, that points to Deacon, because I doubt if the girl would have thought of such a thing, but needless to say, when the two of them were told to show a specimen of their printing, it wasn't a mite like the writing on the form. Whichever of them it was, either they were pretty clever, or they got somebody else to do it for them.

"You say you've heard already about what happened that night. What you want to know is the stories Cranton and Deacon told about it. Here's where Cranton, to my mind, shows up better than Deacon, unless he was very deep indeed. He told a perfectly consistent tale from start to finish. It was Deacon's plan first and last. Cranton was to come down in a car and be under Mrs. Wilbraham's window at the time mentioned in the telegram. Deacon would then throw out the emerald necklace, and Cranton would go straight off with it to London and get it broken up and sold, dividing the loot fifty-fifty with Deacon, less £50 he'd given him on account. Only he said that what came out of the window was only the jewel-case and not the emeralds, and he accused Deacon of taking the stuff himself and rousing the house on purpose to put the blame on him—on Cranton, that is. And of course, if that was Deacon's plan, it was a very good one. He would get the stuff and the kudos as well.

"The trouble was, of course, that none of this came out till some time after Cranton had been arrested, so that when Deacon was taken and made his first statement to the police, he didn't know what story he'd got to meet. The first account he gave was very straightforward and simple, and the only trouble about it was that it obviously wasn't true. He said he woke up in the night and heard somebody moving about in the garden, and at once said to his wife: 'I believe there's somebody after the plate.' Then, he said, he went downstairs, opened the back door and looked out, in time to see somebody on the terrace under Mrs. Wilbraham's window. Then (according to him) he rushed back indoors and upstairs, just quick enough to catch a fellow making off through Mrs. Wilbraham's window."

"Hadn't Mrs. Wilbraham locked her door?"

"No. She never did, on principle—afraid of fire, or something. He said he shouted loudly to alarm the house, and then the old lady woke up and saw him at the window. In the meantime the thief had climbed down by the ivy and got away. So he rushed off downstairs and found the footman just coming out of the back door. There was a bit of confusion about the back door part of the story, because Deacon didn't explain, first go-off, how he happened to be in Mrs. Wilbraham's bedroom at all. His very first tale, to Sir Charles, had been that he went straight out when he heard the noise in the garden, but by the time the police got him, he'd managed to fit the two accounts together, and said that he'd either been too upset at the time to explain himself clearly or else that everybody else had been too upset to understand what he said. Well, that was all right, until they started to unearth all the history of his having met Cranton before, and the telegram and so on. Then Cranton, seeing that the game was up, told his tale in full, and of course, that made it pretty awkward for Deacon. He couldn't deny it altogether, so he now admitted knowing Cranton, but said it was Cranton who had tried to tempt him into stealing the emeralds, while he had been perfectly sea-green incorruptible. As for the telegram, he denied that altogether, and put it on Elsie. And he denied the £50 altogether, and it's a fact that they never traced it to him.

"Of course, they cross-examined him pretty fiercely. They wanted to know, first, why he hadn't warned Sir Charles about Cranton and secondly, why he'd told a different tale at first. He declared that he thought Cranton had given up all idea of the theft, and he didn't want to frighten anybody; but that when he heard noises in the garden, he guessed what was happening. He also said that afterwards he was afraid to own up to knowing Cranton for fear he should be accused of complicity. But it sounded a pretty thin story, and neither the judge nor the jury believed a word of it. Lord Bramhill spoke very severely to him after the verdict, and said that if it hadn't been his first offence, he'd have given him the heaviest sentence it was in his power to bestow. He called it aggravated larceny of the very worst type, being committed by a servant in a position of trust, in a dwelling-house and his master's dwelling-house at that, and accompanied by the opening of a window, which made it into burglary, and then he had violently resisted arrest, and so forth, and so on; and in the end he gave Deacon eight years' penal servitude and told him he was lucky to get off with that. Cranton was an old offender and might have got a lot more, but the judge said he was unwilling to punish him much more heavily than Deacon, and gave him ten years. So that was that. Cranton went to Dartmoor, and served his full time as a perfectly good old lag, without giving much trouble to anybody. Deacon, being a first offender, went to Maidstone, where he set up to be one of those model prisoners—which is a kind you always want to look out for, because they are always up to some mischief or other. After nearly four years—early in 1918, it was—this nice, refined, well-conducted convict made a brutal attack on a warder and broke prison. The warder died, and of course the whole place was scoured for Deacon, without any success. I daresay, what with the War and one thing and another, they hadn't as many men to carry on the job as they ought to have had. Anyhow, they didn't find him, and for two years he enjoyed the reputation of being about the only man who had ever broken prison successfully. Then his bones turned up in one of those holes—dene-holes, I think they call them, in a wood in North Kent, so they found it was one up to the prison system after all. He was still in his convict clothes and his skull was all smashed in, so he must have tumbled over during the night—probably within a day or two of his escape. And that was the end of him."

"I suppose there's no doubt he was guilty."

"Not the slightest. He was a liar from beginning to end, and a clumsy liar at that. For one thing, the ivy on the Red House showed clearly enough that nobody had climbed down by it that night—and in any case, his final story was as full of holes as a sieve. He was a bad lot, and a murderer as well, and the country was well rid of him. As for Cranton, he behaved pretty well for a bit after he came out. Then he got into trouble again for receiving stolen goods, or goods got by false pretences or something, and back he went into quod. He came out again last June, and they kept tabs on him till the beginning of September. Then he disappeared, and they're still looking for him. Last seen in London—but I shouldn't be surprised if we'd seen the last of him today. It's my belief, and always was, that Deacon had the necklace, but what he did with it, I'm damned if I know. Have another spot of beer, my lord. It won't do you any harm."

"Where do you think Cranton was, then, between September and January?"

"Goodness knows. But if he's the corpse, I should say France, at a guess. He knew all the crooks in London, and if anybody could wangle a forged passport, he could."

"Have you got a photograph of Cranton?"

"Yes, my lord, I have. It's just come. Like to have a look at it?"

"Rather!"

The Superintendent brought out an official photograph from a bureau which stood, stacked neatly with documents, in a corner of the room. Wimsey studied it carefully.

"When was this taken?"

"About four years ago, my lord, when he went up for his last sentence. That's the latest we have."

"He had no beard then. Had he one in September?"

"No, my lord. But he'd have plenty of time to grow one in four months."

"Perhaps that's what he went to France for."

"Very likely indeed, my lord."

"Yes—well—I can't be dead positive, but I think this is the man I saw on New Year's Day."

"That's very interesting," said the Superintendent.

"Have you shown the photograph to any of the people in the village?"

Mr. Blundell grinned ruefully.

"I tried it on the Wilderspins this afternoon, but there! Missus said it was him, Ezra said 'twas nothing like him—and a bunch of neighbours agreed heartily with both of them. The only thing is to get a beard faked on to it and try 'em again. There's not one person in a hundred can swear to a likeness between a bearded face and one that's clean-shaven."

"H'm, too true. Defeat thy favour with an usurped beard. . . . And of course you couldn't take the body's finger-prints, since he had no hands."

"No, my lord, and that's a sort of an argument, in a way, for it's being Cranton."

"If it *is* Cranton, I suppose he came here to look for the necklace, and grew a beard so that he shouldn't be recognized by the people that had seen him in court."

"That's about it, my lord."

"And he didn't come earlier simply because he had to let his beard grow. So much for my bright notion that he might have received some message within the last few months. What I can't understand is that stuff about Batty Thomas and Tailor Paul. I've been trying to make out something from the inscriptions on the bells, but I might as well have left it alone. Hear the tolling of the bells, iron bells—though I'd like to know when church bells were ever made of iron—what a world of solemn thought their monody compels! Was Mr. Edward Thorpe at his brother's wedding, do you know?"

"Oh, yes, my lord. He was there, and a terrible row he made with Mrs. Wilbraham after the theft. It upset poor Sir Charles very much. Mr. Edward as good as told the old lady that it was all her own fault, and he wouldn't hear a word against Deacon. He was certain Elsie Bryant and Cranton had fixed it all up between them. I don't believe myself that Mrs. Wilbraham would ever have cut up so rough if it weren't for the things Mr. Edward said to her, but she was—is—a damned obstinate old girl, and the more he swore it was Elsie, the more *she* swore it was Deacon. You see, Mr. Edward had recommended Deacon to his father——"

"Oh, had he?"

"Why, yes. Mr. Edward was working in London at the time—quite a lad, he was, only twenty-three—and hearing that Sir Charles was wanting a butler, he sent Deacon down to see him."

"What did he know about Deacon?"

"Well, only that he did his work well and looked smart. Deacon was a waiter in some club that Mr. Edward belonged to, and it seems he mentioned that he wanted to try private service, and that's how Mr. Edward came to think of him. And, naturally, having recommended the fellow, he had to stick up for him. I don't know if you've met Mr. Edward Thorpe, but if you have, my lord, you'll know that anything that belongs to him is always perfect. He's never been known to make a mistake, Mr. Edward hasn't—and so, you see, he couldn't possibly have made a mistake about Deacon."

"Oh, yes?" said Wimsey. "Yes, I've met him. Frightful blithering ass. Handy thing to be, sometimes. Easily cultivated. Five minutes' practice before the glass every day, and you will soon acquire that vacant look so desirable for all rogues, detectives and Government officials. However, we will not dwell on Uncle Edward. Let us return to our corpse. Because, Blundell, after all, even if it is Cranton, come to look for emeralds—who killed him, and why?"

"Why," returned the policeman, "supposing he found the emeralds all right and somebody lammed him on the head and took them off him. What's wrong with that?"

"Only that he doesn't seem to have been lammed on the head."

"That's what Dr. Baines says; but we don't know that he's right."

"No—but anyway, the man was killed somehow. Why kill him, when you'd already got him tied up and could take the emeralds without any killing at all?"

"To prevent him squealing. Stop! I know what you're going to say—Cranton wasn't in a position to squeal. But he was, don't you see. He'd already been punished for the theft—they couldn't do anything more to him for that, and he'd only to come and tell us where the stuff was to do himself quite a lot of good. You see his game. He could have done the sweet injured innocence stunt. He'd say: 'I always told you Deacon had the stuff, so the minute I could manage it, I went down to Fenchurch to find it, and I did find it—and of course I was going to take it straight along to the police-station like a good boy, when Tom, Dick or Harry came along and took it off me. So I've come and told you all about it, and when you lay your hands on Tom, Dick or Harry and get the goods you'll remember it was me gave you the office.' Oh, yes—that's what he could have done, and the only thing we'd have been able to put on him would be failing to report himself, and if he'd put us on to getting the emeralds, he'd be let off light enough, you bet. No! anybody as wanted those emeralds would have to put Cranton where he couldn't tell any tales. That's clear enough. But as to who it was, that's a different thing."

"But how was this person to know that Cranton knew where the necklace was? And how did he know, if it comes to that? Unless it really was he who had them after all, and he hid them somewhere in Fenchurch instead of taking them to London. It looks to me as though this line of argument was going to make Cranton the black sheep after all."

"That's true. How'd he come to know? He can't have got the tip from anybody down here, or they'd have got the stuff for themselves, and not waited for him. They've had long enough to do it, goodness knows. But why should Cranton have left the stuff behind him?"

"Hue and cry. Didn't want to be caught with it on him. He may have parked it somewhere when he drove off, meaning to come back and fetch it later. You never know. But the longer I look at these photographs, the more positive I feel that the man I met was Cranton. The official description agrees, too—colour of eyes and all that. And if the corpse isn't Cranton, what's become of him?"

"There you are," said Mr. Blundell. "I don't see as we can do much more till we get the reports from London. Except, of course, as regards the burying. We ought to be able to get a line on that. And what you say about Miss Thorpe's notion—I mean, as to the wreaths and that—may have something in it. Will you have a chat with this Mrs. Gates, or shall I? I think you'd better tackle Mr. Ashton. You've got a good excuse for seeing him, and if I went there officially, it might put somebody on his guard. It's a nuisance, the churchyard being so far from the village. Even the Rectory doesn't overlook it properly, on account of the shrubbery."

"No doubt that circumstance was in the mind of the murderer. You mustn't quarrel with your bread and butter, Superintendent. No difficulty, no fun."

"Fun?" said the Superintendent. "Well, my lord, it's nice to be you. How about Gates?"

"You'd better do Gates. If Miss Thorpe's leaving tomorrow, I can't very well call without looking a nosey parker. And Mr. Thorpe doesn't approve of me. I daresay he's issued an order: No Information. But *you* can invoke all the terrors of the law."

"Not much, I can't. Judges' rules and be damned. But I'll have a try. And then there's——"

"Yes, there's Will Thoday."

"Ah! . . . but if Miss Thorpe's right, he's out of it. He was laid up in bed from New Year's Eve till the 14th of January. I know that for certain. But somebody in his house may have noticed something. It'll be a bit of a job getting anything out of them, though. They've had a taste of the dock once, and they'll get frightened, ten to one, the minute they see me."

"You needn't worry about that. You can't very well frighten them worse than they're frightened already. Go and read the Burial Service to them and watch their reactions."

"Oh!" said the Superintendent. "Religion's a bit out of my line, except on Sundays. All right—I'll take on that part of it. Maybe, if I don't mention that dratted necklace . . . but there, my mind's that full of it, it'll be a mercy if it don't slip out."

Which shows that policemen, like other people, are at the mercy of their sub-conscious preoccupations.

THE FOURTH PART

Lord Peter Dodges with Mr. Blundell and Passes Him

"Dodging" is taking a retrograde movement, or moving a place backwards out of the ordinary hunting course. . . . She will be seen to dodge with a bell, and pass a bell alternately throughout her whole work.

TROYTE

"WELL NOW, ma'am," said Superintendent Blundell.

"Well, officer?" retorted Mrs. Gates.

It is said, I do not know with how much reason, that the plain bobby considers "officer" a more complimentary form of address than "my man," or even "constable"; while some people, of the Disraelian school of thought, affirm that an unmerited "Sergeant" is not taken amiss. But when a highly-refined lady, with a grey glacé gown and a grey glacé eye, addresses a full-blown Superintendent in plain clothes as "officer," the effect is not soothing, and is not meant to be so. At this rate, thought Mr. Blundell, he might just as well have sent a uniformed inspector, and had done with it.

"We should be greatly obliged, ma'am," pursued Mr. Blundell, "for your kind assistance in this little matter."

"A little matter?" said Mrs. Gates. "Since when have murder and sacrilege been considered little matters in Leamholt? Considering that you have had nothing to do for the last twenty years but run in a few drunken labourers on market days, you seem to take your new responsibilities very coolly. In my opinion, you ought to call in the assistance of Scotland Yard. But I suppose, since being patronized by the aristocracy, you consider yourself quite competent to deal with any description of crime."

"It does not lie with me, ma'am, to refer anything to Scotland Yard. That is a matter for the Chief Constable."

"Indeed?" said Mrs. Gates, not in the least disconcerted. "Then why does the Chief Constable not attend to the business himself? I should prefer to deal directly with him."

The Superintendent explained patiently that the interrogation of witnesses was not, properly speaking, the duty of the Chief Constable.

"And why should I be supposed to be a witness? I know nothing about these disgraceful proceedings."

"Certainly not, ma'am. But we require a little information about the late Lady Thorpe's grave, and we thought that a lady with your powers of observation would be in a position to assist us."

"In what way?"

"From information received, ma'am, it appears probable that the outrage may have been committed within a very short period after Lady Thorpe's funeral. I understand that you were a frequent visitor at the graveside after the melancholy event——"

"Indeed? And who told you that?"

"We have received information to that effect, ma'am."

"Quite so. But from whom?"

"That is the formula we usually employ, ma'am," said Mr. Blundell, with a dim instinct that the mention of Hilary would only make bad worse. "I take it, that is a fact, is it not?"

"Why should it not be a fact? Even in these days, some respect may be paid to the dead, I trust."

"Very proper indeed, ma'am. Now can you tell me whether, on any occasion when you visited the grave, the wreaths presented the appearance of having been disturbed, or the earth shifted about, or anything of that kind?"

"Not," said Mrs. Gates, "unless you refer to the extremely rude and vulgar behaviour of that Mrs. Coppins. Considering that she is a Nonconformist, you would think she would have more delicacy than to come into the churchyard at all. And the wreath itself was in the worst possible taste. I suppose she was entitled to send one if she liked, considering the great and many favours she had always received from Sir Charles' family. But there was no necessity whatever for anything so large and ostentatious. Pink hot-house lilies in January were entirely out of place. For a person in her position, a simple bunch of chrysanthemums would have been ample to show respect, without going out of her way to draw attention to herself."

"Just so, ma'am," said the Superintendent.

"Merely because," pursued Mrs. Gates, "I am here in a dependent position, that does not mean that I could not have afforded a floral tribute quite as large and expensive as Mrs. Coppins'. But although Sir Charles and his lady, and Sir Henry and the late Lady Thorpe after them, were always good enough to treat me rather as a friend than a servant, I know what is due to my position, and should never have dreamed of allowing my modest offering to compete in any way with those of the Family."

"Certainly not, ma'am," agreed the Superintendent, heartily.

"I don't know what you mean by 'Certainly not,'" retorted Mrs. Gates. "The Family themselves would have raised no objection, for I may say that they have always looked on me as one of themselves, and seeing that I have been housekeeper here thirty years, it is scarcely surprising that they should."

"Very natural indeed, ma'am. I only mean that a lady like yourself would, of course, take the lead in setting an example of good taste and propriety, and so forth. My wife," added Mr. Blundell, lying with great determination and an appearance of the utmost good faith, "my wife is always accustomed to say to our girls, that for an example of ladylike behaviour, they cannot do better than look up to Mrs. Gates of the Red House at Fenchurch. Not——" (for Mrs. Gates looked a little offended)—"that Mrs. Blundell would presume to think our Betty and Ann in any way equal to *you*, ma'am, being only one of them in the post-office and the other a clerk in Mr. Compline's office, but it does young people no harm to look well above themselves, ma'am, and my wife always says that if they will model themselves upon Queen Mary, or—since they cannot have very much opportunity of studying her Gracious Majesty's behaviour—upon Mrs. Gates of the Red House, they can't fail to grow up a credit to their parents, ma'am."

Here Mr. Blundell—a convinced Disraelian—coughed. He thought he had done that rather well on the spur of the moment, though, now he came to think of it, "deportment" would have been a better word than "behaviour."

Mrs. Gates unbent slightly, and the Superintendent perceived that he would have no further trouble with her. He looked forward to telling his wife and family about this interview. Lord

Peter would enjoy it, too. A decent sort of bloke, his lordship, who would like a bit of a joke.

"About the wreath, ma'am," he ventured to prompt.

"I am telling you about it. I was disgusted—really *disgusted,* officer, when I found that Mrs. Coppins had had the *impertinence* to remove my wreath and put her own in its place. There were, of course, a great many wreaths at Lady Thorpe's funeral, some of them extremely handsome, and I should have been quite content if my little tribute had been placed on the roof of the hearse, with those of the village people. But Miss Thorpe would not hear of it. Miss Thorpe is always very thoughtful."

"A very nice young lady," said Mr. Blundell.

"Miss Thorpe is one of the Family," said Mrs. Gates, "and the Family are always considerate of other people's feelings. True gentlefolk always are. Upstairs are not."

"That's very true indeed, ma'am," said the Superintendent, with so much earnestness that a critical listener might almost have supposed the remark to have a personal application.

"My wreath was placed upon the coffin itself," went on Mrs. Gates, "with the wreaths of the Family. There was Miss Thorpe's wreath, and Sir Henry's, of course, and Mr. Edward Thorpe's and Mrs. Wilbraham's and mine. There was quite a difficulty to get them all upon the coffin, and I was quite willing that mine should be placed elsewhere, but Miss Thorpe insisted. So Mrs. Wilbraham's was set up against the head of the coffin, and Sir Henry's and Miss Thorpe's and Mr. Edward's *on* the coffin, and mine was given a position at the foot—which was practically the same thing as being on the coffin itself. And the wreaths from the Servants' Hall and the Women's Institute were on one side and the Rector's wreath and Lord Kenilworth's wreath were on the other side. And the rest of the flowers were placed, naturally, on top of the hearse."

"Very proper, I'm sure, ma'am."

"And consequently," said Mrs. Gates, "after the funeral, when the grave was filled in, Harry Gotobed took particular notice that the Family's wreaths (among which include mine) were placed in suitable positions on the grave itself. I directed Johnson the chauffeur to attend to this—for it was a very rainy day, and it would not have been considerate to ask one of the maids to go—and he assured me that this was done. I have always found Johnson sober and conscientious in his work, and I believe him to be a perfectly truthful man, as such people go. He described to me exactly where he placed the wreaths, and I have no doubt that he carried out his duty properly. And in any case, I interrogated Gotobed the next day, and he told me the same thing."

"I daresay he did," thought Mr. Blundell, "and in his place I'd have done the same. I wouldn't get a fellow into trouble with this old cat, not if I knew it." But he merely bowed and said nothing.

"You may judge of my surprise," went on the lady, "when, on going down the next day after Early Service to see that everything was in order, I found Mrs. Coppins' wreath—not at the side, where it should have been—but *on* the grave, as if she were somebody of importance, and *mine* pushed away into an obscure place and actually covered up, so that nobody could see the card at all. I was extremely angry, as you may suppose. Not that I minded in the least where my poor little remembrance was placed, for that can make no difference to anybody, and it is the thought that counts. But I was so much incensed by the woman's insolence—merely because I had felt it necessary to speak to her one day about the way in which her children behaved in the post-office. Needless to say, I got nothing from her but impertinence."

"That was on the 5th of January, then?"

"It was the morning after the funeral. That, as you say, would be Sunday the fifth. I did not accuse the woman without proof. I had spoken to Johnson again, and made careful inquiries of Gotobed, and they were both positive of the position in which the wreaths had been left the night before."

"Mightn't it have been some of the school-children larking about, ma'am?"

"I could well believe anything of *them*," said Mrs. Gates; "they are always ill-behaved, and I have frequently had to complain to Miss Snoot about them, but in this case the insult was too pointed. It was quite obviously and definitely aimed at myself, by that vulgar woman. Why a small farmer's wife should give herself such airs, I do not know. When I was a girl, village people knew their place, and kept it."

"Certainly," replied Mr. Blundell, "and I'm sure we were all much happier in those days. And so, ma'am, you never noticed any disturbance except on that one occasion?"

"And I should think that was quite enough," replied Mrs. Gates. "I kept a very good look-out after that, and if anything of a similar kind had occurred again, I should have complained to the police."

"Ah, well," said the Superintendent, as he rose to go, "you see, it's come round to us in the end, and I'll have a word with Mrs. Coppins, ma'am, and you may be assured it won't happen again. Whew! What an old catamaran!" (this to himself as he padded down the rather neglected avenue beneath the budding horse-chestnuts). "I suppose I had better see Mrs. Coppins."

Mrs. Coppins was easily found. She was a small, shrewish woman with light hair and eyes which boded temper.

"Oh, yes," she said, "Mrs. Gates did have the cheek to say it was me. As if I'd have touched her mean little wreath with a hay-fork. Thinks she's a lady. No real lady would think twice about where her wreath was or where it wasn't. Talking that way to me, as if I was dirt! Why shouldn't we give Lady Thorpe as good a wreath as we could get? Ah! she was a sweet lady—a *real* lady, she was—and her and Sir Henry were that kind to us when we were a bit put about, like, the year we took this farm. Not that we were in any real difficulty—Mr. Coppins has always been a careful man. But being a question of capital at the right moment, you see, we couldn't just have laid our hand on it at the moment, if it hadn't been for Sir Henry. Naturally, it was all paid back—with the proper interest. Sir Henry said he didn't want interest, but that isn't Mr. Coppins' way. Yes—January 5th, it would be—and I'm quite sure none of the children had anything to do with it, for I asked them. Not that my children would go to do such a thing, but you know what children are. And it's quite true that her wreath was where she said it was, last thing on the evening of the funeral, for I saw Harry Gotobed and the chauffeur put it there with my own eyes, and they'll tell you the same."

They did tell the Superintendent so, at some considerable length; after which, the only remaining possibility seemed to be the school-children. Here, Mr. Blundell enlisted the aid of Miss Snoot. Fortunately, Miss Snoot was not only able to reassure him that none of her scholars was in fault ("for I asked them all very carefully at the time, Superintendent, and they assured me they had not, and the only one I might be doubtful of is Tommy West, and he had a broken arm at the time, through falling off a gate"); she was also able to give valuable and unexpected help as regards the time at which the misdemeanour was committed.

"We had a choir-practice that night, and when it was over—that would be about half-past seven—the rain had cleared up a little, and I thought I would just go and give another little look at dear Lady Thorpe's resting-place; so I went round with my torch, and I quite well remember seeing Mrs. Coppins' wreath standing up against the side of the grave next the church, and thinking what a beautiful one it was and what a pity the rain should spoil it."

The Superintendent felt pleased. He found it difficult to believe that Mrs. Coppins or anybody else had gone out to the churchyard on a dark, wet Saturday night to remove Mrs. Gates' wreath. It was surely much more reasonable to suppose that the burying of the corpse had been the disturbing factor, and that brought the time of the crime down to some hour between 7.30 p.m. on the Saturday and, say, 8.30 on the Sunday morning. He thanked Miss Snoot very much and, looking at his watch, decided that he had just about time to go along to Will Thoday's. He was pretty sure to find Mary at home, and, with luck, might catch Will himself when he came home to dinner. His way led him past the churchyard. He drove slowly, and, glancing over the churchyard wall as he went, observed Lord Peter Wimsey, seated in a reflective manner and apparently meditating among the tombs.

"'Morning!" cried the Superintendent cheerfully. "'Morning, my lord!"

"Oy!" responded his lordship. "Come along here a minute. You're just the man I wanted to see."

Mr. Blundell stopped his car at the lych-gate, clambered out, grunting (for he was growing rather stout), and made his way up the path.

Wimsey was sitting on a large, flat tombstone, and in his hands was about the last thing the Superintendent might have expected to see, namely, a large reel of line, to which, in the curious, clumsy-looking but neat and methodical manner of the fisherman, his lordship was affixing a strong cast adorned with three salmon-hooks.

"Hullo!" said Mr. Blundell. "Bit of an optimist, aren't you? Nothing but coarse fishing about here."

"Very coarse," said Wimsey. "Hush! While you were interviewing Mrs. Gates, where do you think I was? In the garage, inciting our friend Johnson to theft. From Sir Henry's study. Hist! not a word!"

"A good many years since he went fishing, poor soul," said Mr. Blundell, sympathetically.

"Well, he kept his tackle in good order all the same," said Wimsey, making a complicated knot and pulling it tight with his teeth. "Are you busy, or have you got time to look at something?"

"I was going along to Thoday's, but there's no great hurry. And, by the way, I've got a bit of news."

Wimsey listened to the story of the wreath.

"Sounds all right," he said. He searched in his pocket, and produced a handful of lead sinkers, some of which he proceeded to affix to his cast.

"What in the world are you thinking of catching with that?" demanded Mr. Blundell. "A whale?"

"Eels," replied his lordship. He weighed the line in his hand and gravely added another piece of lead.

Mr. Blundell, suspecting some kind of mystification, watched him in discreet silence.

"That will do," said Wimsey, "unless eels swim deeper than ever plummet sounded. Now come along. I've borrowed the keys of the church from the Rector. He had mislaid them, of course, but they turned up eventually among the Clothing Club accounts."

He led the way to the cope-chest beneath the tower, and threw it open.

"I have been chattin' with our friend Mr. Jack Godfrey. Very pleasant fellow. He tells me that a complete set of new ropes was put in last December. One or two were a little dicky, and they didn't want to take any chances over the New Year peal, so they renewed the lot while they were about it. These are the old ones, kept handy in case of sudden catastrophe. Very neatly coiled and stowed. This whopper belongs to Tailor Paul. Lift 'em out carefully—eighty feet or so of rope is apt to be a bit entanglin' if let loose on the world. Batty Thomas. Dimity. Jubilee. John. Jericho. Sabaoth. But where is little Gaude? Where and oh, where is she? With her sallie cut short and her rope cut long, where and oh, where can she be? No—there's nothing else in the chest but the leather buffets and a few rags and oilcans. No rope for Gaude. *Gaudeamus igitur, juvenes dum sumus.* The mystery of the missing bell-rope. *Et responsum est ab omnibus: Non est inventus—-a* or *-um.*"

The Superintendent scratched his head and gazed vaguely about the church.

"Not in the stove," said Wimsey. "My first thought, of course. If the burying was done on Saturday, the stoves would be alight, but they'd be banked down for the night, and it would have been awkward if our Mr. Gotobed had raked out anything unusual on Sunday morning with his little scraper. As a matter of fact, he tells me that one of the first things he does on Sunday morning is to open the top thing-ma-jig on the stove and take a look inside to see that the flue-pipe is clear. Then he stirs it up a-top, rakes it out at the bottom door and sets it drawing for the day. I don't *think* that was where the rope went. I hope not, anyway. I think the murderer used the rope to carry the body by, and didn't remove it till he got to the graveside. Hence these salmon-hooks."

"The well?" said Mr. Blundell, enlightened.

"The well," replied Wimsey. "What shall we do, or go fishing?"

"I'm on; we can but try."

"There's a ladder in the vestry," said Wimsey. "Bear a hand. Along this way—out through the vestry-door—and here we are. Away, my jolly boys, we're all bound away. Sorry! forgot this was consecrated ground. Now then—up with the cover. Half a jiff. We'll sacrifice half a brick to the water-gods. Splosh!—it's not so very deep. If we lay the ladder over the mouth of the well, we shall get a straight pull."

He extended himself on his stomach, took the reel in his left hand and began to pay the line cautiously out over the edge of the ladder, while the Superintendent illumined the proceedings with a torch.

The air came up cold and dank from the surface of the water. Far below a circle of light reflected the pale sky and the beam of the torch showed hooks and line working steadily downwards. Then a tiny break in the reflection marked the moment when the hooks touched the water.

A pause. Then the whirr of the reel as Wimsey rewound the line.

"More water than I thought. Where are those leads? Now then, we'll try again."

Another pause. Then:

"A bite, Super, a bite! What's the betting it's an old boot? It's not heavy enough to be the rope. Never mind. Up she comes. Ahoy! up she rises! Sorry, I forgot again. Hullo, ullo, ullo! What's this? Not a boot, but the next thing to it. A hat! Now then, Super! Did you measure the head of the corpse? You did? Good! then we shan't need to dig him up again to see if his hat fits. Stand by with the gaff. Got him! Soft felt, rather the worse for wear and water. Mass production. London maker. Exhibit One. Put it aside to dry. Down she goes again. . . . *And* up she comes. Another tiddler. Golly! what's this? Looks like a German sausage. No, it isn't. No, it isn't. It's a sallie. Sallie in our alley. She is the darling of my heart. Little Gaude's sallie. Take her up tenderly, lift her with care. Where the sallie is, the rest will be. . . . Hoops-a-daisy! . . . I've got it. . . . It's caught somewhere. . . . No, don't pull too hard, or the hook may come adrift. Ease her. Hold her. . . . Damn! . . . Sorry, undamn! I mean, how very provoking, it's got away. . . . *Now* I've got it. . . . Was that the ladder cracking or my breastbone, I wonder? Surprisin'ly sharp edge a ladder has. . . . There now, there now! there's your eel—all of a tangle. Catch hold. Hurray!"

"It's not all here," said the Superintendent, as the slimy mass of rope was hauled over the edge of the well.

"Probably not," said Wimsey, "but this is one of the bits that were used to do the tying. He's cut it loose and left the knots in."

"Yes. Better not touch the knots, my lord. They might tell us something about who tied 'em."

"Take care of the knots and the noose will take care of itself. Right you are. Here we go again."

In process of time, the whole length of the rope—as far as they could judge—lay before them in five sections, including the sallie.

"Arms and ankles tied separately. Then body tied up to something or other and the slack cut off. And he removed the sallie because it got in the way of his knots. H'm!" said Mr. Blundell. "Not very expert work, but effective, I dare say. Well, my lord, this is a very interesting discovery of yours. But—it's a bit of a facer, isn't it? Puts rather a different complexion on the crime, eh?"

"You're right, Super. Well, one must face up to things, as the lady said when she went to have hers lifted. Hullo! what the——"

A face, perched in a bodiless sort of way on the churchyard wall, bobbed suddenly out of sight as he turned, and then bobbed up again.

"What the devil do you want, Potty?" demanded the Superintendent.

"Oh, nothing," replied Potty. "I don't want nothing. Who're you goin' to hang with that there, mister? That's a rope, that is. They've got eight on 'em hanging up the tower there," he added, confidentially. "Rector don't let me go up there no more, because they don't want nobody to know. But Potty Peake knows. One, two, three, four, five, six, seven, eight—all hung up by the neck. Old Paul, he's the biggest—Tailor Paul—but there did ought to be nine tailors by rights. I can count, you see; Potty can count. I've counted 'em over time and again on my fingers. Eight. And one is nine. And one is ten—but I ain't telling you *his* name. Oh, no. He's waiting for the nine tailors—one, two, three, four——"

"Here, you, hop it!" cried the Superintendent, exasperated. "And don't let me catch you hanging round here again."

"Who's a-hanging? Listen—you tell me, and I'll tell you. There's Number Nine a-coming, and that's a rope to hang him, ain't it, mister? Nine of 'em, and eight's there already. Potty knows. Potty can say. But he won't. Oh, no! Somebody might be listening." His face changed to its usual vacant look and he touched his cap.

"Good-day, sir. Good-day, mister. I got to feed the pigs, that's Potty's work. Yes, that's right. They pigs did ought to be fed. 'Morning, sir; 'morning, mister."

He slouched away across the fields towards a group of outhouses some distance away.

"There!" said Mr. Blundell, much vexed. "He'll go telling everybody about this rope. He's got hanging on the brain, ever since he found his mother hanging in the cow-house when he was a kid. Over at Little Dykesey, that was, a matter of thirty year back. Well, it can't be helped. I'll get these things taken along to the station, and come back later on for Will Thoday. It'll be past his lunch-time now."

"It's past mine, too," said Wimsey, as the clock chimed the quarter past one. "I shall have to apologize to Mrs. Venables."

. . . . . .

"So you see, Mrs. Thoday," said Superintendent Blundell, pleasantly, "if anybody can help us over this awkward business it's you."

Mary Thoday shook her head.

"I'm sure I would if I could, Mr. Blundell, but there! how can I? It's right enough to say I was up all night with Will. I hardly had my clothes off for a week, he was that bad, and the night after they laid poor Lady Thorpe to rest, he was just as bad as could be. It turned to pneumonia, you know, and we didn't think as we should ever pull him through. I'm not likely to forget that night, nor the day neither. Sitting here, listening to old Tailor Paul and wondering if he was going to ring for Will before the night was out."

"There, there!" said her husband, embarrassed, and sprinkling a great quantity of vinegar on his tinned salmon, "it's all over now, and there's no call to get talking that way."

"Of course not," said the Superintendent. "Not but what you had a pretty stiff time of it, didn't you, Will? Delirious and all that kind of thing, I'll lay. I know what pneumonia is, for it carried off my old mother-in-law in 1922. It's a very trying thing to nurse, is pneumonia."

"So 'tis," agreed Mrs. Thoday. "Very bad he was, that night. Kept on trying to get out of his bed and go to church. He thought they was ringing the peal without him, though I kept on telling him that was all rung and finished with New Year's Day. A terrible job I had with him, and nobody to help me, Jim having left us that very morning. Jim was a great help while he was here, but he had to go back to his ship. He stayed as long as he could, but of course he's not his own master."

"No," said Mr. Blundell. "Mate on a merchantman, isn't he? How's he getting along? Have you heard from him lately?"

"We had a postcard last week from Hong Kong," said Mary, "but he didn't say much. Only that he was well and love to the children. He hasn't sent nothing but postcards this voyage, and he must be terrible busy, for he's such a man for writing letters as a rule."

"They'll be a bit shorthanded, maybe," said Will. "And it's an anxious time for men in his line of business, freights being very scarce and hard to come by. It'll be all this depression, I suppose."

"Yes, of course. When do you expect him back?"

"Not for I don't know when," replied Will. The Superintendent looked sharply at him, for he seemed to detect a note almost of satisfaction in the tone. "Not if trade's decent, that is. You see, his ship don't make regular trips. She follows cargo, as they call it, tramping round from port to port wherever there's anything to be picked up."

"Ah, yes, of course. What's the name of the ship, again?"

"The *Hannah Brown*. She belongs to Lampson & Blake of Hull. Jim is doing very well, I'm told, and they set great store by him. If anything happened to Captain Woods, they'd give the ship to Jim. Wouldn't they, Will?"

"So he says," replied Thoday uneasily. "But it don't do to count on anything these days."

The contrast between the wife's enthusiasm and the husband's lack of it was so marked that Mr. Blundell drew his own conclusions.

"So Jim's been making trouble between 'em, has he?" was his unspoken comment. "That explains a lot. But it doesn't help me much. Better change the subject."

"Then you didn't happen to see anything going on at the church that night?" he said. "No lights moving about? Nothing of that kind?"

"I didn't move from Will's bedside all night," replied Mrs. Thoday, with a hesitating glance at her husband. "You see, he was so ill, and if I left him a minute, he'd be throwing the clothes off and trying to get up. When it wasn't the peal that was in his mind, it was the old trouble—you know."

"The old Wilbraham affair?"

"Yes. He was all muddled up in his head, thinking the—the—that dreadful trial was on and he had to stand by me."

"That'll *do!*" cried Thoday, suddenly, pushing his plate away so violently that the knife and fork clattered from the plate upon the table. "I won't have you fretting yourself about that old business no more. All that's dead and buried. If it come up in my mind when I wasn't rightly in my senses, I can't help that. God knows, I'd be the last to put you in mind of it if I'd been able to help myself. You did ought to know that."

"I'm not blaming you, Will."

"And I won't have nothing more said about it in my house. Why do you want to come worrying her this way, Mr. Blundell? She's told you as she don't know a thing about this chap that was buried, and that's all there is to it. What I may have said and done, when I was ill, don't matter a hill of beans."

"Not a scrap," admitted the Superintendent, "and I'm very sorry such an allusion should have come up, I'm sure. Well, I won't keep you any longer. You can't assist me and that's all there is to it. I'm not saying it isn't a disappointment, but a policeman's job's all disappointments, and one must take the rough with the smooth. Now I'll be off and let the youngsters come back to their tea. By the way, what's gone with the parrot?"

"We've put him in the other room," said Will, with a scowl. "He's taken to shrieking fit to split your head."

"That's the worst of parrots," said Mr. Blundell. "He's a good talker, though. I've never heard a better."

He bade them a cheerful good evening and went out. The two Thoday children—who had been banished to the woodshed during the discussion of murders and buryings, unsuited to their sex and tender years—ran down to open the gate for him.

"Evening, Rosie," said Mr. Blundell, who never forgot anybody's name, "evening, Evvie. Are you being good girls at school?"

But, the voice of Mrs. Thoday calling them at that moment to their tea, the Superintendent received but a brief answer to his question.

. . . .

Mr. Ashton was a farmer of the old school. He might have been fifty years old, or sixty or seventy, or any age. He spoke in a series of gruff barks, and held himself so rigidly that if he had swallowed a poker it could only have produced unseemly curves and flexions in his figure. Wimsey, casting a thoughtful eye upon his hands, with their gnarled and chalky joints, concluded, however, that his unbending aspect was due less to austerity than to chronic arthritis. His wife was considerably younger than himself; plump where he was spare, bounce-about where he was stately, merry where he was grave, and talkative where he was monosyllabic. They made his lordship extremely welcome and offered him a glass of home-made cowslip wine.

"It's not many that makes it now," said Mrs. Ashton. "But it was my mother's recipe, and I say, as long as there's peggles to be got, I'll make my peggle wine. I don't hold by all this nasty stuff you get at the shops. It's good for nothing but to blow out the stomach and give you gas."

"Ugh!" said Mr. Ashton, approvingly.

"I quite agree with you, Mrs. Ashton," said his lordship. "This is excellent." And so it was. "It is another kindness I have to thank you for." And he expressed his gratitude for the first-aid given to his car the previous January.

"Ugh!" said Mr. Ashton. "Pleased, I'm sure."

"But I always hear of Mr. Ashton engaged in some good work or other," went on his lordship. "I believe he was the good samaritan who brought poor William Thoday back from Walbeach the day he was taken ill."

"Ugh!" repeated Mr. Ashton. "Very fortunate we happened to see him. Ugh! Very bad weather for a sick man. Ugh! Dangerous thing, influenza."

"Dreadful!" said his wife. "Poor man—he was quite reeling with it as he came out of the Bank. I said to Mr. Ashton, 'How terrible bad poor Will do look, to be sure! I'm sure he's not fit to go home.' And sure enough, we hadn't got but a mile or so out of the town when we saw his car drawn up by the side of the road, and him quite helpless. It was God's mercy he didn't drive into the Drain and kill himself. And with all that money on him, too! Dear, dear! What a terrible loss it would have been. Quite helpless and out of his head he was, counting them notes over and dropping of them all over the place. 'Now, Will,' I said, 'you just put them notes back in your pocket and keep quiet and we'll drive you home. And you've no call to worry about the car,' I said, 'for we'll stop at Turner's on the way and get him to bring it over next time he comes to Fenchurch. He'll do it gladly, and he can go back on the bus.' So he listened to me and we got him into our car and brought him home. And a hard time he had, dear, dear! He was prayed for in church two weeks running."

"Ugh!" said Mr. Ashton.

"What he ever wanted to come out for in such weather I can't think," went on Mrs. Ashton, "for it wasn't market day, and we wouldn't have been there ourselves, only for Mr. Ashton having to see his lawyer about Giddings' lease, and I'm sure if Will had wanted any business done, we'd have been ready to do it for him. Even if it was the Bank, he could have trusted us with it, I should think. It's not as though Mr. Ashton couldn't have taken care of two hundred pounds, or two thousand, for that matter. But Will Thoday was always very close about his business."

"My dear!" said Mr. Ashton, "ugh! It may have been Sir Henry's business. You wouldn't have him anything but close about what's not, rightly speaking, his affair."

"And since when, Mr. Ashton," demanded his lady, "has Sir Henry's family banked at the London and East Anglia? Let alone that Sir Henry was always a deal too considerate to send a sick man out to do business for him in a snowstorm? I've told you before that I don't believe that two hundred pounds had anything to do with Sir Henry, and you'll find out one of these days I'm right, as I always am. Aren't I, now?"

"Ugh!" said Mr. Ashton. "You make a lot of talk, Maria, and some of it's bound to be right. Funny if it wasn't, now and again. Ugh! But you've no call to be interfering with Will's money. You leave that to him."

"That's true enough," admitted Mrs. Ashton, amiably. "I do let my tongue run on a bit, I'll allow. His lordship must excuse me."

"Not at all," said Wimsey. "In a quiet place like this, if one doesn't talk about one's neighbours, what is there to talk about?

And the Thodays are really your only near neighbours, aren't they? They're very lucky. I'll be bound, when Will was laid up, you did a good bit of the nursing, Mrs. Ashton."

"Not as much as I'd have liked," said Mrs. Ashton. "My daughter was took ill at the same time—half the village was down with it, if it comes to that. I managed to run in now and again, of course—'twouldn't be friendly else—and our girl helped Mary with the cooking. But what with being up half the night——"

This gave Wimsey his opportunity. In a series of tactful inquiries he led the conversation to the matter of lights in the churchyard.

"There, now!" exclaimed Mrs. Ashton. "I always thought as there might be something in that tale as little Rosie Thoday told our Polly. But children do have so many fancies, you never know."

"Why, what tale was that?" asked Wimsey.

"Ugh! foolish nonsense, foolish nonsense," said Mr. Ashton. "Ghosts and what not."

"Oh, *that's* foolish enough, I dare say," retorted his lady, "but you know well enough, Luke Ashton, that the child might be telling the truth, ghost or no ghost. You see, your lordship, it's this way. My girl Polly—she's sixteen now and going out to service next autumn, for whatever people may say and whatever airs they may give themselves, I will maintain there's nothing like good service to train a girl up to be a good wife, and so I told Mrs. Wallace only last week. It's not standing behind a counter all day selling ribbons and bathing-dresses (if they call them dresses, with no legs and no backs and next to no fronts neither) will teach you how to cook a floury potato, let alone the tendency to fallen arches and varicose veins. Which," added Mrs. Ashton triumphantly, "she couldn't hardly deny, suffering sadly from her legs as she do."

Lord Peter expressed his warm appreciation of Mrs. Ashton's point of view and hinted that she had been about to say that Polly——

"Yes, of course. My tongue do run on and no mistake, but Polly's a good girl, though I say it, and Rosie Thoday's always been a pet of Polly's, like, ever since she was quite a baby and Polly only seven. Well, then, it was a good time ago, now—when would it be, Luke? End of January, maybe, near enough—it was pretty near dark at six o'clock, so it couldn't be much later—well, call it end of January—Polly comes on Rosie and Evvie sitting together under the hedge just outside their place, both of them crying. 'Why, Rosie,' says Polly, 'what's the matter?' And Rosie says, Nothing, now that Polly's come and can they walk with her to the Rectory, because their Dad has a message for Rector. Of course, Polly was willin' enough, but she couldn't understand what they was cryin' about, and then, after a bit—for you know how difficult it is to get children to tell you what they're frightened on—it comes out that they're afraid to go past the churchyard in the dark. Well, Polly being a good girl, she tells 'em there's no call to be frighted, the dead being in the arms of our Saviour and not having the power to come out o' their graves nor to do no harm to nobody. But that don't comfort Rosie, none the more for that, and in the end Polly makes out that Rosie's seen what she took to be the spirit of Lady Thorpe a-flittin' about her grave. And it seems the night she see her was the night of the funeral."

"Dear me," said Wimsey. "What exactly did she see?"

"No more than a light, by what Polly could make out. That was one of the nights Will Thoday was very bad, and it seems Rosie was up and about helping her mother—for she's a good, handy child, is Rosie—and she looks out o' the window and sees the light just a-rising out of where the grave would be."

"Did she tell her mother and father?"

"Not then, she didn't. She didn't like to, and I remember well, as a child I was just the same, only with me it was a funny sort of thing that used to groan in the wash-house, which I took to be bears—but as to telling anybody, I'd ha' died first. And so would Rosie, only that night her father wanted her to go a message to the Rectory and she tried everything to get off doing it, and at last he got angry and threatened to take a slipper to her. Not that he meant it, I don't suppose," said Mrs. Ashton, "for he's a kind man as a rule, but he hadn't hardly got over his illness and he was fratchety, like, as sick people will be. So then Rosie made up her mind to tell him what she seen. Only that made him angrier still, and he said she was to go and no more nonsense, and never to speak about ghosts, and such like to him again. If Mary had been there, she'd a-gone, but she was out getting his medicine from Dr. Baines, and the bus don't come back till half-past seven and Will wanted the message sent particular, though I forget now what it were. So Polly told Rosie it couldn't have been Lady Thorpe's spirit, for that was at rest, and if it had been, Lady Thorpe wouldn't do harm to a living soul; and she said Rosie must a-seen Harry Gotobed's lantern. But it couldn't well a-been that, for by what the child said it was one o'clock in the morning past that Rosie see the light. Dear me an' all! I'm sure if I'd a-known then what I know now, I'd a-paid more attention to it."

Superintendent Blundell was not best pleased when this conversation was repeated to him.

"Thoday and his wife had better be careful," he observed.

"They told you the exact truth, you know," said Wimsey.

"Ah!" said Mr. Blundell. "I don't like witnesses to be so damned particular about exact truth. They get away with it as often as not, and then where are you? Not but what I did think of speaking to Rosie, but her mother called her away double quick—and no wonder! Besides, I don't care, somehow, for pumping kids about their parents. I can't help thinking of my own Betty and Ann."

And if that was not quite the exact truth, there was a good deal of truth in it; for Mr. Blundell was a kindly man.

THE FIFTH PART

Tailor Paul Is Called Before with a Single

The canal has been dangerously ignored. Each year of the Republic, our family have reported to the Capital that there were silted channels and weakened dykes in our neighbourhood. My husband and Mai-da's father have just interviewed the present President. They were received politely, but their conclusion is that nothing will be done.

NORA WALN: THE HOUSE OF EXILE

LORD PETER WIMSEY sat in the schoolroom at the Rectory, brooding over a set of underclothing. The schoolroom was, in fact, no longer the schoolroom, and had not been so for nearly twenty years. It had retained its name from the time when the Rector's daughters departed to a real boarding-school. It was now devoted to Parish Business, but a fragrance of long-vanished governesses still clung about it—governesses with straight-fronted corsets and high-necked frocks with bell sleeves, who wore their hair *à la* Pompadour. There was a shelf of battered lesson-books, ranging from *Little Arthur's England* to Hall & Knight's *Algebra,* and a bleached-looking Map of Europe still adorned one wall. Of this room, Lord Peter had been made free, "except," as Mrs. Venables explained, "on Clothing-Club nights, when I am afraid we shall have to turn you out."

The vest and pants were spread upon the table, as though the Clothing Club, in retiring, had left some forlorn flotsam and jetsam behind. They had been washed, but there were still faint discolorations upon them, like the shadow of corruption, and here and there the fabric had rotted away, as the garments of mortality will, when the grave has had its way with them. Wafted in through the open window came the funeral scent of jonquils.

Wimsey whistled gently as he examined the underclothes, which had been mended with scrupulous and economical care. It puzzled him that Cranton, last seen in London in September, should possess a French vest and pants so much worn and so carefully repaired. His shirt and outer garments—now also clean and folded—lay on a chair close at hand. They, too, were well-worn, but they were English. Why should Cranton be wearing second-hand French underclothes?

Wimsey knew that it would be hopeless to try tracing the garments through the makers. Underwear of this mark and quality was sold by the hundred thousand in Paris and throughout the provinces. It lay stacked up outside the great linen-drapers' shops, marked "Occasions," and thrifty housewives bought it there for cash. There was no laundry-mark; the washing had doubtless been done at home by the housewife herself or the *bonne à tout faire*. Holes here and there had been carefully darned; under the armpits, patches of a different material had been neatly let in; the wrists of the vest, frayed with use, had been over-sewn; buttons had been renewed upon the pants. Why not? One must make economies. But they were not garments that anyone would have gone out of his way to purchase, even at a second-hand dealer's. And it would be hard for even the most active man to reduce his clothes to such a state of senility in four months' wear.

Lord Peter thrust his fingers into his hair till the sleek yellow locks stood upright. "Bless his heart!" thought Mrs. Venables, looking in upon him through the window. She had conceived a warm maternal affection for her guest. "Would you like a glass of milk, or a whisky-and-soda, or a cup of beef-tea?" she suggested, hospitably. Wimsey laughed and thanked her, but declined.

"I hope you won't catch anything from those dreadful old clothes," said Mrs. Venables. "I'm sure they can't be healthy."

"Oh, I don't expect to get anything worse than brain-fever," said Wimsey. "I mean"—seeing Mrs. Venables look concerned—"I can't quite make out about these underthings. Perhaps you can suggest something." Mrs. Venables came in, and he laid his problem before her.

"I'm sure I don't know," said Mrs. Venables, gingerly examining the objects before her. "I'm afraid I'm not a Sherlock Holmes.

I should think the man must have had a very good, hard-working wife, but I can't say more."

"Yes, but that doesn't explain why he should get his things in France. Especially as everything else is English. Except, of course, the ten-centime piece, and they're common enough in this country."

Mrs. Venables, who had been gardening and was rather hot, sat down to consider the question.

"The only thing I can think of," she said, "is that he got his English clothes as a disguise—you said he came here in disguise, didn't you? But, of course, as nobody would see his underneaths, he didn't bother to change them."

"But that would mean that he came from France."

"Perhaps he did. Perhaps he was a Frenchman. They often wear beards, don't they?"

"Yes; but the man I met wasn't a Frenchman."

"But you don't know he was the man you met. He may be somebody quite different."

"Well, he *may*," said Wimsey, dubiously.

"He didn't bring any other clothes with him, I suppose?"

"No; not a thing. He was just a tramping out-of-work. Or he said he was. All he brought was an old British trench-coat, which he took with him, and a toothbrush. He left that behind him. Can we wangle a bit of evidence out of that? Can we say that he must have been murdered because, if he had merely wandered away, he would have taken his toothbrush with him? And if he was the corpse, where is his coat? For the corpse had no coat."

"I can't imagine," replied Mrs. Venables, "and that reminds me, do be careful when you go down the bottom of the garden. The rooks are building and they *are* so messy. I should wear a hat if I were you. Or there's always an old umbrella in the summer-house. Did he leave his hat behind too?"

"In a sense he did," said Wimsey. "We've found that, in rather a queer place. But it doesn't help us much."

"Oh!" said Mrs. Venables, "how tiresome it all is. I'm sure you'll wear your brains right out with all these problems. You mustn't overdo yourself. And the butcher says he has some nice calf's liver today, only I don't know if you can eat it. Theodore is very fond of liver-and-bacon, though I always think it's rather rich. And I've been meaning to say, it's very good of that nice manservant of yours to clean the silver and brass so beautifully, but he really shouldn't have troubled. I'm quite used to giving Emily a hand with it. I hope it isn't very dull for him here. I understand he's a great acquisition in the kitchen and extraordinarily good at music-hall imitations. Twice as good as the talkies, Cook says."

"Is he indeed?" said Wimsey. "I had no idea of it. But what I don't know about Bunter would fill a book."

Mrs. Venables bustled away, but her remarks remained in Wimsey's mind. He put aside the vest and pants, filled a pipe and wandered down the garden, pursued by Mrs. Venables with an ancient and rook-proof linen hat, belonging to the Rector. The hat was considerably too small for him, and the fact that he immediately put it on, with expressions of gratitude, may attest the kind heart which, despite the poet, is frequently found in close alliance with coronets; though the shock to Bunter's system was severe when his master suddenly appeared before him, wearing this grotesque headgear, and told him to get the car out and accompany him on a short journey.

"Very good, my lord," said Bunter. "Ahem! there is a fresh breeze, my lord."

"All the better."

"Certainly, my lord! If I may venture to say so, the tweed cap or the grey felt would possibly be better suited to the climatic conditions."

"Eh? Oh! Possibly you are right, Bunter. Pray restore this excellent hat to its proper place, and, if you should see Mrs. Venables, give her my compliments and say that I found its protection invaluable. And Bunter, I rely upon you to keep a check upon your Don Juan fascinations and not strew the threshold of friendship with the wreckage of broken hearts."

"Very good, my lord."

On returning with the grey felt, Bunter found the car already out and his lordship in the driving-seat.

"We are going to try a long shot, Bunter, and we will begin with Leamholt."

"By all means, my lord."

They sped away up the Fenchurch Road, turned left along the Drain, switchbacked over Frog's Bridge without mishap and ran the twelve or thirteen miles to the little town of Leamholt. It was market day, and the Daimler had to push her way decorously through droves of sheep and pigs and through groups of farmers, who stood carelessly in the middle of the street, disdaining to move till the mudguards brushed their thighs. In the centre of one side of the market-place stood the post-office.

"Go in here, Bunter, and ask if there is any letter here for Mr. Stephen Driver, to be left till called for."

Lord Peter waited for some time, as one always waits when transacting business in rural post-offices, while pigs lurched against his bumpers and bullocks blew down his neck. Presently, Bunter returned, having drawn a blank despite a careful search conducted by three young ladies and the postmaster in person.

"Well, never mind," said Wimsey. "Leamholt is the post town, so I thought we ought to give it the first chance. The other possibilities are Holport and Walbeach, on this side of the Drain. Holport is a long way off and rather unlikely. I think we will try Walbeach. There's a direct road from here—at least, as direct as any fen road ever is. . . . I suppose God could have made a sillier animal than a sheep, but it is very certain that He never did. . . . Unless it's cows. Hoop, there, hup! hup! get along with you, Jemima!"

Mile after mile the flat road reeled away behind them. Here a windmill, there a solitary farm-house, there a row of poplars strung along the edge of a reed-grown dyke. Wheat, potatoes, beet, mustard and wheat again, grassland, potatoes, lucerne, wheat, beet and mustard. A long village street with a grey and ancient church tower, a red-brick chapel, and the Vicarage set in a little oasis of elm and horse-chestnut, and then once more dyke and windmill, wheat, mustard and grassland. And as they went, the land flattened more and more, if a flatter flatness were possible, and the windmills became more numerous, and on the right hand the silver streak of the Wale River came back into view, broader now, swollen with the water of the Thirty-foot and of Harper's Cut and St. Simon's Eau, and winding and spreading here and there, with a remembrance of its ancient leisure. Then, ahead of the great circle of the horizon, a little bunch of spires and roofs and a tall tree or so, and beyond them the thin masts of shipping. And so, by bridge and bridge, the travellers came to Walbeach, once a great port, but stranded now far inland with the silting of the marshes and the choking of the Wale outfall; yet with her maritime tradition written unerringly upon her grey stones and timber warehouses, and the long lines of her half-deserted quays.

Here, at the post-office in the little square, Lord Peter waited in the pleasant hush that falls on country towns where all days but market days are endless sabbaths. Bunter was absent for some time, and, when he emerged, did so with a trifle less than his usual sedateness, while his usually colourless face was very slightly flushed about the cheek-bones.

"What luck?" inquired Wimsey, genially.

To his surprise, Bunter replied by a hasty gesture enjoining silence and caution. Wimsey waited till he had taken his place in the car and altered his question to:

"What's up?"

"Better move on quickly, my lord," said Bunter, "because, while the manœuvre has been attended with a measure of success, it is possible that I have robbed His Majesty's Mails by obtaining a postal packet under false pretences."

Long before this handsome period had thundered to its close, the Daimler was running down a quiet street behind the church.

"What *have* you been doing, Bunter?"

"Well, my lord, I inquired, as instructed, for a letter addressed to Mr. Stephen Driver, poste restante, which might have been lying here some time. When the young person inquired how long a time, I replied, according to our previous arrangement, that I had intended to visit Walbeach a few weeks ago, but had been prevented from doing so, and that I understand that an important letter had been forwarded to me at this address under a misapprehension."

"Very good," said Wimsey. "All according to Cocker."

"The young person, my lord, then opened a species of safe or locker, and searched in it, and after the expiration of a considerable period, turned round with a letter in her hand and inquired what name I had said."

"Yes? These girls are very bird-witted. It would have been more surprising if she hadn't asked you to repeat the name."

"Quite so, my lord. I said, as before, that the name was Stephen or Steve Driver, but at the same time I observed from where I was standing that the letter in her hand bore a blue stamp. There was only the counter between us, and, as you are aware, my lord, I am favoured with excellent sight."

"Let us always be thankful for blessings."

"I hope I may say that I always am, my lord. On seeing the blue stamp, I added quickly (calling to mind the circumstances of the case) that the letter had been posted in France."

"Very good, indeed," said Wimsey, nodding approval.

"The young person, my lord, appeared to be puzzled by this remark. She said, in a doubtful tone, that there was a letter from

France which had been lying in the post-office for three weeks, but that it was addressed to another person."

"Oh, hell!" said Wimsey.

"Yes, my lord; that thought passed through my own mind. I said, 'Are you quite sure, miss, that you have not mistaken the handwriting?' I am happy to say, my lord, that the young person —being young, and, no doubt, inexperienced, succumbed to this somewhat elementary strategy. She answered immediately, 'Oh, no—it's as plain as print: M. Paul Taylor.' At that point——"

"Paul Taylor!" cried Wimsey, in sudden excitement. "Why, that was the name——"

"Precisely, my lord. As I was about to say, at that point it was necessary to act promptly. I said at once: 'Paul Taylor? Why, that is the name of my chauffeur.' You will excuse me, my lord, if the remark should appear to carry any disrespectful implication, seeing that you were at that moment in the car and might conceivably be supposed to be the person alluded to, but in the momentary agitation of my spirits, my lord, I was not in a position to think as quickly or as clearly as I should have wished."

"Bunter," said his lordship, "I warn you that I am growing dangerous. Will you say at once, yes or no, did you get that letter?"

"Yes, my lord, I did. I said, of course, that since the letter for my chauffeur was there, I would take it to him, adding some facetious observations to the effect that he must have made a conquest while we were travelling abroad and that he was a great man for the ladies. We were quite merry on the subject, my lord."

"Oh, were you?"

"Yes, my lord. At the same time, I said, it was exceedingly vexatious that my own letter should have gone astray, and I requested the young person to institute another search. She did so, with some reluctance, and in the end I went away, after remarking that the postal system in this country was very undependable and that I should certainly write to *The Times* about it."

"Excellent. Well, it's all very illegal, either way, but we'll get Blundell to put it right for us—I'd have suggested his doing it himself, but it was such a shot at a venture that I didn't think he'd cotton to it, and I hadn't a devil of a lot of faith in it myself. And anyway——" here Wimsey was seized with an uprush of candour to the lips—"anyway, it was *my* jolly old idea and I wanted us to have the fun of it ourselves. Now, don't start apologizing any more. You were perfectly brilliant in two places and I'm as bucked as hell. What's that? It mayn't be the right letter? Rot!

It *is* the right letter. It's damn well got to be the right letter, and we're going to go straight along to the Cat and Fiddle, where the port is remarkable and the claret not to be despised, to celebrate our deed of darkness and derring-do."

Accordingly, within a very short time, Wimsey and his follower found themselves established in a dark old upper room, facing away from the square and looking out upon the squat, square church tower, with the rooks wheeling over it and the seagulls swooping and dipping among the gravestones. Wimsey ordered roast lamb and a bottle of the far-from-despicable claret and was soon in conversation with the waiter, who agreed with him that things were very quiet.

"But not so quiet as they used to be, sir. The men working on the Wash Cut make a difference to the town. Oh, yes, sir—the Cut's nearly finished now, and they say it will be opened in June. It will be a good thing, so they say, and improve the draining very much. It's hoped as it will scour the river out ten feet or more and take the tide up again to the head of the Thirty-foot Drain, like it was in the old days, by what they tell us. Of course, I don't know about that, sir, for it seems that was in Oliver Cromwell's time, and I've only been here twenty year, but that's what the Chief Engineer says. They've brought the Cut to within a mile of the town now, sir, and there's to be a great opening in June, with a gala and a cricket match and sports for the young people, sir. And they say as they're asking the Duke of Denver to come down and open the Cut, but we haven't heard yet if he'll come."

"He'll come all right," said Wimsey. "Dash it, he shall come. He does no work and it will do him good."

"Indeed, sir?" said the waiter, a little dubiously, not knowing the cause of this certainty, but unwilling to offend. "Yes, sir, it would be much appreciated in the town if he was to come. Will you take another potato, sir?"

"Yes, please," said Wimsey. "I'll make a point of jogging old Denver up to do his duty. We'll all come. Great fun. Denver shall present gold cups to all the winners and I will present silver rabbits to all the losers, and with luck somebody will fall into the river."

"That," said the waiter, seriously, "will be very gratifying."

Not till the port (Tuke Holdsworth '08) was set upon the table did Wimsey draw the letter from his pocket and gloat upon it. It was addressed in a foreign hand to "M. Paul Taylor, Poste Restante, Walbeach, Lincolnshire, Angleterre."

"My family," observed Lord Peter, "have frequently accused me of being unrestrained and wanting in self-control. They little know me. Instead of opening this letter at once, I reserve it for Superintendent Blundell. Instead of rushing off at once to Superintendent Blundell, I remain quietly at Walbeach and eat roast mutton. It is true that the good Blundell is not at Leamholt today, so that nothing would be gained if I did rush back, but still —it just shows you. The envelope bears a post-mark which is only half-decipherable, but which I make out to be something ending in y in the department of either Marne or Seine-et-Marne—a district endeared to many by the recollection of mud, blood, shell-holes and trench-feet. The envelope is of slightly worse quality than even the majority of French envelopes, and the writing suggests that it was carried out with what may be called a post-office pen and ink to match, by a hand unaccustomed to the exercise. The ink and pen mean little, for I have never yet encountered in any part of France a pen and ink with which any normal person could write comfortably. But the handwriting is suggestive, because, owing to the system of State education in that country, though all the French write vilely, it is rare to find one who writes very much more vilely than the rest. The date is obscure, but, since we know the time of arrival, we may guess the time of dispatch. Can we deduce anything further from the envelope?"

"If I may be allowed to say so, my lord, it is possibly a little remarkable that the name and address of the sender does not appear on the back."

"That is well observed. Yes, Bunter, you may have full marks for that. The French, as you have no doubt often noticed, seldom head their letters with an address as we do in England, though they occasionally write at the foot some such useless indication as 'Paris' or 'Lyon,' without adding the number of the house and the name of the street. They do, however, frequently place these necessary indications on the flap of the envelope, in the hope that they may be thrown into the fire and irrecoverably lost before the letter is answered or even read."

"It has sometimes occurred to me, my lord, to be surprised at that habit."

"Not at all, Bunter. It is quite logical. To begin with, it is a fixed idea with the French that the majority of letters tend to be lost in the post. They put no faith in Government departments, and I think they are perfectly right. They hope, however, that, if the post-office fails to deliver the letter to the addressee it may, in time, return it to the sender. It seems a forlorn hope, but they are again perfectly right. One must explore every stone and leave no avenue unturned. The Englishman, in his bluff, hearty way, is content that under such circumstances the post-office should violate his seals, peruse his correspondence, extract his signature and address from the surrounding verbiage, supply a fresh envelope and return the whole to him under the blushing pseudonym of 'Hubbykins' or 'Dogsbody' for the entertainment of his local postman. But the Frenchman, being decorous, not to say secretive, by nature, thinks it better to preserve his privacy by providing, on the exterior of the missive, all the necessary details for the proper functioning of this transaction. I do not say he is wrong, though I do think it would be better if he wrote the address in both places. But the fact that this particular letter provides no address for return does perhaps suggest that the sender was not precisely out for publicity. And the devil of it is, Bunter, that ten to one there will be no address on the inside, either. No matter. This is very excellent port. Be good enough to finish the bottle, Bunter, because it would be a pity to waste it and if I have any more I shall be too sleepy to drive."

They took the direct road back from Walbeach to Fenchurch, following the bank of the river.

"If this country had been drained intelligently and all of a piece," remarked Wimsey, "by running all the canals into the rivers instead of the rivers into the canals, so as to get a good scour of water, Walbeach might still be a port and the landscape would look rather less like a crazy quilt. But what with seven hundred years of greed and graft and laziness, and perpetual quarrelling between one parish and the next, and the mistaken impression that what suits Holland must suit the fens, the thing's a mess. It answers the purpose, but it might have been a lot better. Here's the place where we met Cranton—if it was Cranton. By the way, I wonder if that fellow at the Sluice saw anything of him. Let's stop and find out. I love dawdling round locks."

He twisted the car across the bridge and brought it to a standstill close beside the sluice-keeper's cottage. The man came out to see what was wanted and was lured, without difficulty, into a desultory conversation, beginning with the weather and the crops and going on to the Wash Cut, the tides and the river. Before very long, Wimsey was standing on the narrow wooden foot-bridge that ran across the Sluice, gazing down thoughtfully into the green water.

The tide was on the ebb and the gates partly open, so that a slow trickle ran through them as the Wale water discharged itself sluggishly towards the sea.

"Very picturesque and pretty," said Wimsey. "Do you ever get artists and people along here to paint it?"

The sluice-keeper didn't know as he did.

"Some of those piers would be none the worse for a bit of stone and mortar," went on Wimsey; "and the gates look pretty ancient."

"Ah!" said the sluice-keeper. "I believe you." He spat into the river. "This here sluice has been needing repairs—oh! a matter of twenty year, now. And more."

"Then why don't they do it?"

"Ah!" said the sluice-keeper.

He remained lost in melancholy thought for some minutes, and Wimsey did not interrupt him. Then he spoke, weightily, and with long years of endurance in his voice.

"Nobody knows whose job this here sluice is, seemin'ly. The Fen Drainage Board, now—they say as it did oughter be done by the Wale Conservancy Board. And *they* say the Fen Drainage Board did oughter see to it. And now they've agreed to refer it, like, to the East Level Waterways Commission. But they ain't made their report yet." He spat again and was silent.

"But," said Wimsey, "suppose you got a lot of water up this way, would the gates stand it?"

"Well, they might and they mightn't," replied the sluice-keeper. "But we don't get much water up here these days. I have heard tell as it was different in Oliver Cromwell's time, but we don't get a great lot now."

Wimsey was well used to the continual intrusion of the Lord Protector upon the affairs of the Fen, but he felt it to be a little unjustified in the present case.

"It was the Dutchmen built this sluice, wasn't it?" he said.

"Ah!" agreed the sluice-keeper. "Yes, that's who built this sluice. To keep the water out. In Oliver Cromwell's time this country was all drownded every winter, so they say. So they built this sluice. But we don't get much water up nowadays."

"You will, though, when they've finished the New Wash Cut."

"Ah! so they say. But I don't know. Some says it won't be no different. And some says as it'll drown the land round about Walbeach. All I know, they've spent a sight of money, and where's it coming from? To my mind, things was all very well as they was."

"Who's responsible for the Wash Cut? The Fen Drainage Board?"

"No, that's the Wale Conservancy, that is."

"But it must have occurred to them that it might make a difference to this sluice. Why couldn't they do it all at the same time?"

The fenman gazed at Wimsey with a slow pity for his bird-witted feebleness of mind.

"Ain't I telling yew? They don't rightly know if it did oughter be paid for by the Fen Drainage or the Wale Conservancy. Why," and a note of pride crept into his tone, "they've had five law actions about this here sluice. Ah! they took one on 'em up to Parliament, they did. Cost a heap of money, so they say."

"Well, it seems ridiculous," said Wimsey. "And with all this unemployment about, too. Do you get many of the unemployed tramping round this way?"

"Times we do, times we don't."

"I remember meeting a chap along the Bank last time I was down here—on New Year's Day. I thought he looked a bit of a tough nut."

"Oh, him? Yes. He got took on at Ezra Wilderspin's place, but he soon had enough o' that. Didn't want to do no work. Half on 'em don't. He came along askin' for a cup o' tea, but I told him to get out. It wasn't tea he was lookin' for. Not him. I know his sort."

"I suppose he'd come from Walbeach."

"I suppose he had. He said so, anyhow. Said he'd been trying to get work on the Wash Cut."

"Oh? He told me he was a motor mechanic."

"Ah!" The sluice-keeper spat once more into the tumbling water. "They'd say anything."

"He looked to me as though he'd worked a good bit with his hands. Why shouldn't there be work for men on the Cut? That's what I was saying."

"Yes, sir, it's easy to say them things. But with plenty o' skilled men out of a job, they don't need to go taking on the like of him. That's where it is, you see."

"Well," said Wimsey, "I still think that the Drainage Board and the Conservancy Board and the Commission between them ought to be able to absorb some of these men and give you a fresh set of gates. However, it's not my business, and I'll have to be pushing along."

"Ah!" said the sluice-keeper. "New gates? Ah!"

He remained hanging on the rail and spitting thoughtfully into the water till Wimsey and Bunter had regained the car. Then he came hobbling after them.

"What I says is," he observed, leaning so earnestly over the door of the Daimler that Wimsey hurriedly drew back his feet, thinking that the usual expectoration was about to follow, "what I says is, Why don't they refer it to Geneva? See? Why don't they refer it to Geneva? Then we might get it, same time as they gets disarmament, see?"

"Ha, ha!" said Wimsey, rightly supposing this to be irony. "Very good! I must tell my friends about that. Good work, what? Why don't they refer it to Geneva? Ha, ha!"

"That's right," said the sluice-keeper, anxious that the point of the jest should not be lost. "Why don't they refer it to Geneva? See?"

"Splendid!" said Wimsey. "I won't forget that. Ha, ha, ha!"

He gently released the clutch. As they moved away, he glanced back and saw the sluice-keeper convulsed by the remembrance of his own wit.

. . . .

Lord Peter's misgivings about the letter were duly confirmed. He honourably submitted it, unopened, to Superintendent Blundell, as soon as the latter returned from attendance at the Quarter Sessions where he had been engaged all day. The Superintendent was alarmed by Wimsey's unorthodox raid on the post-office, but pleased by his subsequent discretion, and readily allowed him full credit for zeal and intelligence. Together they opened the envelope. The letter, which bore no address, was written on thin paper of the same poor quality as the envelope, and began:

"*Mon cher mari*——"

"Hey!" said Mr. Blundell. "What's that mean? I'm not much of a French scholar, but doesn't *mari* mean 'husband'?"

"Yes. 'My dear husband,' it begins."

"I never knew that Cranton—dash it!" exclaimed Mr. Blundell. "Where does Cranton come into this? I never heard of his having any wife at all, let alone a French one."

"We don't know that Cranton comes into it at all. He came to

St. Paul and asked for a Mr. Paul Taylor. This, presumably, is addressed to the Paul Taylor he asked for."

"But they said Paul Taylor was a bell."

"Tailor Paul is a bell, but Paul Taylor may be a person."

"Who is he, then?"

"God knows. Somebody with a wife in France."

"And the other chap, Batty Something—is he a person?"

"No, he's a bell. But he may be a person, too."

"They can't both be persons," said Mr. Blundell, "it's not reasonable. And where is this Paul Taylor, anyhow?"

"Perhaps he was the corpse."

"Then where's Cranton? They can't," added the Superintendent, "both be the corpse. That's not reasonable, either."

"Possibly Cranton gave one name to Wilderspin and another to his correspondent."

"Then what did he mean by asking for Paul Taylor at Fenchurch St. Paul?"

"Perhaps that was the bell, after all."

"See here," said Mr. Blundell, "it doesn't seem reasonable to me. This Paul Taylor or Tailor Paul can't be both a bell and a person. At least, not both at once. It sounds kind of, well, kind of batty to me."

"Why bring Batty into it? Batty is a bell. Tailor Paul is a bell. Paul Taylor is a person, because he gets letters. You can't send letters to a bell. If you did you'd be batty. Oh, bother!"

"Well, I don't understand it," said Mr. Blundell. "Stephen Driver, he's a person, too. You don't say he's a bell, do you? What I want to know is, which of 'em all is Cranton. If he's been and fixed himself up with a wife in France between this and last September—I mean, between this and January—no, I mean between September and January—I mean—here, dash it all, my lord, let's read the blooming letter. You might read it out in English, would you? My French is a bit off, these days."

> "My dear husband [Wimsey translated],—You told me not to write to you, without great urgency, but three months are past and I have no news of you. I am very anxious, asking myself if you have not been taken by the military authorities. You have assured me that they could not now have you shot, the War being over so long ago, but it is known that the English are very strict. Write, I beseech you, a little word to say that you are safe. It begins to be very difficult to do the work of the farm alone, and we have had great trouble with the Spring sowing. Also the red cow is dead. I am

obliged to carry the fowls to market myself, because Jean is too exigent, and prices are very low. Little Pierre helps me as much as he can, but he is only nine. Little Marie has had the whooping-cough and the Baby also. I beg your pardon if I am indiscreet to write to you, but I am very much troubled. Pierre and Marie send kisses to their papa.

"Your loving wife,

"SUZANNE."

Superintendent Blundell listened aghast; then snatched the paper from Wimsey, as though he mistrusted his translation and thought to tear out some better meaning from the words by mere force of staring at them.

"Little Pierre—nine years old—kisses to their papa—and the red cow's dead—t'cha!" He did a little arithmetic on his fingers. "Nine years ago, Cranton was in gaol."

"Step-father, perhaps?" suggested Wimsey.

Mr. Blundell paid no heed. "Spring sowing—since when has Cranton turned farmer? And what's all that about military authorities? And the War. Cranton never was in the War. There's something here I can't make head or tail of. See here, my lord—this can't be Cranton. It's silly, that's what it is. It can't be Cranton."

"It begins to look as if it wasn't," said Wimsey. "But I still think it was Cranton I met on New Year's Day."

"I'd better get on the telephone to London," said Mr. Blundell. "And then I'll have to be seeing the Chief Constable about this. Whatever it is, it's got to be followed up. Driver's disappeared and we've found a body that looks like his and we've got to do something about it. But France—well, there! How we're to find this Suzanne I don't know, and it'll cost a mint of money."

THE SIXTH PART

Monsieur Rozier Hunts the Treble Down

The remaining bell . . . does nothing but plain hunting, and is therefore said to be "in the hunt with the Treble."

TROYTE ON CHANGE-RINGING

THERE ARE harder jobs in detective work than searching a couple of French departments for a village ending in "y," containing a farmer's wife whose first name is Suzanne, whose children are Pierre, aged nine, Marie and a baby of unknown age and sex, and whose husband is an Englishman. All the villages in the Marne district end, indeed, in "y," and Suzanne, Pierre and Marie are all common names enough, but a foreign husband is rarer. A husband named Paul Taylor would, of course, be easily traced, but both Superintendent Blundell and Lord Peter were pretty sure that "Paul Taylor" would prove to be an alias.

It was about the middle of May when a report came in from the French police which looked more hopeful than anything previously received. It came through the Sûreté, and originated with M. le commissaire Rozier of Château-Thierry in the department of Marne.

It was so exceedingly promising that even the Chief Constable, who was a worried gentleman with an itch for economy, agreed that it ought to be investigated on the spot.

"But I don't know whom to send," he grumbled. "Dashed expensive business, anyhow. And then there's the language. Do you speak French, Blundell?"

The Superintendent grinned sheepishly. "Well, sir, not to say speak it. I could ask for a spot of grub in an *estaminet*, and maybe swear at the garsong a bit. But examining witnesses—that's a different question."

"I can't go myself," said the Chief Constable, sharply and hastily, as though anticipating a suggestion that nobody had had the courage to make. "Out of the question." He tapped his fingers on his study table and stared vaguely over the Superintendent's head at the rooks wheeling high over the elms at the end of the garden. "You've done your best, Blundell, but I think we had better hand the thing over, lock, stock and barrel, to Scotland Yard. Perhaps we ought to have done so earlier."

Mr. Blundell looked chagrined. Lord Peter Wimsey, who had come with him, ostensibly in case help should be needed to translate the commissaire's letter, but actually because he was determined not to be left out of anything, coughed gently.

"If you would entrust the inquiry to me, sir," he murmured, "I could pop over in two ticks—at my own expense, of course," he added, insinuatingly.

"I'm afraid it would be rather irregular," said the Chief Constable, with the air of one who only needs to be persuaded.

"I'm more reliable than I look, really I am," said his lordship. "And my French is my one strong point. Couldn't you swear me in as a special constable, or something? with a natty little armlet and a truncheon? Or isn't interrogation part of a special constable's duties?"

"It is not," said the Chief Constable. "Still," he went on, "still—I suppose I might stretch a point. And I suppose"—he looked hard at Wimsey—"I suppose you'll go in any case."

"Nothing to prevent me from making a private tour of the battle-fields," said Wimsey, "and of course, if I met one of my old Scotland Yard pals knocking round there, I might join up with him. But I really think that, in these hard times, we ought to consider the public purse, don't you, sir?"

The Chief Constable was thoughtful. He had no real wish to call in Scotland Yard. He had an idea that a Yard man might make himself an officious nuisance. He gave way. Within two days, Wimsey was being cordially received by M. le commissaire Rozier. A gentleman who has "*des relations intimes*" with the Paris Sûreté, and who speaks perfect French, is likely to be well received by country *commissaires de police*. M. Rozier produced a bottle of very excellent wine, entreated his visitor to make himself at home, and embarked upon his story.

"It does not in any way astonish me, milord, to receive an

inquiry concerning the husband of Suzanne Legros. It is evident that there is there a formidable mystery. For ten years I have said to myself, 'Aristide Rozier, the day will come when your premonitions concerning the so-called Jean Legros will be justified.' I perceive that the day is at hand, and I congratulate myself upon my foresight."

"Evidently," said Wimsey, "M. le commissaire possesses a penetrating intelligence."

"To lay the matter clearly before you, I am obliged to go back to the summer of 1918. Milord served in the British Army? Ah! then milord will remember the retreat over the Marne in July. *Quelle histoire sanglante!* On that occasion the retreating armies were swept back across the Marne pell-mell and passed in disorder through the little village of C——y, situated upon the left bank of the river. The village itself, you understand, milord, escaped any violent bombardment, for it was behind the front-line trenches. In that village lived the aged Pierre Legros and his granddaughter Suzanne. The old man was eighty years of age and refused to leave his home. His grandchild, then aged twenty-seven, was a vigorous and industrious girl, who, single-handed, kept the farm in a sort of order throughout the years of conflict. Her father, her brother, her affianced husband had all been killed.

"About ten days after the retreat, it was reported that Suzanne Legros and her grandfather had a visitor at the farm. The neighbours had begun to talk, you understand, and the curé, the reverend Abbé Latouche, now in paradise, thought it his duty to inform the authorities here. I myself, you comprehend, was not here at that time; I was in the Army; but my predecessor, M. Dubois, took steps to investigate the matter. He found that there was a sick and wounded man being kept at the farm. He had suffered a severe blow upon the head and various other injuries. Suzanne Legros, and her grandfather, being interrogated, told a singular story.

"She said that, on the second night after the retreat had passed through the village, she went to a distant outhouse and there found this man lying sick and burning with fever, stripped to his underclothing, with his head roughly bandaged. He was dirty and blood-stained and his clothes were bedaubed with mud and weeds as though he had been in the river. She contrived to carry him home with the old man's help, washed his wounds and nursed him as best she might. The farm is a couple of kilometres distant from the village itself, and she had no one whom she could send for assistance. At first, she said, the man had raved in French about the incidents of the battle, but afterwards he had fallen into a heavy stupor, from which she could not rouse him. When seen by the curé and by the commissaire he lay inert, breathing heavily and unconscious.

"She showed the clothing in which she had found him—a vest, under-pants, socks, and shirt of regulation army pattern, very much stained and torn. No uniform; no boots; no identity disc; no papers. It seemed evident that he had been in the retreat and had been obliged to swim across the river in making his way back from the front line—this would account for the abandoning of his boots, uniform and kit. He seemed to be a man of some thirty-five or forty years of age, and when first seen by the authorities, he had a dark beard of about a week's growth."

"Then he had been clean-shaven?"

"It would seem so, milord. A doctor from the town was found to go out and see him, but he could only say that it appeared to be a severe case of injury to the brain from the wound in the head. He advised ameliorative measures. He was only a young student of small experience, incapacitated from the Army by reason of frail health. He has since died.

"It was at first supposed that they had only to wait till the man came to himself to learn who he was. But when, after three more weeks of coma, he slowly regained consciousness, it was found that his memory, and, for some time, his speech also, was gone. Gradually, the speech was regained, though for some time he could express himself only in a thick and mumbling manner, with many hesitations. It seemed that there were injuries to the locutory centres in the brain. When he was well enough to understand and make himself understood, he was, naturally, interrogated. His replies were simply that his mind was a blank. He remembered nothing of his past—but nothing. He did not know his name, or his place of origin; he had no recollection of the War. For him, his life began in the farm-house at C——y."

M. Rozier paused impressively, while Wimsey registered amazement.

"Well, milord, you will understand that it was necessary to report the case at once to the Army authorities. He was seen by a number of officers, none of whom could recognize him, and his portrait and measurements were circulated without result. It was thought at first that he might be an Englishman—or even a

Boche—and that, you understand, was not agreeable. It was stated, however, that when Suzanne first found him, he had deliriously muttered in French, and the clothes found upon him were undoubtedly French also. Nevertheless, his description was issued to the British Army, again without result, and, when the Armistice was signed, inquiries were extended to Germany. But they knew nothing of him there. Naturally, these inquiries took some time, for the Germans had a revolution, as you know, and everything was much disordered. In the meanwhile, the man had to live somewhere. He was taken to hospital—to several hospitals —and examined by psychologists, but they could make nothing of him. They tried—you understand, milord—to set traps for him. They suddenly shouted words of command at him in English, French and German, thinking that he might display an automatic reaction. But it was to no purpose. He seemed to have forgotten the War."

"Lucky devil!" said Wimsey, with feeling.

"*Je suis de votre avis.* Nevertheless, a reaction of some kind would have been satisfying. Time passed, and he became no better. They sent him back to us. Now you know, milord, that it is impossible to repatriate a man who has no nationality. No country will receive him. Nobody wanted this unfortunate man except Suzanne Legros and her *bon-papa.* They needed a man to work on the farm and this fellow, though he had lost his memory, had recovered his physical strength and was well suited for manual labour. Moreover, the girl had taken a fancy to him. You know how it is with women. When they have nursed a man, he is to them in a manner their child. Old Pierre Legros asked leave to adopt this man as his son. There were difficulties—*que voulez-vous?* But, *enfin,* since something had to be done with the man, and he was quiet and well-behaved and gave no trouble, the consent was obtained. He was adopted under the name of Jean Legros and papers of identity were made out for him. The neighbours began to be accustomed to him. There was a man—a fellow who had thought of marrying Suzanne—who was his enemy and called him *sale Boche*—but Jean knocked him down one evening in the *estaminet* and after that there was no more heard of the word *Boche.* Then, after a few years, it became known that Suzanne had the wish to marry him. The old curé opposed the match—he said it was not known but that the man was married already. But the old curé died. The new one knew little of the circumstances. Besides, Suzanne had already thrown her bonnet over the windmill. Human nature, milord, is human nature. The civil authorities washed their hands of the matter; it was better to regularize the position. So Suzanne Legros wedded this Jean, and their eldest son is now nine years of age. Since that time there has been no trouble—only Jean still remembers nothing of his origin."

"You said in your letter," said Wimsey, "that Jean had now disappeared."

"Since five months, milord. It is said that he is in Belgium, buying pigs, cattle, or I know not what. But he has not written, and his wife is concerned about him. You think you have some information about him?"

"Well," said Wimsey, "we have a corpse. And we have a name. But if this Jean Legros has conducted himself in the manner you describe, then the name is not his, though the corpse may be. For the man whose name we have was in prison in 1918 and for some years afterwards."

"Ah! then you have no further interest in Jean Legros?"

"On the contrary. An interest of the most profound. We still have the corpse."

"*A la bonne heure*," said M. Rozier cheerfully. "A corpse is always something. Have you any photograph? any measurements? any marks of identification?"

"The photograph will assuredly be of little use, since the corpse when found was four months old and the face had been much battered. Moreover, his hands had been removed at the wrists. But we have measurements and two medical reports. From the latest of these, recently received from a London expert, it appears that the scalp bears the mark of an old scar, in addition to those recently inflicted."

"Aha! that is perhaps some confirmation. He was, then, killed by being beaten on the head, your unknown?"

"No," said Wimsey. "All the head-injuries were inflicted after death. The expert opinion confirms that of the police-surgeon on this point."

"He died, then, of what?"

"There is the mystery. There is no sign of fatal wound, or of poison, or of strangling, nor yet of disease. The heart was sound; the intestines show that he had not died of starvation—indeed, he was well-nourished, and had eaten a few hours before his death."

"*Tiens!* an apoplexy, then?"

"It is possible. The brain, you understand, was in a somewhat putrefied condition. It is difficult to say with certainty, though there are certain signs that there had been an effusion of blood into the cortex. But you comprehend that, if a thundering apoplexy killed this man, it was not so obliging as to bury him also."

"Perfectly. You are quite right. Forward, then, to the farm of Jean Legros."

The farm was a small one, and did not seem to be in too flourishing a state. Broken fences, dilapidated outhouses and ill-weeded fields spoke of straitened means and a lack of the necessary labour. The mistress of the house received them. She was a sturdy, well-muscled woman of some forty years of age, and carried in her arms a nine-months-old child. At the sight of the commissaire and his attendant gendarme a look of alarm came unmistakably into her eyes. Another moment, and it had given place to that expression of mulish obstinacy which no one can better assume at will than the French peasant.

"M. le commissaire Rozier?"

"Himself, madame. This gentleman is milord Vainsé, who has voyaged from England to make certain inquiries. It is permitted to enter?"

It was permitted, but at the word "England" the look of alarm had come again; and it was not lost on either of the men.

"Your husband, Mme. Legros," said the commissaire, coming brusquely to the point, "he is absent from home. Since how long?"

"Since December, M. le commissaire."

"Where is he?"

"In Belgium."

"Where, in Belgium?"

"Monsieur, in Dixmude, as I suppose."

"You suppose? You do not know? You have had no letter from him?"

"No, monsieur."

"That is strange. What took him to Dixmude?"

"Monsieur, he had taken the notion that his family lived perhaps at Dixmude. You know, without doubt, that he had lost his memory. *Eh, bien!* in December, one day, he said to me, 'Suzanne, put a record on the gramophone.' I put on the record of a great *diseuse*, reciting *Le Carillon*, poem of Verhaeren, to music. *C'est un morceau très impressionnant*. At that moment, filled with emotion where the carillons are named turn by turn, my husband cried out: 'Dixmude! there is then a town of Dixmude in Belgium?' 'But certainly,' I replied. He said, 'But that name says something to me! I am convinced, Suzanne, that I have a beloved mother residing in Dixmude. I shall not rest till I have gone to Belgium to make inquiries about this dear mother.' M. le commissaire, he would listen to nothing. He went away, taking with him our small savings, and since that time I have heard nothing from him."

"*Histoire très touchante*," said the commissaire, drily. "You have my sympathy, madame. But I cannot understand that your husband should be a Belgian. There were no Belgian troops engaged at the third Battle of the Marne."

"Nevertheless, monsieur, his father may have married a Belgian. He may have Belgian relations."

"*C'est vrai*. He left you no address?"

"None, monsieur. He said he would write on his arrival."

"Ah! And he departed how? By the train?"

"Oh, yes, monsieur."

"And you have made no inquiries? From the mayor of Dixmude, for example?"

"Monsieur, you understand that I was sufficiently embarrassed. I did not know where to begin with such an inquiry."

"Nor of us, the police, who exist for that? You did not address yourself to us?"

"M. le commissaire, I did not know—I could not imagine—I told myself every day, 'Tomorrow he will write,' and I waited, *et enfin*——"

"*Et enfin*—it did not occur to you to inform yourself. *C'est bien remarquable*. What gave you the idea that your husband was in England?"

"In England, monsieur?"

"In England, madame. You wrote to him under the name of Paul Taylor, did you not? At the town of Valbesch in the county of Laincolonne?" The commissaire excelled himself in the rendering of these barbarian place-names. "At Valbesch in Laincolonne you address yourself to him in the name of Paul Taylorrrr—*voyons, madame, voyons*, and you tell me now that you suppose him to be all the time in Belgium. You will not deny your own handwriting, I suppose? Or the names of your two children? Or the death of the red cow? You do not imagine that you can resurrect the cow?"

"Monsieur——"

"Come, madame. During all these years you have been lying to the police, have you not? You knew very well that your husband was not a Belgian but an Englishman? That his name was actually Paul Taylor? That he had not lost his memory at all? Ah! you think that you can trifle with the police in that way? I assure you, madame, that you will find it a serious matter. You have falsified papers, that is a crime!"

"Monsieur, monsieur——"

"That is your letter?"

"Monsieur, since you have found it, I cannot deny it. But——"

"Good, you admit the letter. Now, what is this about falling into the hands of the military authorities?"

"I do not know, monsieur. My husband—monsieur, I implore you to tell me, where is my husband?"

The commissaire Rozier paused, and glanced at Wimsey, who said:

"Madame, we are greatly afraid that your husband is dead."

"*Ah, mon dieu! je le savais bien.* If he had been alive, he would have written to me."

"If you will help us by telling us the truth about your husband, we may be able to identify him."

The woman stood looking from one to the other. At last she turned to Wimsey.

"You, milord, you are not laying a trap for me? You are sure that my husband is dead?"

"Come, come," said the commissaire, "that makes no difference. You must tell the truth, or it will be the worst for you."

Wimsey took out of the attaché case which he had brought with him the underclothing which had been found upon the corpse.

"Madame," he said, "we do not know whether the man who wore these is your husband, but on my honour, the man who wore these is dead and they were taken from his body."

Suzanne Legros turned the garments over, her work-hardened fingers slowly tracing each patch and darn. Then, as though the sight of them had broken down something in her, she dropped into a chair and laid her head down on the mended vest and burst into loud weeping.

"You recognize the garments?" asked the commissaire presently, in a milder tone.

"Yes, they are his, I mended these garments myself. I understand that he is dead."

"In that case," said Wimsey, "you can do him no harm by speaking."

When Suzanne Legros had recovered herself a little, she made her statement, the commissaire calling in his attendant gendarme to take a shorthand note of it.

"It is true that my husband was not a Frenchman or a Belgian. He was an Englishman. But it is true also that he was wounded in the retreat of 1918. He came to the farm one night. He had lost much blood and was exhausted. Also his nerves were shattered, but it is not true that he had lost his memory. He implored me to help him and to hide him, because he did not want to fight any more. I nursed him till he was well and then we arranged what we should say."

"It was shameful, madame, to harbour a deserter."

"I acknowledge it, monsieur, but consider my position. My father was dead, my two brothers killed, and I had no one to help me with the farm. Jean-Marie Picard, that was to have married me, was dead also. There were so few men left in France, and the War had gone on so long. And also, monsieur, I grew to love Jean. And his nerves were greatly deranged. He could not face any more fighting."

"He should have reported to his unit and applied for sick leave," said Wimsey.

"But then," said Suzanne, simply, "they would have sent him back to England and separated us. And besides, the English are very strict. They might have thought him a coward and shot him."

"It appears, at least, that he made you think so," said Monsieur Rozier.

"Yes, monsieur. I thought so and he thought so too. So we arranged that he should pretend to have lost his memory, and since his French accent was not good, we decided to make out that his speech was affected by his injury. And I burnt his uniform and papers in the copper."

"Who invented the story—you or he?"

"He did, monsieur. He was very clever. He thought of everything."

"And the name also?"

"The name also."

"And what was his real name?"

She hesitated. "His papers were burnt, and he never told me anything about himself."

"You do not know his name. Was it then not Taylor?"

"No, monsieur. He adopted that name when he went back to England."

"Ah! and what did he go to England for?"

"Monsieur, we were very poor, and Jean said that he had property in England which could be disposed of for a good sum, if only he could get hold of it without making himself known. For, you see, if he were to reveal himself he would be shot as a deserter."

"But there was a general amnesty for deserters after the War."

"Not in England, monsieur."

"He told you that?" said Wimsey.

"Yes, milord. So it was important that nobody should know him when he went to fetch the property. Also there were difficulties which he did not explain to me, about selling the goods—I do not know what they were—and for that he had to have the help of a friend. So he wrote to this friend and presently he received a reply."

"Have you that letter?"

"No, monsieur. He burnt it without showing it to me. This friend asked him for something—I did not quite understand that, but it was some sort of guarantee, I think. Jean shut himself up in his room for several hours the next day to compose his answer to the letter, but he did not show that to me, either. Then the friend wrote back and said he could help him, but it would not do for Jean's name to appear—neither his own name nor the name of Legros, you understand. So he chose the name of Paul Taylor, and he laughed very much when the idea came to him to call himself so. Then the friend sent him papers made out in the name of Paul Taylor, British subject. I saw those. There was a passport with a photograph; it was not very much like my husband, but he said they would not pay great attention to it. The beard was like his."

"Had your husband a beard when you first knew him?"

"No, he was clean-shaven, like all the English. But of course, he grew his beard when he was ill. It altered him very much, because he had a small chin, and with the beard it looked bigger. Jean took with him no luggage; he said he would buy clothes in England, because then he would again look like an Englishman."

"And you know nothing of the nature of this property in England?"

"Nothing whatever, monsieur."

"Was it land, securities, valuables?"

"I know nothing about it, monsieur. I asked Jean often, but he would never tell me."

"And you expect us to believe that you do not know your husband's real name?"

Again the hesitation. Then: "No, monsieur, I do not know. It is true that I saw it upon his papers, but I burnt those and I do not now remember it. But I think it began with a C, and I should know it if I saw it again."

"Was it Cranton?" asked Wimsey.

"No, I do not think it was that, but I cannot say what it was. As soon as he was able to speak at all, he told me to give him his papers, and I asked him then what his name was, because I could not pronounce it—it was English and difficult—and he said that he would not tell me his name then, but I could call him what I liked. So I called him Jean, which was the name of my *fiancé*, who was killed."

"I see," said Wimsey. He hunted through his pocketbook and laid the official photograph of Cranton before her. "Is that your husband as you first knew him?"

"No, milord. That is not my husband. It is not in the least like him." Her face darkened. "You have deceived me. He is not dead and I have betrayed him."

"He is dead," said Wimsey. "It is this man who is alive."

. . . . . .

"And now," said Wimsey, "we are no nearer than before to a solution."

"*Attendez*, milord. She has not yet told all she knows. She does not trust us, and she is concealing the name. Only wait, and we shall find means to make her speak. She still thinks that her husband may be alive. But we shall convince her. We shall have this man traced. It is some months old, the trail, but it will not be too difficult. That he started from here by train to go to Belgium I already know, by my inquiries. When he sailed for England, it was doubtless from Ostend—unless, *voyons*, milord, what resources could this man command?"

"How can I tell? But we believe that this mysterious property had to do with an emerald necklace of many thousands of pounds value."

"*Ah, voilà!* It would be worth while to spend money, then. But this man, you say he is not the man you thought. If that other man was the thief, how does this one come into it?"

"There is the difficulty. But look! There were two men concerned in the theft: one, a London *cambrioleur*, the other, a domestic servant. We do not know which of them had the jewels; it is a long story. But you heard that this Jean Legros wrote to a friend in England, and that friend may have been Cranton, the burglar. Now Legros cannot have been the servant who stole the jewels in the first place, for that man is dead. But before dying, the thief may have communicated to Legros the secret of where the emeralds are hidden, and also the name of Cranton. Legros then writes to Cranton and proposes a partnership to find the jewels. Cranton does not believe, and asks for proof that Legros really knows something. Legros sends a letter which satisfies Cranton, and Cranton in turn procures the necessary papers for Legros. Then Legros goes to England and meets Cranton. Together they go and discover the jewels. Then Cranton kills his confederate, so as to have all for himself. How is that, monsieur? For Cranton also has disappeared."

"It is very possible, milord. In that case, both the jewels and the murderer are in England—or wherever this Cranton may be. You think, then, that the other dead man, the servant, communicated the hiding-place of the necklace—to whom?"

"Perhaps to some fellow-prisoner who was only in gaol for a short term."

"And why should he do that?"

"In order that this fellow-prisoner should provide him with a means to escape. And the proof is that the servant did break prison and escape, and afterwards his dead body was found in a pit many miles from the prison."

"Aha! the affair begins to outline itself. And the servant—how did he come to be found dead? Eh?"

"He is supposed to have fallen over the edge of the pit in the dark. But I begin to think that he was killed by Legros."

"Milord, our thoughts chime together. Because, *voyez-vous*, this story of desertion and military authorities will not hold water. There is more than a desertion behind this change of name and this fear of the British police. But if the man was an old gaolbird, and had committed a murder into the bargain, the thing understands itself. Twice he changes his name, so that he shall not be traced even to France, because he, Legros, under his English name, had enlisted after his release from prison and the records of your Army might reveal him. Only, if he was in the Army, it is strange that he should have found the leisure to plan a prison-breaking for his comrade and commit murder. No, there are still difficulties, but the outline of the plot is clear and will develop itself more clearly still as we proceed. In the meanwhile, I will undertake inquiries here and in Belgium, I think, milord, we must not confine ourselves to the ordinary passenger-routes, or even to the ports. A motorboat might well make the journey to the coast of Laincolonne. Your police, also, will make inquiries on their part. And when we have shown the progress of Legros from the front door of his house to his grave in England, then, I think, Mme. Suzanne will speak a little more. And now, milord, I beg you will honour us by sharing our dinner tonight. My wife is an excellent cook, if you will condescend to a *cuisine bourgeoise* garnished with a tolerable *vin de Bourgogne*. Monsieur Delavigne of the Sûreté informs me that you have the reputation of a *gourmet*, and it is only with a certain diffidence that I make the suggestion, but it would give Mme. Rozier unheard-of delight if you would give her the pleasure of making your acquaintance."

"Monsieur," said Lord Peter, "I am infinitely obliged to you both."

THE SEVENTH PART

Plain Hunting

First, Lucus Mortis; then Terra Tenebrosa; next, Tartarus; after that, Terra Oblivionis; then Herebus; then Barathrum; then Gehenna; and then Stagnum Ignis.

J. SHERIDAN LEFANU: WYLDER'S HAND

"WELL," SAID Superintendent Blundell, "if that's how it is, we've got to find Cranton. But it's a funny thing to me. From what they tell me, I wouldn't have thought Cranton was the man for that sort of job. He's never been suspected of killing anyone, and he never looked to me like a killer. And you know, my lord, that it's very rare for one of them sort of smart burglars to go all off the rails and take to violence. What I mean, it isn't in them, as a rule, if you get my meaning. It's true he went for Deacon in the dock but that was more of a scrimmage, as you might say, and I don't think he meant much harm. Supposing as it was the other chap that killed Cranton? He might have changed clothes with him to prevent identification."

"So he might. But what becomes of that old scar on the head? That seems to fit in with the body being this fellow they call Jean Legros. Unless Cranton had a scar too."

"He'd no scar up to last September," said the Superintendent thoughtfully. "No, I reckon you're right, and that won't work. Some of the measurements seem a bit different, too—though of course, it's not easy to be as accurate as all that when you're comparing a live man with a four-months-old corpse. And there were so many teeth gone and busted from the corpse that we've not got much out of that, either. No, we've got to find Cranton. If he's alive, he's lying uncommon low. Looks as though he'd done something pretty bad—I give you that."

The conversation took place in the churchyard, where Mr. Blundell had been undertaking an exhaustive search for unspecified clues. The Superintendent thoughtfully decapitated a nettle, and resumed:

"Then there's that chap Will Thoday. I can't make him out at all. I'll swear he knows something—but what *can* he know? It's as certain as anything can be that he was sick in bed when it all happened. He sticks to that, and says he knows nothing. What can you do with a man who says he knows nothing? Why, nothing. And as for his wife, *she* couldn't have tied a man up and buried him. She's not a powerful sort of woman by any means. And I've got hold of the children. It went against me to do it, but I did it all the same. And they say their Mother and Dad were both in the house all night. There's one other person might know something, and that's James Thoday. Look here, my lord, here's a queer thing. James Thoday left Fenchurch St. Paul on January 4th, early in the morning, to join his ship. He was seen to go, all right—the station-master saw him. But he never got to Hull that day. I've been on to Lampson & Blake, and they say they had a wire from him to say he couldn't get back in time, but would arrive on the Sunday night—which he did. Had some story of being taken suddenly ill—and they say he looked ill enough when he did arrive. I've told them to get in touch with him as quick as they can."

"Where was the wire sent from?"

"London. From a post-office near Liverpool street. About the time when the train Jim Thoday took at Dykesey would get up there. Looks as though he'd been taken queer on the way up."

"He might have picked up influenza from his brother."

"So he might. Still, he was fit to sail the next day, and it looks funny, don't you think? He'd have had plenty of time to go up to London and come down here again. He wouldn't come to Dykesey, of course, but he might have come part of the way by train and done the rest by car or motor-bike or what-not."

Wimsey whistled. "You think he was in with Will over the thing. Yes, I see. Will is in a conspiracy with Legros to get the emeralds—is that it? And he gets 'flu and can't do the job himself, so he arranges with Brother Jim to do it for him. Then Jim meets Legros and kills him and buries him and vamooses with the emeralds to Hong Kong. Well, that would explain one thing, and that is, why those infernal stones haven't been put on the European market. He could easily get rid of them over in the

East. But look here, Super—how did Will Thoday get in touch with Legros in the first place? It was easy enough when we put it all on Cranton, because he could have got the papers and things made out for Legros by one of his pals in Town. But you can't imagine that Thoday produced forged papers and provided Legros with his passage facilities and all that. How would a fellow like that know how to set about it?"

Mr. Blundell shook his head.

"But there's that two hundred pounds," he said.

"So there is, but that was after Legros had started."

"And when Legros was killed, the money was returned to the bank."

"Was it?"

"Oh, yes. I had a word with Thoday. He made no difficulties. He said he had an idea of purchasing a bit of land and starting to farm again on his own, but that, after his illness, he gave up the idea, thinking that for some time he wouldn't be strong enough. He gave me permission to go over his bank account. It was all in order—no suspicious withdrawals of money up to that £200 on December 31st, and that was paid in again in January, as soon as he was able to get about. And it's true about the land, too. He did think of buying it. All the same, £200 all in one-pound notes——"

The Superintendent broke off, and made a sudden dive behind a tall tombstone. There was a squeak and a scuffle. Mr. Blundell emerged, rather flustered. His large hand held Potty Peake's coat-collar in a firm grip.

"Now, you clear off," said the Superintendent, giving his captive a rough, but not unkindly, shake. "You get yourself into trouble, my lad, hanging round the churchyard and listening to private conversations. See?"

"Ar!" said Potty, "you needn't choke a fellow. You needn't choke poor Potty. If you knowed what Potty knows——"

"What do you know?"

Potty's eyes gleamed cunningly.

"I seen him—Number Nine—I seen him a-talking to Will in the church. But the Tailors was too much for him. Him with the rope—he got him, and he'll get you too. Potty knows. Potty ain't lived all these years, in and out of the church, for nothing."

"Who was talking to Will in the church?"

"Why, him!" Potty jerked his head towards the Thorpe grave. "Him they found over there. The black-bearded man. There's eight in the belfry and one in the grave. That makes nine. You think Potty can't count, but he can. But him as calls the peal—you won't get him, oh, no!"

"See here," said Wimsey, "you're a clever fellow, Potty. When did you see Will Thoday talking to the black-bearded man? See if you can count that far."

Potty Peake grinned at him. "Potty can count all right," he said, with great satisfaction. "Oh, yes." He began an elaborate calculation on his fingers. "Ah! it was a Monday night, that's when it was. There was cold pork and beans for dinner—that's good, cold pork and beans. Ah! Parson he preached about thankfulness. Be thankful for Christmas, he says. There was roast fowl Christmas Day and boiled pork and greens Sunday and be thankful, that's what Parson says. So Potty slips out at night, fo to be thankful again. You got to go to church to be thankful proper, ain't you, sir? And there was the church door standing open. So Potty creeps in, careful-like, see? And there's a light in the vestry. Potty was frightened. There's things hanging in the vestry. Ah! So Potty hides behind ole Batty Thomas, and then Will Thoday comes in, and Potty hears them talking in the vestry. 'Money,' Will says. 'Tis a great wickedness, is money. And then Will Thoday he cries out—he fetches a rope from the chest and—ah! Potty's afraid. He thinks about hanging. Potty don't want to see no one hanged. Potty runs away. He looks in at the vestry window, and there's the black-bearded man a-laying on the floor, and Will a-standing over him with the rope. Ah, dear! oh, dear! Potty don't like ropes. Potty's allus a-dreamin' of ropes. One, two, three, four, five, six, seven, eight—and this one's nine. Potty seen him a-hangin' there. Ooh!"

"I think you was a-dreaming all the time," said the Superintendent. "There's nobody been hanged that I know of."

"I see him a-hanging," persisted Potty. "Terrible it were. But don't you pay no attention. 'Tis only one o' poor Potty's dreams." His face changed. "You lemme go, mister. I gotter feed my pigs."

"Bless my heart," said Superintendent Blundell. "And what do you suppose we're to make of that?"

Wimsey shook his head.

"I think he saw something—or how did he know that the rope was gone from the cope-chest? But as for hanging, no! He's crazed about hanging. Got a hanging complex, or whatever they call it. The man wasn't hanged. Which Monday night do you suppose Potty meant?"

"Can't be January 6th, can it?" said the Superintendent. "The body was buried on the 4th, as far as we can make out. And it can't very well be December 30th, because Legros only got here on January 1st—if that was Legros you saw. And besides, I can't make out whether he means Sunday or Monday, with his boiled pork."

"I can," said Wimsey. "He had boiled pork and greens on Sunday, and Parson told him to be thankful and so he was. And on Monday, he had the pork cold with beans—probably the tinned variety if I know the modern country-woman—and he felt thankful again. So he went down to the church to be thankful in the proper place. It would be some time in the evening, as there was a light in the vestry."

"That's right. Potty lives with an aunt of his—a decent old soul, but not very sharp. He's always slipping out at night. They're cunning as the devil, these naturals. But which evening was it?"

"The day after Parson had preached on thankfulness," said Wimsey. "Thankfulness for Christmas. That looks like December 30th. Why not? You don't know that Legros didn't get here before January 1st. That's when Cranton got here."

"But I thought we'd washed Cranton out of it," objected Mr. Blundell, "and put Will Thoday in his place."

"Then who was it I met on the road over the bridge?"

"That must have been Legros."

"Well, it may be—though I still think it was Cranton, or his twin-brother. But if I met Legros on January 1st, he can't have been hanged by Will Thoday on December 30th. And in any case, he wasn't hanged. And," said Wimsey, triumphantly, "we still don't know how he did die!"

The Superintendent groaned.

"What I say is, we've got to find Cranton, anyhow. And as for December 30th, how are you going to be sure of that, anyway?"

"I shall ask the Rector which day he preached about thankfulness. Or Mrs. Venables. She's more likely to know."

"And I'd better see Thoday again. Not that I believe a single word Potty says. And how about Jim Thoday? How does he come into it now?"

"I don't know. But one thing I'm sure of, Super. It was no sailor put those knots into Gaude's rope. I'll take my oath on that."

"Oh, well!" said the Superintendent.

. . . . . .

Wimsey went back to the house and found the Rector in his study, busily writing out a touch of Treble Bob Major.

"One moment, my dear boy," he said, pushing the tobacco-jar towards his guest, "one moment. I am just pricking this little touch to show Wally Pratt how to do it. He has got himself 'imbrangled' as they call it—fine old English word, that. Now what has the foolish lad done here? The ninth lead should bring Queen's change—let me see, let me see—51732468, 15734286—that's the first thirds and fourths all right—51372468, 15374286—and that's the first fourths and thirds—13547826—ah! here is the trouble! The eighth should be at home. What has happened?—To be sure! What a beetle-headed cuckoo I am! He has forgotten to make the bob. She can't come home till she's called." He ran a red-ink line down the page and started to write figures furiously. "There! 51372468, 15374286—and *now* she comes home like a bird!—13572468. That's better. Now it should come round at the second repeat. I will just check it. Second to fifth, third to second—yes, yes—that brings 15263748, with Tittums at the end of the second course, and repeated once again brings it round. I will just jot down the lead-ends for him to check it by. Second to third, third to fifth, fourth to second, fifth to seventh, sixth to fourth, seventh to eighth, eighth to sixth for the plain lead. Then the bob. Plain, bob, bob, three plain and a bob. I cannot understand why red ink should distribute itself so lavishly over one's person. There! I have a large smear on my cuff! Call her in the middle, in and out and home. Repeat twice. A lovely little touch." He pushed aside several sheets of paper covered with figures, and transferred a quantity of red ink from his fingers to his trouser-legs. "And now, how are you getting along? Is there anything I can do to help you?"

"Yes, padre. You can tell me on which Sunday this winter you preached about thankfulness."

"Thankfulness? Well, now, that's rather a favourite subject of mine. Do you know, I find people very much disposed to grumble—I do indeed—and when you come to think of it, they might all be very much worse off. Even the farmers. As I said to them last Harvest Festival—oh! you were asking about my Thankfulness sermon—well, I nearly always preach about it at Harvest Festival. . . . Not so long ago as that? . . . Let me think. My memory is getting very unreliable, I fear . . ." He made a dive for the door. "Agnes, my dear! Agnes! Can you spare us a moment? . . . My wife is sure to remember. . . . My dear, I am so sorry to interrupt you, but can you recollect when I last preached about Thankfulness? I touched on the subject in my Tithe sermon, I remember—would you be thinking of that? Not that we have had any trouble about tithe in this parish. Our farmers are very sensible. A man from St. Peter came to talk to me about it, but I pointed out to him that the 1918 adjustment was made in the farmers' interests and that if they thought they had reason to complain of the 1925 Act, then they should see about getting a fresh adjustment made. But the law, I said, is the law. Oh, on the matter of tithe I assure you I am adamant. Adamant."

"Yes, Theodore," said Mrs. Venables, with rather a wry smile, "but if you didn't so often advance people money to pay the tithe with, they mightn't be as reasonable as they are."

"That's different," said the Rector, hurriedly, "quite different. It's a matter of principle, and any small personal loan has nothing to do with it. Even the best of women don't always grasp the importance of a legal principle, do they, Lord Peter? My sermon dealt with the principle. The text was: 'Render unto Caesar.' Though whether Queen Anne's Bounty is to be regarded as Caesar or as God—and sometimes, I admit, I feel that it is a little unfortunate that the Church should appear to be on Caesar's side, and that disestablishment and disendowment——"

"A Caesarian operation is indicated, so to speak?" suggested Wimsey.

"A——? Oh, yes! Very good," said the Rector. "My dear, that is very good, don't you think? I must tell the Bishop—no, perhaps not. He is just a leetle bit strait-laced. But it is true—if only one could separate the two things, the temporal and the spiritual—but the question I ask myself is always, the churches themselves—the buildings—our own beautiful church—what would become of it in such a case?"

"My dear," said Mrs. Venables, "Lord Peter was asking about your sermons on Thankfulness. Didn't you preach one on the Sunday after Christmas? About thankfulness for the Christmas message? Surely you remember. The text was taken from the Epistle for the day: 'Thou art no more a servant, but a son.' It was about how happy we ought to be as God's children and about making a habit of saying 'Thank-you, Father' for all the pleasant things of life, and being as pleasant-tempered as we should wish our own children to be. I remember it so well, because Jackie and Fred Holiday got quarrelling in church over those prayer-books we gave them and had to be sent out."

"Quite right, my dear. You always remember everything. That was it, Lord Peter. The Sunday after Christmas. It comes back to me very clearly now. Old Mrs. Giddings stopped me in the porch afterwards to complain that there weren't enough plums in her Christmas plum-pudding."

"Mrs. Giddings is an ungrateful old wretch," said his wife.

"Then the next day *was* the 30th December," said Wimsey. "Thanks, Padre, that's very helpful. Do you recollect Will Thoday coming round to see you on the Monday evening, by any chance?"

The Rector looked helplessly at his wife, who replied readily enough:

"Of course he did, Theodore. He came to ask you something about the New Year's peal. Don't you remember saying how queer and ill he looked? Of course, he must have been working up for that attack of 'flu, poor man. He came late—about 9 o'clock—and you said you couldn't understand why he shouldn't have waited till the morning."

"True, true," said the Rector. "Yes, Thoday came round to me on the Monday night. I hope you are not—well! I mustn't ask indiscreet questions, must I?"

"Not when I don't know the answers," said Wimsey, with a smile and a shake of the head. "About Potty Peake, now. Just how potty is he? Can one place any sort of reliance on his account of anything?"

"Well," said Mrs. Venables, "sometimes one can and sometimes one can't. He gets mixed up, you know. He's quite truthful, as far as his understanding goes, but he gets fancies and then tells them as if they were facts. You can't trust anything he says about ropes or hanging—that's his little peculiarity. Otherwise—if it was a question of pigs, for instance, or the church organ—he's quite good and reliable."

"I see," said Wimsey. "Well, he has been talking a good bit about ropes and hanging."

"Then don't believe a word of it," replied Mrs. Venables, robustly. "Dear me! here's that Superintendent coming up the drive. I suppose he wants you."

Wimsey caught Mr. Blundell in the garden and headed him away from the house.

"I've seen Thoday," said the Superintendent. "Of course he denies the whole story. Says Potty was dreaming."

"But how about the rope?"

"There you are! But that Potty was hiding behind the churchyard wall when you and I found the rope in the well, and how much he may have heard, I don't know. Anyway, Thoday denies it, and short of charging him with the murder, I've got to take his word for it. You know these dratted regulations. No bullying of witnesses. That's what they say. And whatever Thoday did or didn't do, he couldn't have buried the body, so where are you? Do you think any jury is going to convict on the word of a village idiot like Potty Peake? No. Our job's clear. We've got to find Cranton."

. . . .

That afternoon, Lord Peter received a letter.

"*Dear Lord Peter,*—I have just thought of something funny you ought to know about, though I don't see how it can have anything to do with the murder. But in detective stories the detective always wants to know about anything funny, so I am sending you the paper. Uncle Edward wouldn't like me writing to you, because he says you encourage me about wanting to be a writer and mixing myself up in police work—he *is* a silly old stick-in-the-mud! So I don't suppose Miss Garstairs—that's our H.M.—would let me send you a letter, but I'm putting this into one to Penelope Dwight and I do hope she sends it on all right.

"I found the paper lying in the belfry on the Saturday before Easter Day and I meant to show it to Mrs. Venables because it was so funny, but Dad dying made me forget all about it. I thought it must be some rubbish of Potty Peake's, but Jack Godfrey says it isn't Potty's writing, but it's quite mad enough to be him, isn't it? Anyway, I thought you might like to have it. I don't see how Potty could have got hold of that foreign paper, do you?

"I hope you are getting on well with the investigations. Are you still at Fenchurch St. Paul? I am writing a poem about the founding of Tailor Paul. Miss Bowler says it is quite good and I expect they will put it in the School magazine. That will be one in the eye for Uncle Edward, anyhow. He can't stop me being printed in the School Mag. Please write if you have time and tell me if you find out anything about the paper.

"Yours sincerely,

"HILARY THORPE."

"A colleague, as Sherlock Holmes would say, after my own heart," said Wimsey, as he unfolded the thin enclosure. "Oh, lord! 'I thought to see the fairies in the fields'—a lost work by Sir James Barrie, no doubt! Literary sensation of the year. 'But I saw only the evil elephants with their black backs.' This is neither rhyme nor reason. Hum! there is a certain dismal flavour about it suggestive of Potty, but no reference to hanging, so I conclude that it is not his—he surely couldn't keep King Charles' Head out of it so long. Foreign paper—wait a minute! I seem to know the look of that paper. By God, yes! Suzanne Legros' letter! If the paper isn't the dead spit of this, I'm a Dutchman. Let me think. Suppose this was the paper Jean Legros sent to Cranton, or Will Thoday, or whoever it was? Blundell had better have a look at it. Bunter, get the car out. And what do you make of this?"

"Of this, my lord? I should say that it was written by a person of no inconsiderable literary ability, who had studied the works of Sheridan Lefanu and was, if I may be permitted the expression, bats in the belfry, my lord."

"It strikes you that way? It does not look to you like a cipher message, or anything of that kind?"

"It had not occurred to me to regard it in that light, my lord. The style is cramped, certainly, but it is cramped in what I should call a consistent manner, suggestive of—ah!—literary rather than mechanical effort."

"True, Bunter, true. It certainly isn't anything simple and bucolic of the every-third-word type. And it doesn't look as if it was meant to be read with a grid, because, with the possible exception of 'gold,' there isn't a single word in it that's significant—or could be significant of anything but moonshine. That bit about the moon is rather good, of its kind. Mannered, but imaginative. 'Frail and faint as a sickle of straw.' Alliteration's artful aid, what? 'So then came minstrels, having gold trumpets, harps and drums. These played very loudly beside me, breaking that spell.' Whoever wrote that had an ear for cadence. Lefanu, did you say? That's not a bad shot, Bunter. It reminds me a little of that amazing passage in *Wylder's Hand* about Uncle Lorne's dream."

"That was the passage I had in mind, my lord."

"Yes. Well—in that case the victim was due to 'be sent up again, at last, a thousand, a hundred, ten and one, black marble steps, and then it will be the other one's turn.' He *was* sent up again, Bunter, wasn't he?"

"From the grave, my lord? I believe that was so. Like the present unknown individual."

"As you say—very like him. 'Hell gapes, Erebus now lies open,' as our correspondent has it. 'The mouths of Death wait on thy end.' Does he mean anything by that, Bunter?"

"I could not say, my lord."

"The word 'Erebus' occurs in the Lefanu passage too, but there, if I remember rightly, it is spelt with an H. If the man who wrote this got his inspiration there, he knew enough, at any rate, about Erebus to be familiar with both spellings. All very curious, Bunter mine. We'll go along to Leamholt and get the two sheets of paper put side by side."

. . . . . .

There was a great wind blowing over the Fen, and immense white clouds sailing fast in the wide blue dome of sky. As they drew up before the police-station at Leamholt, they met the Superintendent just about to step into his own car.

"Coming to see me, my lord?"

"I was. Were you coming to see me?"

"Yes."

Wimsey laughed.

"Things are moving. What have you got?"

"We've got Cranton."

"No!"

"Yes, my lord. They've run him to earth in a place in London. I heard from them this morning. Seems he's been ill, or something. Anyway, they've found him. I'm going up to interrogate him. Would you like to come?"

"Rather! Shall I run you up there? Save the force a bit of money, you know, on train-fares. And be quicker and more comfortable."

"Thank you very much, my lord."

"Bunter, wire to the Rector that we have gone to Town. Hop in, Super. You will now see how safe and swift modern methods of transport are when there is no speed-limit. Oh, wait a moment. While Bunter is wiring, have a look at this. It reached me this morning."

He handed over Hilary Thorpe's letter and the enclosure.

"Evil elephants?" said Mr. Blundell. "What in the name of goodness is all this about?"

"I don't know. I'm hoping your friend Cranton can tell us."

"But it's potty."

"I don't think Potty could rise to such heights. No, I know what you mean—don't trouble to explain. But the paper, Superintendent, the paper!"

"What about it? Oh, I get you. You think this came from the same place as Suzanne Legros' letter. I shouldn't wonder if you're right. Step in and we'll have a look. By jove, my lord, and you *are* right. Might have come out of the same packet. Well, I'll be—— Found in the belfry, you say. What do you think it all means, then?"

"I think this is the paper that Legros sent to his friend in England—the 'guarantee' that he composed, shut up in his room for so many hours. And I think it's the clue to where the emeralds were hidden. A cipher, or something of that sort."

"Cipher, eh? It's a queer one, then. Can you read it?"

"No, but I jolly well will. Or find somebody who can. I'm hoping that Cranton will read it for us. I bet he won't, though," added his lordship, thoughtfully. "And even if we do read it, it isn't going to do us much good, I'm afraid."

"Why not?"

"Why, because you can bet your sweet life that the emeralds were taken away by whoever it was killed Legros—whether it was Cranton or Thoday or somebody else we don't know about yet."

"I suppose that's a fact. Anyhow, my lord, if we read the cipher and find the hiding-place, and the stuff's gone, that'll be pretty good proof that we're working along the right lines."

"So it will. But," added Wimsey, as the Superintendent and Bunter piled into the car and were whisked away out of Leamholt at a speed which made the policeman gasp, "if the emeralds are gone, and Cranton says he didn't take them, and we can't prove he did, and we can't find out who Legros really was, or who killed him, why then—where are we?"

"Just where we were before," said Mr. Blundell.

"Yes," said Wimsey. "It's like Looking-Glass Country. Takes all the running we can do to stay in the same place."

The Superintendent glanced about him. Flat as a chess-board, and squared like a chess-board with intersecting dyke and hedge, the Fen went flashing past them.

"Very like Looking-Glass Country," he agreed, "same as the picture in the book. But as for staying in the same place—all I can say is, it don't look like it, my lord—not where you're concerned."

THE EIGHTH PART

Lord Peter Follows His Course Bell to Lead

I will again urge on the young conductor the great advantage that it will be to him to write out touches or even whole peals . . . whereby he will gain a great insight into the working of the bells.

TROYTE ON CHANGE-RINGING

"WELL, OF course," admitted Mr. Cranton, grinning up ruefully from his pillow into Lord Peter's face, "if your lordship recognizes me, that's done it. I'll have to come clean, as the sheet said to the patent washer. It's a fact I was in Fenchurch St. Paul on New Year's Day, and a lovely place it is to start a happy New Year in, I don't think. And it's true I failed to report myself as from last September. And if you ask me, I think it's damned slack of you flatties not to have dug me out earlier. What we pay rates and taxes for I don't know."

He stopped and shifted restlessly.

"Don't waste your breath in giving us lip," said Chief Inspector Parker of the C.I.D., kindly enough. "When did you start growing that face-fungus? In September? I thought so. What was the idea? You didn't think it was becoming, did you?"

"I didn't," said Mr. Cranton. "Went to my heart, I may say, to disfigure myself. But I thought, 'They'll never know Nobby Cranton with his handsome features all hidden in black hair.' So I made the sacrifice. It's not so bad now, and I've got used to it, but it looked horrible while it was growing. Made me think of those happy times when I lived on His Majesty's bounty. Ah! and look at my hands. They've never got over it. I ask you, how can a gentleman carry on with his profession after all those years of unrefined manual labour? Taking the bread out of a man's mouth, I call it."

"So you had some game on, which started last September," said Parker, patiently. "What was it, now? Anything to do with the Wilbraham emeralds, eh?"

"Well, to be frank, it was," replied Nobby Cranton. "See here, I'll tell you the truth about that. I didn't mind—I never *have* minded—being put inside for what I did do. But it's offensive to a gentleman's feelings when his word isn't believed. And when I said I never had those emeralds, I meant what I said. I never did have them, and you know it. If I had had them, I wouldn't be living in a hole like this, you can bet your regulation boots. I'd have been living like a gentleman on the fat of the land. Lord!" added Mr. Cranton, "I'd have had 'em cut up and salted away before you could have said 'knife.' Talk about tracing them—you'd never have traced them the way I'd have worked it."

"So you went to Fenchurch St. Paul to try and find them, I suppose?" suggested Wimsey.

"That's right, I did. And why? Because I knew they must be there. That swine—you know who I mean——"

"Deacon?"

"Yes, Deacon." Something that might have been fear and might have been mere anger twisted the sick man's face. "He never left the place. He couldn't have got them away before you pinched him. You watched his correspondence, didn't you? If he'd packed them up and posted them, you'd have known it, eh? No. He had them there—somewhere—I don't know—but he had them. And I meant to get them, see? I meant to get them, and I meant to bring them along and show 'em to you and make you take back what you said about my having had them. Pretty silly, you'd have looked, wouldn't you, when you had to own up that I was right?"

"Indeed?" said Parker. "That was the idea, was it? You were going to find the stuff and bring it along like a good little boy?"

"That's right."

"No idea of making anything out of them, of course?"

"Oh, dear, no," replied Mr. Cranton.

"You didn't come to us in September and suggest that we should help you to find them?"

"Well, I didn't," agreed Mr. Cranton. "I didn't want to be bothered with a lot of clumsy cops. It was my own little game, see? All my own work, as the pavement-artists say."

"Delightful," said Parker. "And what made you think you knew where to look for them?"

"Ah!" said Mr. Cranton, cautiously. "Something Deacon once said gave me an idea. But he was a liar about that, too. I never met such a liar as that fellow was. He was so crooked, you could have used his spine for a safety-pin. It serves me right for having to do with menials. A mean, sneaking spirit, that's what you find in that sort. No sense of honour at all."

"Very likely," said the Chief Inspector. "Who is Paul Taylor?"

"There you are!" said Mr. Cranton, triumphantly. "Deacon said to me——"

"When?"

"In the—oh, well!—in the dock, if you will excuse my mentioning such a vulgar place. 'Want to know where those shiners are?' he said. 'Ask Paul Taylor or Batty Thomas'—and grinned all over his face. 'Who're they?' said I. 'You'll find 'em in Fenchurch,' he said, grinning still more. 'But you aren't likely to see Fenchurch again in a hurry,' he said. So then I biffed him one—excuse the expression—and the blinking warder interfered."

"Really?" said Parker, incredulously.

"Cross my heart and wish I may die," said Mr. Cranton. "But when I got down to Fenchurch, you see, I found there were no such people—only some rubbish about bells. So I dismissed the matter from my mind."

"And sneaked off on the Saturday night. Why?"

"Well, to be frank with you," replied Mr. Cranton, "there was an individual in that place I didn't like the looks of. I got the idea that my face struck a chord in her mind, in spite of the exterior decorations. So, not wishing for argument—which is always ungentlemanly—I went quietly away."

"And who was the penetrating individual?"

"Why, that woman—Deacon's wife. We had stood shoulder to shoulder, as you might say, under unfortunate circumstances, and I had no wish to renew the acquaintance. I never expected to see *her* in that village, and, candidly, I thought she showed a lack of taste."

"She came back when she married a man named Thoday," said Wimsey.

"Married again, did she?" Cranton's eyes narrowed. "Oh, I see. I didn't know that. Well, I'm damned!"

"Why the surprise?"

"Why?—Oh, well—somebody wasn't too particular, that's all."

"See here," said Parker, "you may as well tell the truth now. Did that woman have anything to do with the theft of the emeralds?"

"How should I know? But to be frank, I don't believe she did. I think she was just a plain fool. Deacon's catspaw. I'm sure the fellow put her on to find out about the stuff, but I don't think she was wise to what she was doing. Honestly, I don't think so, because I can't see that man Deacon giving his game away. But hell! What do I know about it?"

"You don't think she knows where the stuff is?"

Cranton thought for a moment. Then he laughed.

"I'd pretty well take my oath she doesn't."

"Why?"

He hesitated.

"If she knew and was straight, she'd have told the police, wouldn't she? If she knew and was crooked, she'd have told me or my pals. No. You won't get it out of her."

"H'm! You say you think she recognized you?"

"I got a sort of idea that she was beginning to find my face familiar. Mind you, it was only a kind of hunch I got. I might have been wrong. But I anticipated argument, and I have always considered argument ill-bred. So I went away. In the night. I was working for the blacksmith—an excellent fellow, but crude. I didn't want any argument with him, neither. I just went quietly home to think things out, and then I got laid up with rheumatic fever, and it's left my heart dickey, as you see."

"Quite so. How did you get rheumatic fever?"

"Well, wouldn't anybody get rheumatic fever, if he'd fallen into one of those cursed dykes? I never saw such a country, never. Country life never did suit me—particularly in the blasted middle of winter, with a thaw going on. I was damn nearly found dead in a ditch, which is no end for a gentleman."

"You didn't investigate the matter of Batty Thomas and Tailor Paul any further, then?" said Parker, placidly putting aside the eloquence which Mr. Cranton seemed ready to lavish on any side-issue. "I am referring to the bells. You did not, for instance, visit the belfry, to see if the emeralds were hidden up there?"

"No, of course I didn't. Besides," went on Mr. Cranton, much too hastily, "the confounded place was always locked."

"You tried it, then?"

"Well, to be frank, I may just have laid my hand on the door, so to speak."

"You never went up into the bell-chamber?"

"Not me."

"Then how do you account for that?" demanded Parker, suddenly producing the mysterious cipher and thrusting it under the sick man's eyes.

Mr. Cranton turned extremely white.

"That?" he gasped. "That?—I never——" He fought for breath. "My heart—here, give me some of the stuff in that glass——"

"Give it him," said Wimsey, "he's really bad."

Parker gave him the medicine with a grim face. After a time the blue pallor gave place to a healthier colour, and the breathing became more natural.

"That's better," said Cranton. "You startled me. What did you say? That? I never saw that before."

"You're lying," said the Chief Inspector, curtly. "You have seen it. Jean Legros sent it to you, didn't he?"

"Who's he? Never heard of him."

"That's another lie. How much money did you send him to get him to England?"

"I tell you I never heard of him," repeated Cranton, sullenly. "For God's sake, can't you leave me alone? I tell you I'm ill."

He looked ill enough. Parker swore under his breath.

"Look here, Nobby, why not come across with the truth? It'll save us bothering you. I know you're ill. Cough it up and get it over."

"I know nothing about it. I've told you—I went down to Fenchurch and I came away again. I never saw that paper and I never heard of Jean what's-his-name. Does that satisfy you?"

"No, it doesn't."

"Are you charging me with anything?"

Parker hesitated. "Not as yet," he said.

"Then you've got to take my answer," said Mr. Cranton, faintly, but as one who is sure of his position.

"I know that," said Parker, "but, hang it, man! do you *want* to be charged? If you'd rather come down with us to the Yard——"

"What's the idea? What have you got to charge me with? You can't try me for stealing those bloody emeralds all over again. I haven't got them. Never seen them——"

"No; but we might charge you with the murder of Jean Legros."

"No—no—no!" cried Cranton. "It's a lie! I never killed him. I never killed anybody. I never——"

"He's fainted," said Wimsey.

"He's dead," said Superintendent Blundell, speaking for the first time.

"I hope to goodness not," said Parker. "No—it's all right, but he looks pretty queer. Better get hold of that girl. Here, Polly!"

A woman came in. She gave one resentful glance at the three men and hurried across to Cranton.

"If you've killed him," she muttered, "it's murder. Coming and threatening one that's as sick as him. You get out, you great bullies. He's done nobody any harm."

"I'll send the doctor along," said Parker. "And I'll be coming to see him again. And when I do come, see that I find him here all right. Understand? We shall want him elsewhere, you know, as soon as he's fit to be moved. He hasn't reported himself since last September."

The girl shrugged a disdainful shoulder, and they left her bending over the sick man.

"Well, Superintendent," said Parker, "I'm afraid that's the best we can do for you at the moment. The man's not shamming—he's really ill. But he's holding something out on us. All the same, I don't think it's murder, somehow. That wouldn't be like Cranton. He knew that paper all right."

"Yes," said Wimsey. "Produced quite a reaction, didn't it? He's frightened about something, Charles. What is it?"

"He's frightened about the murder."

"Well," said Blundell, "it looks to me as though he did it. He admits he was there, and that he ran away on the night the body was buried. If he didn't do it, who did? He could have got the key of the crypt from the sexton all right, we know that."

"So he could," said Wimsey, "but he was a stranger to the place. How did he know where the sexton kept his tools? Or where to find the bell-rope? He might have noticed the well, of course, in the day-time, but it's funny that he should have had the whole scheme so pat. And where does Legros come into it? If Deacon told Cranton in the dock where to find the emeralds, where was the sense of bringing Legros to England? He didn't want him. And, if he did for some reason need Legros, and killed him to get the emeralds, where are the emeralds? If he sold them, you ought to have found it out by now. If he's still got them, you'd better have a hunt for them."

"We'll search the house," said Parker, dubiously, "but I don't somehow think he's got them. He wasn't alarmed about the emeralds. It's a puzzle. But we'll turn the place upside-down, and if they're there, we'll get them."

"And if you do," said Blundell, "then you can arrest that chap for the murder. Whoever's got the emeralds did the murder. I'm sure of that."

"Where thy treasure is, there shall thy heart be also," said Wimsey. "The heart of this crime is down at St. Paul. That's my prophecy, Charles. Will you have a bet on it?"

"No, I won't," said the Chief Inspector. "You're right too often, Peter, and I've no money to waste."

. . . .

Wimsey went back to Fenchurch St. Paul and shut himself up with the cipher. He had untwisted cryptograms before, and he felt certain that this would prove to be a simple one. Whether the inventor was Cranton or Jean Legros or Will Thoday or any other person connected with the affair of the Wilbraham emeralds, he was hardly likely to be an expert in the art of secret writing. Yet the thing had the signs of a cunning hand about it. He had never seen a secret message that looked so innocent. Sherlock Holmes' Little Dancing Men were, by comparison, obviously secretive.

He tried various simple methods, such as taking every second, third or fourth letter, or skipping letters in accordance with a set combination of figures, but without result. He tried assigning a number to each letter and adding the results, word by word and sentence by sentence. This certainly produced enough mathematical problems to satisfy a Senior Wrangler, but none of them seemed to make sense. He took all the bell-inscriptions and added them up also, with and without the dates, but could find nothing significant. He wondered whether the book contained the whole of what was on the bells. Leaving his papers strewn over the table, he went to the Rector to borrow the keys of the belfry. After a slight delay, caused by the keys having been taken downstairs by mistake for the keys of the wine-cellar, he secured them and made his way to the church.

He was still puzzled about the finding of the cryptogram. The keys jingled together in his hand—the two great keys of the West and South doors, all by themselves on a steel chain, and then, in a bunch on a ring together, the keys of the crypt and vestry, the key of the belfry, the key of the ringing-chamber and the key that unlocked the counterpoise of the belfry. How had Cranton known where to find them? He could, of course, have taken them from the sexton's house—if he had known already. But if "Stephen Driver" had been asking questions about the church keys, somebody would have taken notice of it. The sexton had the key of the West door and of the crypt. Had he the other keys as well? Wimsey suddenly turned back and shot the question through the study window at the Rector, who was struggling with the finances of the Parish Magazine.

Mr. Venables rubbed his forehead.

"No," he said at last. "Gotobed has the West-door key and the key of the crypt, as you say, and he also has the key of the belfry stair and of the ringing-chamber, because he rings the single bell for Early Service and sometimes deputizes for Hezekiah when he's ill. And Hezekiah has the keys of the South porch and the belfry stair and the ringing-chamber, too. You see, Hezekiah was sexton before Gotobed, and he likes to keep his privilege of ringing the passing-bell, though he's too old for the other work, and he has the necessary keys. But neither of them has the key to the counterpoise. They don't need it. The only people who have that are Jack Godfrey and myself. I have a complete set of everything, of course, so that if one of the others is lost or mislaid, I can supply it."

"Jack Godfrey—has he the key of the crypt as well?"

"Oh, no—he doesn't need that."

Curiouser and curiouser, thought Wimsey. If the man who left the paper in the bell-chamber was the same man who buried the body, then either he took *all* the Rector's keys, or he had access to *two* sets, and those two sets had to be Jack Godfrey's (for the key of the counterpoise) and Gotobed's (for the key of the crypt). And if the man had been Cranton, then how did he *know*? Of course, the criminal might have brought his own spade (though that added to the complication). If so, he must have had either the Rector's keys or Jack Godfrey's. Wimsey went round to the back and got hold of Emily and Hinkins. They were both quite sure that they had never seen the man who called himself Stephen Driver inside the Rectory gates, much less inside the

Rector's study, which was the proper place for the keys when they were in their proper place.

"But they weren't there at all, my lord," said Emily, "because, if you remember, they keys was missing on New Year's night, and it wasn't till near a week after we found them in the vestry—bar the key of the church porch and that was in the lock where Rector left it after choir-practice."

"After choir-practice? On the Saturday?"

"That's right," said Hinkins. "Only, don't you remember, Emily, Rector said it couldn't have been him as left it, because it was gone a-missing, and he didn't have it on Saturday and had to wait for Harry Gotobed?"

"Well, I don't know," said Emily, "but that's where it was. Harry Gotobed said he found it there when he went to ring for Early Service."

More confused than ever, Wimsey trotted back to the study window. Mr. Venables, arrested with a carrying-figure at the tip of his pen, was at first not very clear in his recollection, but said presently that he believed Emily was right.

"I must have left the keys in the vestry the week before," he suggested, "and whoever left the church last after choir-practice must have found the church key and used it—but who that would be, I don't know, unless it was Gotobed. Yes, it would be Gotobed, because he would wait behind to make up the stoves. But it was funny that he should leave the key in the lock. Dear me! You don't think it could have been the murderer, do you?"

"I do, indeed," said Wimsey.

"There now!" exclaimed the Rector. "But if I left the keys in the vestry, how did he get in to find them? He couldn't get in without the church key. Unless he came to choir-practice. Surely, nobody belonging to the choir——"

The Rector looked horribly distressed. Wimsey hastened to comfort him.

"The door would be unlocked during choir-practice. He might have slipped in then."

"Oh, yes—of course! How stupid I am! No doubt that is what occurred. You have relieved my mind very much."

Wimsey had not, however, relieved his own mind. As he resumed his way to the church, he turned the matter over. If the keys had been taken on New Year's Eve, then Cranton had not taken them. Cranton had not arrived till New Year's Day. Will

Thoday had come, unnecessarily, to the Rectory on December 30th, and might have taken the keys then, but he had certainly not been in the church on the night of January 4th to restore them. It remained possible that Will Thoday had taken the keys and the mysterious James Thoday had returned them—but in that case, what was Cranton doing in the business? And Wimsey felt sure that Cranton knew something about the paper found in the bell-chamber.

Meditating thus, Wimsey let himself into the church, and, unlocking the door in the tower, made his way up the spiral stair. As he passed through the ringing-chamber, he noticed with a smile that a new board had made its appearance on the wall, announcing that: "On New Year's morning, 19—, a Peal of 15,840 Kent Treble Bob Major was Rung in 9 hours and 15 Minutes, the Ringers being: Treble, Ezra Wilderspin; 2, Peter D. B. Wimsey; 3, Walter Pratt; 4, Henry Gotobed; 5, Joseph Hinkins; 6, Alfred Donnington; 7, John P. Godfrey; Tenor, Hezekiah Lavender; Theodore Venables, Rector, assisting. Our Mouths shall shew forth Thy Praise." He passed up through the great, bare clock-chamber, released the counterpoise and climbed again till he came out beneath the bells. There he stood for a moment, gazing up into their black mouths while his eyes grew accustomed to the semi-darkness. Presently their hooded silence oppressed him. A vague vertigo seized him. He felt as though they were slowly collapsing together and coming down upon him. Spellbound, he spoke their names: Gaude, Sabaoth, John, Jericho, Jubilee, Dimity, Batty Thomas and Tailor Paul. A soft and whispering echo seemed to start from the walls and die stealthily among the beams. Suddenly he shouted in a great voice: "Tailor Paul!" and he must somehow have hit upon a harmonic of the scale, for a faint brazen note answered him, remote and menacing, from overhead.

"Come!" said Wimsey, pulling himself together, "this won't do. I'm getting as bad as Potty Peake, coming here and talking to the bells. Let's find the ladder and get to work."

He switched on his torch and turned it on the dim corners of the belfry. It showed him the ladder, and it showed him something else also. In the gloomiest and dustiest corner of the floor, there was a patch that was not so dusty. He stepped eagerly forward, the menace of the bells forgotten. Yes, there was no mistake. A portion of the floor had at some fairly recent time been scrubbed, for the dust which in other places lay centuries thick was here only a thin film.

He knelt to examine it, and new thoughts went swooping and turning through his brain like bats. Why should anybody trouble to swab the floor of a belfry, unless to remove some very sinister stain? He saw Cranton and Legros climbing to the belfry, with the cipher in their hands for guidance. He saw the green glint of the jewels, dragged from their old hiding-place in the light of the lantern. He saw the sudden leap, the brutal blow, and the blood gushing to the floor, the cipher fluttering, unheeded, into a corner. And then the murderer, trembling and glancing over his shoulder, as he snatched the emeralds from dead fingers, took up the body and stumbled panting down the creaking ladders. The sexton's spade from the crypt, the bucket and scrubbing-brush from the vestry, or wherever they were kept, the water from the well——

There he stopped. The well? The well meant the rope, and what had the rope to do with this? Had it been used merely as a convenient means to carry the corpse? But the experts had been so sure that the victim had been bound before he was dead. And besides, there were the blow and the blood. It was all very well making horrible pictures for one's self, but there had been no blow till the man had been dead too long to leave any pool of blood. And if there was no blood, why scrub the floor?

He sat back on his heels and looked up again to the bells. If their tongues could speak, they could tell him what they had seen, but they had neither speech nor language. Disappointed, he again took up the torch and searched further. Then he broke out into harsh and disgusted laughter. The whole cause of the mystery revealed itself absurdly. An empty quart beer-bottle lay there, rolled into an obscure place behind a quantity of worm-eaten beams that were stacked against the wall. Here was a pretty ending to his dreams! Some unlicenced trespasser on consecrated ground—or possibly some workman legitimately engaged in repairs to the bell-cage—had spilt his beer and had tidily removed the stains, while the bottle, rolling out of sight, had been forgotten. No doubt that was all. Yet a lingering suspicion caused Wimsey to take up the bottle very carefully, by means of a finger inserted into the neck. It was not very dusty. It could not, he thought, have lain there long. It would bear somebody's finger-prints—perhaps.

He examined the rest of the floor very carefully, but could find only a few jumbled footprints in the dust—large, male prints, he thought. They might be Jack Godfrey's or Hezekiah Lavender's, or anybody's. Then he took the ladder and made an exhaustive search of the bells and timbers. He found nothing. No secret mark. No hiding-place for treasure. And nothing whatever suggestive of fairies or elephants, enchanters or Erebus. After several dirty and fatiguing hours, he descended again, carrying the bottle as his sole reward.

. . . .

Curiously enough, it was the Rector who solved the cipher. He came into the schoolroom that night as the hall-clock struck eleven, thoughtfully bearing a glass of hot toddy in one hand and an old-fashioned foot-muff in the other.

"I do hope you are not working yourself to death," he said, apologetically. "I have ventured to bring a little comfort for the inner man. These nights of early summer are so chilly. And my wife thinks you might like to put your feet in this. There is always a draught under that door. Allow me—it is slightly moth-eaten, I fear, but still affords protection. Now, you must not let me disturb you. Dear me! What is that? Are you pricking out a peal? Oh, no—I see they are letters, not figures. My eyesight is not as good as it was. But I am rudely prying into your affairs."

"Not a bit, padre. It does look rather like a peal. It's still this wretched cipher. Finding that the number of letters formed a multiple of eight, I had written it out in eight columns, hoping forlornly that something might come of it. Now you mention it, I suppose one might make a simple sort of cipher out of a set of changes."

"How could you do that?"

"Well, by taking the movements of one bell and writing the letters of your message in the appropriate places and then filling up the places of the other bells with arbitraries. For instance. Take a Plain Course of Grandsire Doubles,[1] and suppose you want to convey the simple and pious message 'Come and worship.' You would select one bell to carry the significants—let us say, No. 5. Then you would write out the beginning of your plain course,

[1] "Doubles" is the name given to a set of changes rung on 5 bells, the tenor (No. 6) being rung last or "behind" in each change.

and wherever No. 5 came you would put in one letter of your message. Look."

He rapidly scribbled down the two columns:

1 2 3 4 5 6	
2 1 3 5 4 6	. . . C . .
2 3 1 4 5 6	. . . . O .
3 2 4 1 5 6	. . . . M .
3 4 2 5 1 6	. . . E . .
4 3 5 2 1 6	. . A . . .
4 5 3 1 2 6	. N . . . .
5 4 1 3 2 6	D . . . . .
5 1 4 2 3 6	W . . . . .
1 5 2 4 3 6	. O . . . .
1 2 5 3 4 6	. . R . . .
2 1 5 4 3 6	. . S . . .
2 5 1 3 4 6	. H . . . .
5 2 3 1 4 6	I . . . . .
5 3 2 4 1 6	P . . . . .
etc.	

"Then you could fill up the other places with any sort of nonsense letters—say X L O C M P, J Q I W O N, N A E M M B, T S H E Z P, and so on. Then you would write the whole thing out in one paragraph, dividing it so as to look like words."

"Why?" inquired the Rector.

"Oh, just to make it more difficult. You could write, for example, 'XLOC MPJQI. WON NAE M MBTS! HEZP?' and so on to the end. It wouldn't matter what you did. The man who received the message and had the key would simply divide the letters into six columns again, run his pencil along the course of No. 5, and read the message."

"Dear me!" said Mr. Venables, "so he would! How very ingenious. And I suppose that with a little further ingenuity, the cipher might be made to convey some superficial and misleading information. I see, for instance, that you already have the word WON and the Scotch expression NAE. Could not the idea be extended further, so that the entire passage might appear completely innocuous?"

"Of course it could. It might look like this." Wimsey flicked Jean Legros' communication with his finger.

"Have you——? But pardon me. I am unwarrantably interfering. Still—have you tried this method on the cryptogram?"

"Well, I haven't," admitted Wimsey. "I've only just thought of it. Besides, what would be the good of sending a message like that to Cranton, who probably knows nothing about bell-ringing? And it would take a bell-ringer to write it, and we have no reason to suppose that Jean Legros was a ringer. It is true," he added thoughtfully, "that we have no reason to suppose he was not."

"Well, then," said the Rector. "Why not try? You told me, I think, that this paper was picked up in the belfry. Might not the person to whom it was sent, though not himself a ringer and not knowing how to interpret it, have connected it in his mind with the bells and supposed that the key was to be found in the belfry? No doubt I am very foolish, but it appears to me to be possible."

Wimsey struck his hand on the table.

"Padre, that's an idea! When Cranton came to Fenchurch St. Paul, he asked for Paul Taylor, because Deacon had told him that Tailor Paul or Batty Thomas knew where the emeralds were. Come on! Have at it. We'll ask Tailor Paul ourselves."

He picked up the paper on which he had already written the cryptogram in eight columns.

"We don't know what method the fellow used, or which bell to follow. But we'll take it that the bell is either Batty Thomas or Tailor Paul. If the method is Grandsire Triples, it can't be Tailor Paul, for the Tenor would be rung behind the whole way and we should find the message running down the last column. And it's not like to be Grandsire Major, because you never ring that method here. Let us try Batty Thomas. What does the 7th bell give us? GHILSTETHCWA. That's not very encouraging. For form's sake we'll try the other bells. No. No. No. Could the man possibly have started off with a bob or single?"

"Surely not."

"Well, you never know. He's not pricking a peal, he's only making a cipher and he might do something unusual on purpose."

His pencil traced the letters again.

"No. I can't make anything of it. Wash out Grandsires. And I think we can probably wash out Stedman's, too—that would keep the significants too close together. Try Kent Treble Bob, and we'll take Tailor Paul first, since the Tenor is the usual observation bell for that method. She starts in the 7th place, H. Then 8th place, E. Back to 7th, S; to 6ths, I; to 4ths, T. 'HESIT.'

Well, it's pronounceable, at any rate. Dodge up into 6ths place, T again. Down to 5ths, E; to 4ths, T; to 3rds, H. 'HESITTETH.' Hullo, Padre! we've got two words, anyhow. 'He sitteth.' Perhaps 'He' is the necklace. We'll carry on with this."

The Rector, his glasses sliding down his long nose with excitement, pored over the paper as the pencil made its rapid way down the letters.

"'He sitteth between'—it's part of a verse from Psalm xcix—there, what did I tell you? 'He sitteth between the Cherubims.' Now, what can that mean? Oh, dear! there is some mistake—the next letter should be a B—'be the earth never so unquiet.'"

"Well, it isn't a B; it's another T. There isn't a B anywhere. Wait a moment. THE is coming—no, THEI—no, as you were. It's THE ISLES. I can't help it, Padre. It couldn't come like that by accident. Just a second, and we'll have it all sorted out and then you can say what you like. . . . Oy! what's happened here at the end? Oh, dash it! I was forgetting. This must be the end of the lead. Yes"—he calculated rapidly—"it is, and we've got to make the 3rds and 4ths. There you are. Message complete; and what it means is more than I can tell you."

The Rector polished his glasses and stared.

"It's verses from three psalms," he said. "Most singular. 'He sitteth between the cherubims'; that's Ps. xcix. 1. Then 'The isles may be glad thereof'; that's Ps. xcvii. 1. Both those psalms begin alike: 'Dominus regnavit,' 'The Lord is King.' And then we get, 'as the rivers in the south,' That's Ps. cxxvi. 5, 'In convertendo,' 'When the Lord turned the captivity of Sion.' This is a case of *obscurum per obscuriora*—the interpretation is even more perplexing than the cipher."

"Yes," said Wimsey. "Perhaps the figures have something to do with it. We have 99. 1. 97. 1. 126. 5. Are they to be taken as one figure 9919711265? or to be left as they are? or re-divided? The permutations are almost endless. Or perhaps they ought to be added. Or converted into letters on some system we haven't discovered yet. It can't be a simple a = 1 substitution. I refuse to believe in a message that runs I I A I G I A B F E. I shall have to wrestle with this quite a lot more. But you have been simply marvellous, Padre. You ought to take to deciphering codes as a profession."

"It was pure accident," said Mr. Venables, simply, "and due entirely to my failing vision. That is a curious thing. It has given me the idea for a sermon about evil being over-ruled for good.

ITHOUGHT	LYCLOUDB	NYTEARSB
TOSEETHE	UTNOBLIN	EFORETHE
FAIRIESI	DEYEOFAM	THINMOON
NTHEFIEL	ORTALWAS	ROSEUPFR
DSBUTISA	PERMITTE	AILANDFA
WONLYTHE	DTOSPYTH	INTASASI
EVILELEP	EMSOTHEN	CKLEOFST
HANTSWIT	CAMEMINS	RAWNOWTH
HTHEIRBL	TRELSHAV	OUGHTHEE
ACKBACKS	INGGOLDT	NCHANTER
WOEHOWTH	RUMPETSH	GNASHHIS
ATSIGHTA	ARPSANDD	TEETHVAI
WEDMETHE	RUMSTHES	NLYYETSH
ELVESDAN	EPLAYEDV	ALLHERET
CEDALLAR	ERYLOUDL	URNASTHE
OUNDANDA	YBESIDEM	SPRINGRE
BOUTWHIL	EBREAKIN	TURNSOHW
EIHEARDV	GTHATSPE	RETCHEDM
OICESCAL	LLSOTHED	ANHELLGA
LINGCLEA	REAMVANI	PESEREBU
RLYAHHOW	SHEDWHER	SNOWLIES
ITRIEDTO	EATITHAN	OPENTHEM
SEETHROW	KEDHEAVE	OUTHSOFD
OFFTHEUG	NISHEDMA	EATHWAIT
		ONTHYEND

But I should never have thought of the possibility that one might make a cipher out of change-ringing. Most ingenious."

"It could have been done still more ingeniously," said Wimsey. "I can think of lots of ways to improve it. Suppose—but I won't waste time with supposing. The point is, what the dickens is one to do with 99. 1. 97. 1. 126. 5.?"

He clutched his head between his hands, and the Rector, after watching him for a few minutes, tiptoed away to bed.

THE NINTH PART

Emily Turns Bunter from Behind

Let the bell that the Treble turns from behind make thirds place, and return behind again.

RULES FOR CHANGE-MAKING
ON FOUR BELLS

"I SHOULD like," panted Emily between her sobs, "to give my week's warning."

"Good gracious, Emily!" cried Mrs. Venables, pausing as she passed through the kitchen with a pail of chicken-feed, "what on earth is the matter with you?"

"I'm sure," said Emily, "I ain't got no fault to find with you and Rector as has always been that kind, but if I'm to be spoken to so by Mr. Bunter, which I'm not his servant and never want to be and ain't no part of my duties, and anyway how was I to know? I'm sure I'd have cut my right hand off rather than disoblige his lordship, but I did ought to have been told and it ain't my fault and so I told Mr. Bunter."

Mrs. Venables turned a little pale. Lord Peter presented no difficulties, but Bunter she found rather alarming. But she was of the bulldog breed, and had been brought up in the knowledge that a servant was a servant, and that to be afraid of a servant (one's own or anybody else's) was the first step to an Avernus of domestic inefficiency. She turned to Bunter, standing white and awful in the background.

"Well, now, Bunter," she said, firmly. "What is all this trouble about?"

"I beg your pardon, madam," said Bunter in a stifled manner. "I fear that I forgot myself. But I have been in his lordship's service now for going on fifteen years (counting my service under him in the War), and such a thing has never yet befallen me. In the sudden shock and the bitter mortification of my mind, I spoke with considerable heat. I beg, madam, that you will overlook it. I should have controlled myself better. I assure you that it will not occur again."

Mrs. Venables put down the chicken-pail.

"But what was it all about?"

Emily gulped, and Bunter pointed a tragic finger at a beer-bottle which stood on the kitchen table.

"That bottle, madam, was entrusted to me yesterday by his lordship. I placed it in a cupboard in my bedroom, with the intention of photographing it this morning, before despatching it to Scotland Yard. Yesterday evening, it seems that this young woman entered the room during my absence, investigated the cupboard and removed the bottle. Not content with removing it, she dusted it."

"If you please, 'm," said Emily, "how was I to know it was wanted? A nasty, dirty old thing. I was only a-dusting the room, 'm, and I see this old bottle on the cupboard shelf, and I says to myself, 'Look at that dusty old bottle, why, however did that get there? It must have got left accidental.' So I takes it down and when Cook see it she says, 'Why, whatever have you got there, Emily? That'll just do,' she says, 'to put the methylated.' So I gives it a dust——"

"And now the finger-prints have all gone," concluded Bunter in a hollow tone, "and what to say to his lordship I do not know."

"Oh, dear! oh, dear!" said Mrs. Venables, helplessly. Then she seized on the one point of domestic economy which seemed to call for inquiry. "How did you come to leave your dusting so late?"

"If you please, 'm, I don't know how it was. I got all behind yesterday, somehow, and I said to myself, 'Better late than never,' and I'm sure if I'd only have known——"

She wept loudly, and Bunter was touched.

"I am sorry I expressed myself with so much acerbity," he said, "and I take blame to myself for not removing the key from the cupboard door. But you will understand my feelings, madam, when I think of his lordship innocently waking to a new day, if I may say so, and not knowing of the blow which is in store for him. It goes to my heart, if you will pardon my mentioning the organ in such a connection. There, madam, is his morning tea, only waiting for my hand to put the boiling water to it, and I feel, madam, as though it were the hand of a murderer which no perfumes of Arabia—supposing such to be suitable to my situation—

could sweeten. He has rung twice," added Bunter, in desperate tones, "and he will know by the delay that something of a calamitous nature has occurred——"

"Bunter!"

"My lord!" cried Bunter, in a voice like prayer.

"What the devil has happened to my tea? What the——? Oh, I beg your pardon, Mrs. Venables. Excuse my language and my bath-robe, won't you? I didn't know you were here."

"Oh, Lord Peter!" exclaimed Mrs. Venables, "such a dreadful thing's happened. Your man is so terribly upset, and this silly girl —she meant well of course and it's all a mistake—but we've dusted all the finger-prints off your bottle!"

"Wah-ha-ha!" sobbed Emily. "Oh-oh! Wah-ha-ha! I did it. I dusted it. I didn't know—ho-ho."

"Bunter," said his lordship, "what is the verse about the struck eagle stretched upon the plain, Never through something clouds to soar again? It expresses my feelings exactly. Take up my tea and throw the bottle in the dust-bin. What's done cannot be undone. In any case the finger-prints were probably of no importance. William Morris once wrote a poem called *The Man Who Never Laughed Again*. If the shout of them that triumph, the song of them that feast, should never again be heard upon my lips, you will know why. My friends will probably be devoutly thankful. Let it be a warning to you never to seek for happiness out of a bottle. Emily, if you cry any more, your young man won't know you on Sunday. Don't worry about the bottle, Mrs. Venables—it was a beastly bottle, anyhow, and I always loathed the sight of it. It is a beautiful morning for early rising. Allow me to carry the chicken-pail. I beg you will not give another thought to the bottle, or Emily either. She's a particularly nice girl, isn't she? What is her surname, by the way?"

"Holliday," said Mrs. Venables. "She's a niece of Russell's, the undertaker, you know, and some sort of relation to Mary Thoday, though of course everybody is, in this village, related to somebody or the other, I mean. It comes of being such a small place, though now that they all have motor-bicycles and the 'buses running twice a week it isn't so bad, and there won't be so many unfortunate creatures like Potty Peake. All the Russells are very nice, superior people."

"Just so," said Lord Peter Wimsey. He did a certain amount of thinking as he spooned out mash into the chicken trough.

. . . .

He spent the early part of the morning in fresh unavailing study of the cryptogram, and as soon as he thought the pubs would be open, went round to the Red Cow for a pint of beer.

"Bitter, my lord?" inquired Mr. Donnington with his hand upon the tap.

Wimsey said No, not today. He would have a bottle of Bass for a change.

Mr. Donnington produced the Bass, observing that his lordship would find it in very nice condition.

"Condition is nine-tenths of the bottle," said Wimsey, "and a lot of it depends upon the bottling. Who are your bottlers?"

"Griggs of Walbeach," said Mr. Donnington. "Very sound people they are, too; I've got no complaints to make. Just you try for yourself—though you can tell by the look of it, if you see what I mean. Clear as a bell—though, of course, you have to be able to trust your cellarman. I had a chap once that never could be taught not to pack his Bass 'ead down in the basket, same as if it was stout. Now stout will stand being stood on its 'ead, though it's not a thing I ever would do myself and I don't recommend it, but Bass *must* be stood right ways up and not shook about if you're to do justice to the beer."

"Very true indeed," said Wimsey. "There's certainly nothing wrong with this. Your health. Won't you take something yourself?"

"Thank you, my lord, I don't mind if I do. Here's luck. Now, that," said Mr. Donnington, raising the glass to the light, "is as nice a glass of Bass as you could wish to see."

Wimsey asked whether he did much with quart bottles.

"Quarts?" said Mr. Donnington. "No. Not with quarts, I don't. But I believe Tom Tebbutt down at the Wheatsheaf does a bit. Griggs bottles for him, too."

"Ah!" said Wimsey.

"Yes. There's one or two prefers quarts. Though, mind you, most of the business about here is draught. But there's a farmer here and there as likes the quarts delivered at their homes. Ah! in the old days they all did their own brewing—there's plenty farms now with the big brewing coppers still standing, and there's a few as still cures their own sides of bacon—Mr. Ashton's one on 'em, he won't have nothing new-fangled. But what with these chain stores and their grocery vans, and the girls all wanting to be off to the pictures in their silk stockings and so many things coming in tins, it's not many places where you can see a bit of real home-cured. And look at the price of pig-feed. What I say is, the farmers did ought to have some protection. I was brought up a Free Trader myself, but times has changed. I don't know if you've ever thought of these things, my lord. They may not come your way. Or—there—I'm forgetting. Maybe you sit in the 'Ouse of Lords, now. Harry Gotobed will have it that that's so, but I said as he was mistook—but there! you'll know better than me about that."

Wimsey explained that he was not qualified to sit in the House of Lords. Mr. Donnington observed with pleasure that in that case the sexton owed him half a crown, and while he made a note of the fact on the back of an envelope, Wimsey escaped and made his way to the Wheatsheaf.

Here, by exercising a certain amount of tact, he obtained a list of those households to which Bass was regularly supplied in quarts. Most of the names were those of farmers in outlying places, but as an afterthought, Mrs. Tebbutt mentioned one which made Wimsey prick up his ears.

"Will Thoday, he had a few while Jim was at home—a dozen or so, it might be. He's a nice chap, is Jim Thoday—makes you laugh by the hour telling his tales of foreign parts. He brought back that there parrot for Mary, though as I says to her, that bird ain't no proper example for the children. How it do go on, to be sure. I'm sure, if you'd heard what it said to Rector the other day! I didn't know where to look. But it's my belief, Rector didn't understand half of it. He's a real gentleman, is Mr. Venables, not like old parson. He was a kind man, too, but different from Rector, and they say he used to swear something surprising in a clergyman. But there, poor man! He had a bit of a weakness, as they say. 'Do as I say, don't do as I do'—that's what he used to say in his sermons. Terrible red in the face he were, and died sudden, of a stroke."

Wimsey tried in vain to steer the conversation back to Jim Thoday. Mrs. Tebbutt was fairly launched into reminiscences of Old Rector, and it was half an hour before he was able to make his way out of the Wheatsheaf. Turning back towards the Rectory, he found himself at Will Thoday's gate. Glancing up the path, he saw Mary, engaged in hanging out washing. He suddenly determined on a frontal attack.

"I hope you'll forgive me, Mrs. Thoday," he said, when he had announced himself and been invited to enter, "if I take your mind back to a rather painful episode. I mean to say, bygones are bygones and all that and one hates digging anything up, what? But when it comes to dead bodies in other people's graves and so on, well, sometimes one gets wondering about them and all that sort of thing, don't you know."

"Yes, indeed, my lord. I'm sure if there's anything I can do to help, I will. But as I told Mr. Blundell, I never knew a thing about it, and I can't imagine how it came there. That was the Saturday night he was asking me about, and I'm sure I've thought and thought, but I couldn't call to mind as I'd seen anything."

"Do you remember a man who called himself Stephen Driver?"

"Yes, my lord. Him that was at Ezra Wilderspin's. I remember seeing him once or twice. They said at the inquest that the body might have been him."

"But it wasn't," said Wimsey.

"Wasn't it, my lord?"

"No. Because we've found this chap Driver and he's still alive and kicking. Had you ever seen Driver before he came here?"

"I don't think so, my lord; no, I can't say as I ever did."

"He didn't remind you of anybody?"

"No, my lord."

She appeared to be answering quite frankly, and he could not see any signs of alarm in voice or expression.

"That's odd," said Wimsey, "because he says that he ran away from St. Paul because he thought you had recognized him."

"Did he? Well, that's a strange thing, my lord."

"Did you ever hear him speak?"

"I don't think I ever did, my lord."

"Suppose he hadn't been wearing a beard, now—would he remind you of anybody?"

Mary shook her head. Like most people, she found the effort of imagination beyond her.

"Well, do you recognize this?"

He took out a photograph of Cranton, taken at the time of the Wilbraham emeralds affair.

"That?" Mrs. Thoday turned pale. "Oh, yes, my lord. I remember him. That was Cranton, that took the necklace and was sent to prison same time as—as my first husband, my lord. I expect you know all about that. That's his wicked face. Oh, dear! it's given me quite a turn, seeing that again."

She sat down on a bench and stared at the photograph.

"This isn't—it couldn't be Driver?"

"That's Driver," said Wimsey. "You had no idea of it?"

"That I never had, my lord. If I'd ever had such a thought, I'd have spoken to him, don't you fear! I'd have got out of him where he put those emeralds to. You see, my lord, that was what went so hard against my poor husband, this man saying as my husband had kept the necklace himself. Poor Jeff, there's no doubt he was tempted—all through my fault, my lord, talking so free—and he did take the jewels, I'm sorry to say. But he didn't have them afterwards. It was this Cranton had them all the time. Don't you think it hasn't been a bitter hard cross to me, my lord, all these years, knowing as I was suspected? The jury believed what I said, and so did the judge, but you'll find some as thinks now that I had a hand in it and knew where the necklace was. But I never did, my lord, never. If I'd been able to find it, I'd have crawled to London on my hands and knees to give it back to Mrs. Wilbraham. I know what poor Sir Henry suffered with the loss of it. The police searched our place, and I searched it myself, over and over——"

"Couldn't you take Deacon's word for it?" asked Wimsey, softly.

She hesitated, and her eyes clouded with pain.

"My lord, I did believe him. And yet, all the same—well! it was such a terrible shock to me that he could have done such a thing as rob a lady in the master's house, I didn't know but what he mightn't perhaps have done the other too. I didn't rightly know what to believe, if you understand me, my lord. But *now* I feel quite sure that my husband was telling the truth. He was led away by this wicked Cranton, there's no doubt of that, but that he was deceiving us all, afterwards, I don't believe. Indeed, my lord, I don't think he was—I'm quite sure of it in my own mind."

"And what do you suppose Cranton came down here for?"

"Doesn't that show, my lord, that it was him as hid them after all? He must have got frightened and hid them away in some place that night, before he got away."

"He says himself that Deacon told him in the dock that the emeralds were here, and he was to ask Tailor Paul and Batty Thomas to find them for him."

Mary shook her head. "I don't understand that, my lord. But if my husband had said such a thing to him then, Cranton wouldn't have kept quiet about it. He'd have told the jury, he was that mad with Jeff."

"Would he? I'm not so sure. Suppose Deacon told Cranton

where to find the emeralds, don't you think Cranton would have waited in the hope of getting hold of them when he came out of prison? And mightn't he have come down here last January to look for them? And then, thinking you'd spotted him, mightn't he have run away in a fright?"

"Well, my lord, I suppose he might. But then, who would that poor dead man be?"

"The police think he may have been an accomplice of Cranton's, who helped him to find the emeralds and was killed for his pains. Do you know whether Deacon made any friends among the other convicts or the warders at Maidstone?"

"I couldn't say, I'm sure, my lord. He was allowed to write now and again, of course, but naturally he wouldn't tell anybody a thing like that, because his letters would be read."

"Naturally. I wondered whether perhaps you'd had a message from him at some time—through a released prisoner, or anything like that?"

"No, my lord, never."

"Have you ever seen this writing?"

He handed her the cryptogram.

"That writing? Why, of course——"

"Shut up, you fool! Shut up, you bloody fool! Come on, Joey! Show a leg there!"

"Good lord!" exclaimed Wimsey, startled. Peering round the door into the inner room, he encountered the bright eye of a grey African parrot fixed knowingly upon him. At sight of a stranger, the bird stopped talking, cocked its head aslant, and began to sidle along its perch.

"Damn your eyes!" said his lordship, pleasantly. "You made me jump."

"Aw!" said the bird, with a long, self-satisfied chuckle.

"Is that the bird your brother-in-law gave you? I've heard about him from Mrs. Tebbutt."

"Yes, my lord, that's him. He's a wonderful talker, but he does swear and that's the truth."

"I've no use for a parrot that doesn't," said Wimsey. "Seems unnatural. Let me see—what were we——? Oh, yes, that bit of writing. You were just saying——"

"I said, of course I'd never seen it before, my lord."

Wimsey could have sworn that she had been going to say just the opposite. She was looking at—no, not at, but through and past him, with the face of someone who sees an incredible catastrophe approaching.

"It's queer-looking stuff, isn't it?" she went on, in a flat voice. "Don't seem to mean anything. What made you think I should know anything about the like of that?"

"We had an idea that it might have been written by some man your late husband knew at Maidstone. Did you ever hear of anyone called Jean Legros?"

"No, my lord. That's a French name, isn't it? I've never seen a Frenchman, except a few of those Beljums that came over here in the War."

"And you never knew anyone called Paul Taylor?"

"No, never."

The parrot laughed heartily.

"Shut up, Joey!"

"Shut up, you fool! Joey, Joey, Joey! Scratch a poll, then. Aw!"

"Oh, well," said Wimsey. "I just wondered."

"Where did that come from?"

"What? Oh, this? It was picked up in the church, and we had an idea it might be Cranton's. But he says it isn't, you know."

"In the *church?*"

As though the word were a cue, the parrot picked it up, and began muttering excitedly:

"Must go to church. Must go to church. The bells. Don't tell Mary. Must go to church. Aw! Joey! Joey! Come on, Joey! Must go to church."

Mrs. Thoday stepped hurriedly into the other room and flung a cloth over the cage, while Joey squawked protestingly.

"He goes on like that," she said. "Gets on my nerves. He picked it up the night Will was so bad. They were ringing the peal, and it worried him, like, that he couldn't be there. Will gets that angry with Joey when he starts mocking him. Shut up, now, Joey, do."

Wimsey held out his hand for the cryptogram, which Mary surrendered—reluctantly, he thought, and as though her thoughts were elsewhere.

"Well, I mustn't bother you any more, Mrs. Thoday. I just wanted to clear up that little point about Cranton. I expect you are right after all, and he just came down here to go snoop about on his own. Well, you aren't likely to be bothered with him again. He's ill, and in any case, he'll have to go back to prison to work out his time. Forgive my bargin' along and botherin' you about what's best forgotten."

But all the way back to the Rectory, he was haunted by Mary Thoday's eyes and by the hoarse muttering voice of the parrot: "The bells! the bells! Must go to the church! Don't tell Mary!"

. . . . . .

Superintendent Blundell clicked his tongue a good deal over all this.

"It's a pity about the bottle," he said. "Don't suppose it would have told us anything, but you never know. Emily Holliday, eh? Of course, she's a cousin of Mary Thoday's. I'd forgotten that. That woman beats me—Mary, I mean. Damned if I know what to make of her, or her husband either. We're in touch with those people at Hull, and they're arranging to get James Thoday shipped back to England as soon as possible. We told them he might be wanted as a witness. Best way to work it—he can't skip his orders; or, if he does, we'll know there's something wrong and go after him. It's a queer business altogether. As regards that cipher, what do you say to sending it along to the Governor of Maidstone? If this fellow Legros or Taylor or whatever he is was ever in there, they may be able to spot the handwriting."

"So they may," said Wimsey, thoughtfully. "Yes, we'll do that. And I'm hoping we'll hear from M. Rozier again soon. The French haven't any of our inhibitions about dealing with witnesses."

"Lucky them, my lord," replied Mr. Blundell, with fervour.

THE TENTH PART

Lord Peter Is Called Wrong

And he set the cherubims within the inner house: and they stretched forth the wings of the cherubims.

1 KINGS VI. 27

And above were costly stones.

1 KINGS VII. 11

"I HOPE," said the Rector on the following Sunday morning, "there is nothing wrong with the Thodays. Neither Will nor Mary was at Early Service. I've never known them both miss before, except when he was ill."

"No more they were," said Mrs. Venables. "Perhaps Will has taken a chill again. These winds are very treacherous. Lord Peter, do have another sausage. How are you getting along with your cipher?"

"Don't rub it in, I'm hopelessly stuck."

"I shouldn't worry," said Mr. Venables. "Even if you have to lie still a whole pull now and again, you'll soon find yourself back in the hunt."

"I wouldn't mind that," said Wimsey. "It's lying behind the whole way that gets on my nerves."

"There's always something that lies behind a mystery," said the Rector, mildly enjoying his little witticism. "A solution of some kind."

"What I say is," observed Mrs. Venables darkly, "there are always wheels within wheels."

"And where there's a wheel, there's usually a rope," added his lordship.

"Unhappily," said the Rector, and there was a melancholy pause.

. . . .

Anxiety about the Thodays was somewhat allayed by their appearance together at Matins, but Wimsey thought he had never seen two people look so ill and unhappy. In wondering about them, he lost all consciousness of what was going on about him, sat down for the Venite, lost the Psalms for the day, embarked on a loud and solitary "For thine is the Kingdom" at the end of the second "Our Father," and only pulled himself together when Mr. Venables came down to preach his sermon. As usual, Mr. Gotobed had failed to sweep the chancel properly, and a hideous crunching of coke proclaimed the Rector's passage to the pulpit. The Invocation was pronounced, and Wimsey sank back with a sigh of relief into the corner of the pew, folded his arms and fixed his gaze firmly on the roof.

"Who hast exalted thine only Son with great triumph into the Heavens. Those words are from the collect for the day. What do they mean to us? What picture do we make of the glory and triumph of Heaven? Last Thursday we prayed that we also might in heart and mind thither ascend and continually dwell, and we hope that after death we shall be admitted—not only in heart and mind but in soul and body—to that blessed state where cherubim and seraphim continually sing their songs of praise. It is a beautiful description that the Bible gives us—the crystal sea and the Lord sitting between the cherubims, and the angels with their harps and crowns of gold, as the old craftsmen imagined them when they built this beautiful roof that we are so proud of—but do we, do you and I really believe———?"

It was hopeless. Wimsey's thoughts were far away again. "He rode upon the cherubim and did fly. He sitteth between the cherubims." He was suddenly reminded of the little architect who had come down to advise about the church roof at Duke's Denver. "You see, your Grace, the rot has got into the timbers; there are holes behind those cherrybims you could put your hand in." *He sitteth between the cherubims.* Why, of course! Fool that he was—climbing up among the bells to look for cherubims when they were here over his head, gazing down at him, their blank golden eyes blind with excess of light. The cherubim? Nave and aisle were thick with cherubim, as autumn leaves in Vallombrosa. Nave and aisle—"the *isles* may be glad thereof"—and then the third text—"as the rivers in the *south.*" Between the cherubims in the south aisle—what could be clearer than that? In his excitement he nearly shot out of his seat. It only remained to discover which particular pair of cherubims was concerned, and that ought not to be very difficult. The emeralds themselves would be gone, of course, but if one could find even the empty hiding-place, that would prove that the cryptogram was connected with the necklace and that all the queer tragedy brooding over Fenchurch St. Paul was in some way connected with the emeralds too. Then, if the handwriting of the cryptogram could be traced back to Maidstone Gaol and to Jean Legros, they would know who Legros was, and with luck they would also link him up with Cranton. After that, if Cranton could escape from the murder charge, he would be a lucky man.

Over the Sunday beef and Yorkshire pudding, Wimsey tackled the Rector.

"How long ago was it, sir, that you took away the galleries from the aisles?"

"Let me see," said Mr. Venables, "about ten years ago, I think. Yes, that is right. Ten years. Hideous, cumbersome things they were. They ran right across the aisle windows, obscuring all the upper tracery and blocking the light, and were attached to the arcading. As a matter of fact, what with those horrible great pews, like bathing machines, sprouting up from the floor, and the heavy galleries, you could scarcely see the shafts of the pillars at all."

"Or anything else," said his wife. "I always used to say it was regular blind man's holiday underneath those galleries."

"If you want to see what it was like," added the Rector, "go and look at Upwell Church near Wisbech. You'll find the same sort of gallery in the north aisle there (though ours was larger and uglier), and they have an angel roof, too, though not as fine as ours, because their angels are only attached to the roof itself, instead of being on the hammer-beams. In fact, you can't see the angels in their north aisle at all, unless you climb up into the gallery."

"I suppose there was the usual amount of opposition when you took the galleries down?"

"A certain amount, of course. There are always some people who oppose any change. But it did seem absurd, when the church was far too large for the parish in any case, to have all that unnecessary seating. There was plenty of room for the school-children in the aisle."

"Did anybody sit in the gallery besides the school-children?"

"Oh, yes. The Red House servants and a few of the oldest inhabitants, who had been there from time immemorial. Indeed, we really had to wait for one poor old soul to die before we embarked on the improvements. Poor old Mrs. Wilderspin, Ezra's grandmother. She was ninety-seven and came regularly to church every Sunday, and it would have broken her heart to have turned her out."

"Which side did the Red House servants sit?"

"At the west end of the south aisle. I never liked that, because one couldn't see what they were doing, and sometimes their behaviour wasn't as reverent as it might have been. I do not think the House of God is a proper place for flirtation, and there was so much nudging and giggling that it really was very unseemly."

"If that woman Gates had done her duty and sat with the servants it would have been all right," said Mrs. Venables, "but she was far too much of a lady. She always has to have her own seat, just inside the south door, for fear she should feel faint and have to go out."

"Mrs. Gates is not a robust woman, my dear."

"Rubbish!" said Mrs. Venables. "She eats too much and gets indigestion, that's all."

"Perhaps you are right, my dear."

"I can't stand the woman," said Mrs. Venables. "The Thorpes ought to sell that place, but apparently they can't under Sir Henry's will. I don't see how it can be kept up, and the money would be more use to Hilary Thorpe than that great tumble-down house. Poor little Hilary! If it hadn't been for that horrible old Wilbraham creature and her necklace—I suppose there's no hope of recovering the necklace, Lord Peter, after all this time?"

"I'm afraid we're a day after the fair. Though I'm pretty sure it was in this parish up to last January."

"In the parish? Where?"

"I think it was in the church," said Wimsey. "That was a very powerful sermon of yours this morning, Padre. Very inspiring. It inspired me to guess the riddle of the cryptogram."

"No!" exclaimed the Rector. "How did it do that, I wonder?"

Wimsey explained.

"Good gracious! How very remarkable! We must investigate the place at once."

"Not at once, Theodore."

"Well, no, my dear, I didn't mean today. I'm afraid it wouldn't do to take ladders into the church on Sunday. We are still rather touchy here about the Fourth Commandment. Besides, I have the Children's Service this afternoon and three baptisms, and

Mrs. Edwards is coming to be churched. But, Lord Peter, how do you suppose the emeralds got up in the roof?"

"Why, I was just thinking about that. Isn't it true that this fellow Deacon was arrested after church on Sunday morning? I expect he got some idea of what was going to happen to him, and concealed his loot somehow during the service."

"Of course, he was sitting up there that morning. Now I understand why you asked so many questions about the gallery. What a sad villain the man must have been! He really did—what is that word they use when one malefactor deceives another?"

"Double-cross?" suggested Wimsey.

"Ah! that is the very expression I was looking for. He did double-cross his accomplice. Poor man! I mean the accomplice. Ten years in prison for a theft of which he never enjoyed the fruits. One cannot help feeling some sympathy for him. But in that case, Lord Peter, who constructed the cryptogram?"

"I think it must have been Deacon, because of the bell-ringing."

"Ah, yes. And then he gave it to this other man, Legros. Why did he do that?"

"Probably as an inducement to Legros to help him to escape from Maidstone."

"And Legros waited all these years before making use of it?"

"Legros obviously had very good reasons for keeping out of England. Eventually he must have passed the cryptogram on to somebody here—Cranton, perhaps. Possibly he couldn't decipher it himself, and in any case he wanted Cranton's help to get back from France."

"I see. Then they found the emeralds and Cranton killed Legros. How sad it makes me to think of all this violence for the sake of a few stones!"

"It makes me still sadder to think of poor Hilary Thorpe and her father," said Mrs. Venables. "You mean to say that while they needed that money so badly, the emeralds were hidden in the church all the time, within a few feet of them?"

"I'm afraid so."

"And where are they now? Has this man Cranton got them? Why hasn't somebody found them by now? I can't think what the police are doing."

. . . .

Sunday seemed an unusually long day. On the Monday morning, a great many things happened at once.

The first thing was the arrival of Superintendent Blundell, in great excitement.

"We've got that letter from Maidstone," he announced, "and whose do you suppose the writing is?"

"I've been thinking it over," said Wimsey. "I think it must have been Deacon's."

"There!" said Mr. Blundell, disappointed. "Well, you're quite right, my lord; it is."

"It must be the original cipher," said Wimsey. "When we found out that it had to do with bell-ringing, I realized that Deacon must be the author. To have two bell-ringing convicts in Maidstone Gaol at once seemed rather too much of a coincidence. And then, when I showed the paper to Mrs. Thoday, I felt sure that she recognized the writing. It might have meant that Legros had written to her, but it was still more likely that she knew it to be her husband's."

"Well, then, how did it come to be written on that foreign paper?"

"Foreign paper is much of a muchness," said Wimsey. "Did Lady Thorpe ever have a foreign maid? Old Lady Thorpe, I mean."

"Sir Charles had a French cook," said the Superintendent.

"At the time of the theft?"

"Yes. She left them when the War broke out, I remember. She wanted to get back to her family, and they scraped her across on one of the last boats."

"Then that's clear enough. Deacon invented his cryptogram before he actually hid the emeralds. He couldn't have taken it into prison with him. He must have handed it to somebody——"

"Mary," said the Superintendent, with a grim smile.

"Perhaps. And she must have sent it to Legros. It's all rather obscure."

"Not so obscure as that, my lord." Mr. Blundell's face grew still grimmer. "I thought it was a bit reckless, if you'll excuse me, showing that paper to Mary Thoday. She's skipped."

"Skipped?"

"First train to town this morning. And Will Thoday with her. A precious pair."

"Good God!"

"You may say so, my lord. Oh, we'll have them, don't you fear. Gone off, that's what they've done, and the emeralds with them."

"I admit," said Wimsey, "I didn't expect that."

"Didn't you?" said Mr. Blundell. "Well, I didn't either, or I'd have kept a sharper eye on them. And by the way, we know now who that Legros fellow was."

"You're a perfect budget of news today, Super."

"Ah! well—we've had a letter from your friend M. Rozier. He had that woman's house searched, and what do you think they found? Legros' identification disc—no less. Any more guesses coming, my lord?"

"I might make a guess, but I won't. I'll buy it. What was the name?"

"Name of Arthur Cobbleigh."

"And who's Arthur Cobbleigh when he's at home?"

"You hadn't guessed that, then?"

"No—my guess was quite different. Go on, Super. Spill the beans."

"Well, now. Arthur Cobbleigh—seems he was just a bloke. But can you guess where he came from?"

"I've given up guessing."

"He came from a little place near Dartford—only about half a mile from the wood where Deacon's body was found."

"Oho! now we're coming to it."

"I got on the 'phone straight away as soon as this letter came. Cobbleigh was a chap aged somewhere about twenty-five in 1914. Not a good record. Labourer. Been in trouble once or twice with the police for petty thieving and assault. Joined up in the first year of the War and considered rather a good riddance. Last seen on the last day of his leave in 1918, and that day was just two days after Deacon's escape from prison. Left his home to rejoin his unit. Never seen again. Last news of him, 'Missing believed killed' in the retreat over the Marne. Officially, that is. Last actual news of him—over there!"

The Superintendent jerked his thumb in the general direction of the churchyard.

Wimsey groaned.

"It makes no sense, Super, it makes no sense! If this man Cobbleigh joins up in the first year of the War, how on earth could he have been elaborately in league with Deacon, who went to Maidstone in 1914? There was no time. Damn it! You don't get a man out of quod in a few spare hours spent on leave. If Cobbleigh had been a warder—if he'd been a fellow-convict—if he'd been anything to do with the prison, I could understand it. Had he a relation in the gaol or anything of that sort? There must have been something more to it than that."

"Must there? Look here, my lord, how's this? I've been working this thing out coming over, and this is what I make out of it. Deacon bust away from a working-party, didn't he? He was found still wearing his prison dress, wasn't he? Doesn't that show his escape wasn't planned out elaborately beforehand? They'd have found him fast enough, if he hadn't gone and pitched down that dene-hole, wouldn't they? Now, you listen to this, and see if it don't hold water. I can see it plain as a pike-staff. Here's this Cobbleigh—a hard nut, by all accounts. He's walking through the wood on the way from his mother's cottage, to take the train at Dartford for wherever he might be going to join up with the troops going back to France. Somewhere on that moor he finds a chap lurking about. He collars him, and finds he's pinched the escaped convict that everybody's looking for. The convict says, 'Let me go, and I'll make you a rich man,' see? Cobbleigh's got no objection to that. He says, 'Lead me to it. What is it?' The convict says, 'The Wilbraham emeralds, that's what it is.' Cobbleigh says, 'Coo! tell us some more about that. How'm I to know you ain't kidding me? You tell us where they are and we'll see about it.' Deacon says, 'No fear—catch me telling you, without you helps me first.' Cobbleigh says, 'You can't help yourself,' he says, 'I only got to give you up and then where'll you be?' Deacon says, 'You won't get much out o' that. You stick by me and I'll put hundreds of thousands of pounds in your hands.' They go on talking, and Deacon, like a fool, lets out that he's made a note of the hiding-place and has it on him. 'Oh, have you?' says Cobbleigh, 'then you damn well take that.' And lams him over the head. Then he goes over him and finds the paper, which he's upset to find he can't make head or tail of. Then he has another look at Deacon and sees he's done him in good and proper. 'Oh, hell!' says he, 'that's torn it. I better shove him out of the way and clear off.' So he pops him down the hole and makes tracks for France. How's that, so far?"

"Fine, full-blooded stuff," said Wimsey. "But why should Deacon be carrying a note of the hiding-place about with him? And how did it come to be written on foreign paper?"

"I don't know. Well, say it was like you said before. Say he'd given the paper to his wife. He spills his wife's address, like a fool, and then it all happens the way I said. Cobbleigh goes back to France, deserts, and gets taken care of by Suzanne. He keeps quiet about who he is, because he don't know whether Deacon's body's been found or not and he's afraid of being had up for murder if he goes home. Meanwhile, he's stuck to the paper—no, that's wrong. He writes to Mrs. Deacon and gets the paper out of her."

"Why should she give it up?"

"That's a puzzler. Oh, I know! I've got it this time. He tells her he's got the key to it. That's right. Deacon told him, 'My wife's got the cipher, but she's a babbling fool and I ain't trusted her with the key. I'll give you the key and that'll show you I know what I'm talking about.' Then Cobbleigh kills him, and when he thinks it's safe he writes over to Mary and she sends him the paper."

"The original paper?"

"Why, yes."

"You'd think she'd keep that and send him a copy."

"No. She sends the original, so that he can see it's in Deacon's writing."

"But he wouldn't necessarily know Deacon's writing."

"How's she to know that? Cobbleigh works out the cipher and they help him to get across."

"But we've been into all that and decided the Thodays couldn't do it."

"All right, then. The Thodays bring Cranton into it. Cobbleigh comes over, anyhow, under the name of Paul Taylor, and he comes along to Fenchurch and they get the emeralds. Then Thoday kills him, and *he* takes the emeralds. Meanwhile, along comes Cranton to see what's happening and finds they've been ahead of him. He clears off and the Thodays go about looking innocent till they see we're getting a bit close on their trail. Then *they* clear."

"Who did the killing, then?"

"Any one of them, I should say."

"And who did the burying?"

"Not Will, anyhow."

"And how was it done? And why did they want to tie Cobbleigh up? Why not kill him straight off and with a bang on the head? Why did Thoday take £200 out of the bank and put it back again? When did it all happen? Who was the man Potty Peake saw in the church on the night of the 30th? And, above all, why was the cipher found in the belfry, of all places?"

"I can't answer everything at once, can I? That's the way it was done between 'em, you can take it from me. And now I'm going to have Cranton charged, and get hold of those precious Thodays, and if I don't put my hand on the emeralds among them, I'll eat my hat."

"Oh!" said Wimsey, "that reminds me. Before you came, we were just going to look at the place where Deacon hid those jolly old emeralds. The Rector solved the cipher——"

"Him?"

"He. So, just for fun, and by way of shutting the stable door after the steed was stolen, we're going to climb up aloft and have a hunt among the cherubims. In fact, the Rector is down at the church, champing his bit at this very moment. Shall we go?"

"Sure—though I haven't a lot of time to waste."

"I don't suppose it will take long."

The Rector had procured the sexton's ladder and was already up in the south aisle roof, covering himself with cobwebs as he poked about vaguely among the ancient oak.

"The servants sat just about here," he said, as Wimsey came in with the Superintendent. "But now I come to think of it, we had the painters up here last year, and they ought to have found anything there was to be found."

"Perhaps they did," said Wimsey; and Mr. Blundell uttered a low moan.

"Oh, I hope not. I really think not. They are most honest men." Mr. Venables came down from the ladder. "Perhaps you had better try. I am not clever about these things."

"Beautiful old work this is," said his lordship. "All pegged together. There's a lot of this old rafter work down at Duke's Denver, and when I was a kid I made rather a pretty cache for myself in a corner of the attic. Used to keep tiddley-winks counters in it and pretend it was a pirate's hoard. Only it was a dickens of a job getting them out again. I say! Blundell! do you remember that wire hook you found in the corpse's pocket?"

"Yes, my lord. We never made out what that was for."

"I ought to have known," said Wimsey. "I made a thing very like it for the pirate's hoard." His long fingers were working over the beams, gently pulling at the thick wooden pegs which held them together. "He must have been able to reach it from where he sat. Aha! what did I tell you? This is the one. Wriggle her gently and out she comes. Look!"

He wrenched at one of the pegs, and it came out in his hand. Originally, it had passed right through the beam and must have been over a foot in length, tapering from the size of a penny-piece at one end to something over half-an-inch at the other. But at some time it had been sawn off about three inches from the thick end.

"There you are," said Wimsey. "An old schoolboy cache originally, I expect. Some kid got pushing it from the other end and found it was loose. Probably shoved it clean out. At least, that's what I did, up in the attic. Then he took it home and sawed six inches or so out of the middle of it. Next time he comes to church he brings a short rod with him. He pushes the thin end back again into place with the rod, so that the hole doesn't show from the other side. Then he drops in his marbles or whatever he wanted to hide, and plugs up the big end again with this. And there he is, with a nice little six-inch hidey-hole where nobody would ever dream of looking for it. Or so he thinks. Then—perhaps years afterwards—along comes friend Deacon. He's sitting up here one day, possibly a little bored with the sermon (sorry, Padre!). He starts fidgeting with the peg, and out it comes—only three inches of it. Hullo! says he, here's a game! Handy place if you wanted to pop any little thing away in a hurry. Later on, when he does want to pop his little shiners away in a hurry, he thinks of it again. Easy enough. Sits here all quiet and pious, listening to the First Lesson. Puts his hand down at his side, slips out the plug, slides the emeralds out of his pocket, slips them into the hole, pops back the plug. All over before his reverence says 'Here endeth.' Out into the sunshine and slap into the arms of our friend the Super here and his merry men. 'Where are the emeralds?' they say. 'You can search me,' says he. And they do, and they've been searching ever since."

"Amazing!" said the Rector. Mr. Blundell uttered a regrettable expression, remembered his surroundings and coughed loudly.

"So now we see what the hook was for," said Wimsey. "When Legros, or Cobbleigh, whichever you like to call him, came for the loot——"

"Stop a minute," objected the Superintendent. "That cipher didn't mention anything about a hole, did it? It only mentioned cherubims. How did he know he needed a hook to get necklaces out of cherubims?"

"Perhaps he'd had a look at the place first. But of course, we know he did. That must have been what he was doing when Potty Peake saw him and Thoday in the church. He spotted the place then, and came back later. Though why he should have waited five days I couldn't tell you. Possibly something went wrong. Anyway, back he came, armed with his hook, and hitched the necklace out. Then, just as he was coming down the ladder, the accomplice took him from behind, tied him up, and—and then—and then did away with him by some means we can't account for."

The Superintendent scratched his head.

"You'd think he might have waited for a better place to do it in, wouldn't you, my lord? Putting him out here in the church, and all that bother of burying him and what not. Why didn't he go while the going was good, and shove Cobbleigh into the dyke or something on the way home?"

"Heaven knows," said Wimsey. "Anyhow, there's your hiding-place and there's the explanation of your hook." He thrust the end of his fountain pen into the hole. "It's quite a deep—no, by jove, it's not! it's only a shallow hole after all, not much longer than the peg. We can't, surely, have made a mistake. Where's my torch? Dash it! (Sorry, Padre.) Is that wood? or is it——? Here, Blundell, find me a mallet and a short, stout rod or stick of some kind—not too thick. We'll have this hole clear."

"Run across to the Rectory and ask Hinkins," suggested Mr. Venables, helpfully.

In a few minutes' time, Mr. Blundell returned, panting, with a short iron bar and a heavy wheel-spanner. Wimsey had shifted the ladder and was examining the narrow end of the oaken peg on the east side of the beam. He set one end of the bar firmly against the peg and smote lustily with the spanner. An ecclesiastical bat, startled from its resting-place by the jar, swooped out with a shriek, the tapered end of the peg shot smartly through the hole and out at the other side, and something else shot out with it—something that detached itself in falling from its wrapping of brown paper and cascaded in a flash of green and gold to the Rector's feet.

"Bless my heart!" cried Mr. Venables.

"The emeralds!" yelled Mr. Blundell. "The emeralds, by God! And Deacon's fifty pounds with them."

"And we're wrong, Blundell," said Lord Peter. "We've been wrong from start to finish. Nobody found them. Nobody killed anybody for them. Nobody deciphered the cryptogram. We're wrong, wrong, out of the hunt and wrong!"

"But we've got the emeralds," said the Superintendent.

3

A SHORT TOUCH OF

STEDMAN'S TRIPLES

FIVE PARTS

840

BY THE PART ENDS

5 6 1 2 3 4
3 4 1 5 6 2
6 2 1 3 4 5
4 5 1 6 2 3
2 3 1 4 5 6

TREBLE THE OBSERVATION.

Call her the last whole turn, out quick, in slow, the second half turn and out slow.

Four times repeated.

TROYTE

THE FIRST PART

The Quick Work

The work of each bell is divided in three parts, viz. the quick work, dodging, and slow work.

TROYTE ON CHANGE-RINGING

LORD PETER WIMSEY passed a restless day and night and was very silent the next day at breakfast.

At the earliest possible moment he got his car and went over to Leamholt.

"Superintendent," he said, "I think I have been the most unmitigated and unconscionable ass that ever brayed in a sleuth-hound's skin. Now, however, I have solved the entire problem, with one trivial exception. Probably you have done so too."

"I'll buy it," said Mr. Blundell. "I'm like you, my lord. I'm doing no more guessing. What's the bit you haven't solved, by the way?"

"Well, the murder," said his lordship, with an embarrassed cough. "I can't quite make out who did that, or how. But that, as I say, is a trifle. I know who the dead man was, why he was tied up, where he died, who sent the cryptogram to whom, why Will Thoday drew £200 out of the bank and put it back again, where the Thodays have gone and why and when they will return, why Jim Thoday missed his train, why Cranton came here, what he did and why he is lying about it and how the beer bottle got into the belfry."

"Anything else?" asked Mr. Blundell.

"Oh, yes. Why Jean Legros was silent about his past, what Arthur Cobbleigh did in the wood at Dartford, what the parrot was talking about and why the Thodays were not at Early Service on Sunday, what Tailor Paul had to do with it and why the face of the corpse was beaten in."

"Excellent," said Mr. Blundell. "Quite a walking library, aren't you, my lord? Couldn't you go just a step further and tell us who we're to put the handcuffs on?"

"I'm sorry. I can't do that. Dash it all, can't I leave one little tit-bit for a friend?"

"Well," said Mr. Blundell, "I don't know that I ought to complain. Let's have the rest of it and perhaps we'll be able to do the last bit on our own."

Lord Peter was silent for a moment.

"Look here, Super," he said at last. "This is going to be a dashed painful sort of story. I think I'd like to test it a bit before I come out with it. Will you do something yourself, first? You've got to do it in any case, but I'd rather not say anything till it is done. After that, I'll say anything you like."

"Well?"

"Will you get hold of a photograph of Arthur Cobbleigh and send it over to France for Suzanne Legros to identify?"

"That's got to be done, naturally. Matter of routine."

"If she identifies it, well and good. But if she's stubborn and refuses, will you give her this note, just as it is, and watch her when she opens it?"

"Well, I don't know about doing that personally, my lord, but I'll see that this Monsieur Rozier does it."

"That will do. And will you also show her the cryptogram?"

"Yes, why not? Anything else?"

"Yes," said Wimsey, more slowly. "The Thodays. I'm a little uncomfortable about the Thodays. You're trailing them, I suppose?"

"What do you think?"

"Exactly. Well, when you've put your hands on them, will you let me know before you do anything drastic? I'd rather like to be there when you question them."

"I've no objection to that, my lord. And this time they'll have to come across with some sort of story, judge's rules or no judge's rules, even if it breaks me."

"You won't have any difficulty about that," said Wimsey. "Provided, that is, you catch them within a fortnight. After that, it will be more difficult."

"Why within a fortnight?"

"Oh, come!" expostulated his lordship. "Isn't it obvious? I show Mrs. Thoday the cipher. On Sunday morning neither she nor her husband attends Holy Communion. On Monday they depart to London by the first train. My dear Watson, it's staring you in the face. The only real danger is——"

"Well?"

"The Archbishop of Canterbury. A haughty prelate, Blundell. An arbitrary prince. But I don't suppose they'll think about him, somehow. I think you may risk him."

"Oh, indeed! And how about Mr. Mussolini and the Emperor of Japan?"

"Negligible. Negligible," replied his lordship, with a wave of the hand. "Likewise the Bishop of Rome. But get on to it, Blundell, get on to it."

"I mean to," said Mr. Blundell, with emphasis. "They'll not get out of the country, that's a certainty."

"So it is, so it is. Of course, they'll be back here by tomorrow fortnight, but that will be too late. How soon do you expect Jim Thoday back? End of the month? Be sure he doesn't give you the slip. I've an idea he may try to."

"You think he's our man?"

"I don't know, I tell you. I don't want him to be. I rather hope it's Cranton."

"Poor old Cranton," said the Superintendent, perversely, "I rather hope it isn't. I don't like to see a perfectly good jewel-thief stepping out of his regular line, so to speak. It's disconcerting, that's what it is. Besides, the man's ill. However, we shall see about that. I'll get on to this Cobbleigh business and settle it."

"Right!" said Wimsey. "And I think, after all, I'll ring up the Archbishop. You never know."

"Dotty!" said Mr. Blundell to himself. "Or pulling my leg. One or the other."

. . . .

Lord Peter Wimsey communicated with the Archbishop, and appeared to be satisfied with the result. He also wrote to Hilary Thorpe, giving her an account of the finding of the emeralds. "So you see," he said, "your Sherlocking was very successful. How pleased Uncle Edward will be." Hilary's reply informed him that old Mrs. Wilbraham had taken the necklace and restored the money paid in compensation—all without comment or apology. Lord Peter haunted the Rectory like an unhappy ghost. The Superintendent had gone to town in pursuit of the Thodays. On Thursday things began to happen again.

Telegram from Commissaire Rozier to Superintendent Blundell:
Suzanne Legros no knowledge Cobbleigh identifies photograph in sealed envelope as her husband identification supported by mayor here do you desire further action.

Telegram from Superintendent Blundell to Lord Peter Wimsey:
Suzanne Legros rejects Cobbleigh identifies sealed photograph who is it unable trace Thodays in London.

Telegram from Superintendent Blundell to Commissaire Rozier:
Please return papers immediately detain Legros pending further information.

Telegram from Lord Peter Wimsey to Superintendent Blundell:
Surely you know by this time try all churches registrars.

Telegram from Superintendent Blundell to Lord Peter Wimsey:
Vicar St. Andrews Bloomsbury says asked perform marriage by licence William Thoday Mary Deacon both of that parish was it Deacon.

Telegram from Lord Peter Wimsey to Superintendent Blundell:
Yes of course you juggins charge Cranton at once.

Telegram from Superintendent Blundell to Lord Peter Wimsey:
Agree juggins but why charge Cranton Thodays found and detained for inquiry.

Telegram from Lord Peter Wimsey to Superintendent Blundell:
Charge Cranton first joining you in town.

After dispatching this wire, Lord Peter summoned Bunter to pack up his belongings and asked for a private interview with Mr. Venables, from which both men emerged looking distressed and uneasy.

"So I think I'd better go," said Wimsey. "I rather wish I hadn't come buttin' into this. Some things may be better left alone, don't you think? My sympathies are all in the wrong place and I don't like it. I know all about not doing evil that good may come. It's doin' good that evil may come that is so embarrassin'."

"My dear boy," said the Rector, "it does not do for us to take too much thought for the morrow. It is better to follow the truth and leave the result in the hand of God. He can foresee where we cannot, because He knows all the facts."

"And never has to argue ahead of His data, as Sherlock Holmes would say? Well, Padre, I dare say you're right. Probably I'm tryin' to be too clever. That's me every time. I'm sorry to have made so much unpleasantness, anyhow. And I really would rather go away now. I've got that silly modern squeamishness that doesn't like watchin' people suffer. Thanks awfully for everything. Good-bye."

. . . .

Before leaving Fenchurch St. Paul, he went and stood in the churchyard. The grave of the unknown victim still stood raw and black amid the grass, but the grave of Sir Henry and Lady Thorpe had been roofed in with green turves. Not far away there was an ancient box tomb; Hezekiah Lavender was seated on the slab, carefully cleaning the letters of the inscription. Wimsey went over and shook hands with the old man.

"Makin' old Samuel fine and clean for the summer," said Hezekiah. "Ah! Beaten old Samuel by ten good year, I have. I says to Rector, 'Lay me aside old Samuel,' I says, 'for everybody to see as I beaten him.' An' I got Rector's promise. Ah! so I have. But they don't write no sech beautiful poetry these here times."

He laid a gouty finger on the inscription, which ran:

Here lies the Body of SAMUEL SNELL
That for fifty Years pulled the Tenor Bell.
Through Changes of this Mortal Race
He Laid his Blows and Kept his Place
Till Death that Changes all did Come
To Hunt him Down and Call him Home.
His Wheel is broke his Rope is Slackt
His Clapper Mute his Metal Crackt,
Yet when the great Call summons him from Ground
He shall be Raised up Tuneable and Sound.

. MDCXCVIII .
Aged 76 years

"Ringing Tailor Paul seems to be a healthy occupation," said Wimsey. "His servants live to a ripe old age, what?"

"Ah!" said Hezekiah. "So they du, young man, so they du, if so be they're faithful tu 'un an' don't go a-angerin' 'un. They bells du know well who's a-haulin' of 'un. Wunnerful understandin' they is. They can't abide a wicked man. They lays in wait to overthrow 'un. But old Tailor Paul can't say I ain't done well by her an' she allus done well by me. Make righteousness your course bell, my lord, an' keep a-follerin' on her an' she'll see you through your changes till Death calls you to stand. Yew ain't no call to be afeard o' the bells if so be as yew follows righteousness."

"Oh, quite," said Wimsey, a little embarrassed.

He left Hezekiah and went into the church, stepping softly as though he feared to rouse up something from its sleep. Abbot Thomas was quiet in his tomb; the cherubim, open-eyed and open-mouthed, were absorbed in their everlasting contemplation; far over him he felt the patient watchfulness of the bells.

THE SECOND PART

Nobby Goes In Slow and Comes Out Quick

It is a frightful plight. Two angels buried him . . . in Vallombrosa by night; I saw it, standing among the lotus and hemlock.

J. SHERIDAN LEFANU: WYLDER'S HAND

MR. CRANTON was in an infirmary as the guest of His Majesty the King, and looked better than when they had last seen him. He showed no surprise at being charged with the murder of Geoffrey Deacon, twelve years or so after that gentleman's reputed decease.

"Right!" said Mr. Cranton. "I rather expected you'd get on to it, but I kept on hoping you mightn't. I didn't do it, and I want to make a statement. Do sit down. These quarters aren't what I could wish for a gentleman, but they seem to be the best the Old Country can offer. I'm told they do it much prettier in Sing Sing. England, with all thy faults I love thee still. Where do you want me to begin?"

"Begin at the beginning," suggested Wimsey, "go on till you get to the end and then stop. May he have a fag, Charles?"

"Well, my lord and—no," said Mr. Cranton. "I won't say gentlemen. Seems to go against the grain, somehow. Officers, if you like, but not gentlemen. Well, my lord and officers, I don't need to tell you that I'm a deeply injured man. I said I never had those shiners, didn't I? And you see I was right. What you want to know is, how did I first hear that Deacon was still on deck? Well, he wrote me a letter, that's how. Somewhere about last July, that would be. Sent it to the old crib, and it was forwarded on—never you mind who by."

"Gammy Pluck," observed Mr. Parker, distantly.

"I name no names," said Mr. Cranton. "Honour among—gentlemen. I burnt that letter, *being* an honourable gentleman, but it was some story, and I don't know that I can do justice to it. Seems that when Deacon made his get-away, after an unfortunate encounter with a warder, he had to sneak about Kent in a damned uncomfortable sort of way for a day or two. He said the stupidity of the police was almost incredible. Walked right over him twice, he said. One time they trod on him. Said he'd never realized so vividly before why a policeman was called a flattie. Nearly broke his fingers standing on them. Now I," added Mr. Cranton, "have rather small feet. Small and well-shod. You can always tell a gentleman by his feet."

"Go on, Nobby," said Mr. Parker.

"Anyhow, the third night he was out there lying doggo in a wood somewhere, he heard a chap coming along that wasn't a flattie. Rolling drunk, Deacon said he was. So Deacon pops out from behind a tree and pastes the fellow one. He said he didn't mean to do him in, only put him out, but he must have struck a bit harder than what he meant. Mind you, that's only what he said, but Deacon always was a low kind of fellow and he'd laid out one man already and you can't hang a chap twice. Anyway, he found he'd been and gone and done it, and that was that.

"What he wanted, of course, was duds, and when he came to examine the takings, he found he'd bagged a Tommy in uniform with all his kit. Well, that wasn't very surprising, come to think of it. There were a lot of those about in 1918, but it sort of took Deacon aback. Of course, he knew there was a war on—they'd been told all about that—but it hadn't, as you might say, come home to him. This Tommy had some papers and stuff on him and a torch, and from what Deacon could make out, looking into the thing rather hurriedly in a retired spot, he was just coming off his leaf and due to get back to the Front. Well, Deacon thought, any hole's better than Maidstone Gaol, so here goes. So he changes clothes with the Tommy down to his skin, collars his papers and what not, and tips the body down the hole. Deacon was a Kentish man himself, you see, and knew the place. Of course, he didn't know the first thing about soldiering—however, needs must and all that. He thought his best way was to get up to Town and maybe he'd find some old pal up there to look after him. So he tramped off—and eventually he got a lift on a lorry or something to a railway station. He did mention the name, but I've forgotten it. He picked some town he'd never been in—a small place.

Anyway, he found a train going to London and he piled into it. That was all right; but somewhere on the way, in got a whole bunch of soldiers, pretty lit-up and cheery, and from the way they talked, Deacon began to find out what he was up against. It came over him, you see, that here he was, all dressed up as a perfectly good Tommy, and not knowing the first thing about the War, or drill or anything, and he knew if he opened his mouth he'd put his foot in it."

"Of course," said Wimsey. "It'd be like dressing up as a Freemason. You couldn't hope to get away with it."

"That's it. Deacon said it was like being among people talking a foreign language. Worse; because Deacon did know a bit about foreign languages. He was an educated sort of bloke. But this Army stuff was beyond him. So all he could do was to pretend to be asleep. He said he just rolled up in his corner and snored, and if anybody spoke to him he swore at them. It worked quite well, he said. There was one very persistent bloke, though, with a bottle of Scotch. He kept on shoving drinks at Deacon and he took a few, and then some more, and by the time he got to London he was pretty genuinely sozzled. You see, he'd had nothing to eat, to speak of, for a coupla days, except some bread he'd managed to scrounge from a cottage."

The policeman who was taking all this down in shorthand scratched stolidly on over the paper. Mr. Cranton took a drink of water and resumed.

"Deacon said he wasn't very clear what happened to him after that. He wanted to get out of the station and go off somewhere, but he found it wasn't so easy. The darkened streets confused him, and the persistent fellow with the bottle of Scotch seemed to have taken a fancy to him. This bloke talked all the time, which was lucky for Deacon. He said he remembered having some more drinks and something about a canteen, and tripping over something and a lot of chaps laughing at him. And after that he must really have fallen asleep. The next thing he knew, he was in a train again, with Tommies all round him, and from what he could make out, they were bound for the Front."

"That's a very remarkable story," said Mr. Parker.

"It's clear enough," said Wimsey. "Some kindly soul must have examined his papers, found he was due back and shoved him on to the nearest transport, bound for Dover, I suppose."

"That's right," said Mr. Cranton. "Caught in the machine, as you might say. Well, all he could do was to lie doggo again. There were plenty of others who seemed to be dog-tired and fairly well canned and he wasn't in any way remarkable. He watched what the others did, and produced his papers at the right time and all that. Fortunately, nobody else seemed to belong to his particular unit. So he got across. Mind you," added Mr. Cranton, "I can't tell you all the details. I wasn't in the War myself, being otherwise engaged. You must fill up the blanks for yourself. He said he was damned seasick on the way over, and after that he slept in a sort of cattle-wagon and finally they bundled him out at last in the dark at some ghastly place or other. After a bit he heard somebody asking if there was anyone belonging to his unit. He knew enough to say 'Yes, sir' and stand forward—and then he found himself foot-slogging over a filthy road full of holes with a small party of men and an officer. God! he said it went on for hours and he thought they must have done about a hundred miles, but I daresay that was an exaggeration. And he said there was a noise like merry hell going on ahead, and the ground began to shake, and he suddenly grasped what he was in for."

"This is an epic," said Wimsey.

"I can't do justice to it," said Mr. Cranton, "because Deacon never knew what he was doing and I don't know enough to make a guess. But I gather he walked straight into a big strafe. Hell let loose, he said, and I shouldn't wonder if he began to think kindly of Maidstone Gaol and even of the condemned cell. Apparently he never got to the trenches, because they were being shelled out of them and he got mixed up in the retreat. He lost his party and something hit him on the head and laid him out. Next thing he knew he was lying in a shell-hole along with somebody who'd been dead some time. I don't know. I couldn't follow it all. But after a bit he crawled out. Everything was quiet and it was coming on dark, so he must have lost a whole day somehow. He'd lost his sense of direction, too, he said. He wandered about, and fell in and out of mud and holes and wire, and in the end he stumbled into a shed where there was some hay and stuff. But he couldn't remember much about that, either, because he'd had a devil of a knock on the head and he was getting feverish. And then a girl found him."

"We know all about that," said the Superintendent.

"Yes, I daresay you do. You seem to know a lot. Well, Deacon was pretty smart about that. He got round the soft side of the girl and they made up a story for him. He said it was fairly easy pretending to have lost his memory. Where the doctor blokes made a mistake was trying to catch him out with bits of Army drill. He'd never done any, so of course he didn't have to pretend not to recognize it. The hardest part was making out that he didn't know any English. They nearly got him on that, once or twice. But he did know French, so he did his best to seem intelligent about that. His French accent was pretty good, but he pretended to have lost his speech, so that any mumbling or stammering might be put down to that, and in the intervals he practised talking to the girl till he was word-perfect. I must say, Deacon had brains."

"We can imagine all that part," said Parker. "Now tell us about the emeralds."

"Oh, yes. The thing that started him on that was getting hold of an old English newspaper which had a mention of the finding of a body in the dene-hole—his own body, as everyone thought. It was a 1918 paper, of course, but he only came across it in 1924—I forget where. It turned up, the way things do. Somebody'd used it to wrap up something sometime, and I think he came across it in an *estaminet*. He didn't bother about it, because the farm was doing pretty well—he'd married the girl by then, you see—and he was quite happy. But later on, things began to go badly, and it worried him to think about those sparklers all tucked away doing no good to anybody. But he didn't know how to start getting hold of them, and he got a vertical breeze up every time he thought of that dead warder and the chap he'd thrown down the hole. However, in the end, he called to mind yours truly, and figured it out that I'd be out on my own again. So he wrote me a letter. Well, as you know, I wasn't out. I was inside again, owing to a regrettable misunderstanding, so I didn't get the letter for some time, my pals thinking it wasn't quite the sort of thing to send to the place where I was. See? But when I came out again, there was the letter waiting for me."

"I wonder he made *you* his confidant," observed Parker. "There had been—shall we say, ungentlemanly words passed on the subject."

"Ah!" said Mr. Cranton. "There had, and I had something to say about that when I wrote back. But you see, he'd nobody else to go to, had he? When all's said and done, there's nobody like Nobby Cranton to handle a job like that in a refined and competent manner. I give you my word I nearly told him to go and boil himself, but in the end I said, No! let bygones be bygones. So I promised to help the blighter. I told him I could fix him up with money and papers and get him across all right. Only I told him he'd have to give me a bit more dope on the thing first. Otherwise, how was I to know he wouldn't double-cross me again, the dirty skunk?"

"Nothing more likely," said Parker.

"Ah! and he did, too, blast his worm-eaten little soul! I said he'd have to tell me where the stuff was. And would you believe it, the hound wouldn't trust me! Said, if he told me that, I might get in and pinch the bleeding lot before he got there!"

"Incredible!" said Parker. "Of course you wouldn't do such a thing as that."

"Not me," replied Nobby. "What do *you* think?" He winked. "Well, we went on writing backwards and forwards till we reached what they call an impasse. At last he wrote and said he'd send me a what d'you call—a cipher, and if I could make out from that where the shiners were, I was welcome. Well, he sent the thing, and I couldn't make head or tail of it, and I told him so. Then he said, All right; if I didn't trust him I could go down to Fenchurch and ask for a tailor called Paul as lived next door to Batty Thomas, and they'd give me the key, but, he says, you'd do better to leave it to me, because I know how to handle them. Well, I didn't know, only I thought to myself if these two chaps come in on it they'll want their share, and they might turn sour on me, and it seemed to me I was safer with Deacon, because he stood to lose more than I did. Call me a mug if you like, but I sent him over the money and some perfectly good papers. Of course, he couldn't come as Deacon and he didn't want to come as Legros, because there might be a spot of trouble over that, and he suggested his papers should be made out as Paul Taylor. I thought it a bit silly myself, but he seemed to think it would be a good joke. Now, of course, I know why. So the papers were made out, with a lovely photograph—a real nice job, that was. Might have been anybody. As a matter of fact, it was a composite. It looked very convincing, and had quite a look of all sorts of people. Oh, yes! and I sent him some clothes to meet him at Ostend, because he said his own things were too Frenchy. He came across on the 29th December. I suppose you got on to that?"

"Yes," said Blundell, "we did, but it didn't help us a lot."

"That bit went all right. He sent me a message from Dover. Telephoned from a public call-box—but I'll forgive you for not tracing that. He said he was going straight through and would come along up to London with the stuff next day or the day after, or as soon as he could. Anyway, he would get a message through somehow. I wondered whether I oughtn't to go down to Fenchurch myself—mind you, I never trusted him—but I wasn't altogether keen, in spite of my face-fungus. I'd grown that on spec, you understand. I didn't want you people following me about too much. And besides, I had one or two other irons in the fire. I'm coming clean, you see."

"You'd better," said Parker, ominously.

"I didn't get any message on the 30th, nor yet on the 31st, and I thought I'd been had proper. Only I couldn't see what he had to gain by double-crossing me. He needed me to handle the goods—or so I thought. Only then it struck me he might have picked up some other pal over at Maidstone or abroad."

"In that case, why bring you into it at all?"

"That's what I thought. But I got so windy, I thought I'd better go down to the place and see what was happening. I didn't want to leave a trail, so I went over to Walbeach—never mind how, that's off the point——"

"Probably Sparky Bones or the Fly-Catcher," put in Parker, thoughtfully.

"Ask no questions and you'll hear no lies. My pal decanted me a few miles out and I footslogged it. I made out I was a tramp labourer, looking for work on the New Cut. Thank God, they weren't taking on any hands, so they didn't detain me."

"So we gathered."

"Ah! I suppose you would go nosey-parkering round there. I got a lift part of the way to Fenchurch and walked the rest. Beastly country it is, too, as I said before. I'm not doing my hiking thereabouts, I can tell you."

"That was when we ran across one another, I think," said Wimsey.

"Ah! and if I'd known who I had the pleasure of stopping I'd have walked off home," said Mr. Cranton, handsomely. "But I didn't know, so I trotted along and—but there! I expect you know that part of it."

"You got a job with Ezra Wilderspin and made inquiries for Paul Taylor."

"Yes—and a nice business that was!" exclaimed Nobby with indignation. "Mr. Paul Bleeding Taylor and Mr. Batty Thomas! Bells, if you please! And not a hide nor hair of *my* Paul Taylor to be seen or heard of. I tell you, that made me think a bit. I didn't know if he'd been and gone, or if he'd been pinched on the way, or if he was lurking about round the corner or what. And that chap Wilderspin—he was a good hand at keeping a hardworking man's nose to the grindstone, curse him! 'Driver, come here!' 'Steve, do this!' I didn't have a minute to call my own. All the same, I started to think quite a lot about that cipher. I took the idea that maybe it had to do with those bells. But could I get into the confounded belfry? No, I couldn't. Not openly, I mean. So I made out to do it one night and see if I could make sense of the thing up there. So I made a couple or so of picklocks, the forge being handy for the job, and on Saturday night I just let myself quietly out of Ezra's back-door.

"Now, look here. What I'm going to tell you is Gospel truth. I went down to that church a bit after midnight, and the minute I put my hand on the door, I found it was open. What did I think? Why, I thought Deacon must be in there on the job. Who else was it likely to be, that time of night? I'd been in the place before and made out where the belfry door was, so I went along nice and quiet, and that was open, too. 'That's all right,' I thought, 'Deacon's here, and I'll give him Tailor Paul and Batty Thomas for not keeping me posted.' I got up into a sort of place with ropes in it—damn nasty, I thought they looked. And then there was a ladder and more ropes a-top of that. And then another ladder and a trap-door."

"Was the trap-door open?"

"Yes, and I went up. And I didn't half like it, either. Do you know, when I got up into the next place—Gee! there was a queer feel about it. Not a sound, but like as if there might be people standing round. And dark! It was a pitch-black beast of a night and raining like hell, but I never met anything like the blackness of that place. And I felt as if there was hundreds of eyes watching me. Talk about the heebie-jeebies! Well, there!

"After a bit, with still not a sound, I sort of pulled myself together and put my torch on. Say, have you ever been up in that place? Ever seen those bells? I'm not what you'd call fanciful in a general way, but there was something about the bells that gave me the fantods."

"I know," said Wimsey, "they look as if they were going to come down on you."

"Yes, *you* know," said Nobby, eagerly. "Well, I'd got to where I wanted, but I didn't know where to begin. I didn't know the first thing about bells, or how to get to them or anything. And

I couldn't make out what had happened to Deacon. So I looked round on the floor with the torch and—Boo!—there he was!"

"Dead?"

"Dead as a door-nail. Tied up to a big kind of post, and a look on his face—there! I don't want to see a face like that again. Just as though he'd been struck dead and mad all at one go, if you see what I mean."

"I suppose there's no doubt he was dead?"

"Dead?" Mr. Cranton laughed. "I never saw anyone deader."

"Stiff?"

"No, not stiff. But cold, my God! I just touched him. He swung on the ropes and his head had fallen over—well, it looked as if he'd got what was coming to him, anyhow, but worse. Because, to do them justice, they're pretty quick on the drop, but he looked as if it had lasted for a good long time."

"Do you mean the rope was round his neck?" demanded Parker, a little impatiently.

"No. He wasn't hanged. I don't know what killed him. I was just looking to see, when I heard somebody starting to come up the tower. I didn't stop, you bet. There was another ladder, and I legged it up that as high as I could go, till I got to a sort of hatch leading out on to the roof, I suppose. I squatted inside that and hoped the other fellow wouldn't take it into his head to come up after me. I wasn't keen on being found up there at all, and the body of my old pal Deacon might want some explaining. Of course, I could have told the truth, and pointed out that the poor bloke was cold before I got there, but me having pick-locks in my pocket rather jiggered up that bit of the alibi. So I sat tight. The chap came up into the place where the body was and started moving round and shuffling about, and once or twice he said 'Oh, God!' in a groaning sort of voice. Then there was a nasty soft sort of thump, and I reckoned he'd got the body down on the floor. Then after a bit I heard him pulling and hauling, and presently his steps went across the floor, very slow and heavy, and a bumping noise, like he was dragging old Deacon after him. I couldn't see him at all from where I was, because from my corner I could only see the ladder and the wall opposite, and he was right away on the other side of the room. After that there was more scuffling, and a sort of bumping and sliding, and I took it he was getting the body down the other ladder. And I didn't envy him the job, neither.

"I waited up there and waited, till I couldn't hear him any more, and then I began to wonder what I should do next. So I tried the door on to the roof. There was a bolt inside, so I undid that and stepped out. It was raining like blazes and pitch-black, but out I crawled and got to the edge of the tower and looked over. How high is that cursed tower? Hundred and thirty feet, eh? Well, it felt like a thousand and thirty. I'm no cat-burglar, nor yet a steeplejack. I looked down, and I saw a light moving about right away up the other end of the church, miles away beneath me in the graveyard. I tell you I hung on to that blinking parapet with both hands and I got a feeling in my stomach as though me and the tower and everything was crumbling away and going over. I was glad I couldn't see more than I did.

"Well, I thought, you'd better make tracks, Nobby, while the dirty work's going on down there. So I came in again carefully and bolted the door after me and started to come down the ladder. It was awkward going in the dark and after a bit I switched my torch on, and I wished I hadn't. There I was, and those bells just beneath me—and, God! how I hated the look of them. I went all cold and sweaty and the torch slipped out of my hand and went down, and hit one of the bells. I'll never forget the noise it made. It wasn't loud, but kind of terribly sweet and threatening, and it went humming on and on, and a whole lot of other notes seemed to come out of it, high up and clear and close—right in my ears. You'll think I'm loopy, but I tell you that bell was alive. I shut my eyes and hung on to the ladder and wished I'd chosen a different kind of profession—and that'll show you what a state I was in."

"You've got too much imagination, Nobby," said Parker.

"You wait, Charles," said Lord Peter. "You wait till you get stuck on a ladder in a belfry in the dark. Bells are like cats and mirrors—they're always queer, and it doesn't do to think too much about them. Go on, Cranton."

"That's just what I couldn't do," said Nobby, frankly. "Not for a bit. It felt like hours, but I daresay it wasn't more than five minutes. I crawled down at last—in the dark, of course, having lost the torch. I groped round after it and found it, but the bulb had gone, naturally, and I hadn't any matches. So I had to feel for the trap-door, and I was terrified of pitching right down. But I found it at last, and after that it was easier, though I had a nasty time on the spiral staircase. The steps are all worn away, and I slipped about, and the walls were so close I couldn't breathe. My man had left all the doors open, so I knew he'd be coming back, and that didn't cheer me up much, either. When I was out in the church I hared it for all I was worth to the door. I tripped over something on the way, too, that made an awful clatter. Something like a big metal pot."

"The brass ewer at the foot of the font," said Wimsey.

"They didn't ought to keep it there," said Mr. Cranton, indignantly. "And when I got out through the porch, I had to pussyfoot pretty gently over that beastly creaking gravel. In the end I got away and then I ran—golly, how I ran! I hadn't left anything behind at Wilderspin's, bar a shirt they'd lent me and a tooth-brush I'd bought in the village, and I wasn't going back there, I ran and ran like hell, and the rain was something cruel. And it's a hell of a country. Ditches and bridges all over the place. There was a car came past one time, and trying to get out of the light, I missed my footing and rolled down the bank into a ditch full of water. Cold? It was like an ice-bath. I fetched up at last in a barn near a railway station and shivered there till morning, and presently a train came along, so I got on that. I forget the name of the place, but it must have been ten or fifteen miles away from Fenchurch. By the time I got up to London I was in a fever, I can tell you; rheumatic fever, or so they said. And you see what it's done to me. I pretty nearly faded out, and I rather wish I had. I'll never be fit for anything again. But that's the truth and the whole truth, my lord and officers. Except that when I came to look myself over, I couldn't find Deacon's cipher. I thought I'd lost it on the road, but if you picked it up in the belfry, it must have come out of my pocket when I pulled the torch out. I never killed Deacon, but I knew I'd have a job to prove I didn't, and that's why I spun you a different tale the first time you came."

"Well," said Chief Inspector Parker, "let's hope it'll be a lesson to you to keep out of belfries."

"It will," replied Nobby fervently. "Every time I see a church tower now it gives me the jim-jams. I'm done with religion, I am, and if I ever go inside a church-door again, you can take and put me in Broadmoor."

THE THIRD PART

Will Thoday Goes In Quick and Comes Out Slow

For while I held my tongue, my bones consumed away through my daily complaining.

PSALM XXXII. 3

WIMSEY THOUGHT he had never seen such utter despondency on any face as on William Thoday's. It was the face of a man pushed to the last extremity, haggard and grey, and pinched about the nostrils like a dead man's. On Mary's face there was anxiety and distress, but something combative and alert as well. She was still fighting, but Will was obviously beaten.

"Now then, you two," said Superintendent Blundell, "let's hear what you have to say for yourselves."

"We've done nothing we need be ashamed of," said Mary.

"Leave it to me, Mary," said Will. He turned wearily to the Superintendent. "Well," he said, "you've found out about Deacon, I suppose. You know that he done us and ours a wrong that can't be put right. We been trying, Mary and me, to put right as much as we can, but you've stepped in. Reckon we might have known we couldn't keep it quiet, but what else could we do? There's been talk enough about poor Mary down in the village, and we thought the best thing was to slip away, hoping to make an honest woman of her without asking the leaves of all they folk with long tongues as 'ud only be too glad to know something against us. And why shouldn't we? It weren't no fault of ours. What call have you got to stop us?"

"See here, Will," said Mr. Blundell, "it's rough luck on you, and I'm not saying as 'tisn't, but the law's the law. Deacon was a bad lot, as we all know, but the fact remains somebody put him away, and it's our job to find out who did it."

"I ain't got nothing to say about that," said Will Thoday, slowly. "But it's cruel hard if Mary and me——"

"Just a moment," said Wimsey. "I don't think you quite realize the position, Thoday. Mr. Blundell doesn't want to stand in the way of your marriage, but, as he says, somebody did murder Deacon, and the ugly fact remains that you were the man with the best cause to do it. And that means, supposing a charge were laid against you, and brought into court—well, they might want this lady to give evidence."

"And if they did?" said Will.

"Just this," said Wimsey. "The law does not allow a wife to give evidence against her husband." He waited while this sank in. "Have a cigarette, Thoday. Think it out."

"I see," said Thoday, bitterly. "I see. It comes to this—there ain't no end to the wrong that devil done us. He ruined my poor Mary and brought her into the dock once, and he robbed her of her good name and made bastards of our little girls, and now he can come between us again at the altar rails and drive her into the witness-box to put my neck in the rope. If ever a man deserved killing, he's the one, and I hope he's burning in hell for it now."

"Very likely he is," said Wimsey, "but you see the point. If you don't tell us the truth now——"

"I've nothing to tell you but this," broke out Thoday in a kind of desperation. "My wife—and she *is* my wife in God's sight and mine—she never knew nothing about it. Not one word. And she knows nothing now, nothing but the name of the man rotting in that grave. And that's the truth as God sees us."

"Well," said Mr. Blundell, "you'll have to prove that."

"That's not quite true, Blundell," said Wimsey, "but I dare say it could be proved. Mrs. Thoday——"

The woman looked quickly and gratefully at him.

"When did you first realize that your first husband had been alive till the beginning of this year, and that you were, therefore, not legally married to Will Thoday here?"

"Only when you came to see me, my lord, last week."

"When I showed you that piece of writing in Deacon's hand?"

"Yes, my lord."

"But how did that——?" began the Superintendent. Wimsey went on, drowning his voice.

"You realized then that the man buried in Lady Thorpe's grave must be Deacon."

"It came over me, my lord, that that must be the way of it.

I seemed to see a lot of things clear that I hadn't understood before."

"Yes. You'd never doubted till that moment that Deacon had died in 1919?"

"Not for a moment, my lord. I'd never have married Will else."

"You have always been a regular communicant?"

"Yes, my lord."

"But last Sunday you stayed away."

"Yes, I did, my lord. I couldn't come there, knowing as me and Will wasn't properly married. It didn't seem right, like."

"Of course not," said Wimsey. "I beg your pardon, Superintendent. I'm afraid I interrupted you," he added, blandly.

"That's all very well," said Mr. Blundell. "You said you didn't recognize that writing when his lordship showed it to you."

"I'm afraid I did. It wasn't true—but I had to make up my mind quick—and I was afraid——"

"I'll bet you were. Afraid of getting Will into trouble, hey? Now, see here, Mary, how did you know that paper wasn't written donkey's years ago? What made you jump so quick to the idea Deacon was the corpse in the Thorpe grave? Just you answer me that, my girl, will you?"

"I don't know," she said, faintly. "It came over me all of a sudden."

"Yes, it did," thundered the Superintendent. "And why? Because Will had told you about it already, and you knew the game was up. Because you'd seen that there paper before——"

"No, no!"

"I say, Yes. If you hadn't have known something, you'd have had no cause to deny the writing. You knew *when* it was written —now, didn't you?"

"That's a lie!" said Thoday.

"I really don't think you're right about that, Blundell," said Wimsey, mildly, "because, if Mrs. Thoday had known about it all along, why shouldn't she have gone to Church last Sunday morning? I mean, don't you see, if she'd brazened it out all those months, why shouldn't she do it again?"

"Well," retorted the Superintendent, "and how about Will? He's been going to church all right, ain't he? You aren't going to tell me *he* knew nothing about it either."

"Did he, Mrs. Thoday?" inquired Wimsey, gently.

Mary Thoday hesitated.

"I can't tell you about that," she said at last.

"Can't you, by God?" snapped Mr. Blundell. "Well, now, will you tell me——?"

"It's no good, Mary," said Will. "Don't answer him. Don't say nothing. They'll only twist your words round into what you don't mean. We've got nothing to say and if I got to go through it, I got to go through it and that's all about it."

"Not quite," said Wimsey. "Don't you see that if you tell us what you know, and we're satisfied that your wife knows nothing—then there's nothing to prevent your marriage from going through straight away? That's right, isn't it, Super?"

"Can't hold out any inducement, my lord," said the Superintendent, stolidly.

"Of course not, but one can point out an obvious fact. You see," went on Wimsey, "somebody *must* have known something, for your wife to have jumped so quickly to the conclusion that the dead man was Deacon. If she hadn't already been suspicious about you—if *you* were perfectly ignorant and innocent the whole time—then *she* had the guilty knowledge. It would work all right that way, of course. Yes, I see now that it would. If she knew, and told you about it—then *you* would be the one with the sensitive conscience. *You* would have told *her* that you couldn't kneel at the altar with a guilty woman——"

"Stop that!" said Thoday. "You say another word and I'll—— Oh, my God! it wasn't that, my lord. She never knew. I did know. I'll say that much, I won't say no more, only that. As I hope to be saved, she never knew a word about it."

"As you hope to be saved?" said Wimsey. "Well. Well. And you did know, and that's all you've got to tell us?"

"Now, look here," said the Superintendent, "you'll have to go a bit further than that, my lad. When did you know?"

"When the body was found," replied Thoday, "I knew then." He spoke slowly, as though every word were being wrenched out of him. He went on more briskly: "That's when I knew who it was."

"Then why didn't you say so?" demanded Blundell.

"What, and have everybody know me and Mary wasn't married? Likely, ain't it?"

"Ah!" said Wimsey. "But why didn't you get married then?"

Thoday shifted uncomfortably in his chair.

"Well, you see, my lord—I hoped as Mary needn't ever know. It was a bitter hard thing for her, wasn't it? And the children. We couldn't ever put that right, you see. So I made up my mind to say nothing about it and take the sin—if it was a sin—on my shoulders. I didn't want to make no more trouble for her. Can't you understand that? Well, then—when she found it out, through seeing that there paper——" He broke off and started again. "You see, ever since the body was found I'd been worried and upset in my mind, like, and I daresay I was a bit queer in my ways and she'd noticed it—when she asked me if the dead man was Deacon after all, why, then I told her as it was, and that's how it all came about."

"And how did you know who the dead man was?"

There was a long silence.

"He was terribly disfigured, you know," went on Wimsey.

"You said you thought he was—that he'd been in prison," stammered Thoday, "and I said to myself——"

"Half a mo'," broke in the Superintendent, "when did you ever hear his lordship say that? It wasn't brought out at the inquest, nor yet at the adjournment, because we were most particularly careful to say nothing about it. Now then!"

"I heard something about it from Rector's Emily," said Thoday, slowly. "She happened to hear something his lordship said to Mr. Bunter."

"Oh, *did* she?" snapped Mr. Blundell. "And how much more did Rector's Emily overhear, I'd like to know. That beer-bottle, now! Who told her to dust the finger-prints off it—come, now!"

"She didn't mean no harm about that," said Will. "It was nothing but girl's curiosity. You know how they are. She came over next day and told Mary all about it. In a rare taking, she was."

"Indeed!" said the Superintendent, unbelievingly. "So *you* say. Never mind. Let's go back to Deacon. You heard that Emily heard something his lordship said to Mr. Bunter about the dead man having been in prison. Was that it? And what did you think of that?"

"I said to myself, it must be Deacon. I said, here's that devil come out of his grave to trouble us again, that's what I said. Mind you, I didn't exactly know, but that's what I said to myself."

"And what did you imagine he had come for?"

"How was I to know? I thought he'd come, that's all."

"You thought he'd come after the emeralds, didn't you?" said the Superintendent.

For the first time a look of genuine surprise and eagerness came into the haunted eyes. "The emeralds? Was *that* what he was after? Do you mean he had them after all? Why, we always thought the other fellow—Cranton—had got them."

"You didn't know that they had been hidden in the church?"

"*In the church?*"

"We found them there on Monday," explained his lordship, placidly, "tucked away in the roof."

"In the roof of the church? Why, then *that* was what he—— The emeralds found? Thank God for that! They'll not be able to say now as Mary had any hand in it."

"True," said Wimsey. "But you were about to say something else, I rather fancy. 'That was what he——' What? 'That was what he was after when I found him in the church.' Was that it?"

"No, my lord. I was going to say—— I was just going to say, that was what he did with them." A fresh wave of anger seemed to sweep over him. "The dirty villain! He did double-cross that other fellow after all."

"Yes," agreed his lordship. "I'm afraid there's not much to be said in favour of the late Mr. Deacon. I'm sorry, Mrs. Thoday, but he was really rather an unsatisfactory person. And you're not the only one to suffer. He married another woman over in France, and she's left with three small children too."

"Poor soul!" said Mary.

"The damned scoundrel!" exclaimed Will. "If I'd have known that, I'd——"

"Yes?"

"Never mind," growled the farmer. "How did he come to be in France? How did he——?"

"That's a long story," said Wimsey, "and rather far from the point at issue. Now, let's get your story clear. You heard that the body of a man who might have been a convict had been found in the churchyard, and though the face was quite unrecognizable, you were—shall we say inspired?—to identify him with Geoffrey Deacon, whom you had supposed to have died in 1918. You said nothing about it till your wife, the other day, saw a bit of Deacon's handwriting, which might have been written at any time, and was—shall we again say inspired?—with the same idea. Without waiting for any further verification, you both rushed away to town to get remarried, and that's the only explanation you can give. Is that it?"

"That's all I can say, my lord."

"And a damned thin story too," observed Mr. Blundell, truculently. "Now, get this, Will Thoday. You know where you stand as well as I do. You know you're not bound to answer any questions now unless you like. But there's the inquest on the body; we can have that re-opened, and you can tell your story to the coroner. Or you can be charged with the murder and tell it to a judge and jury. Or you can come clean now. Whichever you like. See?"

"I've nothing more to say, Mr. Blundell."

"I tell thee all, I can no more," observed Wimsey thoughtfully. "That's a pity, because the public prosecutor may get quite a different sort of story fixed in his mind. He may think, for instance, that you knew Deacon was alive because you had met him in the church on the night of December 30th."

He waited to see the effect of this, and resumed:

"There's Potty Peake, you know. I don't suppose he's too potty to give evidence about what he saw and heard that night from behind Abbot Thomas' tomb. The black-bearded man and the voices in the vestry and Will Thoday fetching the rope from the cope-chest. What took you into the church, by the way? You saw a light, perhaps. And went along and found the door open, was that it? And in the vestry, you found a man doing something that looked suspicious. So you challenged him and when he spoke you knew who it was. It was lucky that the fellow didn't shoot you, but probably you took him unawares. Anyway, you threatened to give him up to justice and then he pointed out that that would put your wife and children in an unpleasant position. So you indulged in a little friendly chat—did you speak?—In the end, you compromised. You said you would keep quiet about it and get him out of the country with £200 in pocket, but you hadn't got it at the moment and in the meantime you would put him in a place of safety. Then you fetched a rope and tied him up. I don't know how you kept him quiet while you went to fetch it. Did you give him a straight left to the jaw, or what? . . . You won't help me? . . . Well, never mind. You tied him up and left him in the vestry while you went round to steal Mr. Venables' keys. It's a miracle you found them in the right place, by the way. They seldom are. Then you took him up into the belfry, because the bell-chamber was nice and handy and had several locks to it, and it was easier than escorting him out through the village. After that you brought him some food—perhaps Mrs. Thoday could throw some light on that. Did you miss a quart bottle of beer or so about that time, Mrs. Thoday? Some of those you got in for Jim? By the way, Jim is coming home and we'll have to have a word with him."

Watching Mary's face, the Superintendent saw it contract suddenly with alarm, but she said nothing. Wimsey went on remorselessly.

"The next day you went over to Walbeach to get the money. But you weren't feeling well, and on the way home you broke down completely and couldn't get back to let Deacon out. That was damned awkward for you, wasn't it? You didn't want to confide in your wife. Of course, there was Jim."

Thoday raised his head.

"I'm not saying anything one way or other, my lord, except this. I've never said one word to Jim about Deacon—not one word. Nor he to me. And that's the truth."

"Very well," said Wimsey. "Whatever else happened, in between December 30th and January 4th, somebody killed Deacon. And on the night of the 4th, somebody buried the body. Somebody who knew him and took care to mutilate his face and hands beyond recognition. And what everybody will want to know is, at what moment did Deacon cease to be Deacon and become the body? Because that's rather the point, isn't it? We know that you couldn't very well have buried him yourself, because you were ill, but the killing is a different matter. You see, Thoday, he didn't starve to death. He died with a full tummy. *You* couldn't have fed him after the morning of December 31st. If you didn't kill him then, who took him his rations in the interval? And who, having fed him and killed him, rolled him down the belfry ladder on the night of the 4th, with a witness sitting in the roof of the tower—a witness who had seen him and recognized him? A witness who——"

"Hold on, my lord," said the Superintendent. "The woman's fainted."

THE FOURTH PART

The Slow Work

Who shut up the sea with doors . . .
and brake up for it my decreed place?
JOB XXXVIII. 8, 10

"HE WON'T say anything," said Superintendent Blundell.

"I know he won't," said Wimsey. "Have you arrested him?"

"No, my lord, I haven't. I've sent him home and told him to think it over. Of course, we could easily get him on being an accessory after the fact in both cases. I mean, he was shielding a known murderer—that's pretty clear, I fancy; and he's also shielding whoever killed Deacon, if he didn't do it himself. But I'm taking the view that we'll be able to handle him better after we've interrogated James. And we know James will be back in England at the end of the month. His owners have been very sensible. They've given him orders to come home, without saying what he's wanted for. They've arranged for another man to take his place and he's to report himself by the next boat."

"Good! It's a damnable business, the whole thing. If ever a fellow deserved a sticky death, it's this Deacon brute. If the law had found him the law would have hanged him, with loud applause from all good citizens. Why should we hang a perfectly decent chap for anticipating the law and doing our dirty work for us?"

"Well, it *is* the law, my lord," replied Mr. Blundell, "and it's not my place to argue about it. In any case, we're going to have a bit of a job to hang Will Thoday, unless it's as an accessory before the fact. Deacon was killed on a full stomach. If Will did away with him on the 30th, or the 31st, why did he go to collect the £200? If Deacon was dead, he wouldn't want it. On the other hand, if Deacon wasn't killed till the 4th, who fed him in the interval? If James killed him, why did he trouble to feed him first? The thing makes no sense."

"Suppose Deacon was being fed by somebody," said Wimsey, "and suppose he said something infuriatin' and the somebody killed him all of a sudden in a frenzy, not meaning to?"

"Yes, but how did he kill him? He wasn't stabbed or shot or clouted over the head."

"Oh, I don't *know*," said Wimsey. "Curse the man! He's a perfect nuisance, dead or alive, and whoever killed him was a public benefactor. I wish I'd killed him myself. Perhaps I did. Perhaps the Rector did. Perhaps Hezekiah Lavender did."

"I don't suppose it was any of those," said Mr. Blundell, stolidly. "But it might have been somebody else, of course. There's that Potty, for instance. He's always wandering round the church at night. Only he'd have to get into the bell-chamber, and I don't see how he could. But I'm waiting for James. I've got a hunch that James may have quite a lot to tell us."

"Have you? Oysters have beards, but they don't wag them."

"If it comes to oysters," said the Superintendent, "there's ways and means of opening 'em—*and* you needn't swallow 'em whole, neither. You're not going back to Fenchurch?"

"Not just at present. I don't think there's very much I can do down there for a bit. But my brother Denver and I are going to Walbeach to open the New Cut. I expect we shall see you there."

. . . .

The only other thing of interest that happened during the next week or so was the sudden death of Mrs. Wilbraham. She died at night and alone—apparently from mere old age—with the emeralds clasped in her hand. She left a will drawn up fifteen years earlier, in which she left the whole of her very considerable estate to her Cousin Henry Thorpe "because he is the only honest man I know." That she should cheerfully have left her only honest relative to suffer the wearing torments of straitened means and anxiety throughout the intervening period seemed to be only what anybody might have expected from her enigmatic and secretive disposition. A codicil, dated on the day after Henry's death, transferred the legacy to Hilary, while a further codicil, executed a few days before her own death, not only directed that the emeralds which had caused all the disturbance should be given to "Lord Peter Wimsey, who seems to be a sensible man and to have acted without interested motives," but also made him

Hilary's trustee. Lord Peter made a wry face over this bequest. He offered the necklace to Hilary, but she refused to touch it; it had painful associations for her. It was, indeed, only with difficulty that she was persuaded to accept the Wilbraham estate. She hated the thought of the testatrix; and besides, she had set her heart on earning her own living. "Uncle Edward will be worse than ever," she said. "He will want me to marry some horrible rich man, and if I want to marry a poor one, he'll say he's after the money. And anyway, I don't want to marry anybody."

"Then don't," said Wimsey. "Be a wealthy spinster."

"And get like Aunt Wilbraham? Not me!"

"Of course not. Be a nice wealthy spinster."

"Are there any?"

"Well, there's me. I mean, I'm a nice wealthy bachelor. Fairly nice, anyway. And it's fun to be rich. I find it so. You needn't spend it all on yachts and cocktails, you know. You could build something or endow something or run something or the other. If you don't take it, it will go to some ghastly person—Uncle Edward or somebody—whoever is Mrs. Wilbraham's next-of-kin, and they'd be sure to do something silly with it."

"Uncle Edward would," said Hilary, thoughtfully.

"Well, you've got a few years to think it over," said Wimsey. "When you're of age, you can see about throwing it into the Thames. But what I'm to do with the emeralds I really don't know."

"Beastly things," said Hilary. "They've killed grandfather, and practically killed Dad, and they've killed Deacon and they'll kill somebody else before long. I wouldn't touch them with a barge-pole."

"I'll tell you what. I'll keep them till you're twenty-one, and then we'll form ourselves into a Wilbraham Estate Disposals Committee and do something exciting with the whole lot."

Hilary agreed; but Wimsey felt depressed. So far as he could see, his interference had done no good to anybody and only made extra trouble. It was a thousand pities that the body of Deacon had ever come to light at all. Nobody wanted it.

. . . .

The New Wash Cut was opened with great rejoicings at the end of the month. The weather was perfect, the Duke of Denver made a speech which was a model of the obvious, and the Regatta was immensely successful. Three people fell into the river, four men and an old woman were had up for being drunk and disorderly, a motor-car became entangled with a trademan's cart and young Gotobed won First Prize in the Decorated Motor-cycle section of the Sports.

And the River Wale, placidly doing its job in the midst of all the disturbance, set to work to scour its channel to the sea. Wimsey, leaning over the wall at the entry to the Cut, watched the salt water moving upward with the incoming tide, muddied and chafing along its new-made bed. On his left, the crooked channel of the old river lay empty of its waters, a smooth expanse of shining mud.

"Doing all right," said a voice beside him. He turned and found that it was one of the engineers.

"What extra depth have you given her?"

"Only a few feet, but she'll do the rest herself. There's been nothing the matter with this river except the silting of the outfall and the big bend below here. We've shortened her course now by getting on for three miles and driven a channel right out into the Wash beyond the mudbanks. She'll make her own outfall now, if she's left to herself. We're expecting her to grind her channel lower by eight or ten feet—possibly more. It'll make all the difference to the town. It's a scandal, the way the thing's been let go. Why, as it is, the tide scarcely gets up higher than Van Leyden's Sluice. After this, it'll probably run up as far as the Great Leam. The whole secret with these Fen rivers is to bring back all the water you can into its natural course. Where the old Dutchmen went wrong was in dispersing it into canals and letting it lie about all over the place. The smaller the fall of the land, the bigger weight of water you need to keep the outfall scoured. You'd think it was obvious, wouldn't you? But it's taken people hundreds of years to learn it."

"Yes," said Wimsey. "I suppose all this extra water will go up the Thirty-Foot?"

"That's right. It's practically a straight run now from the Old Bank Sluice to the New Cut Outfall—thirty-five miles—and this will carry off a lot of the High Level water from Leamholt and Lympsey. At present the Great Leam has to do more work than it should—they've always been afraid to let the Thirty-Foot take its fair proportion of the flood-water in winter, because you see, when it got down to this point it would have overflowed the old river-bed and drowned the town. But now the New Cut will carry it clean off, and that will relieve the Great Leam and obviate the floods round Frogglesham, Mere Wash and Lympsey Fen."

"Oh!" said Wimsey. "I suppose the Thirty-Foot Dyke will stand the strain?"

"Oh, dear, yes," said the engineer, cheerfully. "It was meant to from the beginning. In fact, at one time, it had to. It's only within the last hundred years that the Wale has got so badly silted up. There's been a good deal of shifting in the Wash—chiefly owing to tidal action, of course, and the Nene Outfall Cut, and that helped to cause the obstruction, don't you see. But the Thirty-Foot worked all right in the old days."

"In the Lord Protector's time, I suppose," said Wimsey. "And now you've cleared the Wale Outfall, no doubt the obstruction will go somewhere else."

"Very likely," replied the engineer, with unimpaired cheerfulness. "These mudbanks are always shifting about. But in time I daresay they'll clear the whole thing—unless, of course, they really take it into their heads to drain the Wash and make a job of it."

"Just so," said Wimsey.

"But as far as it goes," continued the engineer, "this looks pretty good. It's to be hoped our dam over there will stand up to the strain. You'd be surprised at the scour you get with these quiet-looking rivers. Anyhow, this embankment is all right—I'll take my oath of that. You watch the tide-mark. We've marked the old low level and the old high level—if you don't see the one lowered and the other raised by three or four feet within the next few months, you can call me—a Dutchman. Excuse me a minute—I just want to see that they're making that dam good over there."

He hurried off to superintend the workmen who were completing the dam across the old course of the river.

"And how about my old sluice-gates?"

"Oh!" said Wimsey, looking round, "it's you, is it?"

"Ah!" The sluice-keeper spat copiously into the rising water. "It's me. That's who it is. Look at all this money they been spending. Thousands. But as for them gates of mine, I reckon I can go and whistle for 'em."

"No answer yet from Geneva?"

"Eh?" said the sluice-keeper. "Oh! Ah! Meaning what I said? Ah! that were a good 'un, weren't it? Why don't they refer it to the League of Nations? Ah! and why don't they? Look at thisher great scour o' water a-comin' up. Where's that a-going to? It's got to go somewhere, ain't it?"

"No doubt," said Wimsey. "I understand it's to go up the Thirty-Foot."

"Ah!" said the sluice-keeper. "Always interfering with things, they are."

"They're not interfering with your gates, anyway."

"No, they ain't, and that's just where it is. Once you starts interferin' with things you got to go on. One thing leads to another. Let 'm bide, that's what I say. Don't go digging of 'em up and altering of 'em. Dig up one thing and you got to dig up another."

"At that rate," objected Wimsey, "the Fens would still be all under water."

"Well, in a manner of speaking, so they would," admitted the sluice-keeper. "That's very true. So they would. But none the more for that, they didn't ought to come a-drowning of us now. It's all right for him to talk about letting the floods out at the Old Bank Sluice. Where's it all a-going to? It comes up, and it's got to go somewhere, and it comes down and it's got to go somewhere, ain't it?"

"At the moment I gather it drowns the Mere Wash and Frogglesham and all those places."

"Well, it's their water, ain't it?" said the sluice-keeper. "They ain't got no call to send it down here."

"Quite," said Wimsey, recognizing the spirit that had hampered the Fen drainage for the last few hundred years, "but as you say yourself, it's got to go somewhere."

"It's their water," retorted the man obstinately, "let 'em keep it. It won't do us no good."

"Walbeach seems to want it."

"Ah! them!" The sluice-keeper spat vehemently. "They don't know what they want. They're always a-wantin' some nonsense or other. And there's always some fool to give it 'em, what's more. All I wants is a new set of gates, but I don't look like getting of 'em. I've asked for 'em time and again. I asked that young feller there. 'Mister,' I says to him, 'how about a new set o' gates for my sluice?' 'That ain't in our contract,' he says. 'No,' I says, 'and drowning half the parish ain't in your contract neither, I suppose.' But he couldn't see it."

"Well, cheer up," said Wimsey. "Have a drink."

He did, however, feel sufficient interest in the matter to speak to the engineer about it when he saw him again.

"Oh, I think it's all right," said that gentleman. "We did, as a matter of fact, recommend that the gates should be repaired and strengthened, but you see, the damned thing's all tied up in some kind of legal bother. The fact is, once you start on a job like this, you never know where it's going to end. It's all piecemeal work. Stop it up in one place and it breaks out in another. But I don't think you need worry about this part of it. What *does* want seeing to is the Old Bank dyke—but that's under a different authority altogether. Still, they've undertaken to make up their embankment and put in some fresh stonework. If they don't, there'll be trouble, but they can't say we haven't warned them."

"Dig up one thing," thought Wimsey, "and you have to dig up another. I wish we'd never dug up Deacon. Once you let the tide in, it's got to go somewhere."

. . . . .

James Thoday, returning to England as instructed by his employers, was informed that the police wanted him as a witness. He was a sturdy man, rather older than William, with bleak blue eyes and a reserved manner. He repeated his original story, without emphasis and without details. He had been taken ill in the train after leaving Fenchurch. He had attributed the trouble to some sort of gastric influenza. When he got to London, he had felt quite unable to proceed, and had telegraphed to that effect. He had spent part of that day huddled over the fire in a public house near Liverpool Street; he thought they might remember him there. They could not give him a bed for the night and, in the evening, feeling a little better, he had gone out and found a room in a back street. He could not recall the address, but it had been a clean, pleasant place. In the morning he found himself fit to continue his journey, though still very weak and tottery. He had, of course, seen English papers mentioning the discovery of the corpse in the churchyard, but knew nothing further about it, except, of course, what he had heard from his brother and sister-in-law, which was very little. He had never had any idea who the dead man was. Would he be surprised to hear that it was Geoffrey Deacon? He would be very much surprised indeed. The news came as a terrible shock to him. That would be a bad job for his people.

Indeed, he looked startled enough. But there had been a tenseness of the muscles about his mouth which persuaded Superintendent Blundell that the shock had been caused, not so much by hearing the dead man's name as by hearing that the police knew it.

Mr. Blundell, aware of the solicitude with which the Law broods over the interests of witnesses, thanked him and proceeded with his inquiries. The public house was found, and substantiated the story of the sick sailor who had sat over the fire all day drinking hot toddies; but the clean and pleasant woman who had let her room to Mr. Thoday was not so easy of identification.

Meanwhile, the slow machinery of the London police revolved and, from many hundreds of reports, ground out the name of a garage proprietor who had hired out a motor-bicycle on the evening of the 4th of January to a man answering to the description of James Thoday. The bicycle had been returned on the Sunday by a messenger, who had claimed and taken away the deposit, minus the charge for hire and insurance. No, not a district messenger: a youth, who looked like an ordinary out-of-work.

On hearing this, Chief Inspector Parker, who was dealing with the London end of the inquiry, groaned dismally. It was too much to expect this nameless casual to turn up. Ten to one, he had pocketed the surplus deposit and would be particularly unwilling to inform the world of the fact.

Parker was wrong. The man who had hired the bicycle had apparently made the fatal mistake of picking an honest messenger. After prolonged inquiry and advertisement a young Cockney made his appearance at New Scotland Yard. He gave his name as Frank Jenkins, and explained that he had only just seen the advertisement. He had been seeking work in various places, and had drifted back to Town in time to be confronted with the police inquiry on a notice board at the Labour Exchange.

He very well remembered the episode of the motor-bike. It had struck him as funny at the time. He had been hanging round a garridge in Bloomsbury in the early morning of January 5th, hoping to pick up a job, when he see a bloke coming along on this here bike. The bloke was short and stocky, with blue eyes and sounded like he might be the boss of some outfit or other—he spoke sharp and quick, like he might be accustomed to giving orders. Yes, he might have been an officer in the mercantile marine, very likely. Come to think of it, he did look a bit like a sailor. He was dressed in a very wet and dirty motoring coat and wore a cap, pulled down over his face, like. This man had said: "Here, sonny, d'you want a job?" On being told "Yes," he had asked: "Can you ride a motor-bike?" Frank Jenkins had replied, "Lead me to it, guv'nor"; whereupon he had been told to take the machine back to a certain garage, to collect the deposit and to bring it to the stranger outside the Rugby Tavern at the corner of Great James Street and Chapel Street, when he would receive something for his pains. He had done his part of the business, and hadn't took more than an hour, all told (returning by 'bus), but when he arrived at the Rugby Tavern, the stranger was not there, and apparently never had been there. A woman said she had seen him walking away in the direction of Guildford Street. Jenkins had hung about till the middle of the morning, but had seen no sign of the man in the motor-coat. He had therefore deposited the money with the landlord of the Tavern, with a message to say that he could wait no longer and had kept back half-a-crown—that being the amount he thought fair to award himself for the transaction. The landlord would be able to tell them if the sum had ever been claimed.

The landlord, being interrogated, brought the matter to mind. Nobody answering the description of the stranger had ever called for the money, which, after a little search and delay, was produced intact in a dirty envelope. Enclosed with it was the garage-proprietor's receipt, made out in the name of Joseph Smith, at a fictitious address.

The next thing was, obviously, to confront James Thoday with Frank Jenkins. The messenger identified his employer immediately; James Thoday persisted, politely, that there was some mistake. What next, thought Mr. Parker.

He put the question to Lord Peter, who said:

"I think it's time for a spot of dirty work, Charles. Try putting William and James alone in a room with a microphone or whatever you call the beastly gadget. It may not be pretty, but you'll probably find that it works."

In these circumstances, therefore, the brothers met for the first time since James had left William on the morning of January 4th. The scene was a waiting-room at Scotland Yard.

"Well, William," said James.

"Well, James," said William.

There was a silence. Then James said:

"How much do they know?"

"Pretty well everything, by what I can make out."

There was another pause. Then James spoke again in a constrained voice:

"Very well. Then you had better let me take the blame. I'm not married, and there's Mary and the kids to be thought of. But in God's name, man, couldn't you have got rid of the fellow without killing him?"

"That," said William, "is just what I was going to ask *you*."

"You mean to say, it wasn't you did away with him?"

"Of course not. I'd be a fool to do it. I'd offered the brute two hundred pounds to go back where he came from. If I hadn't a-been ill, I'd a-got him away all right, and that's what I thought you'd a-done. My God! when he came up out o' that grave, like Judgment Day, I wished you'd killed me along of him."

"But I never laid hand on him, Will, till after he was dead. I saw him there, the devil, with that ghastly look on his face, and I never blamed you for what you'd done. I swear I never blamed you, Will—only for being such a fool as to do it. So I broke his ugly face in, so that no one should ever guess who he was. But they've found out, seemingly. It was cursed bad luck, that grave being opened so soon. Maybe it'd have been better if I'd carried him out and thrown him in the Drain, but it's a long way to go, and I thought we'd be safe enough."

"But, see here, James—if you didn't kill him, who did?"

It was at this point that Superintendent Blundell, Chief Inspector Parker and Lord Peter Wimsey walked in on the pair of them.

THE FIFTH PART

The Dodging

Then whispered they of a violated grave—of a disfigured body.

EDGAR ALLAN POE: BERENICE

THE ONLY difficulty was that the two witnesses who had formerly refused to speak could now hardly speak fast enough and spoke both together. Chief Inspector Parker was obliged to call for silence.

"All right," he said. "You've both been suspecting each other and shielding each other. We've grasped that. Now that we've got that clear, let's have the story. William first." He added the usual caution.

"Well, sir," replied William, briskly, "I don't know as I've much to tell you, because his lordship here seems to have worked it all out surprising neat. What my feelings were when he told me just what I did that night I won't say—but what I do want to make as clear as I can is that my poor wife never knew one thing about it, first to last. Why, that was my whole trouble all the time—how to keep it from her.

"I'll begin right at the beginning, with the night of December 30th. I was just coming home, pretty late for me, from seeing to one of the cows that had gone sick up at Sir Henry's place, and as I was passing the church, I thought I saw somebody a-creeping up to the porch and going in. It was a dark night, of course, but, if you remember, sir, it had begun to snow, and I could see something moving, like, against the white. So I thinks, that's Potty up to his games again—I better send him off home. So I goes up to the church door, and I sees footmarks going all along the path as far as the porch, and there they seems to stop. So I says, Hallo! and looks round about a bit. That's queer, I says to myself, where's the beggar got to? So I goes round the church, and I sees a light a-moving about and going towards the vestry. Well, I thinks, maybe it's Rector. And then I thinks, well, maybe it ain't. So I comes back to the door, and there's no key in it, like there would be in the ordinary way if Rector had been inside. So I pushes the door and it opens. And in I goes. And then I hears somebody a-moving about and bumping, like, up in the chancel. I goes along quiet, having rubber boots on, that I was wearing for the fields, and when I gets round behind the chancel screen I sees a light and hears the bloke in the vestry, so in I goes and there's a fellow a-tugging away at the ladder Harry Gotobed uses for seeing to the lamps and that, what's always kept a-lying along the wall. He had his back to me, and on the table I see a kind of a dark lantern and something else as had no right to be there, and that's a revolver. So I catches hold of the revolver and said, loud and sharp, 'What are you doing there?' And he jumped round pretty damn quick and made a dive for the table. 'No, you don't,' I said, 'I've got your gun and I know how to use it. What are you after?' Well, he started some sort of tale about being out of work and tramping about and wanting a place to sleep in, and I said, 'That won't wash. How about this gun? Hands up,' I said, 'let's see what else you've got on you.' So I went through his pockets and brought out what looked to me like a set of pick-locks. 'Well, my lad,' I said, 'that's quite enough for me. You're for it,' and he looked at me, and laughed like hell, and said, 'Think again, Will Thoday.' And I said, 'How do you know my name?' and then I looked again and said, 'My God, it's Jeff Deacon!' And he said, 'Yes; and you're the man that's married my wife.' And he laughed again. And then it come over me just what it all meant."

"How did he know that?" asked Wimsey. "He didn't get it from Cranton."

"That was the other scoundrel? No, he told me he'd meant to come after Mary, but hearing from some fellow at Leamholt that she was married, he'd thought he'd better have a scout round first. I couldn't make out why he'd come back to the place at all, and he wouldn't tell me. I see now, it was the emeralds. He did say something about me keeping quiet and he'd make it worth my while, but I told him I'd have no truck with him. I asked him where he'd been, but he just laughed and said, 'Never you mind.' And I asked what he wanted in Fenchurch, and he said he wanted money. So I made out that he'd meant to come blackmailing Mary. Well, that made me see red, and I was in half a mind to give him up to the police and take what was coming to us, but when I thought about Mary and the kids—well, I couldn't face it. I was wrong, of course, but when I remembered all the talk there'd been—well, I wanted to spare her that. He knew just how I stood, the devil, and he stood there grinning at me.

"So in the end, I made a devil's bargain with him. I said I'd hide him and give him money to get out of the country, and then I thought what was I to do with him? I'd got his pick-locks all right, but I didn't trust him none the more for that, and I was afraid to go out of the church with him, where we might run up against somebody. And then I got the idea of putting him up in the bell-chamber. So I told him what I meant to do and he agreed. I thought I could get the keys from Rector all right, so, just for the time being, I pushed him into the cupboard where the surplices hang and locked him in. Then I thought that he might easily break his way out while I was over at the Rectory, so I went down and fetched a rope from the chest and came back and tied him up. You see, I didn't believe that tale of his about sleeping in the vestry. Robbing the church was what I thought he was after. And besides, if I went away and left him, what was to stop him getting out and hiding somewhere and slugging me over the head when I got back? I'd no key to the church-door, neither, and he might have made off."

"Good thing for you if he had," suggested Mr. Blundell.

"Yes—so long as nobody else caught him. Anyhow, I got the keys. I put up some story to the Rector—it must have been a pretty lame one—the old gentleman was a bit puzzled, I think. He kept on saying how queer I looked, and insisted on getting me a drop of his port. While he was fetching it, I just nipped the keys off the nail by the door. I know what you're going to say—suppose he'd mislaid them as usual? Well, I'd have had to try the same dodge on Jack Godfrey or else change my plans—but there they were and I didn't bother with any ifs. I went back to the church and untied Deacon's legs and made him walk up the belfry stairs in front of me, like taking a pig to market. It wasn't difficult: I had the revolver, you see."

"And you tied him up to a beam in the bell-chamber?"

"Yes, sir, I did. And wouldn't you a-done? Just think of yourself carrying victuals and stuff up one o' they ladders in the dark, with a murderer roaming loose at the top all ready to bash your head in the moment you popped it up above floor-level. I tied him up good and proper, though it was a bit of a job with the rope being so thick. 'Stay you there,' I said, 'and I'll bring you something to eat in the morning and see you out of the country before you're twenty-four hours older.' He cursed like a devil, but I paid no attention to him. It was all I could do to keep my hand offen him, and I'm often minded to think it's a wonder I didn't kill him then and there."

"But had you made any plans for shipping him off?"

"Yes, I had. I'd been over to Walbeach the day before with Jim here, and we'd had a bit of talk with a pal of his—a queer old skipper on a Dutch cargo boat, that was lying there, taking in some sort of freight—I never rightly gathered what it was—but I got the notion the old boy wouldn't find much come amiss to him."

"You're right there, Will," put in Jim, grinning.

"So I found. It wasn't the best plan, maybe, but it was all I could do in the time. I couldn't think very clear, to tell you the truth. I was terrible put about in my mind and my head was buzzing like a thresher. I suppose 'twas the 'flu coming on. I don't know how I got through that evening at home, looking at Mary and the kids and knowing what I knew. Fortunately, she knew I was worried over the cow and put it all down to that—at least, I thought so. I tossed and turned all night, and the only thing to comfort me was the blessed snow coming down and hiding all they footprints we'd left round the church.

"Next morning I was damned ill, but I couldn't stop to think of that. I slipped out well before daybreak, with some bread and cheese and beer in an old tool-bag. Jim heard me and called out to know what was up. So I said I was going over to see the cow—and so I did, only I took the church on the way.

"Deacon was all right, only very bad-tempered and perished wi' cold, so I left him my old coat—not wanting him to be frozen to death. And I tied him up by his elbows and ankles, leaving his hands free, so as he could help himself to his victuals but not untie himself. Then I went on to see to the cow and found her better. After breakfast I got the old car out and ran her over to Walbeach, feeling worse and worse all the time. I found my skipper just getting ready to sail. I had a word with him, and he agreed to wait till 10 o'clock that night and carry my passenger, no questions asked. Two hundred and fifty pounds was the price he wanted and I agreed to pay it. I got the money and gave him the fifty then and there, promising him the rest when I got Deacon aboard. I got into the car and started back—and you know what happened afterwards."

"That's very clear," said Parker. "I needn't tell you that you were compounding a serious felony by helping a convicted murderer to escape from justice. Speaking as a policeman, I am shocked; speaking as a human being, I have every sympathy for you. Now, you." He turned to Jim. "I imagine your part of it comes in here."

"Yes, sir. Well, as you know, poor Will was brought back in a terrible state and we thought for a day or two he was pretty well gone. He was out of his head and kept on calling out that he must go down to the church, but we put that down to the bell-ringing business. All the time he kept a sort of control over himself and never let out a word about Deacon, but one day, when Mary had gone out of the room, he clutched my hand and said, 'Don't let her know, Jim. Get him away.' 'Get who away?' I said. And he said, 'In the belfry—bitter cold and starving.' And then he sat up in bed and said, quite plain and clear, 'My coat—give me my coat—I must have the keys and the money.' I said, 'All right, Will, I'll see to it'—thinking he was dreaming, and after a bit he seemed to forget about it and go off in a doze. But I thought it was queer, so I had a look in his coat, and there, sure enough, were the Rector's bunch of keys and a whole wad of money.

"Well, I began to think there might be something behind it, so I took the keys, and I thought, before I took them back, I'd just have a look round the church. I went in there——"

"Which day was this?"

"I reckon it was the 2nd of January. I went up into the belfry—right up to the bell-chamber, and—well! there he was!"

"He must have been pretty fed up with things by that time."

"Fed up? He was dead and cold."

"Starved to death?"

"Not he. There was a big bit of cheese beside him and near half a loaf of bread and two bottles of beer, one empty and one full. And he hadn't died of cold, neither, as you might expect. I've seen men that had died of exposure, and they died peaceful—curled up like kittens, mostly, as if they'd gone out in their sleep. No. He'd died on his feet, and whatever it was, he'd seen it coming to him. He'd struggled like a tiger against the ropes, working at them till he could get upright, and they had cut through the stuff of his jacket and through his socks. And his face! My God, sir, I've never seen anything like it. His eyes staring open and a look in them as if he'd looked down into hell. It fair shook me.

"I looked him over—and then I saw Will's old coat lying on the floor, thrown off, it might be, in his struggles—and that didn't look like dying of cold, neither. I couldn't tell what to make of it, for I didn't recognize him, you see. I had a look in his breast pocket, and found some papers. There was some made out in the name of Taylor and some in a French name that I've forgotten. I couldn't make head or tail of it. And then I had a look at his hands."

"Ah!" said Wimsey, "now we're coming to it."

"Yes, my lord. You must remember that I knew Deacon. Not very well, but I knew him. And he carried a big scar on one hand, where he'd fallen down one day, carrying a tray with a glass jug on it. I'd seen that scar, and I'd never forget it. When I saw that, my lord, and knew who 'twas—well, there! I hadn't much doubt about what'd happened. Forgive me, Will—I thought you'd done him in, and as God's my witness, I couldn't blame you. Not that I hold with murder, and it came to me then that things could never be the same betwixt you and me—but I didn't blame you. Only I wished it had happened in a fair fight."

"If it had happened, Jim, it would a-been in a fair fight. I might a-killed him, but I wouldn't a-killed him when he was tied up. You might a-known that."

"Well, so I might. But it seemed to me at the time as there was no way out of it. I had to think quick what to do. I found some old boards and beams in a corner, and I stood them up in front of him, so as if anybody came in they might not notice him—not unless they were looking for something—and then I came away and thought hard. I kept the keys. I knew I'd be wanting them, and Rector is so absent-minded, he'd probably think he'd mislaid them.

"I thought all that day—and then I remembered that Lady Thorpe's funeral was fixed for the Saturday. It seemed to me that I might put him in her grave and that he need never be found, barring accidents. I was due to leave on Saturday morning, and I thought I could fix things so as to have an alibi.

"I had a bad moment on Friday. Jack Godfrey told me they were going to ring a muffled peal for Lady Thorpe, and I was all of a shake, thinking he'd see him when he went up to put the leathers on the bells. By a big stroke of luck, he didn't go till after dark, and I suppose he never looked into that dark corner, or he'd have seen the planks had been moved."

"We know what you did on Saturday," said Parker. "You needn't bother with that."

"No, sir. I had an awful ride with that bike. The acetylene lamp worked none too well, and it was raining like the tropics. Still, I got there—much later than I meant, and I went to work. I cut him down——"

"You needn't tell us that, either. There was a witness on the top of the bell-chamber ladder all the time."

"A witness?"

"Yes—and lucky for you, my lad, he was a highly respectable and gentlemanly burglar with the heart of a rabbit and a wholesome fear of bloodshed—otherwise you might be paying blackmail through the nose. But I will say for Nobby," added Parker reflectively, "that he would consider blackmail beneath him. You got the body down into the churchyard?"

"And glad I was to get it there. Rolling it down the ladders—it gave me the heebie-jeebies. And those bells! I was expecting all the time to hear them speak. I never have liked the sound of bells. There's something—you'd think they were alive, sometimes, and could talk. When I was a boy, I read a story in an old magazine about a bell that called out after a murderer. You'll think I'm soft, talking that way, but it made an impression on me and I can't forget it."

"*The Rosamonde*—I know the story," said Wimsey, gently. "It called, 'Help, Jehan! Help, Jehan!' It gave me the grues, too."

"That's the one, my lord. Anyhow, I got the body down, as I said. I opened the grave and was just going to put him in——"

"You used the sexton's spade, I suppose?"

"Yes, sir. The key of the crypt was on Rector's bunch. As I was saying, I was going to put it in, when I remembered that the grave *might* be opened and the body recognized. So I gave it some good, hard blows with the spade across the face——"

He shuddered.

"That was a bad bit, sir. And the hands. I'd recognized them, and so might other people. I got out my jack-knife, and I—well, there!"

" 'With the big sugar-nippers they nipped off his flippers,' " quoted Wimsey, flippantly.

"Yes, my lord. I made them into a parcel with his papers and slipped it all in my pocket. But I put the ropes and his hat down the old well. Then I filled up the grave and put the wreaths back as tidily as I could, and cleaned the tools. But I can tell you, I didn't care about taking them back into the church. All those gold angels with their eyes open in the darkness—and old Abbot

Thomas lying there on his tomb. When my foot crunched on a bit of coke behind the screen, my heart was in my mouth."

"Harry Gotobed really ought to be more careful with the coke," said Wimsey. "It's not for want of telling."

"That damned parcel of stuff was burning my pocket, too. I went up and had a look at the stoves, but they were all stoked up for the night, and the top nowhere near burnt through. I didn't dare put anything in there. Then I had to go up and clean down the belfry. There'd been beer spilt on the floor. Fortunately, Harry Gotobed had left a bucket of water in the coke-house, so I didn't have to draw any from the well, though I've often wondered if he noticed next day that the water was gone. I made everything as clean as I could, and stacked the planks up where I'd found them, and I took away the beer-bottles——"

"Two of them," said Wimsey. "There were three."

"Were there? I couldn't see but the two. I locked up everything tight, and then I wondered what I'd better do with the keys. Finally, I thought I'd best leave them in the vestry, as though Rector had forgotten them—all but the key of the porch, and I left that in the lock. It was the best I could think of."

"And the parcel?"

"Ah! that. I kept the papers and a lot of money that was with them, but the—those other things—I threw into the Thirty-Foot, twelve miles off from Fenchurch, and the bottles with them. The papers and notes I burnt when I got back to London. There was a good fire—for a wonder—in the waiting-room at King's Cross and nobody much about. I didn't think anybody would look for them there. I didn't quite know what to do with Will's coat, but in the end I posted it back to him with a note. I just said, 'Many thanks for loan. I've put away what you left in the belfry.' I couldn't be more open you see, for fear Mary might undo the parcel and read the letter."

"I couldn't write much to you, for the same reason," said Will. "I thought, you see, you had somehow got Deacon away. It never entered my head that he was dead. And Mary usually reads my letters through before they go, sometimes adding a bit of her own. So I just said: 'Many thanks for all you've done for me'—which might a-been took to refer to you nursing me when I was ill. I see you hadn't took the £200, but I supposed you'd managed some fashion, so I just put that back in the bank where it came from. It was a queer thing to me that your letters had grown so short all of a sudden, but I understand it now."

"I couldn't just feel the same, Will," said Jim. "I didn't blame you, mind—but that rope stuck in my gullet. When did you find out what had happened?"

"Why, when the corpse came up. And—you'll have to forgive *me*, Jim—but, naturally, I fancied you'd done the job yourself, and—why, there! I didn't rightly feel the same, neither. Only I kept on hoping, maybe he'd died natural."

"He didn't do that," said Parker, thoughtfully.

"Then who killed him?" demanded Jim.

"I'm sure you didn't, for one," replied the detective. "If you had, you'd have accepted the suggestion that he died of exposure. And somehow I'm inclined to believe your brother didn't do it either—though you're both accessories after the fact to Deacon's crimes, and you aren't clear of the other thing yet; don't think it. You'd have an awkward time with a prosecuting counsel, both of you. But personally, I'm inclined to believe you both."

"Thank you, sir."

"How about Mrs. Thoday? The truth, mind."

"That's all right, sir. She was uneasy in her mind—I won't say she wasn't, seeing me so queer, especially after the body was found. But it was only when she saw Deacon's handwriting on that paper that the meaning of it all come to her. Then she asked me, and I told her part of the truth. I said I'd found out that the dead man was Deacon and that somebody—not me—must have killed him. And she guessed that Jim was mixed up in it. So I said, maybe, but we must stand together and not make trouble for Jim. And she agreed, only she said we must get married again, because we were living in sin. She's a good woman, and I couldn't reason her out of it, so I gave in about that, and we'd fixed to get it all done quiet-like in London—only you found us out, sir."

"Yes," said Blundell, "you've got to thank his lordship here for that. He seemed to know all about it, and very sorry he was to have to stop you, I must say. Seemed to think whoever put Deacon away ought to get the Wedding March out of Lohengrin and flowers all down the aisle."

"Is there any reason why they shouldn't go on and get married now, Superintendent?"

"I don't know as there is," grunted Mr. Blundell. "Not if these two are telling the truth. Proceedings there may be—you two ain't out of the wood yet, but as to getting married, I don't see no great harm in it. We've got their story, and I don't know as poor Mary can add very much to it."

"Thank you very much, sir," said Will again.

"But as to who *did* kill Deacon," went on the Superintendent, "we don't seem very much forrarder. Unless it was Potty or Cranton, after all. I don't know as I ever heard anything queerer than this business. All these three, a-dodging in and out of that old belfry, one up 'tother come on—there's something behind it yet that we don't understand. And you two——" he turned fiercely on the brothers—"you keep your mouths shut about this. It'll have to come out some time, that's a certainty, but if you get talking and obstruct us in our duty of laying hands on the rightful murderer, you're *for* it. Understand?"

He ruminated, sucking his walrus moustache between his large yellow teeth.

"I'd better go down home and grill Potty, I suppose," he muttered, discontentedly. "But if he done it, how did he do it? That's what beats me."

4

A FULL PEAL OF

KENT TREBLE BOB MAJOR

THREE PARTS

5,376

BY THE COURSE ENDS

6 5 4 3 2
3 4 5 6 2
2 3 6 4 5
3 5 6 4 2
4 2 3 5 6

8TH THE OBSERVATION.

Call her before, middle with a double, wrong with a double and home; wrong with a double and home with a double; middle with a double, wrong and home with a double; before, middle with a double, wrong and home with a double: before, middle with a double and wrong with a double.

Twice repeated.

J. WILDE

THE FIRST PART

The Waters Are Called Out

Of clean beasts, and of beasts that are not clean, and of fowls, and of everything that creepeth upon the earth there went in two and two unto Noah into the ark.

GENESIS VII. 8, 9

THE PUBLIC memory is a short one. The affair of the Corpse in Country Churchyard was succeeded, as the weeks rolled on, by so many Bodies in Blazing Garages, Man-Hunts for Missing Murderers, Tragedies in West-End Flats, Suicide-Pacts in Lonely Woods, Nude Corpses in Caves and Midnight Shots in Fashionable Road-Houses, that nobody gave it another thought, except Superintendent Blundell and the obscure villagers of Fenchurch St. Paul. Even the discovery of the emeralds and the identity of the dead man had been successfully kept out of the papers, and the secret of the Thoday re-marriage lay buried in the discreet breasts of the police, Lord Peter Wimsey and Mr. Venables, none of whom had any inducement to make these matters known.

Potty Peake had been interrogated, but without much success. He was not good at remembering dates, and his conversation, while full of strange hints and prophecies, had a way of escaping from the restraints of logic and playing gruesomely among the dangling bell-ropes. His aunt gave him an alibi, for what her menory and observation were worth, which was not a great deal. Nor did Mr. Blundell feel any great enthusiasm about putting Potty Peake in the dock. It was a hundred to one that he would be pronounced unfit to plead, and the result, in any case, might be to lock him up in an institution. "And you know, old lady," said Mr. Blundell to Mrs. Blundell, "I can't see Potty doing such a thing, poor chap." Mrs. Blundell agreed with him.

As regards the Thodays, the position was highly unsatisfactory. If either were charged separately, there would always be sufficient doubt about the other to secure an acquittal, while, if they were charged together, their joint story might well have the same effect upon the jury that it had already had upon the police. They would be acquitted and left under suspicion in the minds of their neighbours, and that would be unsatisfactory too. Or they might, of course, both be hanged—"and between you and me, sir," said Mr. Blundell to the Chief Constable, "I'd never be easy in my mind if they were." The Chief Constable was uneasy too. "You see, Blundell," he observed, "our difficulty is that we've no real proof of the murder. If you could only be sure what the fellow died of——"

So a period of inaction set in. Jim Thoday returned to his ship; Will Thoday, his marriage ceremony performed, went home and went on with his work. In time the parrot forgot its newly-learnt phrases—only coming out with them at long and infrequent intervals. The Rector carried on with his marryings, churchings and baptisms, and Tailor Paul tolled out a knell or two, or struck her solemn blows as the bells hunted in their courses. And the River Wale, rejoicing in its new opportunity, and swollen by the heavy rains of a wet summer and autumn, ground out its channel inch by inch and foot by foot, nine feet deeper than before, so that the water came up brackish at high tide as far as the Great Leam and the Old Bank Sluices were set open to their full extent, draining the Upper Fen.

And it was needed; for in that summer the water lay on the land all through August and September, and the corn sprouted in the stooks, and the sodden ricks took fire and stank horribly, and the Rector of Fenchurch St. Paul, conducting the Harvest Festival, had to modify his favourite sermon upon Thankfulness, for there was scarcely sound wheat enough to lay upon the altar and no great sheaves for the aisle windows or for binding about the stoves, as was customary. Indeed, so late was the harvest and so dank and chill the air, that the stoves were obliged to be lit for the evening service, whereby a giant pumpkin, left incautiously in the direct line of fire, was found to be par-roasted when the time came to send the kindly fruits of the earth to the local hospital.

Wimsey had determined that he would never go back to Fenchurch St. Paul. His memories of it were disquieting, and he felt that there were one or two people in that parish who would be better pleased if they never saw his face again. But when Hilary Thorpe wrote to him and begged him to come and see her during her Christmas holidays, he felt bound to go. His position with regard to her was peculiar. Mr. Edward Thorpe, as trustee under her father's will and her natural guardian, had rights which no court of law would gainsay; on the other hand Wimsey, as sole trustee to the far greater Wilbraham estate, held a certain advantage. He could, if he chose, make things awkward for Mr. Thorpe. Hilary possessed written evidence of her father's wishes about her education, and Uncle Edward could scarcely now oppose them on the plea of lack of funds. But Wimsey, holding the purse-strings, could refuse to untie them unless those wishes were carried out. If Uncle Edward chose to be obstinate, there was every prospect of a legal dog-fight; but Wimsey did not believe that Uncle Edward would be obstinate to that point. It was in Wimsey's power to turn Hilary from an obligation into an asset for Uncle Edward, and it seemed very possible that he would pocket his principles and take the cash. Already he had shown signs of bowing to the rising sun; he had agreed to take Hilary down to spend Christmas at the Red House, instead of with him in London. It was, indeed, not Mr. Thorpe's fault that the Red House was available; he had done his best to let it, but the number of persons desirous of tenanting a large house in ill-repair, situated in a howling desert and encumbered with a dilapidated and heavily mortgaged property, was not very large. Hilary had her way, and Wimsey, while heartily wishing that the whole business could have been settled in London, liked the girl for her determination to stick to the family estate. Here again, Wimsey was a power in the land. He could put the property in order if he liked and pay off the mortgages, and that would no doubt be a satisfaction to Mr. Thorpe, who had no power to sell under the terms of his trust. A final deciding factor was that if Wimsey did not spend Christmas at Fenchurch, he would have no decent excuse for not spending it with his brother's family at Denver, and of all things in the world, a Christmas at Denver was most disagreeable to him.

Accordingly, he looked in at Denver for a day or two, irritated his sister-in-law and her guests as much as, and no more than, usual and thence, on Christmas Eve, made his way across country to Fenchurch St. Paul.

"They seem," said Wimsey, "to keep a special brand of disgusting weather in these parts." He thrust up his hand against the hood of the car, discharging a deluge of water. "Last time it was snowing and now it's pelting cats and dogs. There's a fate in it, Bunter."

"Yes, my lord," said that long-suffering man. He was deeply attached to his master, but sometimes felt his determined dislike of closed cars to be a trifle unreasonable. "A very inclement season, my lord."

"Well, well, we must push on, push on. A merry heart goes all the way. You don't look very merry, Bunter, but then you're one of those sphinx-like people. I've never seen you upset, except about that infernal beer-bottle."

"No, my lord. That hurt my pride very much, if I may say so. A very curious circumstance, that, my lord."

"Pure accident, I think, though it had a suspicious appearance at the time. Whereabouts are we now? Oh, yes, Lympsey, of course; we cross over the Great Leam here by the Old Bank Sluice. We must be just coming to it. Yes, there it is. By jove! some water coming through here!"

He pulled up the car just beyond the bridge, got out and stood in the downpour staring at the sluice. Its five great gates were open, the iron ratchets on the bridge above drawn up to their full extent. Dark and menacing, the swollen flood-water raced through the sluices, eddying and turning and carrying with them the brown reeds and broken willow-stems and here and there fragments of timber filched from the drowned lands of the Upper Fen. And even while he watched, there came a change. Angry little waves and gurges ruffled the strong flow of the river, with an appearance as of repressed tumult and conflict. A man came out of the gate-house by the bridge and took up his position by the sluice, staring down into the river. Wimsey hailed him.

"Tide coming up?"

"Yes, sir. We has to watch her now if we don't want to get the water all across the causey. But she don't rise very far, not without there's an extraordinary high spring tide. She's just coming up to springs now, so we has to do a bit of manipulation, like." He turned, and began to wind down the sluices.

"You see the idea, Bunter. If they shut this sluice, all the upland water has to go by the Old Leam, which has enough to do as it is. But if they leave it open and the tide's strong enough to carry the flood-water back with it through the sluice, they'll drown all the country above the sluice."

"That's it, sir," said the man with a grin. "And if the flood-water carries the tide back, we might drown *you*. It all depends, you see."

"Then we'll hope you manipulate things in our favour," said Wimsey, cheerfully. The rush of water through the arches was slackening now with the lowering of the sluice-gates, the whirlpools became shallower, and the floating sticks and reeds began to eddy against the piles of the bridge. "Just hold her back for a bit till we get to Fenchurch, there's a good fellow."

"Oh, we'll keep her level, don't you be afraid," said the man, reassuringly. "There ain't nothing wrong wi' *this* here sluice."

He put such marked emphasis on the word "this" that Wimsey looked sharply at him.

"How about Van Leyden's Sluice?"

The man shook his head.

"I dunno, sir, but I did hear as old Joe Massey down there were in a great taking about they old gates of his. There was three gentlemen went down yesterday to look at 'em—from the Conservancy or the Board or something o' that, I reckon. But you can't do nothing much for they gates in flood-time. Mebbe they'll hold, mebbe they won't. It's all according."

"Well, that's jolly," said Wimsey. "Come on, Bunter. Have you made your will? We'd better go while the going's good."

Their way this time lay along the south bank or Fenchurch side of the Thirty-Foot. Dyke and drain were everywhere abrim and here and there the water stood in the soaked fields as though they needed but little more to sink back into their ancient desolation of mere and fen. There was little movement on the long, straight road. Here a shabby car met them, splashed with mud and squirting water from every pot-hole; here a slow farm cart plodded ahead with a load of mangel-wurzels, the driver huddled under the rough protection of a sodden sack, and deaf and blind to overtaking traffic; there a solitary labourer, bent with rheumatism, slouched homeward dreaming of fire and beer at the nearest pub. The air was so heavy with water, that not till they had passed Frog's Bridge did they hear the sweet, dull jangle of sound that told them that the ringers were practising their Christmas peal; it drifted through the streaming rain with an aching and intolerable melancholy, like the noise of the bells of a drowned city pulsing up through the overwhelming sea.

They turned the corner beneath the great grey tower and passed by the Rectory wall. As they neared the gate a blast of familiar toots smote upon their ears, and Wimsey slackened speed as the

Rector's car came cautiously nosing its way into the road. Mr. Venables recognized the Daimler immediately, and stopped his engine with the Morris half-way across the road. His hand waved cheerfully to them through the side-curtains.

"Here you are! here you are again!" he cried in welcoming accents, as Wimsey got out and came forward to greet him. "How lucky I am to have just caught you. I expect you heard me coming out. I always blow the horn before venturing into the roadway; the entrance is so very abrupt. How are you, my dear fellow, how are you? Just going along to the Red House, I expect. They are eagerly looking forward to your visit. You will come and see us often, I hope, while you're here. My wife and I are dining with you tonight. She will be so pleased to meet you again. I said to her, I wondered if I should meet you on the road. What terrible weather, is it not? I have to hurry off now to baptize a poor little baby at the end of Swamp Drove just the other side of Frog's Bridge. It's not likely to live, they tell me, and the poor mother is desperately ill, too, so I mustn't linger, because I expect I shall have to walk up the Drove with all this mud and it's nearly a mile and I don't walk as fast as I did. Yes, I am quite well, thank you, except for a slight cold. Oh, nothing at all—I got a little damp the other day taking a funeral for poor Watson at St. Stephen—he's laid up with shingles, so painful and distressing, though not dangerous, I'm happy to say. Did you come through St. Ives and Chatteris? Oh, you came direct from Denver. I hope your family are all quite well. I hear they've got the floods out all over the Bedford Level. There'll be skating on Bury Fen if we get any frosts after this—though it doesn't look like it at present, does it? They say a green winter makes a fat churchyard, but I always think the extreme cold is really more trying for the old people. But I really must push on now. I beg your pardon? I didn't catch what you said. The bells are a little loud. That's why I blew my horn so energetically; it is difficult sometimes to hear while the ringing is going on. Yes, we're trying some Stedman's tonight. You don't ring Stedman's, I think. You must come along one day and have a try at them. Most fascinating. Wally Pratt is making great strides. Even Hezekiah says he isn't doing so badly. Will Thoday is ringing tonight. I turned over in my mind what you told me, but I saw no reason for excluding him. He did wrong, of course, but I feel convinced that he committed no *great* sin, and it would arouse so much comment in the village if he left the ringers. Gossip is such a wicked thing, don't you think? Dear me!

I am neglecting my duties sadly in the pleasure of seeing you. That poor child! I *must* go. Oh, dear! I hope my engine won't give trouble, it is scarcely warmed up. Oh, please don't trouble. How very good of you. I'm ashamed to trespass on your—ah! she always responds at once to the starting-handle. Well, *au revoir, au revoir!* We shall meet this evening."

He chugged off cheerfully, beaming round at them through the discoloured weather curtains and zig-zagging madly across the road in his efforts to drive one way and look another. Wimsey and Bunter went on to the Red House.

THE SECOND PART

The Waters Are Called Home

Deep calleth unto deep at the noise of thy waterspouts: all thy waves and thy billows are gone over me.

PSALM XLII. 7

CHRISTMAS WAS over. Uncle Edward, sourly and reluctantly, had given way, and Hilary Thorpe's career was decided. Wimsey had exerted himself nobly in other directions. On Christmas Eve, he had gone out with the Rector and the Choir and sung "Good King Wenceslas" in the drenching rain, returning to eat cold roast beef and trifle at the Rectory. He had taken no part in the Stedman's Triples, but had assisted Mrs. Venables to tie wet bunches of holly and ivy to the font, and attended Church twice on Christmas Day, and helped to bring two women and their infants to be churched and christened from a remote and muddy row of cottages two miles beyond the Drain.

On Boxing Day, the rain ceased, and was followed by what the Rector described as "a tempestuous wind called Euroclydon." Wimsey, taking advantage of a dry road and a clear sky, ran over to see his friends at Walbeach and stayed the night, hearing great praises of the New Wash Cut and the improvement it had brought to the harbour and the town.

He returned to Fenchurch St. Paul after lunch, skimming merrily along with Euroclydon bowling behind him. Turning across the bridge at Van Leyden's Sluice, he noticed how swift and angry the river ran through the weir, with flood-water and tide-water meeting the wind. Down by the sluice a gang of men were working on a line of barges, which were moored close against the gates and piled high with sandbags. One of the workmen gave a shout as the car passed over the bridge, and another man, seeing him point and gesticulate, came running from the sluice-head across the road, waving his arms. Lord Peter stopped and waited for him to come up. It was Will Thoday.

"My lord!" he cried, "my lord! Thank God you are here! Go and warn them at St. Paul's that the sluice gates are going. We've done what we can with sandbags and beams, but we can't do no more and there's a message come down from the Old Bank Sluice that the water is over the Great Leam at Lympsey, and they'll have to send it down here or be drowned themselves. She's held this tide, but she'll go the next with this wind and the tide at springs. It'll lay the whole country under water, my lord, and there's no time to lose."

"All right," said Wimsey. "Can I send you more men?"

"A regiment of men couldn't do nothing now, my lord. They old gates is going, and there won't be a foot of dry land in the three Fenchurches six hours from now."

Wimsey glanced at his watch. "I'll tell 'em," he said, and the car leapt forward.

The Rector was in his study when Wimsey burst in upon him with the news.

"Great Heavens!" cried Mr. Venables. "I've been afraid of this. I've warned the drainage authorities over and over again about those gates but they wouldn't listen. But it's no good crying over spilt milk. We must act quickly. If they open the Old Bank Sluice and Van Leyden's Sluice blows up, you see what will happen. All the Upper Water will be turned back up the Wale and drown us ten feet deep or more. My poor parishioners—all those outlying farms and cottages! But we mustn't lose our heads. We have taken our precautions. Two Sundays ago I warned the congregation what might happen and I put a note in the December Parish Magazine. And the Nonconformist minister has co-operated in the most friendly manner with us. Yes, yes. The first thing to do is to ring the alarm. They know what that means, thank God! They learnt it during the War. I never thought I should thank God for the War, but He moves in a mysterious way. Ring the bell for Emily, please. The church will be safe, whatever happens, unless we get a rise of over twelve feet, which is hardly likely. Out of the deep, O Lord, out of the deep. Oh, Emily, run and tell Hinkins that Van Leyden's Sluice is giving way. Tell him to fetch one of the other men and ring the alarm on Gaude and Tailor Paul at once. Here are the keys of the church and belfry. Warn your mistress and get all the valuables taken over to the church. Carry them up the tower. Now keep cool, there's a good girl. I don't think the house will be touched, but one cannot be too careful. Find somebody to help you with this chest—I've secured all the parish registers in it—and see that the church plate is taken up the tower as well. Now, where is my hat? We must get on the telephone to St. Peter and St. Stephen and make sure that they are prepared. And we will see what we can do with the people at the Old Bank Sluice. We haven't a moment to lose. Is your car here?"

They ran the car up to the village, the Rector leaning out perilously and shouting warnings to everyone they met. At the post-office they called up the other Fenchurches and then communicated with the keeper of the Old Bank Sluice. His report was not encouraging.

"Very sorry, sir, but we can't help ourselves. If we don't let the water through there'll be the best part of four mile o' the bank washed away. We've got six gangs a-working on it now, but they can't do a lot with all these thousands o' tons o' water coming down. And there's more to come, so they say."

The Rector made a gesture of despair, and turned to the postmistress.

"You'd best get down to the church, Mrs. West. You know what to do. Documents and valuables in the tower, personal belongings in the nave. Animals in the churchyard. Cats, rabbits and guinea-pigs in *baskets, please*—we can't have them running round loose. Ah! there go the alarm-bells. Good! I am more alarmed for the remote farms than for the village. Now, Lord Peter, we must go and keep order as best we can at the church."

The village was already a scene of confusion. Furniture was being stacked on handcarts, pigs were being driven down the street, squealing; hens, squawking and terrified, were being huddled into crates. At the door of the school-house Miss Snoot was peering agitatedly out.

"When ought we to go, Mr. Venables?"

"Not yet, not yet—let the people move their heavy things first. I will send you a message when the time comes, and then you will get the children together and march them down in an orderly way. You can rely on me. But keep them cheerful—reassure them and don't on any account let them go home. They are far safer here. Oh, Miss Thorpe! Miss Thorpe! I see you have heard the news."

"Yes, Mr. Venables. Can we do anything?"

"My dear, you are the very person! Could you and Mrs. Gates

see that the school-children are kept amused and happy, and give them tea later on if necessary? The urns are in the parish-room. Just a moment, I must speak to Mr. Hensman. How are we off for stores, Mr. Hensman?"

"Pretty well stocked, sir," replied the grocer. "We're getting ready to move as you suggested, sir."

"That's fine," said the Rector. "You know where to go. The refreshment room will be in the Lady chapel. Have you the key of the parish-room for the boards and trestles?"

"Yes, sir."

"Good, good. Get a tackle rigged over the church well for your drinking-water, and be sure and remember to boil it first. Or use the Rectory pump, if it is spared to us. Now, Lord Peter, back to the church."

Mrs. Venables had already taken charge in the church. Assisted by Emily and some of the women of the parish, she was busily roping off areas—so many pews for the school-children, so many other pews near the stoves for the sick and aged, the area beneath the tower for furniture, a large placard on the parclose screen REFRESHMENTS. Mr. Gotobed and his son, staggering under buckets of coke, were lighting the stoves. In the churchyard, Jack Godfrey and a couple of other farmers were marking out cattle-pens and erecting shelters among the tombs. Just over the wall which separated the consecrated ground from the bell-field, a squad of voluntary diggers were digging out a handsome set of sanitary trenches.

"Good lord, sir," said Wimsey, impressed, "anybody would think you'd done this all your life."

"I have devoted much prayer and thought to the situation in the last few weeks," said Mr. Venables. "But my wife is the real manager. She has a marvellous head for organization. Hinkins! right up to the bell-chamber with that plate—it'll be out of the way there. Alf! Alf Donnington! How about that beer?"

"Coming along, sir."

"Splendid—into the Lady chapel, please. You're bringing some of it bottled, I hope. It'll take two days for the casks to settle."

"That's all right, sir. Tebbutt and me are seeing to that."

The Rector nodded, and dodging past some of Mr. Hensman's contingent, who were staggering in with cases of groceries, he went out to the gates, where he encountered P. C. Priest, stolidly directing the traffic.

"We're having all the cars parked along the wall, sir."

"That's right. And we shall want volunteers with cars to run out to outlying places and bring in the women and sick people. Will you see to that?"

"Very good, sir."

"Lord Peter, will you act as our Mercury between here and Van Leyden's Sluice? Keep us posted as to what is happening."

"Right you are," said Wimsey. "I hope, by the way, that Bunter —where is Bunter?"

"Here, my lord. I was about to suggest that I might lend some assistance with the commissariat, if not required elsewhere."

"Do, Bunter, do," said the Rector.

"I understand, my lord, that no immediate trouble is expected at the Rectory, and I was about to suggest that, with the kind help of the butcher, sir, a sufficiency of hot soup might be prepared in the wash-house copper, and brought over in the wheeled watering tub—after the utensil has been adequately scalded, of course. And if there were such a thing as a paraffin-oil stove anywhere——"

"By all means—but be careful with the paraffin. We do not want to escape the water to fall into the fire."

"Certainly not, sir."

"You can get paraffin from Wilderspin. Better send some more ringers up to the tower. Let them pull the bells as they like and fire them at intervals. Oh, here are the Chief Constable and Superintendent Blundell—how good of them to come over. We are expecting a little trouble here, Colonel."

"Just so, just so. I see you are handling the situation admirably. I fear a lot of valuable property will be destroyed. Would you like any police sent over?"

"Better patrol the roads between the Fenchurches," suggested Blundell. "St. Peter is greatly alarmed—they're afraid for the bridges. We are arranging a service of ferryboats. They lie even lower than you do and are, I fear, not so well prepared as you, sir."

"We can offer them shelter here," said the Rector. "The church will hold nearly a thousand at a pinch, but they must bring what food they can. And their bedding, of course. Mrs. Venables is arranging it all. Men's sleeping-quarters on the cantoris side, women and children on the decani side. And we can put the sick and aged people in the Rectory in greater comfort, if all goes well. St. Stephen will be safe enough, I imagine, but if not, we must do our best for them too. And, dear me! We shall rely on you,

Superintendent, to send us victuals by boat as soon as it can be arranged. The roads will be clear between Leamholt and the Thirty-Foot, and the supplies can be brought from there by water."

"I'll organize a service," said Mr. Blundell.

"If the railway embankment goes, you will have to see to St. Stephen as well. Good-day, Mrs. Giddings, good-day to you! We are having quite an adventure, are we not? So glad to see you here in good time. Well, Mrs. Leach! So here you are! How's Baby? Enjoying himself, I expect. You'll find Mrs. Venables in the church. Jack! Jackie Holliday! You must put that kitten in a basket. Run and ask Joe Hinkins to find you one. Ah, Mary! I hear your husband is doing fine work down at the Sluice. We must see that he doesn't come to any harm. Yes, my dear, what is it? I am just coming."

For three hours Wimsey worked among the fugitives—fetching and carrying, cheering and exhorting, helping to stall cattle and making himself as useful as he could. At length he remembered his duty as a messenger and extricating his car from the crowd made his way east along the Thirty-Foot. It was growing dark, and the road was thronged with carts and cattle, hurrying to the safety of Church Hill. Pigs and cattle impeded his progress.

"The animals went in two by two," sang Wimsey, as he sped through the twilight, "the elephant and the kangaroo. Hurrah!"

Down at the sluice, the situation looked dangerous. Barges had been drawn against both sides of the gates and an attempt had been made to buttress the sluice with beams and sandbags, but the piers were bulging dangerously and as fast as material was lowered into the water, it was swept down by the force of the current. The river was foaming over the top of the weir, and from the east, wind and tide were coming up in violent opposition.

"Can't hold her much longer, now, my lord," gasped a man, plunging up the bank and shaking the water from him like a wet dog. "She's going, God help us!"

The sluice-keeper was wringing his hands.

"I told 'em, I told 'em! What will become on us?"

"How long now?" asked Wimsey.

"An hour, my lord, if that."

"You'd better all get away. Have you cars enough?"

"Yes, my lord, thank you."

Will Thoday came up to him, his face white and working.

"My wife and children—are they safe?"

"Safe as houses, Will. The Rector's doing wonders. You'd better come back with me."

"I'll hang on here till the rest go, my lord, thank you. But tell them to lose no time."

Wimsey turned the car back again. In the short time that he had been away the organization had almost completed itself. Men, women, children and household goods had been packed into the church. It was nearly seven o'clock and the dusk had fallen. The lamps were lit. Soup and tea were being served in the Lady chapel, babies were crying, the churchyard resounded with the forlorn lowing of cattle and the terrified bleating of sheep. Sides of bacon were being carried in, and thirty waggon-loads of hay and corn were ranged under the church wall. In the only clear space amid the confusion the Rector stood behind the rails of the Sanctuary. And over all, the bells tumbled and wrangled, shouting their alarm across the country. Gaude, Sabaoth, John, Jericho, Jubilee, Dimity, Batty Thomas and Tailor Paul—awake! make haste! save yourselves! The deep waters have gove over us! They call with the noise of the cataracts!

Wimsey made his way up to the altar-rails and gave his message. The Rector nodded. "Get the men away quickly," he said, "tell them they must come at once. Brave lads! I know they hate to give in, but they mustn't sacrifice themselves uselessly. As you go through the village, tell Miss Snoot to bring the school-children down." And as Wimsey turned to go, he called anxiously after him—"and don't let them forget the other two tea-urns!"

• • • • • • •

The men were already piling into their waiting cars when Lord Peter again arrived at the Sluice. The tide was coming up like a race, and in the froth and flurry of water he could see the barges flung like battering rams against the piers. Somebody shouted: "Get out of it, lads, for your lives!" and was answered by a rending crash. The transverse beams that carried the footway over the weir, rocking and swaying upon the bulging piers, cracked and parted. The river poured over in a tumult to meet the battering force of the tide. There was a cry. A dark figure, stepping hurriedly across the reeling barges, plunged and was gone. Another form dived after it, and a rush was made to the bank. Wimsey, flinging off his coat, hurled himself down to the water's edge. Somebody caught and held him.

"No good, my lord, they're gone! My God! did you see that?"

Somebody threw the flare of a headlight across the river. "Caught between the barge and the pier—smashed like egg-shells. Who is it? Johnnie Cross? Who went in after him? Will Thoday? That's bad, and him a married man. Stand back, my lord. We'll have no more lives lost. Save yourselves, lads, you can do them no good. Christ! the sluice gates are going. Drive like hell, men, it's all up!"

Wimsey found himself dragged and hurtled by strong hands to his car. Somebody scrambled in beside him. It was the sluice-keeper, still moaning, "I told 'em, I told 'em!" Another thunderous crash brought down the weir across the Thirty-Foot, in a deluge of tossing timbers. Beams and barges were whirled together like straws, and a great spout of water raged over the bank and flung itself across the road. Then the Sluice, that held the water back from the Old Wale River, yielded, and the roar of the engines as the cars sped away was lost in the thunder of the meeting and over-riding waters.

. . . .

The banks of the Thirty-Foot held, but the swollen Wale, receiving the full force of the Upper Waters and the spring tide, gave at every point. Before the cars reached St. Paul, the flood was rising and pursuing them. Wimsey's car—the last to start—was submerged to the axles. They fled through the dusk, and behind and on their left, the great silver sheet of water spread and spread.

. . . .

In the church, the Rector, with the electoral roll-call of the parish in his hand, was numbering his flock. He was robed and stoled, and his anxious old face had taken on a look of great pastoral dignity and serenity.

"Eliza Giddings."

"Here I am, Rector."

"Jack Godfrey and his wife and family."

"All here, sir."

"Henry Gotobed and his family."

"All here, sir."

"Joseph Hinkins . . . Louisa Hitchcock . . . Obadiah Holliday . . . Miss Evelyn Holliday. . . ."

The party from the Sluice gathered awkwardly about the door.

Wimsey made his way up to where the Rector stood on the chancel steps, and spoke in his ear.

"John Cross and Will Thoday? That is terrible. God rest them, poor, brave fellows. Will you be good enough to tell my wife and ask her to break the sad news to their people? Will went to try and rescue Johnnie? That is just what I should have expected of him. A dear, good fellow in spite of everything."

Wimsey called Mrs. Venables aside. The Rector's voice, shaking a little now, went on with his call:

"Jeremiah Johnson and his family . . . Arthur and Mary Judd . . . Luke Judson . . ."

Then came a long, wailing cry from the back of the church:

"Will! Oh, Will! He didn't want to live! Oh, my poor children—what shall we do?"

Wimsey did not wait to hear any more. He made his way down to the belfry door and climbed the stair to the ringing-chamber. The bells were still sounding their frenzied call. He passed the sweating ringers and climbed again—up through the clock-chamber, piled with household goods, and up and on to the bell-chamber itself. As his head rose through the floor, the brazen fury of the bells fell about his ears like the blows from a thousand beating hammers. The whole tower was drenched and drunken with noise. It rocked and reeled with the reeling of the bells, and staggered like a drunken man. Stunned and shaken, Wimsey set his foot on the last ladder.

Half-way up he stopped, clinging desperately with his hands. He was pierced through and buffeted by the clamour. Through the brazen crash and clatter there went one high note, shrill and sustained, that was like a sword in the brain. All the blood of his body seemed to rush to his head, swelling it to bursting-point. He released his hold of the ladder and tried to shut out the uproar with his fingers, but such a sick giddiness overcame him that he swayed, ready to fall. It was not noise—it was brute pain, a grinding, bludgeoning, ran-dan, crazy, intolerable torment. He felt himself screaming, but could not hear his own cry. His eardrums were cracking; his senses swam away. It was infinitely worse than any roar of heavy artillery. That had beaten and deafened, but this unendurable shrill clangour was a raving madness, an assault of devils. He could move neither forward nor backwards, though his failing wits urged him, "I must get out—I must get out of this." The belfry heaved and wheeled about him as the bells dipped and swung within the reach of an outstretched hand.

Mouth up, mouth down, they brawled with their tongues of bronze, and through it all that shrill, high, sweet, relentless note went stabbing and shivering.

He could not go down, for his head dizzied and his stomach retched at the thought of it. With a last, desperate sanity, he clutched at the ladder and forced his tottering limbs upward. Foot by foot, rung by rung, he fought his way to the top. Now the trap-door was close above his head. He raised a leaden hand and thrust the bolt aside. Staggering, feeling as though his bones were turned to water, and with blood running from his nose and ears, he fell, rather than stepped, out upon the windy roof. As he flung the door to behind him, the demoniac clamour sank back into the pit, to rise again, transmuted to harmony, through the louvres of the belfry windows.

He lay for some minutes quivering upon the leads, while his senses slowly drifted back to him. At length he wiped the blood from his face, and pulled himself groaningly to his knees, hands fastened upon the fretwork of the parapet. An enormous stillness surrounded him. The moon had risen, and between the battlements the sullen face of the drowned Fen showed like a picture in a shifting frame, like the sea seen through the port-hole of a rolling ship, so widely did the tower swing to the relentless battery of the bells.

The whole world was lost now in one vast sheet of water. He hauled himself to his feet and gazed out from horizon to horizon. To the south-west, St. Stephen's tower still brooded over a dark platform of land, like a broken mast upon a sinking ship. Every house in the village was lit up; St. Stephen was riding out the storm. Westward, the thin line of the railway embankment stretched away to Little Dykesey, unvanquished as yet, but perilously besieged. Due south, Fenchurch St. Peter, roofs and spire etched black against the silver, was the centre of a great mere. Close beneath the tower, the village of St. Paul lay abandoned, waiting for its fate. Away to the east, a faint pencilling marked the course of the Potters Lode Bank, and while he watched it, it seemed to waver and vanish beneath the marching tide. The Wale River had sunk from sight in the spreading of the flood, but far beyond it, a dull streak showed where the land billowed up seaward, and thrust the water back upon the Fenchurches. Inward and westward the waters swelled relentlessly from the breach of Van Leyden's Sluice and stood level with the top of the Thirty-Foot Bank. Outward and eastward the gold cock on the weathervane stared and strained, fronting the danger, held to his watch by the relentless pressure of the wind from off the Wash. Somewhere amid that still surge of waters, the broken bodies of Will Thoday and his mate drifted and tumbled with the wreckage of farm and field. The Fen had reclaimed its own.

. . . . . .

One after another, the bells jangled into silence. Gaude, Sabaoth, John, Jericho, Jubilee, Dimity and Batty Thomas lowered their shouting mouths and were at peace, and in their sudden stillness, Tailor Paul tolled out the Nine Tailors for two souls passed in the night. The notes of the organ rose solemnly.

Wimsey crept down from the tower. Into the ringing-chamber, where old Hezekiah still stood to his bell, streamed light and sound from the crowded church. The Rector's voice, musical and small, came floating up, past the wings of the floating cherubim:

"Lighten our darkness . . ."

THE THIRD PART

The Bells Are Rung Down

The bronze monster had struck him dead.

JULIAN SERMET: THE ROSAMONDE

For fourteen days and nights the Wale River ran backward in its bed and the floods stood in the land. They lay all about Fenchurch St. Stephen, a foot above the railway embankment, so that the trains came through snorting and slowly, sending up a wall of water right and left. St. Peter suffered most, its houses being covered to the sills of the upper windows, and its cottages to the eaves. At St. Paul, everything was flooded eight feet deep, except the mound where church and rectory stood.

The Rector's organization worked brilliantly. Supplies were ample for three days, after which an improvised service of boats and ferries brought in fresh food regularly from the neighbouring towns. A curious kind of desert-island life was carried on in and about the church, which, in course of time, assumed a rhythm of its own. Each morning was ushered in by a short and cheerful flourish of bells, which rang the milkers out to the cowsheds in the graveyard. Hot water for washing was brought in wheeled waterbutts from the Rectory copper. Bedding was shaken and rolled under the pews for the day; the tarpaulins dividing the men's side from the women's side of the church were drawn back and a brief service of hymns and prayer was held, to the accompaniment of culinary clinkings and odours from the Lady chapel. Breakfast, prepared under Bunter's directions, was distributed along the pews by members of the Women's Institute, and when this was over, the duties of the day were put in hand. Daily school was carried on in the south aisle; games and drill were organized in the Rectory garden by Lord Peter Wimsey; farmers attended to their cattle; owners of poultry brought the eggs to a communal basket; Mrs. Venables presided over sewing-parties in the Rectory. Two portable wireless sets were available, one in the Rectory, the other in the church; these tirelessly poured out entertainment and instruction, the batteries being kept re-charged by an ingenious device from the engine of Wimsey's Daimler, capably handled by the Wilderspins. Three evenings a week were devoted to concerts and lectures, arranged by Mrs. Venables, Miss Snoot and the combined choirs of St. Stephen and St. Paul, with Miss Hilary Thorpe and Mr. Bunter (comedian) assisting. On Sundays, the routine was varied by an Early Celebration, followed by an undenominational service conducted by the two Church of England priests and the two Nonconformist ministers. A wedding, which happened to fall due in the middle of the fortnight, was made a gala occasion, and a baby, which also happened to fall due, was baptized "Paul" (for the church) "Christopher" (because St. Christopher had to do with rivers and ferries), the Rector strenuously resisting the parents' desire to call it "Van Leyden Flood."

On the fourteenth day, Wimsey, passing early through the churchyard for a morning swim down the village street, noticed that the level of the water had shrunk by an inch, and returned, waving a handful of laurels from somebody's front garden, as the nearest substitute for an olive-branch. That day they rang a merry peal of Kent Treble Bob Major, and across the sundering flood heard the bells of St. Stephen peal merrily back.

. . . .

"The odour," observed Bunter, gazing out on the twentieth day across the dismal strand of ooze and weed that had once been Fenchurch St. Paul, "is intensely disagreeable, my lord, and I should be inclined to consider it insanitary."

"Nonsense, Bunter," said his master. "At Southend you would call it ozone and pay a pound a sniff for it."

The women of the village looked rueful at the thought of the cleansing and drying that their homes would need, and the men shook their heads over the damage to rick and barn.

The bodies of Will Thoday and John Cross were recovered from the streets of St. Stephen, whither the flood had brought them, and buried beneath the shadow of St. Paul's tower, with all the solemnity of a muffled peal. It was only after they had been laid in the earth that Wimsey opened his mind to the Rector and to Superintendent Blundell.

"Poor Will," he said, "he died finely and his sins died with him. He meant no harm, but I think perhaps he guessed at last how Geoffrey Deacon died and felt himself responsible. But we needn't look for a murderer now."

"What do you mean, my lord?"

"Because," said Wimsey, with a wry smile, "the murderers of Geoffrey Deacon are hanged already, and a good deal higher than Haman."

"Murderers?" asked the Superintendent, quickly. "More than one? Who were they?"

"Gaude, Sabaoth, John, Jericho, Jubilee, Dimity, Batty Thomas and Tailor Paul."

There was an astonished silence. Wimsey added:

"I ought to have guessed. I believe it is at St. Paul's Cathedral that it is said to be death to enter the bell-chamber when a peal is being rung. But I know that if I had stayed ten minutes in the tower that night when they rang the alarm, I should have been dead, too. I don't know exactly what of—stroke, apoplexy, shock—anything you like. The sound of a trumpet laid flat the walls of Jericho and the note of a fiddle will shatter a vessel of glass. I know that no human frame could bear the noise of the bells for more than fifteen minutes—and Deacon was shut up there, roped and tied there, for nine interminable hours between the Old Year and the New."

"My God!" said the Superintendent. "Why, then, you were right, my lord, when you said that Rector, or you, or Hezekiah might have murdered him."

"I was right," said Wimsey. "We did." He thought for a moment and spoke again. "The noise must have been worse that night than it was the other day—think how the snow choked the louvres and kept it pent up in the tower. Geoffrey Deacon was a bad man, but when I think of the helpless horror of his lonely and intolerable death-agony——"

He broke off, and put his head between his hands, as though instinctively seeking to shut out the riot of the bell-voices.

The Rector's mild voice came out of the silence.

"There have always," he said, "been legends about Batty Thomas. She has slain two other men in times past, and Hezekiah will tell you that the bells are said to be jealous of the presence of evil. Perhaps God speaks through those mouths of inarticulate metal. He is a righteous judge, strong and patient, and is provoked every day."

"Well," said the Superintendent, striking a note of cheerful commonplace, "seems as if we didn't need to take any more steps in this matter. The man's dead, and the fellow that put him up there is dead too, poor chap, and that's all there is to it. I don't altogether understand about these bells, but I'll take your word for it, my lord. Matter of periods of vibration, I suppose. Yours seems the best solution, and I'll put it up to the Chief Constable. And that's all there is to it."

He rose to his feet.

"I'll wish you good-morning, gentlemen," he said, and went out.

. . . .

The voice of the bells of Fenchurch St. Paul:
Gaude, Gaudy, Domini in laude.
Sanctus, sanctus, sanctus Dominus Deus Sabaoth.
John Cole made me, John Presbyter paid
me, John Evangelist aid me.
From Jericho to John A-Groate
there is no bell can better my note.
Jubilate Deo. Nunc Dimittis, Domine.
Abbot Thomas set me here
and bade me ring both loud and clear.
Paul is my name, honour that same.

Gaude, Sabaoth, John, Jericho, Jubilee, Dimity,
Batty Thomas and Tailor Paul.

Nine Tailors Make a Man.